GOD RIDDANCE

ROBIN BANKS

God Riddance
© Copyright 2018 by Robin Banks. All rights reserved.

Written by Robin Banks.
Cover Illustration © Copyright 2018 by Robin Banks.
Cover design by Robin Banks.

ISBN: 9781980892052

For updates, new releases, useful links, and other information:

https://www.amazon.com/Robin-Banks/e/B01MU5VWGL
https://www.facebook.com/HeinleinsFinches
https://godsbastard.wordpress.com/heinleins-finches/

Contents

1. ADAIR

I should have been doing my homework, but Frankie was twirling.

They'd borrowed my skirt, at long last. They had put it on with some trepidation, but I thought that, once they had taken that first step, they'd throw themself headlong into their skirted state the same way they threw themself into everything else.

They didn't. Instead, they spent roughly an age and a half sitting on our bed, stroking the skirt, their eyes oscillating wildly between it and my face, and between green and brown, until I nudged them.

"Love, it's not a cat."

They stared at me, their eyes enormous and lost. "What?"

"You don't have to pet it, and you can get up without disturbing it. Come on. Off you go. You're missing out on the sunshine."

They got up, looked at me for a last dose of reassurance, took a deep breath, and strode out of the patio doors. After three steps, they turned around to see where I was at. The skirt lagged behind the motion, like heavy gypsy skirts are wont to do. They froze and looked at it in some alarm. Having ascertained that it was still present and correct, they looked up at me with a final question in their eyes.

I nodded. "You look great, love."

They beamed at me so artlessly that my heart melted on the spot, and then they were off.

I picked up my books and sat on the ground, leaning against the patio doors. The books were mostly for show, a vain attempt at assuaging my conscience. I had work to do, and I knew that, one day soon, I would regret not doing it. But I also knew that if I missed this moment, I would regret that for the rest of my natural life.

It was a perfect fall day. The trees around our glade were blushing scarlet, bathed in golden sunshine, and in the middle of them Frankie frolicked in their first skirt. They'd started out rushing and skipping from thing to thing, checking out everything and nothing: fallen leaves, a mark on a tree trunk, a paw print in a patch of mud. Then they'd forgotten that grown-ups needed a reason to move, and just let themself go. It wasn't quite dancing, but it wasn't quite not-dancing, either. I didn't care, anyway: it was beautiful, it gave them joy, and I was there to see it. Life could not have been better.

The knock at our door came way too soon. It was Ben's not-so-secret knock, so I knew that there was no cause for alarm, but I also knew that the moment was over, and mourned its passing.

I bellowed, "Come in!" without getting up.

Ben joined me at the patio door. He was still careful not to step outside, as if the ground could pick him up and sweep him away, but he was getting braver about standing near the edge. I took that as the indication that he trusted himself more, or that he didn't want to die quite as much. Either way, it seemed like a good sign.

My optimism evaporated when I saw him watching Frankie. I didn't expect Ben to be as enthusiastic as I was about Frankie's sartorial excursions, but I thought he'd be supportive, or at least as indifferent as he was to pretty much anything people did that didn't harm anyone. Instead, he looked supremely unimpressed.

I could tell that Frankie had noticed by the narrowing of their eyes. They didn't let that dull their shine, though: instead of frowning back, they pirouetted on the spot, their arms wide open, the skirt flying upwards past their knees. When they had enough of that, they stopped and smiled at Ben. "What do you think?"

Ben pulled his mouth this way and that. "I don't know, man. It's a look, I guess."

I braced myself for incoming shit, but Frankie kept their cool.

"You got a problem with it?"

"I don't wanna piss you off, but a hockey top with a flouncy skirt? Not a traditional combination. But it's your clothes, man. If you like it, go for it."

Frankie's face split into a grin. "Your problem with me wearing a skirt is that I'm not coordinated enough?"

Ben shrugged. "Look, I'm not really fashion conscious, you know? But I grew up with a mom, an older sister, three aunts, and four girl cousins. The guys in my family don't really get speaking parts, as a rule, so I heard a whole load of talk about clothes." He pointed at me. "You should put one of his shirts on. They would go."

"Man, there's no way in hell I could do them up. She's half my width."

"Could you, like, put a plain t-shirt on underneath, and then the shirt on unbuttoned? Layered, like."

That was when the tension I've been holding dissolved into guffaws. The two of them looked at me as if I'd lost it, which I had, but in a good way. The world behind us could be a shitty, shitty place, but my partner and my best friend having an earnest discussion about how to best accessorize a gypsy skirt while scratching the stubble on their chins was the sort of thing that made it all tolerable.

"What's up with her?" mumbled Ben.

Frankie beamed. "It's the sunshine. It gets to his head."

They started twirling again, seeing how high they could get the skirt to fly. They were getting better at it, though I didn't know how they were managing it: just watching them made my head spin. They were so pretty, though, and so full of joy, that they took my breath away. Maybe that was why I felt so dizzy.

I was so taken by the scene that I didn't hear the noise until it was way too close to us. When I did, I panicked. "Frankie! Swarm!"

They didn't stop to check if I was right: they just loped towards me, a wild smile on their face, their hair and skirt streaming behind them. They got to our door just as I was getting up, wrapped an arm around my waist, and pulled me inside.

Ben shut the doors an inch away from my nose. "Seal it up, Gio!"

Frankie elbowed him without letting go of me. "Not yet. You've got to check this out! It's so cool!"

The buzzing intensified and, all of a sudden, the air in front of our door was filled with a shimmering, dancing, living curtain. I still didn't know what those creatures were: they looked a little bit like butterflies, a little bit like hummingbirds, and a whole lot like something straight out of a cartoon. Whatever they were, they couldn't survive on our side of the portal: the one that had sneaked through had withered and died within seconds, breaking Frankie's heart in the process. They were so upset that they nearly cried. That sudden death didn't make much sense, because the creatures were clearly not magical: if they were, they wouldn't have made it into our glade. My circle of protection was as solid as ever. It was solid enough for the wyvern to smack into it with an audible thump.

Ben jumped a foot in the air. "What the fuck was that?"

Frankie shrugged, and cuddled me a bit tighter in the process. "Just a wyvern. You'll see it when it gets up. They normally try to get through the circle a few times before giving up. They're not that bright, but they do learn. The hummingflies—"

"The what now?"

"Hummingflies. Fits them better than butterbirds, don't you think? Anyway, they are way smarter: they have learnt to use the circle to protect themselves. They know that if they get in the wyverns can't get at them. I think it's pretty cool, but Gio is worried about the ecological impact."

Ben looked at me as if I was weird. In the context of the conversation we were having, it was somewhat insulting.

I put on my best declaiming voice and let him have it. "Think about it. If the size of the hummingfly population is controlled by wyvern predation, and we remove that factor, there is no knowing what may happen. For all we know, they are a pest species that could cause untold damage."

Frankie squeaked, "But they are so pretty!"

"So are you, but having swarms of you all over the place would be problematic."

Torn between preening and scoffing, they opted to give me a kiss on the neck. They didn't hurry it, either.

I ignored them, with some effort, and carried on with my lecture. "Then you have to consider the impact on the wyvern population of removing hummingflies as a food source. Assuming that there is a wyvern population: we've only ever seen one at a time. It could have been the same one. I didn't get close enough to tell. Damn thing has a whole load of teeth. And, if it can breathe fire, I don't know if the circle would stop it."

Ben stared at the wyvern. It had managed to stand up, and was flapping its wings and banging its head against the circle, hissing in frustration. "Yannow, there are not too many people who, faced with what is essentially a fucking dragon not ten yards away from them, would worry about the ecological blah-blah of the situation."

Frankie mumbled, "Déformation professionnelle" under their breath.

I was tempted to elbow them in the guts for it, but their French accent never failed to give me the squiggles. I leaned into them instead, and let that be their punishment.

Ben gave us his pro forma eye roll. "That's it. I give up on you. Just remember to shut the whole thing down before you get distracted, OK? Ms. Anzengruber may be mellow, but she won't appreciate a dragon in the house. Even a hummingwhatnot is likely to set her off. You know how she feels about portals."

Frankie gave me a squeeze, but they didn't need to: I knew that Ben was right. We'd been taking liberties of late. The more comfortable we got with magic and the opportunities it brought us, the more careless we became. It wasn't a good attitude: we still knew next to nothing about it, and learning via trial and error could prove way too costly. We'd already come close to fucking everything up once; we needed to do our best not to repeat that mistake.

I removed my intention, and the portal closed down. The fall scene outside our patio doors was replaced with a Maine spring morning: bright, but awfully slushy. Ms. Anzengruber's lawn, or what was left of it, had just started to appear through the snow. It looked more suitable to wallowing than twirling, but it was a backdrop rather more conducive to intellectual pursuits. We sighed in unison. Then we turned away from it, and towards our real lives.

Life wasn't so bad, that spring. The days were tumbling over each other in a rush to get us to finals week, but I didn't mind that: for the first time in my life, I felt prepared. I knew I was going to pass. Hell, if some freak disaster made me fuck up, I knew I could ask for make-up exams. With my grades, there was no way the University wouldn't help me. My teachers were cool, anyway, and my health was improving. I could be cautiously optimistic that everything would go just fine, and I would ace my courses.

Frankie was doing well, too. They had a good chance of getting straight As. It was no surprise to me, because they were extremely intelligent, quick to grasp concepts, and had an excellent – though highly selective – memory. The only reason their school record had been so poor was that the adults in their life let them down. As long as they could focus on a subject, they could learn it as easily as anything. The trick was to find a way to make them interested in something; their motivation had to come from the inside, because deadlines and grades did nothing for them. As their curiosity was all-consuming, that wasn't really a problem.

Our only worry about finals week had been that it would mean Ben's graduation. It was great for him, obviously, but we'd not been looking forward to seeing him go. He was our best friend, and the best housemate anyone could wish for. When he decided to stay on for his Master's, we practically threw a party. When he got a Teaching Assistantship, he threw a party back at us. It was a good party, too: I could only remember about half of it. We were going to lose him for a few weeks in the summer, because he was going up north to visit what was left of his family, but then he'd come back to us for at least a year. I could live with that.

Our only other concern had been the fact that our work was going to dry up for the summer. The commons we worked at was shut for the holidays, so we were facing three and a half months with no income. Frankie might be able to find something to tide them over, but I needed to take a full-time field class that was going to eat most of August and obliterated my chances of finding a legal job. I could feed us on next to no money, but there was an abyss between "cheap" and "free." Most importantly, we still had to pay our rent. There was no way in hell we were going to give up our home, because we loved it too much, but we would have rather done that than let Ms. Anzengruber down. She was the best landlady in the universe and the kindest person who ever lived, and she would have let us stay for free if our situation became desperate, but we couldn't do that to her.

Those were the normal challenges we faced, the ones faced by scores of students. We could talk about them without anyone raising an eyebrow. Our situations might have been a bit more extreme than that of the average student, but there was nothing exceptional about university students being concerned about their grades, finances, and future. Most students had families that supported them, more or less, and homes to go back to if everything else failed, but our challenges were still relatively normal.

The rest of the stuff we had to deal with was anything but. We couldn't talk about it – not to other students, not to our teachers, not even to the therapist Frankie and I saw once a fortnight in a desperate bid to keep our shit together. Nobody would believe us if we told them about Frankie's lie-detecting superpower. They'd think that we were making shit up. If they didn't, that would be even worse: once we explained that Frankie's superpower was the result of the wishes Frankie's god-fathers had placed upon them when they were a tiny baby, we would probably find ourselves in an institution somewhere, staring at padded walls. Even my budding teleportation ability might not get us out of that.

We could have found a way to prove our claims. Frankie could have turned their power into some kind of parlor trick with minimal effort, but they had no inclination to do so. I could have tried to 'port in front of people, but public performances weren't really my thing. I still struggled to form complete sentences if more than one person was listening to me. I didn't really rate my chances at anything more complicated than that.

The most unequivocal proofs of the supranatural fuckery afoot lived in the woods behind our house, in the little shelter Ben and Frankie had built for them. Anyone who met them would have had to choose whether to believe our story, or find an alternative explanation for three talking raccoons. We would have never squealed on them, though, even though they deserved it. We hardly saw them, anyway; as soon as spring had sprung, they'd stopped coming round. Frankie thought that it was because the long days made it harder for them to pop over without getting spotted by our neighbors, but I didn't buy that. I reckoned that the little bastards just didn't need us quite as badly, and I was glad of that. I'd never trusted them. Frankie and Ben pined after them, though, and celebrated every visit as if it was a reason to party. I didn't really mind, because Frankie's happiness was one of my favorite things, and every reason for it was a good one, so I kept my reservations to myself.

All in all, our life was looking up. It wasn't normal, perhaps, but neither were we, so it all worked out fine.

2. First Few Desperate Hours

Frankie and I emerged triumphant from our last final. We knew we'd passed, we were done with homework for weeks, the sun was shining, life was fucking glorious, and all I wanted to do was throw them down on the grass right in the middle of campus and kiss the ever-loving shit out of them.

We might have gotten away with it. Most people who looked at us assumed that Frankie was an unusually pretty boy and I was an unusually ugly girl. They might have been bemused by our odd pairing, but they would probably not have felt the urge to kick our queer asses. That risk was ever-present, though, and even without it, sucking face in public just wasn't seemly. We still had a ton of shit to do, anyway.

Frankie had interviews to arrange; they had applied to literally every summer job going, even those they were unqualified for, out of a combination of optimism and desperation. Their theory was that all they were wasting was their time, which was what they were trying to sell in the first place. If they couldn't sell it, they might as well give it away. I could see where they were coming from, but I could tell that they were not being entirely honest – with themself, if not with me. Every rejection hurt them, even the inevitable ones, and I found it hard to understand where that hurt was coming from.

I could be crushed by any failure, but that was because I literally had no self-worth. My brain's accounting system was set up so that I had to constantly achieve in order to be worth a damn. To stay still was to fall behind. To make things more fun, everything I'd ever achieved throughout my whole life could be obliterated by a single failure, however minor, and render me wholly worthless. A year with Frankie and Ben had taught me that my approach wasn't normal, and experience had shown me that it was unhealthy, but that was how my brain worked. I was trying to change it, but it was taking forever. Then again, it had taken me nineteen years to get this fucked up; maybe it would take me as long to unfuck myself.

Frankie wasn't like me, though. They had a few dents, largely thanks to their fucking parents, but they weren't broken. They were almost wholly normal, apart from those parts of them that were abnormally wonderful. Their hurt was coming from a different place, a place I could not see, and my inability to understand what was happening to them, let alone help them, filled me with dread. Between that and the sadness at seeing them hurt, I was cursing the day they'd decided to apply to those damn jobs, and our financial situation for making that a necessity.

The next step would be even worse. They had a handful of interviews to attend, so any further rejection would feel more personal, even if it wasn't. I wasn't sure that I could talk Frankie out of the resulting downers, because I was pretty confident that they weren't talking themself into them. I would try, obviously, but I didn't rate my chances.

That was a problem for another day, though. Our most immediate concern was to unload our textbooks and grab whatever we could get for them. We were going to get fleeced, because the University bookstore bought low and sold high, but there was no way in hell I was going to risk hanging on to them until the following term. If a new edition came out, they'd be worth peanuts.

We made our way to the Student Union, our bags heavy upon our backs but our hearts relatively light. I kept closing my eyes so I could focus on the sunlight warming up my face. I had missed it so much during the winter, and I felt as if it was washing off months of accumulated gloom. Frankie bounced along, chattering about everything and nothing in that broken-dam way they fell into when they were too happy to restrain themself.

Their stream of consciousness dried up when we entered the Union foyer. It was packed, which I expected, but it was also full of market stalls, which I didn't. Most of them sold things we couldn't afford and didn't care for, like fancy clothes and artsy stuff, but one of them sold CDs.

I watched Frankie out of the corner of my eye. They did really well: they steeled their jaw, pointed their eyes straight ahead, and didn't allow their steps to falter. I could tell that it was a struggle for them, though, and I was conflicted between my pride in their resolve and my anger at how unfair the world was. It took so very little to make them ecstatic, and I still couldn't give it to them.

I carried my funk all the way to the bookstore. Frankie, who was a better human being than me, left theirs at the store door and turned their attention to the task ahead. They let me take lead, as they always did when money was going to change hands, but they didn't space out; I could feel them observing and recording every part of the transaction, logging every little detail in their brain.

When it was done, they waited until we were out of earshot before leaning over to whisper in my ear, "Gio, we actually came out on top, didn't we?"

"How did you work that one out?"

"I remember how much we paid to get those books."

"Yet you claim to be bad at numbers."

They snorted. "Remembering worthless trivia doesn't make me a mathematician. My point is that we just got precisely the same amount of money back."

"Yup. You're exceptionally pretty today."

They blushed. "What does that have to do with anything?"

"I think that girl got a bit flustered. I think she liked you quite a bit, love, and you were staring at her very intently. She must have looked at the wrong price list. I hope it won't get her into trouble. I'm sorry, but I didn't feel inclined to correct her."

Their face scrunched up. "Shit. You're sorry? Should I feel sorry, too?"

"I don't know. They're not going to lose any money out of us, but they're not going to make any, either. Basically we just borrowed those books for a term, for free. They were used to start with, and we treated them well. I can live with that."

They beamed. "Me too! You are so fucking good with money! I don't know where I'd be without you!"

Two mental images fought for control of my brain. Without me, maybe they would still be living in a dorm, studying a subject they detested to achieve a qualification they didn't want, all to try and gain the acceptance of parents who'd never shown them any love. Maybe they'd be living with cool people, in a cool place, and having a much cooler life. I didn't like to think about them in either setting, so I pushed the whole thing down and hoped that they wouldn't seek an answer to their question.

I was rescued by the CD stall. They'd forgotten all about it and it took them by surprise. Once it caught their eyes, their heart followed.

They stopped and took a deep breath. "Mind if I take a look? I'll only be a minute."

"You don't need my permission, love."

They looked down at me, a grave look on their face. "I just want to look. I won't buy anything."

That drove an ice pick through my heart. "Frankie, I'm not going to stop you spending your money if that's what you want to do."

They nodded. "Right. But I don't want you to think—"

"Go! Go before I change my mind, and decide I'm the boss of you!"

They flashed me a half-smile and dashed off.

I loved to watch them looking at music and books; they were so focused, so alive, and so expressive. I liked to guess what they were looking at from their responses. The perfunctory flicking through was probably rap, though it could have been opera. The disgusted twist of their mouth was either Supertramp or the Bee Gees; I'd not found anything yet that repulsed them half as much. The widening of their eyes suggested that they'd found the folk or country section; either guitars or fiddles were involved, for sure.

I knew that they'd landed on something special when they froze, lifted a CD with both hands as if it were a holy relic, and nearly charged towards me holding it. Thankfully, they remembered that running off with unpaid merchandise was not the done thing. They stared at me instead, their face glowing with awe and their body vibrating with excitement, until I walked over to them.

They shoved the CD in my face and hissed, "The Mountain Goats have released a new album!"

"On CD? Isn't that a waste of digital audio?"

They flopped as if someone had cut their strings. "Gio, every time you clean the house I have to suffer through ninety minutes of the Ramones."

"Sure, but they're on a tape, where they belong. Hi-fi reproductions of lo-fi music are illogical."

"You're a Vulcan! And a snob!"

"Frankie, have I ever dissed your music?"

They stuck their chin in the air. "Not in so many words. But you don't deem it deserving of being digitally remastered."

"Come on, love! This wasn't mastered in the first place! The guy has a guitar he found at a thrift store, a boom box, and laryngitis."

"Listen, now—"

"Are you going to get it?"

Their exasperation evaporated, and was replaced with shock. "You mean that."

"Of course. You love them. You've passed all your exams. We actually have money in our pockets, for a change, and half of it is yours. You deserve a treat. So? Are you going to get it?"

They looked about to throw themself at me, but stopped themself and smiled a brave little smile. "No. I don't have to buy it. I can request it from the library, borrow it when they get it, and copy it on a tape, where it belongs." They stuck their tongue out at me.

"Careful what you do with that."

"Why, are you going to cut it off?"

I leaned right into them and whispered, "Are you kidding? I love that thing. I know just where to put it."

They blushed crimson, put the CD back in its slot with the tiniest of flinches, and carried on browsing. I stood next to them, trying to recover. Making salacious comments never failed to wind me up more than it ever did them, but sometimes I just couldn't stop myself.

I had managed to make them somewhat distracted, though, which is how they ended up elbowing a tiny woman right in the temple. It wasn't a hard blow and they apologized quickly, profusely, and charmingly, so I was confident that it wasn't going to be an issue. I was sure of it when the woman responded with a smile, and Frankie's invisible antenna shot up.

I had seen this scene before, but it never failed to enchant me. It was the standard meet-cute scene from a Hollywood romance, if Hollywood romances were acted by puppies. The only word I knew that accurately described Frankie's body language was "ebullient," but that failed to express the sheer animal abandon with which they immersed themself into the experience. Their entire body was involved in communicating their joy at finding a new friend to play with.

We both had our own specialized radars. I had my pervdar, alerting me of incoming trouble, and they had their gaydar. I was entirely flummoxed as to why that was: they had no inner sense of gender, and only really understood it in others as a kind of convoluted and largely pointless performance art, so I could not figure out what their gaydar was picking up. It definitely worked, though, and they never failed to get excited when that happened. Had they a tail, it would have been wagging fast enough to lift them off the ground while they barked "Queer! Queer! Queer!" at the top of their voices. It was cute as hell, though some people found it a bit overwhelming.

Happily, the tiny woman seemed to be into it. As Frankie smiled and giggled and bobbed and weaved, she mirrored them, although at a scaled-down level. Then something was said that turned their mutual joy up a notch and broke the salutation spell. Frankie whipped around to look at me, grinning like a pumpkin, and pulled me towards them.

"Gio, this is Siri! She plays bass and her girlfriend plays drums!"

Huh. Queer *and* into making music? No wonder Frankie was in heaven.

I resigned myself to some socializing. I was deeply uncomfortable around girls, as a rule. Their playbook was infinitely more complex than the guys', and I could barely navigate the latter. I wasn't going to ruin this for Frankie, though, so I braced myself, put on a smile, and prepared to fail with all the grace I could muster.

Frankie turned to Siri. "This is Gio. She's my boyfriend."

That was the kind of pronouncement we normally saved for a select audience, but Frankie was too excited to modulate their delivery. The guy who'd been standing next to me jumped a foot sideways and gave me a dirty look. I didn't blame him: one never knew how contagious the queer cooties were. Siri seemed mildly taken aback, but rallied quickly. Her smile to me was very pretty, if somewhat shaky. I tried to reciprocate, but I only managed a rictus.

Either I was doing better than I thought, or Frankie didn't care about my shortcomings. They ploughed on, a grin on their face, so excited that they were bouncing on the spot. "I told Siri that maybe we could practice at our place, when Ms. Anzengruber is at work. Ben wouldn't mind, would he?"

I shook my head. "I doubt it. He doesn't mind much of anything."

Siri cut in. "Ms. Anzengruber? The librarian? She's your landlady?"

Frankie beamed. "Yeah! You know her?"

"Yeah! She's an expert on LGBT fiction! I spoke to her a bunch when I was working on my senior project. I thought she was brilliant!" Her eyes widened. "That was before she went weird."

Frankie's grin froze. "Weird?"

"Yeah." She dropped her voice to a conspiratorial whisper. "She's dating a janitor, isn't she?"

Frankie's grin cracked, and its chunks slid towards the floor. "A plumber."

"Yeah, that. I mean, I understand about community outreach, because those people need to know that books exist, you know, but actually dating them is taking it a bit too far, really."

Frankie took a deep breath. "He's my uncle. I introduced them, kinda."

"Oh." Siri covered her mouth with her hands. "I'm sorry."

"Are you sorry about what you said, or about the fact that he's my uncle?"

They looked bereft, and the situation wasn't going to get any better, so I stepped up, literally and metaphorically. I squeezed between the two of them and smiled at Siri.

"I'm sorry, but we have to be anywhere else."

I put my arm through Frankie's and dragged them out. They followed me quite readily, but they still looked concussed, so I found a quiet corner of the lobby to check on them. I leaned them up against a wall and gave them a quick hug.

"Are you OK?"

They blinked. "Yeah. No. Gio, she was horrible."

"Yes, she was."

They stared at me, their huge eyes full of grief and confusion. "But why? She has a girlfriend!"

"Being a lesbian isn't proof against being an asshole, love."

"I don't get it."

"I know you don't. You're alright. We'll find someone you can play music with who's not horrible."

They smiled the tiniest of smiles. "Is that a promise?"

"No. But I'll do my damn best."

Their smile blossomed. "Thank you. You're a darling."

They shook their experience off them, like a dog with water, and we moved on. We walked towards the library side by side, our hands close enough to touch. We did that a lot: instead of holding hands, we'd walk with the back of our hands against each other. It wasn't what we wanted to do, and it probably wasn't totally safe, but it seemed like a reasonable compromise.

When we got to the library steps, Frankie stopped and looked at me. They had their Very Thoughtful Face on and spoke with great care, so I knew that something serious was about to come my way and braced for impact.

"Gio? Do you miss having sex with people with a vagina?"

I spluttered, "That's a very specific way of putting it."

They shrugged. "It's a very specific question. Try as I might, I cannot provide a vagina for your delectation."

"I'm aware of that. I'm perfectly happy with your configuration, but thank you for asking."

They frowned and poked me, but not hard. "That's not what I asked. I know you like my bits. You show me all the time. That doesn't mean you can't miss other kinds of bits, though. It's a completely different question, and it has a yes or no answer. Don't prevaricate."

"When you put it like that... No. While all types of bits have their pros and cons, I always thought that the innie-outie arrangement was optimal."

"Innie-outie? That's how you think of me?"

"Isn't that right? I mean, from a practical standpoint..."

They blushed so fiercely that I worried about their stubble catching fire. "I get it. I've just never heard it put like that."

"Do you mind?"

"No. I mind no part of that. Not the terminology, and not the... None of it. Not in the least."

"And are you happy enough with my configuration? Are you missing anything?"

They stared straight at me, their eyes glowing green. "No. You're perfect."

"That's not the answer to my question."

"OK, then." They took a deep breath. "Gio, I really like what you've got, but between the way you make me feel and the things you do to me, I wouldn't care if you had no genitals at all. You could be totally smooth down there, like a doll, and I'd still be perfectly happy. Though I might get frustrated at not being able to give you back what you give me. I'd have to find ways to get around that, I guess. I sure as hell would try."

I narrowly contained a squeak of delight. "That is the sweetest thing anyone has ever said to me. Ever."

"Well, then you must have dated a whole bunch of—" They blinked. "Sorry. I was going to say something unkind."

"I don't mind you slandering my exes. It wouldn't be slander, anyway: they were universally awful."

"Oh, it wasn't that: I didn't want to cast aspersions about your taste and judgment."

"You can't. I've displayed neither until the happy day I found you."

They smiled so prettily that my heart melted, and so did half my brain. I walked into the Library staring at the ground, trying to recollect myself and failing to.

My pervdar shook me out of my reverie. All of a sudden, for no obvious reason, it started screaming bloody murder. I didn't even consider questioning that feeling. Ignoring it had always brought me trouble. I couldn't see them yet, but someone was gunning for us. We were in their crosshair. We were prey.

I grabbed Frankie's arm. They took a look at my face and all the playfulness disappeared from them. "What is it?"

"I don't know. Trouble."

"Where?"

"Not sure, but close."

We spotted him at the same time, even though we saw two totally different things. I saw a guy leaning against the checkout desk. He was a little older than us, with blue eyes and a mop of blond hair. He wore a university hoodie and looked perfectly unremarkable, apart from his eyes: he was staring at Frankie with a blank expression that shrouded a consuming hunger.

Frankie stopped in their tracks and snorted. "Uncle Jacob? I thought I'd told him where to go."

"He doesn't look anything like Jacob."

"Yeah, well, that's shapeshifters for you. It's definitely him. What do you wanna do?"

"We're going to have to talk to him, I think. Even if it's just to tell him to fuck off again."

"Alright. Do we want to do it here, or find somewhere private?"

"Here is safer. He won't try anything extreme in front of witnesses. Unless he kills the lot of us."

A muscle twitched in their jaw. "Do you think it's going that way?"

"No. I don't know. I don't like stalkers."

"I don't think this is a sex thing."

"It doesn't have to be. You told him you didn't want to see him again, and here he is. That's stalking."

"You might have a point. Let's get this done."

They walked ahead of me. I tried to walk beside them, but they wouldn't let me: they kept speeding up, so they got to Jacob two steps ahead of me.

When they reached him, they didn't hang about. "What do you want?"

Jacob smiled at them. "Frankie, my child—" His voice sounded precisely the same as it always had. Coming from a different mouth, it gave me a serious case of the creeps.

Frankie wasn't fazed by that. "Less of that, thank you. I'm nineteen now. What do you want?"

Jacob lowered his eyes. "I missed your birthday. I wanted to see you, but... Look, I know we got off on the wrong foot."

"That's the understatement of the year."

"I made a slight miscalculation, and you cut me right off. You didn't give me a chance to put things right. Do you think that's fair?"

My heart sank. Appeals to fairness were Frankie's kryptonite, followed only by their inclination towards forgiveness. They were neither weak nor foolish; they just knew that sometimes people fucked up and needed a second chance. I couldn't disagree with them, because it was certainly true of the two of us.

I stifled a sigh. I knew where this was going and I didn't like it, but I wasn't going to try and stop Frankie from doing what they thought was right. When they gave me a sidelong glance, I nodded.

They stuck their chin up in the air. "No. It wasn't fair. But your miscalculation wasn't slight, and then you were horribly rude about Gio. That isn't something I'll put up with. What do you actually want?"

Jacob's blue eyes twinkled. "To reconnect. To try again. In the short term, to have a chat. Have you had lunch?"

Frankie's face went blank. "Give us a moment, OK?" They nudged me with their shoulder and we retreated out of earshot. Jacob stayed put, although he was still staring at us.

Frankie leaned their head down to my ear and whispered, "Are you thinking what I'm thinking?"

"I think so. We can get a free meal out of this."

They beamed. "Yeah. Pizza?"

"No way. I've seen the shit they sell around here."

"And yet you insist that you're not a snob. Mexican?"

"Never had it. Do they do steaks?"

"Almost certainly." They grinned. "Are you after the most expensive item on the menu?"

"Nah. Well, yeah, but mostly I would like to be less anemic."

"That's very practical of you. I'm going to buy all the food I can eat, and then some, just to spite the asshole. Are we really doing this?"

"If you want to."

They nodded. "Let's get it over with, then. If it goes the way I expect it to go, I want him to fuck off home, wherever that may be, as soon as physically possible."

I stayed back while they made arrangements with Jacob. Whatever they suggested, Jacob wasn't happy with it. Frankie wouldn't budge, though, and Jacob eventually nodded his assent and walked off. He threw me one of his smiles on his way out, one of the ones that used to turn my insides into soup. I was relieved to find that it just made me mildly nauseous.

Frankie didn't look much happier. "I swear, that guy remembers everything we've ever done or said anywhere near him. He mentioned how much you like seafood and offered to take us to a fancy place over in Bar Harbor."

"What? Frankie, there's no way I—"

They squeezed my hand. "I know. I categorically refused to have him drive us anywhere. He wasn't happy about that, but he's going to have to learn to live with provincial dining. We're meeting tonight at the Mexican place in town."

"And then what?"

"And then we hear what he has to say, we tell him what we think of it, and we go home with full bellies. It'll be alright. I'm almost sure of it."

"What if it isn't?"

"Then we deal with that."

They looked at me long and hard, until I nodded.

"Alright. But can we get our shit done and go home? Today is going downhill at a rate of knots."

Their eyes darkened. "I'm sorry. Is there anything I can do to fix that?"

"Unless you're not planning to come home with me, I think you've got that covered."

They brightened up enough to pick up their normal pace. We'd just returned last term's library books and hunted down my first batch of summer reads – only twenty books at a time, because Frankie was weirdly obsessed with making me take a break over the summer and had established a quota system – when we got collared by Ms. Anzengruber. She rushed towards us, looking unusually flustered, and patted my arm in lieu of a greeting before latching onto Frankie's.

"One of our interviewees didn't show. We have a free slot. Do you still want to give it a go?"

Frankie recoiled. "What? Now?"

"Yes." She took a look at their expression and sighed. "Dear, it will be exactly the same as doing it later, but it will be over sooner."

"But I'm not ready! I'm not dressed!"

She pursed her lips. "You look dressed enough. Nobody is expecting you in a suit and tie. Just pop into the bathroom and fix your hair, and you'll be fine."

They frowned. "What's wrong with my hair?"

We both just looked at them. They rolled their eyes, but they scooted off. When they came back, they looked marginally less tousled but infinitely more nervous.

Ms. Anzengruber smiled at them. "Come on, dear. It will be good for you either way. You need the experience."

Frankie mumbled their disagreement, but they went along with her. As they walked off, they turned back to look at me a couple of times, their expression torn between determination and fear. I wanted to run up to them, hug the shit out of them, and keep them safe from everything that threatened their happiness, but it wouldn't have helped us in the long run. We both needed to get used to selling ourselves and to being rejected. In the short run, we simply needed the money.

I sat myself at our usual spot in the reading room. The place was packed with too many people displaying too many emotions way too openly. The combination of stress and jubilation was overpowering, but I managed to block it all out. It wasn't that hard, really: all I could think about was Frankie, getting grilled by some asshole in the bowels of the library so we could have a chance at keeping a roof over our heads.

I wished I could spare them all of this. I wished I could make everything easier for them, and for us. I knew they wished that, too; that was how Jacob nearly managed to make them fuck with the fabric of reality when they first met. Now Jacob was on the scene again, almost certainly with some kind of nefarious intention, and I didn't like that one bit. I was almost sure that Frankie had learned that lesson, that they wouldn't trust that asshole or try to find any supranatural shortcuts to get us out of the shit, but I wasn't totally sure. I couldn't be. I knew that desperation could make people do all kinds of things. All I could do was keep an eye on the situation.

I didn't need to keep an eye out for Frankie. Even though I hardly used it, because we were together most of the time, my Frankie-sense was as keen as ever. I could feel exactly where they were in the library in relation to me. I didn't know where that was, but I knew that I could have followed that sensation and found them. I was really tempted to. I couldn't barge in on their interview, but I could be there for them when they got out. I was just about to indulge my urge when I felt them heading back towards me. When they walked into the reading room, I was already on my feet.

My heart rose when I saw them, and sank when I noticed their expression. They tried to smile their brave little smile at me, but it didn't go very far. Their whole body looked enervated, as if they struggled to support their own weight. They nodded towards the exit, so I got up and we headed out together.

We were halfway to the main road when I realized that they weren't going to talk about their interview, or about anything else. They still looked like shit, and their walk had none of its usual bounce. I could have pretended that nothing was wrong, but that was not how we did business.

I nudged them with my elbow. They looked up and flashed me a smile. "I'm sorry. I don't think it went well. I told them the truth."

"Of course you did!"

Their eyes dropped back to the floor. "Yeah, well, I'm not too sure that they liked it. My work experience is practically nonexistent."

"Your work experience is precisely like mine, and you made me apply here last term."

"Yeah, but it's different for you. You're a real book person. I'm not."

I felt sorry for them, because they were clearly miserable, but I also felt that they needed a kick in the butt. Nobody else was there to do the honors, so I decided to give it a go.

"Of course. You're totally right. You pretend to read books, right? You just hold them in front of you for the scholarly air they give you."

They frowned. "Of course I don't. That would be silly."

"Right. So you pretend to be a person?"

They stopped and crossed their arms over their chest. "Gio, what the devil are you on about?"

"If you are a real person, and you really read books, then you are a real book person. If they don't hire you, they're fools. But it is more likely to have to do with competition, love. Half the people left in this hellhole need a job. You'll find something."

They murmured, "And if I don't?"

"Then you can spend a few weeks doing nothing but fucking me, and three weeks looking after me. It'd be nice to come home from class and find my dinner ready, and you wearing an apron. Just an apron, I mean, and not another stitch. Shoes optional."

Their smile got a bit warmer. "I would make you breakfast, too. And pack your lunch."

"No way. If I have to spend my days digging holes in the dirt, the last thing I want to see leaving the house is you in my bed. It's the only thing guaranteed to keep me going all day long."

Their eyes dropped to the floor again, but their smile had returned. By the time we got home, they were back to their normal, bouncy self, although they still looked a bit fragile around the edges. I wasn't sure if spending the evening with a guy we neither liked nor trusted was what we needed. It was what we needed to do, though, and it involved us getting fed properly for once, so I didn't try to talk them out of it.

They hit the shower first. I jumped in as soon as they got out, praying that there would still be enough hot water to wash the day off of me. When I walked out of the shower and saw them sitting on our bed, idly flicking through one of my paperbacks, I nearly had a coronary.

"You're dressed!"

They squinted at me. "Yes. It seemed appropriate. We're going out, and I don't think this town is ready for naked dining yet."

"But you have a shirt on! And you've brushed your hair!"

They tilted their head. "Gio, I love you dearly, but sometimes I worry about the level of interest you show in my hair. Yes, I have brushed it. I also tried to tie it back, but it's not long enough yet."

I kept staring at them, trying to find the words to express the fear clutching at my throat, but all I could do was mouth like a fish out of water.

They half-closed their eyes and flopped on the bed. "I just brushed my hair, Gio. I know it's twice in one day, but it seemed like the thing to do. What's the problem?"

"I didn't realize this was going to be a formal occasion! I have nothing to wear!"

They rolled their eyes. "My shirt, your pants, Ms. Anzengruber's coat. You know the drill. You've done it before. Or come naked. I'm sure I wouldn't be the only person there to appreciate that." They lifted themself up on one elbow and looked at me with sad, brown eyes. "We never dress up. I'm more than fine with that, but I thought you might like it. I thought you missed it."

"I do. Were it just me and you, I would love it. But Jacob will be there."

"I fucking hope so, because he's paying. Are you worried that he's going to judge you for what you wear?"

"Yes. I guess."

"If he's going to judge you, then he'd judge you anyway, even if you wore one of my hoodies – which you look fucking gorgeous in, by the way, particularly when it's all you've got on. But that's another story. Why does it matter more if he judges you when you dress up?"

I had to think about that, but not for very long. "If I don't try, I can't fail."

Frankie sat up and patted the bed next to them. I walked over and tried to sit down, but they wouldn't let me: they grabbed my waist and pulled me over instead, until we were lying side by side. Their eyes looked even sadder and browner close up.

"Gio, I don't know what to do. I want you to come with me, obviously, but I don't want you to have a terrible time."

"I won't. I'll get over it."

They winced. "Try again. You don't believe that."

"Sorry. But it is true, mostly. I'll have fun because I'm out with you, even though it stresses me out. The fun may be more than the stress. It usually is, when you're with me."

They ran their hand through my hair and rested it on the back of my neck. "I get it. I wish it wasn't a thing, though."

"It's less of a thing every day."

"I wish it just went away."

"Me too. I'm sorry."

They frowned. "Don't be. I'm sorry."

"You are? What a surprise!"

Their eyes narrowed. "Are you making fun of me?"

"Yes." They opened their mouth to complain, but I closed the distance between us and kissed them. They held back for a full two seconds before getting into it.

When we came up for air and they opened their eyes, they were green again. They still tried to frown at me. "Gio, that's not fair. You know I can't think when you do that."

"Good. Thinking disturbs the brain."

They nuzzled my neck and whispered in my ear, "We could stay here and fuck all night instead of going out."

"Or we could go out, stuff our faces with steak at Jacob's expense, tell him to fuck off, again, and then come back here."

"And fuck all night?"

"If you want to. No school tomorrow."

"I have two interviews in the afternoon."

"We could pretend it's Sunday. Stay in bed all morning."

They sighed against my neck and sent shivers all the way through me. "You are getting positively debauched in your old age. Roguish, too."

"That a problem?"

"Nope. I love it." They pushed away from me, their eyes sparkling. "But if you spend another five seconds in bed with me, all your planning will go to waste. You're naked under that robe."

"Shockingly enough, yes. I tend to undress whenever I perform my ablutions. I find that it facilitates the process. Clothes come off, soap goes on, as a rule. Water is also involved."

Their lips parted. "You know you're killing me, right?"

"I really hope I'm not." I slipped out of bed, though it was a wrench. It took me all of five minutes to locate Frankie's silk shirt and my best pants. I could feel their eyes on me all the way through it. When I turned around and saw them sprawled on my bed, I nearly got undressed again. We had no time for that, though. I steeled myself and tried to get their body out of my brain.

"I'm going to get Ms. Anzengruber's coat."

They tilted their head. "I'll miss you."

"I'll only be upstairs, love."

"I know. I'll still miss you."

I knew that they meant it. I had to tear myself away from the magnetic pull of their eyes. I barely made it. Even after I closed the door behind me, I could still feel them looking at me. I raced upstairs, knowing full well that my hurrying was for nothing: even if borrowing Ms. Anzengruber's coat took seconds rather than minutes, it would still not leave me enough time to show Frankie just how much into them I was, or to let them get enough into me.

Thinking about that got me a little distracted, to put it mildly. That was how I managed to ignore all the clues: that Ms. Anzengruber's voice sounded hollow when she told me to come in; that her lights were off, even though what was left of the sunset did little more than highlight how gloomy the evening was; that she was sitting on her couch clutching a glass as if her life depended on it, her books and crochet languishing next to her. I only realized that something was terribly wrong when she turned towards me and I saw the dread in her eyes.

I froze where I stood. "What is it? What's wrong?"

"It's fine, Gio. Don't panic."

"I won't panic if you tell me what's wrong."

She patted the couch. I unglued my feet from the floor, walked over, and sat down next to her.

She sighed. "It's good news, really. They got the job."

"What?"

"Frankie got the library job. They got it fair and square. I would have never interfered with the hiring process, and I am overjoyed for them, but we will be working together for over three months." She turned and locked eyes with mine. "Gio, I love them, but I'm going to kill them. I just know I will. And I really don't want to, because I *do* love them."

I flinched. I knew exactly what she meant. I loved Frankie more than life itself and I wanted them to be with me every minute of every day, but most people had to take them in small doses. Ms. Anzengruber really liked things to be quiet and neat, and Frankie simply lacked that mode.

I still tried to reassure her. "They are not that bad."

She fixed her eyes on the wall across the room. "The last time I drove them to campus, they sang a song about an ice cream man all the way there. The song sounded as if it had been intended for two or more people, but they sang all the parts. Repeatedly."

"Yeah, well, they've been really focused on their finals. When they're concentrating but not busy enough, their mental jukebox is basically left to do its own thing, and it can get jammed. They can't really hear it."

"Yes, but I can."

I patted her hand. "You'll be OK. All you have to do is keep them busy."

"And they won't sing about ice cream men?"

"They might still hum a bit."

She put down her glass and turned to stare at me. "How do you cope with it?"

"I can't hear them if I'm reading. I can't hear much of anything. And I don't find it that unpleasant, unless they get stuck on repeat or they sing the backing vocals only; that gets really annoying really fast. When that happens, I put some music on, so they sing along to that instead. But you couldn't really do that at the library."

"Nope." She picked up her glass again and took a swig.

"You can change the tune they sing really easily. You just have to sing a bar of something they know..." She was giving me A Look, so I tried really hard to think of another option. "OK. You just need to send them on quests: they'll be busy, they'll be out of your way, and they'll be super-efficient. If they really get into the zone, they might not even hum."

She squinted. "Quests?"

"Yeah. Whatever you ask them to do, turn it into some kind of expedition. Ask them to find all the books that are out of place, or all the places where the books need to go, and they'll get it done in no time, and thoroughly. Ask them to tidy up a stack, and they'll struggle."

"Even though it's exactly the same task?"

"Yeah. They'll get bored and have to force themself to pay attention. That never works well. You kind of have to think of them as a puppy: you have to keep them busy with something that grabs them, or they'll trash your house."

"Hmm." She pursed her lips, but her eyes were smiling. "I seem to recall comparing them to my dog not so long ago, and you baulking at that."

I could feel my face getting hotter. "Yeah, well, there was more to it than that."

"Indeed. I believe some emotions were mentioned and denied."

"That may have been the case. Would it be easier if I just admitted that you were right and I was wrong?"

She smiled. "It would definitely speed things up. To what do I owe your presence, anyway? Not that I don't enjoy it, but you probably came here for a reason."

I rewound the last ten minutes. "Your coat! Can I borrow it? Frankie and I are going out."

"Sure. But there's a catch."

"Oh?"

She sighed. "Would you tell them about the job? I don't want them to worry when they don't need to, but I don't trust myself to have that conversation with them. I am genuinely happy for them; I'm just not happy for me, and I don't want to hurt their feelings. You know how good they are at picking up on that kind of thing."

"Sure.

She patted my leg, and I took that as my cue to clear off. I left her still sitting in the gloom, but she looked much happier. Resigned, anyway.

I rushed down the stairs to find Frankie rushing up.

"What the hell did you two get up to? You've been ages!"

I put my arm through theirs and dragged them out the door. "Portentous news, love: you've reentered the world of employment."

They stopped dead. "You mean that."

"Of course I do. Ms. Anzengruber just told me, and asked me to pass the news along. She wanted you not to worry."

They threw their arms around me. "That's great!"

"It is! No more applications, no more interviews, and I can come to the library with you every day."

They kissed my neck and whispered in my ear, "You wouldn't rather stay in bed and do fuck-all, for a change?"

"Nah. I'd rather be where the books are."

They dropped me as if I was on fire. "That was true. I thought that maybe you... Is it the only reason you'd come to the library with me?"

They were upset, which upset me. I'd only meant it as a joke, and forgot that it was a truth and that they would see that.

I wrapped my arms around them. "No, you dodo. I want to be with you. I like you better than books."

It took them a couple of seconds to return my hug, but when they did, it was a good one. It was so good that I wanted to march them back into the house and have my way with them, but Jacob was waiting for us.

I disentangled myself, inwardly cursing the gods and their meddling, and pulled Frankie towards our shortcut via the railroad tracks.

We were just going past the beaver pond when they stopped. "Gio? You don't think I only got the job because Ms. Anzengruber helped me out, do you?"

I thanked all the gods for the way in which Frankie had worded their question. I could answer it truthfully without telling them what I didn't want them to know. "No, love. That is definitely out of the question."

We found Jacob sitting at the bar of the restaurant. He was sipping on something extremely pink from a glass the size of a fish bowl, snacking on tortilla chips, and sweet-talking a server who looked extremely taken by him. I was not surprised; he was wearing a face that looked like a combination of the one he wore when we first met him and the one he'd worn at the library. He looked a little bit like a rugged, fair-haired version of Frankie, a little bit like a young Kurt Cobain, and a whole lot like a really hot dude.

His looks did nothing for me, though. Not anymore. Once upon a time, I'd found him almost unbearably attractive. He had managed to wrap up everything I loved about Frankie and everything I missed about guys in an extremely sexy package. Now that I knew what a manipulative piece of shit he could be, I was totally over him. The fact that he picked up and discarded faces more often that I changed my socks added an extra dash of disgust to my dislike for him. I didn't loathe him yet, but I was working up to it.

The server didn't know what I knew, and was clearly unhappy to have us interfering with their buddying courtship. She didn't stand a chance, though: as soon as we walked in, Jacob turned every ounce of his attention on Frankie, erasing her existence from his mind. She looked heartbroken, but she still managed to find us a table. Jacob picked the one furthest from everything and everyone, right at the back of the room. I had some serious misgivings about sitting so close to him and so far from the exits, but I ignored them. I was being paranoid, as usual. He wouldn't have tried anything in a public place. I was almost sure of that.

He was playing nicely for now, anyway; almost too nicely, in fact. I didn't know any of the food, so I let Frankie order for both of us. They knew what kind of stuff I liked, and we were going to pick at each other's food, anyway, so I was perfectly happy with them taking charge. However, I was taken aback when they started ordering stuff and just didn't seem to stop. By the time they were done, they'd ordered half the damn menu. I though Jacob might be vexed, but he wasn't; on the contrary, he smiled at them with an avuncular expression that badly suited his current face.

As soon as the server was out of earshot, he turned towards Frankie with a beaming smile and his charm dialed up to max. "Thank you so much for coming. You don't know how happy you made me."

Frankie blinked. "It's just dinner."

"I know, but... Never mind. We have so much to catch up with. How is school?"

"Great. We finished our finals today. I did alright. Gio is going to ace all his courses, obviously."

Jacob smiled dazzlingly at me, and then switched me off. "Great. And do you have any plans for summer?"

"Gio is taking a class, so she can't get a job. I'm still looking."

Jacob frowned. "Should you be working during your breaks?"

"I like to live in a house and eat all year round. It's probably a bad habit, but I can't seem to break it."

"I could—"

Frankie cut him off. "No. Thank you. We're doing just fine."

Frankie and Jacob locked eyes and didn't let go. They were clearly determined to out-stare each other, neither of them willing to back down. It was the most ludicrously macho thing I'd ever seen Frankie do. I understood it, under the circumstances, but I felt awfully embarrassed by it. I also felt physically uncomfortable; it went on for so long that my eyes started watering in sympathy.

The air between them was starting to sizzle when the server turned up with our starters, breaking their standoff. They both turned towards her to thank her. When she cleared off, they went on as if nothing had happened.

Jacob made small talk while we worked through our starters. When the actual meal turned up, he stopped talking altogether. He hardly touched his food, but he seemed overjoyed at watching us stuff our faces.

I didn't know what I was eating, and I didn't really care: most of it was wonderful, and the sheer amount of it was enough to make me happy. Frankie kept dropping bits and pieces on my plate, and I ate until I just couldn't eat any more. Frankie did a lot better than me, managing to shovel a truly surprising amount of stuff into their belly.

When we were all done, the server reappeared and started to clear up. Watching all that wonderful food being taken away made me want to cry, until Frankie leaned close to me and whispered in my ear, "Wenchlad, we're gonna get a doggy bag."

"Really?"

"Yup. Prepare yourself for Mexican three times a day until it's all gone."

I smiled up at them and they mouthed a half-kiss at me. It made me feel squiggly inside, and all of a sudden I was exhausted. I couldn't wait to be done with the evening and with Jacob. I just wanted to be home with Frankie. There was socializing to be done, though. Truly, there was no such thing as a free lunch.

After asking us twice if we wanted a dessert we couldn't possibly eat, Jacob leaned back in his chair, smiled that creepy smile of his, and set off declaiming.

"I know it's terribly old-fashioned, but I believe that the Greeks were right: self-knowledge is the key to unlocking all other wisdoms. It's the foundation upon which we build the cathedral of our knowledge. Know thyself, and you will know the gods. For your people, the opposite is also true: know the gods, and you will know thyself. Knowing what my people have bestowed upon you lets you discover and explore the ways in which you stand out from the crowd, what makes you different, what makes you special. You must be aware by now that my people aren't allowed to talk to your people about the three wishes."

Frankie snorted. "Isn't that what you're doing right now?"

Jacob beamed. "Yes. I don't think much of rules when they get in the way of what I want."

"And the rest of the time?"

"They can be a convenient tool, I guess, if you don't get too attached to them and don't expect others to follow them. Anyway, you know about the wishes already. That makes the taboo totally futile."

"You might have a point there, but I don't want any of this to backfire." They found my hand under the table. "I don't want any trouble. Not for me, not for Gio, and not for anyone who's attached to me. You get me? Not like the last time."

Jacob raised his hands in a conciliatory gesture. "The last time? Nothing happened! Nobody was harmed in any way!"

"But it could have. And kidnapping people *is* harming them."

"You make is sound so dramatic. It does you credit: that you're determined to protect your consort—"

"No. We protect each other."

Jacob's smile faded for a split second. "Quite so. Do you want to hear what I have to say? My time with you, as you defined it, is very limited."

Frankie glanced at me out of the corner of their eye. I shrugged.

"OK. But I reserve the right to stop you if I don't like how this is going."

Jacob beamed. "Of course. So, I took the liberty to run a little investigation on your behalf, to discover your wishes."

Frankie's hand twitched around mine. "That's creepy as hell. And it can't be on my behalf, because I'd not asked you to do it."

"As you say. Now, I knew that you'd met one of your other makers. There aren't too many of my kind living in this area. It has... limitations. So it was a moment's work to find out who your other godfather was. I was disappointed on your behalf—"

Frankie closed their eyes and spoke through gritted teeth. "If you could find it in your heart to stop doing things on my behalf, that'd be swell."

Jacob's smile flickered offline for a long instant. "Let us not be the victims of semantics. At any rate, your other godfather is an artificer. When I heard that, I was disheartened. Those people have their uses, obviously, but they tend to be woefully limited in their outlook. This time, however, one of them was accidentally useful. The wish he placed on you was awfully pedestrian – a mere fault-finding ability, typical of someone who dedicates himself to menial tasks."

Frankie spluttered. "What? But I have a lie detecting thing!"

"You do and you don't. You can see where pieces don't fit, which is why you can spot lies. If you tried unclogging toilets, or whatever it is that Marin does with his time, you might find yourself good at that, too. Not that I'd recommend it: you can do so much more!" He smiled a smile with too many teeth in it. It made something inside me quake, and gave me an urge to grab Frankie and scurry away. I don't think Jacob picked up on it; he only had eyes for Frankie.

He leaned forward towards them, with a passionate look on his face. I was willing to bet that any onlooker would have thought that he was propositioning them. "I only make one wish for my godchildren: not to be bound by artificial limitations. Your people live their lives shackled by cultural mores, personal habits, and fears, both natural and cultivated. They live bound by rules they make up for themselves. Hardly any of these rules are of any real use, and all of them are limiting."

I found my tongue. "Plenty of mores are useful. The proscriptions against cannibalism and infanticide are mores."

Jacob started, as if surprised to find me still there. "Plenty of societies didn't subscribe to them, and prospered. Morals are contextual."

"Moral relativism is a fun game to play, until someone gets hurt."

He leered. "Yet you cannot argue that morals aren't relative. Not with a straight face, anyway. And my wish isn't for my godchildren to reject all rules offhand. It's merely for them to see them for what they are: convenient fabrications, rather than facts of life. Frankie can see what's really there and what's made up. It's the ability to recognize the difference between the laws of gravity and the rules of the road. On this occasion, my wish intersected rather neatly with the artificer's wish." He turned back to Frankie. "You can see the faults in things, and you can see the differences between laws and rules. Combined, they are at the root of your lie-detecting ability, but the same abilities can go much further: you can see cracks in reality. Both in our individual realities, and in the collective fiction we all sign up to."

Frankie shrugged. "I'm sorry, but I don't get that. What does that do?"

"The most basic application is spotting and using weaknesses in people or objects."

"Using weaknesses? For what?"

Jacob grinned. "To change things beyond all recognition, or to break them utterly. All you need to do is find their weakness, manipulate their weak spot with enough force, and they will shatter before you. And force you have aplenty. You must have noticed by now that you have more energy than most other people."

Frankie blinked. "Yeah. It's kind of a problem."

"On the contrary, child: it's a blessing! You have the means to know exactly where to hit, and the ability to hit with vigor, both metaphorically and literally. You can break anything you want. The glasses on our table, a heart, or reality as we know it. That's what I was trying to show you, when we were interrupted." He flicked a glance at me.

Frankie clutched at my hand and wailed. "What? That's not what you told me! I was just trying to rewind things a bit so we'd be less messed up. I wasn't trying to break anything!"

Jacob shrugged. "The difference between breaking things and changing them is a matter of perspective. Everything changes. So does everyone. The speed and direction of the change is what tends to give people pause. You have the power to force instant changes. Some people will call it 'breaking,' others will thank you. Do you care about their opinion?"

"If it's their shit I'm breaking, yes, of course I do!" They turned to me. "Gio, I didn't know. You have to believe me."

I squeezed their hand. "I do. I get it. You were trying to help. You hate it when you break stuff."

Jacob ignored me completely. "When I first met you, I wasn't sure how far your power could go. I knew you had the ability to really make an impact, but I didn't know how much. I'd grossly underestimated you. Child, nothing and nobody can stand in your way. Not even yourself."

Frankie went perfectly rigid. "I beg your pardon?"

"Destruction is what you're made for – literally. It's your manifest destiny." He leaned forward and whispered lustily, "You needn't be afraid. The acts of creation and destruction are one and the same, two sides of the same coin. To you falls the destruction, is all."

"But I don't want to destroy anything!" Frankie was starting to really freak out. Their eyes were showing so much sclera that they looked more white than brown.

Jacob shrugged. "Look around you. Look at the things in this place. Look at the humans. Look at your consort. Are you telling me that you don't know the words that would hurt them – hurt them so badly that they would never go back to being the person they are right now?"

Frankie stared at me, horrified. "No. I mean, yes, maybe, but I'd never... I wouldn't. Gio, I fucking wouldn't!"

Jacob's smile didn't waver. "Maybe not today. But you know those words right now. You can see them in your mind. It's no different from knowing where to stab them in order to kill them instantly."

"But I don't fucking stab people!"

"Of course. But you are capable of doing so. You're the knife that can cut all bonds. You are a loaded gun. If you had never used your abilities, that wouldn't change them, and it wouldn't change your nature. But that is not the case: you have broken so much already, all around you, instinctively and freely. You have stuck your fingers in so many chinks in so many armors, and you don't even realize it. Was your consort single before they met you?"

"Yes! I'm not a home-breaker!"

"But you broke their solitude. You broke their independence. You broke your way into their heart. You broke so much of their life as it was, and changed it to suit your needs. Was it a bad thing you did?"

All the color drained out of their face. "No. I don't know. Gio?"

They were looking at me in despair, needing reassurance, and for the first time in our life together I couldn't give it to them. They'd made my life infinitely better than it had ever been, but there was no denying that they had changed it beyond recognition. I would have never had the courage to embark in such an upheaval on my own: they said the right things, all the way through, and spurred me through the changes.

They'd said the right things, or the wrong things. My life had become wholly Frankie-centric. They were the lynchpin around which everything else revolved. If they left me, my entire life would fall apart. I thought I had chosen that. All of a sudden, I wasn't so sure.

It wasn't just my life they'd changed. Ben, Marin, Ms. Anzengruber... None of us had survived their encounter with Frankie without undergoing a profound metamorphosis. Our lives had changed for the better, and without any premeditation on Frankie's part, but that just supported Jacob's statement. Frankie hadn't meant to turn our lives upside down: they'd just done so because that was what they did.

Frankie read my face. Their face sank in response, before they shut it down completely.

Jacob leaned back in his seat, his grin manic and feral. "I told you, child: it's your destiny. You are nature's wrecking ball, and you have two choices before you: You can learn to control your gift, or let your gift control you. I can help you learn to use it. Creative destruction is my forte."

Frankie locked eyes with him. "No. You're enjoying this. I'm not. I have no doubt that you'd guide me, but I don't trust you to guide me in the direction I want to go."

Jacob frowned. "That is hurtful, yet nowhere near as hurtful as the words you find on the tip of your tongue, and have to bite back. You could destroy me, same as you could destroy anything else."

Frankie's jaw twitched. "That's what you don't get: I don't want to destroy. You have an agenda. You always did. And I want no part of it."

"Child, if you're not with me, then you're against me." He said it casually, but the words sent a chill down my spine.

Frankie was undaunted. "If that's true, then your world is too black-and-white. I will not be your pawn."

Jacob's smile came back, with more teeth than ever. They looked sharper, too. "I'd intended for you to be my queen. It seemed more in line with your proclivities." He schooled his face back to cordiality. "Child, I realize that this whole thing may be a bit of a shock. Even for an agent of change such as yourself, changing your own self-image can be a challenge. Give it time. Think about it. Oh, I also took the liberty of investigating your consort's wishes."

Frankie's face went completely blank. "You did what?"

"I hardly thought it appropriate to give you a gift of that magnitude without doing the same for your consort. I didn't think you'd appreciate that."

Frankie blinked. "Sticking your nose in Gio's business is not OK. But I can see how you might have thought that."

Jacob shrugged. "It makes no odds. I found very little. I only discovered one wisher – a minor genius loci. I trust you know what that means?"

Frankie glanced at me. "Vaguely. The spirit of a place."

"That's all you need to know about it, really. They are so very limited, unless you find yourself on their territory. I couldn't discover the specific nature of the wish, but it is something to do with a sense of home, an attraction and devotion to a place." Jacob turned towards me. "I understand you're an émigré. I'm sorry. That must be difficult for you. To be a genius loci without a locus..." He trailed off and looked at me with something that was probably intended to approximate sympathy or empathy, but made me want to smack him in the face.

Frankie's hand twitched in mine. They opened their mouth to speak, but I cut them off.

"Thank you. Yes, it is uncomfortable. I need to go home now. Sorry to cut the party short, but."

Jacob's faux concern deepened. "Of course! I understand that this is a lot to take in."

"It is. We'll need to think about it."

Frankie opened their mouth again, but I squeezed their hand. They looked at me for an instant, swallowed, and nodded.

"Yes. I need some time to process this. I'll be in touch."

Jacob beamed, his smile looking almost human. "I'll look forward to that. I want you to realize your full potential. You must know that."

Frankie stared at him for a few seconds, and nodded. I got up and they followed me. Jacob trailed behind. We said a hasty goodbye to him while he settled the bill, only remembered our doggy bags because the server nearly threw them at us, and scuttled the hell out of there and towards home.

Frankie stopped as soon as we were out of sight of the restaurant. "Gio, he was telling the truth. He does want me to realize my full potential."

"I don't doubt it, but I'm pretty sure that you would have come to a different conclusion if you'd put the word 'just' in there. He doesn't *just* want you to realize anything. He has his own agenda, as you said, and he's demonstrably full of shit, anyway."

"But he wasn't lying, and you believed him." They stumbled over the words. They were shaking all over, their eyes still unnaturally wide.

I struggled as hard as I could to find the right words, to give them a truth that might reassure them. "Love, some of what he said is somewhat right, and I'm sure he believes all of it, but he's still full of shit. You change things. So do I. Everyone does. To live is to change, ourselves and those around us."

They shook their head. "It's easy for you to say. You can't break reality, or hurt people."

"Bullshit. Right now, I know exactly the words I could tell you to break your life into pieces. Although it may not work with you, because I don't believe them and you'd know that."

They stuck their chin in the air, a muscle twitching in their jaw. "And those words are?"

"You can't come home with me. Not ever. You're not safe to be around."

They reeled away from me for an instant, then leaned towards me. "You don't mean that!"

"I don't." I walked into their arms and hugged them. "I have a number of theories. None of them are solid and all of them are based on very little, but I want to talk to you about them. At home. In bed. Naked."

"What? Why?"

"Because what Jacob said spooked you, and I want to unspook you. You've never been spooked naked in bed with me. That's half of it."

"And the other half?"

I let go of them and pulled them towards home. "He spooked me, too. I need to feel your skin. I need to remember who we are."

We didn't talk again until we had found our way into our bed and each other's arms. Even then, we let our bodies do the talking for a while. We only went back to words once we'd managed to make our dread dissipate.

Frankie kissed my hair and spoke into it. "I don't like this thing I've got. I don't want to hurt you. Not ever. Not even by accident."

"Anyone can hurt anyone. You're way stronger than me: you could kill me without breaking a sweat."

They pulled back to look at me. "I don't think so. You've got a fierce streak. And I wouldn't, anyway. I never, ever want to hurt you."

"I know. That's the point. The issue is not one of ability, but of intention. Ben is stronger than both of us. Do you think he'd ever hurt us?"

"No. He doesn't have it in him."

"There you go. Neither do you."

"But Jacob was right about me changing your life."

"He was. But I changed your life, too. Love, you were studying accounting when I first met you. You used to make your bed every morning. You brushed your hair."

Their hand ran to their curls. "Again with my hair. I'm going to have to cut it off if you keep this up."

"You don't and you won't. That's not my point, anyway. Of course we've changed each other's lives: we'd have to be a pretty shitty couple not to do that, at least a bit. You didn't manipulate me in order to lead me to this. Love, maybe you can see my weak points. If you do, that doesn't worry me. I know you'd only use that knowledge to keep me safe."

"Because I love you?"

"Because, unlike Jacob, you're not an asshole. Which is one of the reasons why *I* love *you*." I kissed them.

They softened under my kiss, and sighed. "What about that genius loci thing?"

"Right. That further proves my point. Stay where you are."

I pulled away from them and scooted to the far end of the bed. They looked bereft and confused. When I 'ported back to them, they just looked confused.

"Frankie, Jacob said that I have a sense of home, an attraction to it. I do. And it takes me back to you. I've never been able to 'port anywhere else, just towards you. And I feel where you are, all the time. Jacob had it less than half right, because he doesn't understand that home isn't a place: it's where you love and are loved. It's where you're safe."

Frankie's face got all scrunched up, which meant that they had a feeling so big that they didn't want to let it out. "But maybe I put that into you."

"You did. By loving me and taking care of me. By giving me more than I ever dreamed I could have. Of course I want to 'port back to you: being with you makes me feel good. And it's good for me, too. I don't think you could trick me into feeling at home with you any more than I could trick you into believing a lie." I poked their chest, right over their heart. "You'll have to just accept that our love for each other is for real, with all attendant issues."

"Like what?"

"Like the fact that it proves that you're grossly unsuited to being the Doom Of Humankind or some suchlike shit, manifest destiny or not. You might be a human wrecking ball, like Jacob said, but you're also a sweetheart."

They blinked. "What if one day you can't 'port to me?"

"Then I'll have to use my legs, like I did before this started. Stop trying to find holes in my theory, or I'll have to try and find holes in yours."

"Like what?"

"Like the fact that we're both demonstrably shit at fulfilling our destinies. I was raised to be my mother's keeper. You were supposed to become an accountant, for fuck's sake."

They nearly smiled. "And to be a dude."

"That, too. A dude accountant. Can you imagine that? You'd have to wear a suit and brush your hair every day. We've thwarted our destinies up to now. I think we can carry on doing so. Quasi-magical abilities aren't enough to stop us."

"How do you know that?"

"They give us options. All we have to do is not take them. Love, I think Jacob wants you to believe that you have no choice."

"He believes that himself. You know that I'd know if he was lying."

"Sure. But his belief doesn't have to be your reality. He's wrong: about you, about me, and about us. And I don't trust him."

"Neither do I."

"What are you going to do about him?"

"I'm not sure." They wrapped their arms around me. "But there's one thing I'm sure of."

"That I love you?"

"No. I mean, yes, but I was thinking of something else. I have to tell Uncle Marin about this. Maybe I should have told him all along."

"He's going to go ballistic."

"He is. But if he can stop me making a mess of things, it's worth it."

We didn't get a chance to tell Ben about all the crap that had gone down with Jacob before he left. His sister's baby was due any day, so he was out the door as soon as he'd finished his last exam. Well, almost: he still found the time to lecture us on proper household and raccoon management.

It was odd for him to sound authoritative. He was normally so spaced out and so easy-going that anything like a definite statement from him seemed abnormal. He was clearly serious about this, though, and that seriousness was coming through loud and clear. It was kind of hot: he was the gentlest person I'd ever met, but he was fucking built, and the deep rumble in his voice when he tried to be stern had a tendency to do weird things to my insides.

"The kids are not allowed to bake unsupervised. I don't trust them to turn the oven off, and they always confuse the flour and the sugar. I think they do it on purpose."

We nodded – or rather I nodded, and Frankie copied me. They were clearly miles away.

A muscle twitched under Ben's eye. "Frankie, what are the kids not allowed to do?"

Frankie snapped back to reality with a visible jolt. "Hmm... Err..."

"They are not allowed to bake unsupervised. And what are *you* not allowed to do?"

They turned to me, a question in their eyes. I shrugged. I had an idea where this was going, but I could not be sure.

Ben spoke clearly and loudly, emphasizing every syllable. "You're not allowed to supervise them. While you are in here," he gestured to the kitchen area of our garage, "Gio is in charge, of you and of the kids. You're not in charge of them. Gio is. Get it?"

"But—"

"No! They need adult supervision. So do you."

"I'm nineteen!"

"Yes, but you are... you're more suited to creative pursuits, OK? You can make popcorn and watch movies with them." He frowned. "Do not let them watch horror movies, even if they ask nicely. They enjoy them at the time, and then they can't sleep for a week. What are they not allowed to watch, Frankie?"

They sighed. "Horror movies. I am listening, you know?"

"Sure thing."

"But..."

"What?"

"What counts as a horror movie? I mean, vampires are not *that* scary..."

Ben closed his eyes and took a deep breath. "When in doubt, ask Gio. When not in doubt, still ask Gio. If it's rated PG, definitely ask Gio."

"What if I don't know the rating? Ms. Anzengruber's tapes—"

"Ask Gio." He frowned and looked at me. "I'm sorry about this. Maybe I should wait until the kids turn up and take them with me."

I stifled a chortle. "I'm sure your sister would love that. Nothing would make a heavily pregnant mother of four happier than three talking raccoons invading her home."

"My nephews and nieces would love them."

"She'd never forgive you. Go. We'll manage."

"Don't let them get caught. Ms. Anzengruber—"

"She's too busy snogging Marin."

"She only needs to see them once, and we'll all be in the shit. Speaking of which...." He dropped his eyes to the ground and scuffed the floor. "I don't suppose I could ask you to give your portals up for a while? I'll only be gone a couple of weeks. Three at the most. Maybe four."

I thought about four weeks without portals: four weeks without sunny glades, without hummingflies and dragons, without Frankie dancing in our skirt, without an escape from our life. I could manage that, but I really didn't want to.

I was still wracking my brain for the right answer when Ben half-slapped and half-stroked my shoulder. "Don't worry about it. I shouldn't have asked. Just be careful, OK? Don't do anything I wouldn't." He looked at Frankie, who was grinning like a jack-o'-lantern and humming softly to themself. "OK, that's not going to work. Don't do anything that seems like a really bad idea. Ring me if you have any problems. Or if you wanna talk."

"I'll definitely want to talk. I'll miss you."

He flinched. "I'll miss you too. Just, dunno, keep an eye on things, but don't let them run you ragged." He turned to scowl at Frankie. "Do not run Gio ragged. This is supposed to be a holiday for her, too."

Frankie snapped back to reality and crossed their arms over their chest. "You do know that without me around he'd work every hour she could and spend all remaining hours studying, right?"

"Right. You have a point." He slapped their shoulder, but it didn't work: Frankie hugged him anyway. Ben emerged looking extremely flustered. "Look, I'll only be a few weeks. You'll hardly notice I'm gone. I'll bring you back photos of the baby. You'll be fine. Say goodbye to Ms. Anzengruber and Marin for me, OK? Oh, yeah: I left my rent money in an envelope on her step. If you could tell her—"

Frankie recoiled. "Are you kidding? She'll make me eat it!"

"She won't. I can't work for my rent while I'm not here. She'll get that."

"If you're so sure of that, why didn't you tell her yourself?"

Ben mumbled, "I thought she might hear it better coming from you."

"Nope. Not gonna happen."

It took another half hour to get Ben out of the house, into his truck, and on the road. Aside from the fact that he was genuinely concerned about our ability to mind the house, which I couldn't really blame him for, he was conflicted: he wanted to go, but he also wanted to stay. I could understand that: I wanted him to go and to stay, too. Of the three of us, Frankie was the least affected. They knew that Ben would come back, and that was enough for them. They didn't really understand why I was so upset, but they still took care of me. As soon as Ben's truck was out of sight, they wrapped me in a hug.

"He won't be gone long, Gio. And you can ring him every day."

"Not really. That'd cost money."

"Wanting to talk to him and not doing it would cost heartache. Money's cheap by comparison."

"You're a sweetheart, you know that?"

They nodded, a serious look on their face. "I try. I don't always manage, but I trust you to give me pointers when I mess it up."

"You're doing great."

We had a quiet evening. I loved having Frankie all to myself, but the house felt huge and echo-y with just the two of us in it.

Ms. Anzengruber and Marin came back when we'd already gone to bed. Frankie grumbled and rolled over without waking up, but something about their arrival had shaken me up and I just couldn't settle back to sleep. It took me forever to realize what it was: the sound of Ms. Anzengruber's laughter tinkling down the stairs. I'd never heard her laugh like that before. I didn't know she could.

I must have been more worn out from finals than I'd realized, because that Saturday I overslept. Not only that, but I woke up to find that half the morning had gone, and so had Frankie. They'd left their guitar pick necklace on their pillow – their code to let me know that they hadn't run away from me – but I'd not heard them get up. They could have been up for hours. I didn't have anything to do or anywhere to go, but I still felt guilty, as if I had let them down.

I rushed to the toilet, and then to find Frankie. They could only be in the garage.

They weren't.

The bile was already rising in my throat, choking me up, when I remembered that I could feel where they were, if I only thought about it. I calmed myself down as much as I could, and reached out for them. They were upstairs. Of course they were. They were probably talking to Marin. They said they would. All the way up the stairs, I chanted to myself that everything was OK, that I was being ridiculous. Then I peered through the half-opened door, and I saw their face.

My stomach clenched up so tight and so fast that I gasped. They turned around, saw me watching them, and attempted a smile.

"Gio, it's OK. Mostly."

They slid along the couch and patted the cushion next to them. I forced myself to walk over to them, even though I wanted to run. I knew that they wouldn't lie to me and I wanted to let them reassure me, but the worry in their eyes didn't do much to support their statement.

"What is it?"

They wrapped their arm around me. "Jacob. Turns out that he's kind of a big deal. And he's bad news."

Marin nodded curtly. "I don't know him, but I know of him. If he wishes to cause you trouble, you are in danger. Even if he doesn't, you've still got a problem while he's hanging around. He's a trickster."

He said that in the exact same tone of voice my mom would have used to say "He's a Jehovah's Witness" or "He's a communist." I was finding it hard to think through the dust storm my panic was kicking up, but that statement jarred me back to relative mental clarity.

"I thought tricksters were OK, outside of the Judeo-Christian tradition. I mean, they shake things up, but they're kinda fun. Aren't they?"

Marin barked, "They're not! They don't care enough about people. Worse than that, they don't take care of people. They don't care if they break ten heroes in their quest for the right one. And even when they mean to help, their plans only ever work out by accident. They don't think things through. Half the time, they don't care if they fail. There is no relying on them."

"He called you an artificer."

Marin sneered. "He's right, although I'm sure he meant it as an insult. I make stuff. He makes trouble. Each to their own."

A thought suddenly hit me. "Why are you here?"

I couldn't be sure, not through his beard, but he looked like he was blushing. "I was invited to stay over, not that it's any of your business."

"No, that's not what I meant. Why are you here, living with humans, instead of being back home with your own people? Why is Jacob?"

His brow furrowed. "Some of us are here for the novelty value. Your people live fast, and change fast. Within a century, you went from not believing in heavier-than-aircrafts to sending a man to the moon. You are driven by curiosity and by the urge to experiment. You're destroying your own planet in the process, but I guess that can't be helped. Your lives are so short that they give you no chance to develop due caution or foresight. But it is your world, to manage or mismanage as you see fit."

"That's a very laissez-faire attitude for a god."

"Not really. It's the common attitude. It just so happens that the gods you get interested in are those who show an interest in you. It makes sense, though you have a tendency to take it to extremes."

"Jacob definitely seems to be taking an interest in Frankie."

Marin scowled. "Yes. And that is a different story. Some of my people left home simply because nobody there is willing to put up with their crap. They had to choose between toeing the line, being punished, or going into exile. And here they are, in an exile of their own choosing."

My stomach clenched. "I know all about that."

Frankie whipped their head around to look at me, their eyes enormous. "No, you don't."

"Ask my mom. You'll change your mind."

"I won't. You didn't relocate so you could be an asshole and get away with it."

"I'm sure that's not how Jacob sees it. He'd come up with something highfalutin about being authentic to one's true self, with a side dish of one's cosmic obligation to realize one's potential, and some crap about destiny."

Frankie grinned. "That does sound like him. But he's still an asshole, and you're not. Your idea of being yourself doesn't fuck anyone else over. His does. He's only half the problem, anyway."

"What's the other half?"

"Me." They put on a smile that didn't spread a millimeter beyond their mouth. "If what Jacob says is right, I am dangerous. Really dangerous."

I could see the fear gathering in their eyes. I swallowed my own dread and did my best to think of the ways in which this wasn't a fucking disaster. It wasn't a kind of thinking I was used to, but Frankie needed me, so I put my brain to work.

"OK. We've already established that Jacob is an asshole, and that he spews shit."

Frankie snorted. "That's anatomically correct on his part."

"Consistency in that respect may be his only charm. The sum total is that what he says isn't worth worrying about. Frankie, if you ever try and break reality, I'll fucking well stop you. You know that."

Their ears went crimson, and only then it occurred to me that maybe they hadn't told Marin the whole story of what had nearly happened back in March. I shut my mouth and held it shut, while they raced so fast over the hole I'd dug for us that they took us safely to the other side.

"You're probably right. You usually are. All the same, Uncle Marin wants to keep a closer eye on me. Until we know more about the situation, anyway. He says that I should do an internship with him instead of working at the library."

I looked at Marin. Sure enough, his ears were crimson, too. I had no doubt that he wanted to keep an eye on Frankie, but I was pretty damn sure that he also wanted to do Ms. Anzengruber a favor. Marin and I had never gotten along, and for a moment I was tempted to land him in the shit. All I had to do was ask the right question, word it so he couldn't wriggle out of it, and watch him flounder between getting caught in a lie or telling an ugly truth. But that would have landed Ms. Anzengruber in the shit, too, and broken Frankie's heart.

I swallowed my base impulse and comforted myself by patting Frankie's leg. "That's not a bad idea, love. If it's practical. I mean, is it even legal? I'd rather deal with a whole platoon of tricksters than piss off the immigration service. I don't think I could get a visa to Canada."

Marin coughed. "I can sort out Frankie's papers by Monday."

"But it's Saturday! That kind of thing takes months! And you're not going to convince an immigration officer that Frankie needs to learn to do plumbing in order to become a sociologist!"

He rolled his eyes. "I know that. We have people in all the government departments we can't just bribe. How do you think we manage to keep our paperwork in order when we don't age?"

"I don't know. I never thought about it. I mean, you're gods—"

He snorted. "Divinity is no help against bureaucracy."

"And what about the money? We can't ask you to fork out for this."

He shrugged. "I'll pay them the same pittance they would have got from the library. If they cannot make me back what they are costing me, I will stop paying them."

I looked at Frankie. They were plainly unhappy. "What is it, love?"

"I understand that it would be a good idea, because Uncle Marin can keep an eye on me and help me find out about this fucking gift of mine, and I don't mind doing the work. You know I like using tools."

I knew Frankie had liked using a hammer, once, and had ended up with a split thumb in the process, but I nodded. "So?"

"I don't want to let Ms. Anzengruber down. We were going to work together all summer. It was going to be so cool."

I chose my words very carefully. I needed to tell them the best-sounding truth I could summon. "Ms. Anzengruber will understand. She will want you to be safe, first and foremost. You'll see her all the time, anyway. We're always under her feet, literally and metaphorically. Maybe it's a good idea if you don't work with her, too."

They frowned. "I live and work with you, and it's great."

I whispered, "That's a bit different. You do all sort of stuff with me that you don't do with her."

They blushed through a smile. It was the best response I could have wished for.

Marin's response was perfect, too: he looked so uncomfortable that I nearly chuckled. He cleared his throat as if trying to dislodge something he just couldn't swallow. "Think about it, but don't take too long. If you decide to work with me, I'll square it off with Cynthia."

Frankie winced. "When did you start calling her that? It sounds so... familiar."

Marin growled. "Our degree of familiarity is none of your business!"

While Frankie apologized like only they knew how, I realized what had been missing from our conversation. "Where is Ms. Anzengruber, anyway?"

Marin pointed at the French doors at the far end of the room. "There."

She was on the deck, kneeling in a patch of sunshine, staring out towards the woods at the back of the house.

"What the hell is she doing?"

"She's been reading a lot about Zen lately. Decided to take up meditation. Says it helps her keep calm." His voice dropped. "She thought it may help her at work."

Frankie beamed, their good humor entirely restored. "Hey, maybe she can teach me! Then we could do it together!"

While Marin choked on his tongue, I gave Frankie a hug. "Love, I hate to say this, but this isn't the best idea you ever had."

3. Hellhound On My Trail

Marin was true to his word, and Frankie started work with him that very Monday. Despite my protestations, they refused to let me get up to see them off. Every time I tried to stir from our bed, they'd pounce on me and kiss me until I was weak at the knees. They kept that up until they were in danger of being late, so I gave up and let them get ready. They blew me a final kiss before dashing out the door, and, just like that, they were gone.

Being at home without Frankie was perfectly OK for almost the whole morning. I tried to go back to sleep, but I just couldn't, so I got up and luxuriated in the bath. When I'd turned into a prune, I got out and set to tidying up the place. I cleaned our room, reorganized our wardrobe, tidied up the garage, and cleaned the kitchen to within an inch of its life. It was only when I found myself organizing our pantry in alphabetical order that I realized that I wasn't doing well.

I'd not been alone for any length of time for weeks. I worked, lived, and studied with Frankie. The few hours a week when they were busy and I couldn't be with them, I hung out with Ben. The handful of times when they had both been busy, Ms. Anzengruber had always been upstairs. I generally left her alone, but knowing that she was there was enough.

Being alone had never been a problem for me. It was what I was used to. Now, though, I wasn't just alone: I was alone and without Frankie, and with nobody else to fill the gap they'd left. It took me a while to interpret the gnawing, panicky feeling in my stomach as loneliness, because I'd never felt it before. It gave my brain weasels something new to chew on, something else to torture me with, and I had no idea what I could do to stop them.

I tried everything I could think of to steady myself, but nothing worked. The house was empty. Frankie wouldn't be back for hours, and neither would Ms. Anzengruber. Ben wouldn't be back for weeks. The more I thought about it, the faster the brain weasels charged around, stumbling over each other in their effort to let me know that this was just not OK. I desperately wanted to clutch at someone, to feel connected.

I thought about phoning Ben. I could clear that up with Ms. Anzengruber, and pay her back when she got her bill. Just thinking about hearing his voice, about knowing that he was there for me, made me feel better for a while, until it made me feel much worse. I could ring him, and we would talk, and then I'd have to hang up and go back to being here, alone, unable to do anything because of the chaos in my brain.

Frankie could have put me right with a word, or a look. Hell, just seeing them would have put me right. But I couldn't see them, because they were at work. They were out there, and I was at home – but I wasn't, not really. This was just an empty building, with me rattling around in it, alone and disconnected. This wasn't home when Frankie was not here. Home was where they were.

An unbearable sense of wrongness grew inside me until my chest threatened to explode. I closed my eyes against it. When I opened them again, I was in a bathroom. It seemed familiar, though I couldn't be sure. If I looked out the window, I might have been able to work out what campus building I was in. I didn't, because sitting on the floor in front of me was Frankie, my Frankie, and I only had eyes for them.

"Gio? What the hell?"

"I didn't mean to! I was just thinking about you, and..."

They got up and hugged me. "OK. Tell me what you're not telling me."

"I was missing you so much! This is the longest we've been apart in months!"

"I know." They kissed me. "I missed you, too. Did you 'port all the way from the house? That's a hell of a long way."

"Missing you was a bigger hell. My brain got all screwy."

They kissed me again. "It's different, is all. We'll get used to it."

"I don't want to get used to it!"

Their eyes started to turn brown. "I'm sorry. I don't like to be without you, either."

"You didn't just go crazy and accidentally 'port yourself, though."

They chewed their bottom lip. "I can't 'port. I would have done it a dozen times, otherwise. Look, we can work something out. We can hang out at lunchtime, if you want. But you'll have to walk over, or be really careful where you 'port. I haven't told Uncle Marin about that. And if people see you—"

"I know. I told you, I didn't mean to."

"I know. We'll figure it out." They wrapped themself around me. I never wanted them to let go, but they did. "I have to get back to work. Uncle Marin is letting me use screwdrivers." They sounded so proud and so happy that I nearly cried.

"That's great. I'll see you tonight?"

"Of course you will, you boob! But don't go home yet. Go to the library."

"And do what?"

"Aside from the fact that, last I checked, you were rather fond of books, Ms. Anzengruber will be there. You can tell her how much you miss me. Here." They handed me their house key.

43

"OK, but why?"

"Because I'm willing to bet you didn't take yours. You may need an emergency 'porting kit if you're going to be doing this a lot."

"I don't plan to."

"All the same, you might wanna think about it." They gave me a peck, pulled away from me, frowned, and leaned into me again for a proper kiss. When they were done, they let me go and sighed. "I'd rather be screwing you than screws, you know?"

"Are you sure?"

"Positive." They tilted their head. "Did you think I'd gone off you in the six hours since I last saw you?"

I froze. I couldn't answer them. I hadn't thought that, not really, but the brain weasels had chattered about it.

Frankie grabbed the sides of my head and gave me a last kiss. "You really are a boob. I love you. Go see Ms. Anzengruber."

"She'll be busy."

"Then she'll tell you that, but you can still say hello. Go on. It'll make you feel better."

I didn't think they were right, but I took their advice anyway. I should have known better. They had never steered me wrong.

I found Ms. Anzengruber at the main library counter. She took a look at my face and frowned. "That bad?"

"Yes. I miss them so damn much."

"You're lucky, dear. I know that you don't feel like that right now, but to have someone you love so passionately—"

The compassion in her eyes unmade me. I opened my mouth and let everything fall out. "That's not the problem. The problem is that I'm crazy. They go away from me for five minutes, and it feels like the end of the world. And it's not just that. Everything is too much, all the time."

She walked around the counter pushing a trolley full of books. "Walk with me."

"Can I push that?"

"You can, but you may not."

I stopped. "If I'm taking up your time, at least I want to help."

She gave me her librarian's death stare, but I was used to it. I stared back at her until she shook her head and relinquished her hoard.

As we walked down the stacks, she whispered. "Marin says that you're highly strung. He could put it better, but he's not wrong. You are highly sensitive, and you react intensely to a variety of stimuli. I'm sure that it must be hard to deal with, at times."

"Make that most of the time."

"But you deal with it. You are keeping up a great GPA, a job, a very intense relationship, and a social life."

I scoffed at that, and she stopped dead and glared at me. "Ben is your friend, and so am I. Don't you dare discount us."

I felt my cheeks beginning to burn. She patted my arm and walked on.

"You underestimate your achievements. I know that you find many things difficult, but that doesn't detract from the fact that you do them."

"Other people get on with stuff without all the fuss."

"Some do, but many don't. They might avoid the fuss, but they don't achieve half as much. How many students do you know who managed a 4.0 GPA the term they got married?"

It was my turn to stop dead.

She smirked. "Frankie told me, dear. Of course they did: they were about to explode with it! I know it wasn't a conventional ceremony, and I know it's not legally binding, but they believe in it. It was the sweetest thing I ever heard, too. You turned an awful moment in their life into something they can remember with fondness." She pulled me onward. "I still expect the two of you to organize something for the lot of us, when you are good and ready. It doesn't have to be anything grand, but I'll be damned if I let you get away with getting married without inviting me. I want the chance to have a good cry over the two of you."

I managed to convince my eyes to reabsorb the tears that threatened to flood my face. When I'd got myself halfway together, I put my most nonchalant voice on. "I didn't plan it. It just seemed the right thing to do. And anyway, I used to be strongly against the concept of marriage."

"And then?"

"And then I met Frankie."

We wondered around the stacks for the rest of the afternoon, sorting out books and whispering at each other. I was having a lovely time, even though Ms. Anzengruber got oddly distracted as the afternoon progressed. I thought it had to do with the fact that we still had a huge pile of unsorted books, but that couldn't have been it, because with only a half hour to go before the end of her shift, she bailed on me. She came back five minutes later, whisked the book trolley from right under my nose, and dragged me down a hallway towards the darkest recesses of the building. As she dumped me in front of a doorway, she told me that one of her colleagues had a few questions about some foreign language books.

He had a whole bunch of questions, actually. I found it hard to answer them to start with, because I didn't know him and he was listening to me so my tongue didn't work properly, but it got easier as I got into the subjects and forgot myself. I didn't even mind that much when he started asking questions about me, where I'd learnt the languages I spoke, what kinds of books I liked, what I was studying, and why. We chatted about this and that for a good twenty minutes, and most of it wasn't too painful. When he finally waved me out of the office, I spent a little time picking a few books to take home with me, despite Frankie's diktat, and then Ms. Anzengruber was ready to take me home.

She was quiet all the way back. When we got to the bottom of her stairs, instead of saying goodbye, she told me, "I'll pick you up at half eight tomorrow."

"I beg your pardon?"

"Your shift doesn't start until ten, but mine starts at nine. You can walk in if you want, but I'm sure you could entertain yourself while you wait."

"What are you on about?"

"You need something to do, Frankie's post was vacant, and you interviewed very well. You got the job. It's not that surprising, dear: not many of our candidates are fluent in three languages, dabble in another two, and have a background in both sciences and humanities."

"But I didn't interview!"

"You did. You just didn't know that you were doing it. I'm sorry, but I thought it may help."

"But I didn't even apply!"

"You did, last January. You didn't get through, but your application was still on file."

"But I'll be taking a class in August!"

"I know. We'll sort something out. You'd make a fine librarian."

"No way! I'd have to talk to people!"

She peered up at me. "What exactly do you think you're doing right now? You need to keep up with yourself, dear. You're changing faster than you realize."

She patted my arm and left me there, mouthing like a stranded fish, as confused as I'd ever been. I felt dizzy as hell, so I sat myself on the bottom step, trying to think my way through it all and failing.

When Frankie came home, they found me only marginally recovered, but it didn't matter: they were so excited that all other considerations became secondary. They were bouncing so much that they had to give me several short kisses instead of their customary long one.

"I did it, Gio! I went to work! With Uncle Marin! I did plumbing!"

"I know! I saw you! You were using screwdrivers!"

They grabbed my shoulders and stared into my eyes. "Gio. This afternoon, I used a drill."

I felt the urge to check them for damage, but I reined it in. My lack of faith in their abilities would have upset them, and I was sure that Marin carried a first aid kit. If he didn't, he'd learn the error of his ways soon enough.

Frankie gave me a sweaty, dusty kiss and bounded off to take a shower. When Marin limped into the house, he found me still staring at the space they'd occupied. He looked tired, disheveled, and morose. That was so normal for him that it gave me no clues as to how their day had gone. He was carrying a six pack of beer. That wasn't a great sign, it being a Monday, but it wasn't a terrible sign, either. When he handed me one of the bottles, my heart sank: he was undoubtedly trying to cushion me from the news that were to come. Then, out of nowhere, he smiled.

"They're not bad. They could be good. And it's not that fault-finding thing of theirs; that won't be much help until they learn about the kinds of faults we're trying to find. They are keen, they are fast, and they listen. They don't know anything about tools, but that's useful: I don't have to break them out of any bad habit. I know it's only their first day, but... I didn't want to kill them. Not even once."

I stared at him. After a couple of eons, I remembered to close my mouth.

He shrugged. "I know. I didn't expect it, either. You've got yourself a good husband... A good spouse. Whatever else they may be, they're going to be a hard worker, and a good provider."

"They told you that we got married?"

"No. Cynthia did. She had to: I found her in a flood of tears. I made her tell me what was going on."

"Is there anyone who doesn't know about it?"

"Ben, most likely. That kid is so spaced out he'd probably not work it out even if you invited him to the ceremony. Get used to it, kid: you can't live with family and expect to have a private life."

He slapped me on the shoulder and limped off upstairs.

When Frankie came out of the shower, they found me still in the hallway, oscillating between grinning and crying. Once I reassured them that everything was OK, they dragged me straight to our room, where we spent a good hour making things more than OK for both of us.

I never got as crazy as that first Frankieless day. Working helped, because I was kept busy. Having people around me also helped, although they couldn't make up for the lack of Frankie. Frankie helped the most: they worked longer hours than me, but they sorted things out so I could see them at lunchtime. They made sure they were in a toilet stall five minutes after the end of my shift, every day, without fail, so I could 'port to them. What Marin made of their scheduled toileting needs was a mystery to me, but the system worked. I bought Frankie their lunch as my excuse to see them, though eating was a secondary consideration for both of us. The whole thing wasn't totally safe, but that made it more fun.

After lunch, I'd amble back home. Waiting for Frankie's return could be a joy, then. I could pretend that we were normal-ish and get our dinner ready, instead of running around in circles wondering if I'd ever see them again. It was probably one of those improvements Ms. Anzengruber wanted me to notice, but as it amounted to me being able to cope without them for a measly couple of hours, I found it hard to celebrate it. All and still, apart from a couple of minor mishaps on Frankie's part that necessitated no more than a plaster, all was going well. Not according to our original plans, perhaps, but we were used to that.

Jacob turned up at the Library two weeks after we'd told him that Frankie would get in touch. Maybe I should have expected him, but I'd managed to make myself forget all about him, even though I could not forget what he'd told us.

I didn't recognize him at first. I was happily stacking shelves and counting down the minutes to the end of my shift and my lunch with Frankie, when my pervdar kicked in. When I looked up, the input my eyes provided clashed horribly with what my brain was screaming at me. A girl was leaning against a shelf, chewing bubblegum. She was one of those perky, girly girls who never looked entirely human to me. She was so perfect and so plastic that she could have been a Barbie doll come to life. That would have been eerie enough to creep me out, but on top of that she was staring at me so intently that her eyes were drilling holes into my skull. When she smiled, I expected to see her canines sticking over her bottom lip. Her smile was perfectly normal, though, at least from a dentistry point of view. It still made my blood freeze.

"Jacob?"

The smile widened. "You really are a fascinating creature. How did you recognize me?"

His voice turned the situation from eerie to terrifying. It was his voice, unequivocally, but high-pitched enough to match his current body. I had to have some sharp words with my sphincters: all they wanted to do was drop and run.

"It's a gift." The words were out of my mouth before I had a chance to think about how inappropriate they were, under the circumstances.

The focus in Jacob's eyes grew even sharper. "I really should have paid more attention to you. I don't think you could ever be useful, but you could definitely be entertaining."

"Frankie wouldn't appreciate you talking like that."

He grinned. "Frankie doesn't seem to appreciate me talking at all, and I think we all know why that is."

"Because you've been an asshole?"

"Because you got in my way. Frankie and I were getting along perfectly well before you stuck your oar in."

"You tried to manipulate them into fucking with the fabric of reality without explaining the possible consequences!"

"I did. And I would have gotten away with it too, if it weren't for you meddling kids." He winked at me. "I don't intend to repeat that mistake."

"You're going to leave them alone?"

"No. I want you to be on board." He bounced a couple of steps closer, pert and pink. "It's quite simple: Frankie is mine. I made them."

"Their mother and father may disagree."

"Their mother and father gave them a body. I gave them the ability to see reality as it really is and to mold it as they see fit."

"I thought Marin gave them at least half of that."

Jacob's face flickered, like a television set. I only caught the briefest glimpse of the face behind his face, but that was enough to freeze my blood. It didn't look anything like any of the faces he'd worn in front of me. It also didn't look wholly human, and it definitely lacked all humanity.

"Your obsession with details—"

"With the truth, you mean?"

He spoke through gritted teeth. "You are deliberately antagonizing me. Are you sure that's what you want to do?"

I wasn't. Every fiber of my being was screaming at me to shut the fuck up and back the fuck down. There was nothing to be gained by provoking him. Even Marin was scared of him, and Marin could make fireballs. The sensible thing – the strategically sound thing – was to let him believe that I would go along with whatever he wanted, and get him out of my way.

I didn't get a chance to. A weird and deeply unpleasant smile lit his face and he started to walk towards me. There was a whole lot of unnecessary movement to his walk: he was coming straight at me, but his hips were going sideways while his chest was bouncing up and down. It was kind of mesmerizing, like a contortionist's act, but it was also disturbing.

The disturbance escalated when he got close to me, so close that I could smell him, and put his hands on my hips. With his mouth only inches from mine, he whispered, "What do you think would happen if I screamed that you assaulted me?"

"Nobody would believe you. They know me."

"But it would be investigated. You might lose your job. And when you got home—"

"I'd tell Frankie what happened, and they would know that I was telling the truth. You can't get between us with lies."

His face flickered again. Close up, his real face – if that was what that was – was even more dreadful to look at. I felt like I did the first time I met a lion at a circus, and the thing towered over me and roared: my brain knew that I was safe, but my body had no interest in that kind of bullshit. All it knew was that a predator wanted to consume me.

While I tried to talk my heart into not beating out of my chest, Jacob nodded slowly to himself.

"You're right. Of course. How about this, then: if Frankie doesn't come round to my way of thinking, I won't hurt them. I will hurt you instead. Only if they stay with you, you understand; I'm not unreasonable. They can keep you and work with me, they can let you go, or they can watch you pay for their transgressions." He let off a giggle like a peal of wind chimes. "Won't that be fun? They will have to choose between hurting you and losing you – which, presumably, would also hurt you. After all, you're hardly a person without them."

That cut so deeply that I would have gasped, had I been able to breathe.

Jacob's smile grew wider and more sensual. "Oh, pet, does that hurt? How about this: you will have to choose between the fear of being without them forever, and the fear of staying with them." He lifted his mouth to my ear and whispered, "I promise you, if I don't get my way, the pain I will inflict upon you will be exquisite. You tell them that. See how they like this truth."

I was frozen solid, so I didn't recoil when he licked my ear. When he took my earlobe in his mouth and nibbled it, it didn't hurt, but it repulsed me so much that a wave of nausea went through me and sapped the last of my energy. A part of me, staring out of the windows of my eyes like a passenger in a train crash, wondered how far he was willing to go, and whether I could regain the use of my body on time to stop him.

I never found that out: the sound of someone clearing their throat made him step back. Ms. Anzengruber was standing at the end of the stack, glaring at us.

"Gio, need I remind you that you are at work?"

She was talking to me. I needed to say something, but my insides were too mixed up. I nodded instead, then realized that it wasn't the right response and shook my head.

"Is this the appropriate conduct for a Library Aide?"

I shook my head again.

"You better get back to your work, then."

She'd not even looked at Jacob, who still stood in front of me, way too close for comfort and way too happy with himself. I tried to step sideways to get away from him, but it didn't work. He stepped along with me, placed a hand on my belly, right over the knot of vomit I was trying to keep down, and murmured, "I guess that's the end of our games for today. No matter. I will see you soon, pet. Don't forget what I told you."

He turned and bounced off with that jiggly walk of his. Ms. Anzengruber watched him go. When she turned back towards me, I got another shock: I thought I was in for a serious telling off, but she didn't look angry or disappointed. She looked concerned.

Her neat little steps took her to me before I'd had a chance to get a full breath in.

"Gio, do you know that girl?"

I didn't think I could talk without squealing yet, so I nodded instead.

"Have you had problems with her before?"

I nodded.

She sagged. "Dear, you can't let girls grab you like that! Or boys, for that matter. What would you have done if I'd not turned up?"

I shrugged. I had no idea, and just thinking about that made me feel like my insides were made of water.

She sighed. "Come on, dear. Go somewhere quiet and have a sit down, before you fall over."

I managed to find my words. "I'm OK."

"You don't look it."

"Nothing happened."

She raised an eyebrow. "I'm sure that when you tell Frankie—"

"You can't tell them! You can't!"

She blinked. "Dear, are you serious?"

"Yes. Don't tell them. Please!" My lungs went to shit again, but this time it felt different: after weeks of being OK, here was the start of an asthma attack. Just what I needed to make the day complete.

I sat down on the floor, leaning forward against my knees. If I could only think myself into relative calm, I might be able to ward the whole thing off, or to keep it minor. Ms. Anzengruber knew the drill, but she couldn't do anything for me: I needed either a shot of alcohol and a strong coffee, or my inhaler, and I didn't have them. All I had was a broken-down body and a brain that kept running around in circles.

I had no doubts that Jacob was able to make good on his promise. Whether he would actually do that was another story. He knew how our society worked, so he knew that he couldn't just hurt me without an investigation taking place. He might be able to pass the whole thing off as a random crime or to ensure that my body was never found, but that would make Frankie suspicious. I was too boring to have enemies. However, if he thought that he had no hope of turning Frankie to his way of thinking, he might not care about that. All I could be sure of was that he could hurt me, but not that he would. What the fuck was I going to do?

I still hadn't worked it out by the time I was well enough to get up. I knew one thing for sure, though: if I told Frankie about it, I would lose them. They would not risk my welfare, not for anything; not even to stay with me. They couldn't be with me 24-7 to ensure that Jacob wouldn't hurt me – assuming that doing so was within their abilities, which was not something we could bank on – so they wouldn't be with me at all. If they didn't straight-up dump me, they would at least make sure that I was out of their way until the situation was resolved.

I couldn't live with that. Jacob was dead right about one thing: I needed Frankie. A life without them was not a life worth living. Just thinking about it made me sick. I needed to keep them out of it while I worked out a solution, or while I waited for Jacob to get fed up with us. Frankie's powers notwithstanding, we were just two mortals in a world full of them. Maybe he would just grow bored and leave us alone. Until then, I needed to keep my shit together – something I'd already failed to do. Neither Frankie nor Jacob could see me fall apart.

Ms. Anzengruber and I made our way towards the exit. As soon as I could talk, I told her, "Don't tell Frankie. About any of this. Please."

She looked about to argue, but she checked herself and nodded instead. "Do you want to sit down for a bit?"

"No. I'm OK. Going to see Frankie."

She looked really unhappy about that, but, again, she didn't protest. She probably didn't want to agitate me, because I was such a wuss that the least upset sent me crashing. Thinking that made the bile rise in my gullet. I really liked her, and I had been hoping that her opinion of me was at least half-decent. I couldn't worry about that, though, because I had bigger fish to fry. So what if she thought that I was a feeble piece of shit? For a change, it was convenient. She had agreed to keep my secret, and I could trust her to keep her word, which eliminated one of my problems.

I stepped out of the library, leaned against the stair railing, and focused on my second immediate issue: the bullshit with my asthma had made me miss my meeting time with Frankie. I wasn't all that late, but I was late enough that I couldn't 'port to them. I would have to walk, and I would have to take it steady because my lungs were still threatening a mutiny.

I closed my eyes, got my Frankie-sense to point me in the right direction, and started a slow slog towards them. By the time I got there, I was horribly late, and they were frantic.

"Where have you been? What happened?" They threw themself at me, then pulled back. "You look awful. Are you hurt?"

I tried to smile at them. "Asthma. Not bad. OK now."

"Shit. Sit down. You've not had an asthma attack in ages! Do you need anything? Do you have your inhaler?"

I latched on to the last question for dear life. It was the only one I could answer safely. "No. Home. Coat pocket."

Frankie launched into their usual lecture about my inability to take care of my inhaler and, by extension, of myself. I was still feeling miserable and probably looked like rehydrated shit, so they alternated snippets of it with long cuddles. About five minutes into it, I felt so good and so bad that I just fell all to pieces, and found myself weeping on their shoulder. That stopped the lecture altogether, but the cuddling carried on. Marin found us like that and, for a wonder, did not make a fuss. He rolled his eyes, but that was it.

I was not about to make a scene in front of him, so I pushed all my feelings down, sucked the snot back up my nose, and wiped the tears off my face. Frankie didn't want me to walk home, so I crawled to the common room, parked myself on an armchair, and proceeded to stare at a TV screen without taking a damn thing in. Every now and then I'd snap out of my stupor and remember that a psychotic god may be watching me, waiting for the right moment to pounce. The resulting terror would overload my system, and send me back to staring without seeing. By the time Frankie swung round to pick me up, I had ridden that rollercoaster so many times that I couldn't feel much of anything.

I spent the night trying to formulate a strategy. After all the physical and emotional upheavals of the day, I was desperately tired, but I was also desperate not to let Jacob fuck up my life with Frankie. After fussing around me all evening, they'd fallen asleep as soon as their head hit the pillow. They were so beautiful in their sleep, so free and pure, that the mere thought of something taking them away from me made me want to clutch them as hard as my pathetic body allowed. I couldn't do that, though: if I woke them up, I would have to explain to them what was going on, and then I would lose them.

By morning I was utterly exhausted and none the wiser. The only tactic I had come up with was to avoid giving Jacob the opportunity to get to me until he got fed up and moved on to new projects, or new victims. I was safe at home, because my circle of protection was as solid as ever. I could draw circles around the buildings we used the most, and smaller circles around myself if I spent any time in one place. It would raise a few eyebrows if anyone saw me at it, but I could deal with that. All in all, protecting myself against Jacob seemed an easier proposition than defending myself against someone who wasn't a god, which seemed ironic. I would still have to make some changes to my life, like planning my day to minimize unnecessary movements and avoiding spaces where I simply could not draw a circle, but I could work that out.

The biggest change, and the one that concerned me the most, was that I was keeping something from Frankie. I couldn't remember exactly when I'd started telling them almost everything, no matter how uncomfortable, but that was what I did, or tried to do. As far as I knew, they did the same with me. There were some secrets between us, but they were only small, petty ones designed to spare feelings and make cohabitation a little bit smoother. Now I would be keeping a crucial piece of information from them, something that could change the course of our lives, something that I knew they would want to know. Thinking of how upset they'd be if they ever found out made me feel like shit, but it was nothing compared to how I felt thinking about losing them.

By the time the alarm clock woke them up, I had gathered all the resolve I could muster. It wasn't much, but I was used to working with insufficient materials.

For once, I didn't argue when they told me to stay in bed until I had to get up for work. I still missed them as soon as they walked out of our room.

I had an extensive collection of mental slides depicting how they looked while they had a wash, how they twitched while they waited for their coffee, how they spaced out over their breakfast, and so on. I played them while listening to them crash around the house, but it wasn't the same as watching them in real life, and missing that show seemed a terrible waste. I knew that I didn't have my shit together, though, and until I got myself sorted out I needed to keep a low profile. Wrapped up in our bed like a pupa, my profile was as low as I could make it.

As soon as they were ready to get out, they rushed over to give me a last-minute kiss. Watching them peer into our room to see if I was asleep made my heart do cartwheels in my chest. I wanted them to stay right where they were so I could look at them forever. Then they threw themself on the bed next to me, and I wanted to feel them forever, to be so close to them that I couldn't tell where our skins started and ended.

I must have clutched at them a bit too desperately, because they sighed into my hair. "You'll be OK. I'll see you at lunchtime."

I was about to fall apart in their arms, to beg them not to go, when I was saved by the bell, almost literally. Marin had clomped down the stairs while Frankie and I were cuddling, and now he was playing a tune on the horn of his van. Frankie gave me a last peck, and then a last kiss. They were just about to wade back in for a last snog when I stopped them.

"Go! You'll get us both lynched!"

"Alright. But remember that you threw me out, despite my remonstrations and supplications. I'll miss you wretchedly."

"I love you more than life itself."

They grinned. "I'm not sure that's healthy, but I'll take it."

It took them three seconds to get out of bed, out of our room, and out the door. The house felt desperately empty without them in it. I turned off the circle of protection just long enough for Marin to drive out, and then I used my Frankie-sense to follow them to work. I was getting better at pinpointing their location. I didn't know if it was because I was more aware of the lay of the land or my sensor, whatever that was, was getting stronger. Either way, I could pretty much tell where they were on campus, not just in relation to me. It gave me a degree of comfort, but it also made me aware of all the space between us, space that I couldn't cross without putting myself in danger. I could 'port to them, of course, but I couldn't 'port back. I needed another solution, and I needed it fast.

We didn't have enough salt in the house to do what I wanted to do, so I took some of Ben's flour and experimented with it. Marin's instructions for circle-making had specified salt, but the small flour circle I made around myself in the middle of our garage gave me that faint, still sensation that meant that it was working fine. I grabbed two flour bags and stashed them in my school bag. When Ms. Anzengruber picked me up to go to work, I was as ready as I was ever going to be.

I spent the spare time before the start of my shift drawing a circle around the library. There were very few people around campus and nobody saw me, but it took longer than I'd thought and used more flour than I'd anticipated. I used what was left to draw a circle around the car park Ms. Anzengruber used. I would have to do it all again around the buildings we used during term time, but that wasn't going to be that hard: flour was relatively cheap, and if I could hit two buildings per day, I could have most of the campus covered in no time.

Of course, I needed to hit those two buildings without Jacob hitting me first. I also had to hope that the circles I made would stay viable, even though I may not use them for long stretches. Leaving them up would totally mess with Marin's movements.

I was on my way into the library, daydreaming about a highly impractical giant circle around the campus and the town that could keep us safe from all harm, when I realized that there was a gaping hole in my plan: circles stopped gods and sundry fays from coming into an area, but that was it. They didn't forcibly eject them from that space. In fact, they kept them corralled in there.

That fact didn't hit me because my brain had finally engaged: I worked it out when I spotted Jacob, wearing a brand new body and face, loitering near the front desk. Well, either it was Jacob, or I'd picked up another predator.

My stomach tried to make a break for freedom, but I shouted it down. I was safe. Even at that time of day, there were too many people in the library for Jacob to do anything drastic. I just had to do my best not to get cut out of the herd for a handful of hours, and do better tomorrow. Now that the circle was in place, I could turn it off, wait for Jacob to fuck off, turn it back on and leave it on permanently. That meant that I would have to tell Frankie about the circle without telling them why I wanted it to be there, and that Frankie would have to work out a way to tell me if Marin needed to come into the library. Those were worries for tomorrow, though: I needed to focus on the present, and on Jacob. He sure as hell was focused on me.

I tried to walk past him nonchalantly, which worked about as well as I should have expected. He – he was a he for the occasion, a perfect Ken doll to go with the previous day's Barbie – just smiled and followed me, not close enough to touch me but way too close for comfort. When I ducked behind the reserve desk he didn't follow, but he didn't fuck off.

He dogged me all the way through my shift, lurking in plain sight. I never felt in danger, not quite, but I never felt safe, either. I felt hounded.

I was doing alright, though. At the very least, I was managing. I was feeling like shit and spending about 50% of my energy on worrying about Jacob rather than on what I needed to do, but I was managing. I could manage. It was manageable. It wasn't going to be forever, and the one thing life had taught me was that *any*thing is manageable if it isn't forever.

That was the theory, anyway. By the end of my shift, I was perilously near the end of my tether and I'd choked down bile so often that I was probably giving myself a fucking ulcer. As soon as my time was up, I grabbed my crap and raced to the nearest restroom. I hid in a stall in the ladies', because Jacob couldn't follow me in there without changing face again or drawing a whole load of attention. Even so, waiting the handful of minutes until the exact right time for 'porting tensed my nerves up so tight that Frankie could have played a tune on them.

I didn't manage to take a proper breath until I found myself in their arms. I tried not to hold them too tight, to breathe myself into calm, to pretend that I was OK, but I failed spectacularly. Half a second into our hug, they went rigid.

"Gio? What's up?"

"I need a hug."

"I'm getting that, but why?"

"Hugging you is the best thing ever." I thought that may distract them, but it didn't.

They unpeeled me from them and peered into my face. "Gio, I get what you're saying, but I really wanna know what you're not saying. What happened? You're in a state."

I rubbed the tears off my face and started to run my hands through my hair, trying to fix myself up, but they caught them and held them. I tried to turn away, but they wouldn't let go and they wouldn't stop looking at me. Their eyes were getting browner by the second. Seeing them so worried about me made me feel awful for upsetting them, and terrified of the possible consequences of that upset.

"I'm OK. I had a problem at work. I don't want to talk about it. Is that alright?"

"Yeah. I guess. Is it that bad?"

"I don't want to think about it. Please. Can you just hold me?"

Their eyes expanded to their maximum size. "But... Yes. Sorry."

They wrapped themself around me. It felt so fucking good that I wanted it to last forever, but I needed to calm them down, to reassure them that nothing was up, even though something most certainly was. I needed to pretend that I didn't feel like I felt, or they would make my nightmares a reality.

We ate lunch together. I had been a bit distracted when I packed it, so one of the sandwiches was ham and jam, but they either didn't notice or they didn't mind – most likely the former. They were so focused on me that they shoveled their food in their face without even looking at it. On any other day, knowing how much they cared about me would have made me feel instantly better. In the present context, it tore me apart. I loved their willingness to put aside all other concerns to deal with mine, but I needed them not to try and find out what my current concerns were.

For a wonder, Marin saved my ass. He stomped in, rolled his eyes at the two of us holding hands, and grumbled, "Did you ask her?"

Frankie flapped their free arm in the air. "Shush! It's supposed to be a surprise!"

"What kind of surprise are you planning, kid? Sticking a bag over her head and bundling her into the trunk?"

"No! I was just waiting for the right moment, alright?"

Marin snorted. "I don't think build-up is going to improve this, but it's none of my business. Five minutes, then I want you back at work."

As he stomped off, I turned to Frankie. "What's going on?"

"I can't tell you now! It'll ruin it!"

"Ruin what?"

"That's what I can't tell you!"

"Where are you taking me?"

Frankie wailed, "Gio! You're not supposed to know that! It's part of the surprise!" When I did not react, they rolled their eyes. "Alright, then. Have it your way. Uncle Marin is taking Ms. Anzengruber to the seaside this Sunday. She asked him to ask me if I wanted to ask you if you wanted to go along."

My brain managed to parse that sentence on the second pass. "Why didn't she just ask me? We've been working together all day!"

They blushed. "I told Uncle Marin that I wanted to take you out. On a date, you know?"

"Oh. And us going to the seaside with those two is a date?"

They started to gesticulate wildly. "No, you see, they'd be driving us there, but then we'd have all day there on our own. So it'd totally be a date. Us two, at the seaside. But it's a Sunday. We'd miss our Sunday

Morning. Would that be OK?"

"Yeah. Of course it'd be OK, if that's what you want to do."

They beamed. "So we are going out? Together? On a date? For real?"

"Frankie, you've been living with me for months. Why is a day out such a big deal?"

They grabbed my hands. "Because it's our first date! I asked you out and you said yes!"

"What the hell did you think I was going to say? I fucking love you."

Frankie pounced on me and proceeded to kiss every scrap of bare skin they could find, and some that they uncovered just for that purpose. When Marin came back and growled at us, I went to wait for them in the common room. I found enough flour at the bottom of my bag to draw a circle around me, and I felt almost safe, almost able to look forward to the weekend ahead.

4. GOING TO PORT WASHINGTON

On Sunday morning, I waited until Frankie had gone into the bathroom, and snuck up to see Ms. Anzengruber. When I explained to her what I wanted, she wasn't optimistic.

"French braids? Dear, I've not done them since grade school."

"They don't have to be good. They just have to *be*."

"Are you sure?"

"Positive."

She sighed. "Sit down, then."

She had my hair up and looking pretty damn good after only a couple of goes and a few minutes. I was ecstatic, but she was not convinced. She kept looking at me and sucking her teeth.

"That just won't cut it."

"It's fine. I like it." I tried to get up, but she pushed me down again.

"Dear, your hair is reasonable. It's the rest that needs work."

I felt a blush rise as my stomach sank. "Thank you very much! If I could stop being ugly, I would have done so years ago!"

She rolled her eyes. "Now you're being ridiculous. What I mean is that the whole ensemble could be jazzed up a little. I am presuming that your aim is to wow your beau."

My cheeks felt hot enough to melt my eyeballs. "That's part of it. I'd also like us to be able to, you know, be a couple for the day. Out and about, without anyone looking at us twice."

Her face ran through a whole load of emotions, none of them very good, before settling on her most librarianish stare. "Right. That is conveniently in line with what I was thinking. Stay put."

She marched off to her bedroom, returned with a basket full of stuff, and proceeded to assault my face. Every time I thought that she must surely be finished, she'd whip out something else out of her magic basket. When she finally had enough of that, she stared at me hard enough to paralyze me. Eventually, she smiled.

"That will do. Hold on."

She went off again, leaving me more confused than ever. Marin, who'd been hiding behind a magazine at the far end of the couch, peered out to look at me.

"Stop huffing. Cynthia will hear you and tell you what's what."

"But I just wanted my hair done! I didn't want all this crap!"

He nearly smiled. "You'll change your mind when the kid sees you. They won't know what hit them."

"What?"

Instead of explaining himself, Marin ducked back behind his magazine as Ms. Anzengruber charged towards me, bearing an armful of clothes.

"There you go. One of these should do. "

"What are they?"

"Dresses. And, before you launch into a disquisition as to why you can't wear one, I'd suggest trying one of the short ones with jeans underneath. It should tick all the boxes. Now, off you trot. We don't have all day."

"But I didn't—"

I didn't get a chance to defend myself, because she shooed me off. I was stomping down the stairs, feeling pretty morose about everything, when one of the dresses caught my eyes. It was bright green, like Frankie's eyes when they were really happy, and kinda floaty. I took off my shirt, put it on, and walked into our bedroom.

Frankie was sprawled on our bed, catching the sun, looking as liquid as a cat. They opened their eyes slowly and lazily, until they focused on me. Then they recoiled and sat up in a single, panicked movement, and ended up crouched on our pillows, staring at me with their mouth open.

"Gio? Fucking hell!"

"What? You don't like it?"

"No! I mean... It's just... Fucking hell!"

I turned to look at myself in the mirror, and nearly gave myself a coronary. "Holy shit! I look like a girl!"

"You don't." They were still staring at me, their eyes enormous and lost. "You look like a princess. You look like an actual princess. You're coming out like that?"

My stomach sank. "I was going to. But if you don't like it—"

"That's not... You're coming out, looking like that, with me?"

"That was the idea, if you'll have me."

They nodded silently, looking horrified. I wanted to ask them what the problem was but I didn't get a chance, because Ms. Anzengruber and Marin descended upon us and dragged us out.

It took us an hour to get to Castine. Frankie spent the entire journey sitting bolt upright and staring at me out of the corner of their eyes. They only spoke when spoken to, and even then they only managed a few monosyllables. By the time we got there, I felt so despondent that I just wanted to turn around and go back – or, even better, to lie down in front of the car and let Ms. Anzengruber run me over.

Alas, neither was an available option. Ms. Anzengruber gave us instructions as to where and when to meet them at the end of the day, and fucked off with Marin. They looked good together. Familiar. Comfortable.

Meanwhile, Frankie still looked as if they were expecting me to turn on them and bite off their nose. After a few unsuccessful attempts at extracting their opinion as to what we should do first, I gave up and walked off. They walked beside me, keeping step. Every now and then they looked as if they were about to say something, but they always checked themself. When they finally spoke, they blurted out their question as a single, incomprehensible word.

"CanIholdyourhand?"

"What?"

They swallowed. "Your hand. Can I, huh, hold it?"

"Of course you can hold my fucking hand, Frankie! Why the hell do you think I dressed like this?"

They shied away from me. "Sorry. I didn't mean to..."

I grabbed their hand and pulled them onward. "What the hell is wrong with you?"

"Nothing. Sorry."

They held my hand tentatively, as if they were holding a baby bird, and spent so much time looking at me that they kept tripping over their own feet. After I'd stopped them face-planting about a dozen times, I grew weary of that game and made them sit on a bench. They sat as far from me as physically possible and stared off into the distance, looking horrified.

After a few minutes of that nonsense, a thought occurred to me.

"Frankie, have you ever dated an actual girl?"

They flinched. "Yeah. I mean, kinda. Not in a while."

"How long a while?"

"I dunno. About ten years or so. Maybe twelve."

"What? So you've not dated a girl since you were what, seven?"

"Something like that. Maybe eight or nine."

"But you like girls!"

They dropped their eyes to the ground. "Yeah. I mean, I like them as people, and I also like them, you know, theoretically. They're soft, and pretty, and they smell nice. But they're kinda scary, too. They hunt in packs, and they can be really mean. I'm not too good at being a guy—"

"That's because you're not a guy!"

"Yeah, well, I know that now, but I didn't know it back then. I just knew that I wasn't too good at being a guy. The guys didn't seem to mind that half as much as the girls did. I mean, some of the guys weren't great about it, but they were just assholes, and I didn't really care. I didn't like them, either. But I liked a bunch of the girls, and they didn't like me, and even when they did... I don't get them, Gio. They have all these rules you have to follow, only you don't get to know what the rules are beforehand: you break them, and *then* you get told that you've been an asshole."

"They're not all like that."

"I know, but—" They turned around, saw me, and blanched. "I didn't mean to... Sorry."

"Frankie, I'm still me. I'm just dressed up."

"Yeah. Of course. Sorry."

I could see the fear swimming at the bottom of their eyes, like a sea monster hiding in a pool. I cursed inwardly. I would have cursed outwardly, too, but that would have only scared them more. When an idea occurred to me, it seemed like the most ridiculous idea I had ever had. It was also the only idea I had, though, so I decided to give it a shot.

"Love, close your eyes."

They tried to back away from me and nearly fell off the bench. "Why?"

"Because I'm asking you nicely. Please?"

"Alright." They swallowed audibly and closed their eyes with the grim determination of a condemned prisoner.

"Frankie, love, it's me, Gio. You know me. You spent half the morning with your dick in my mouth."

A little smile crept on their lips. "It was only about five minutes."

"It was half of 'Doolittle,' and you know it. I should have punched you."

They sniggered. "Come on, it was funny.

"No, Frankie. Singing along to 'Here Comes Your Man' while someone is sucking you off is not funny."

"It's a little bit funny."

"Only if your taste in humor is very, very low. Anyway, Frankie, it's me. You know me. You live with me. You profess to love me."

"Of course I fucking love you!"

"Good to hear. I love you, too. And today we're going to do something special. Something we've never done before."

I could almost see their ears pricking up. "What?"

"We're going to be spies. Fully incognito. You're going to be a dashing young man—"

"Oh, what? Gio, I don't think I can manage that!"

"Of course you can. You did it for eighteen fucking years."

"Yeah, but it was hard, and I sucked at it!"

"This time it won't be hard. You're doing it because you want to, not because you have to. And anyway, here you're a *foreign* dashing young man. That gives you a fair bit of latitude."

"You do realize that we're probably closer to the Canadian border than to Boston, right? I'm hardly exotic."

"May be so, but you're still 'from away.' Make the most of it. You can speak French if you want."

"If I could do that, I might have gotten a grade higher than a C in high school," they grumbled.

"You can work something out. It's your cover, after all. My cover for the day is being a girl."

They frowned. "A regular girl?"

"You tell me."

They took a big breath. "I think you could be an actual princess, Gio. All done up, but not too much, because you're too classy for that. You'd be foreign, too, but we'd speak English in public because it's rude to do otherwise, right?" Their body was tensing up, but this time it was with excitement rather than fear.

"You want me to be a foreign princess for the day?"

"Yeah! Wouldn't that be cool, Gio?"

"It could be. And what is our mission?"

They crossed their arms, their eyes still shut. "Hmm. You didn't get any instructions?"

"Nope. Just a message to meet you here, today, incognito. That must mean that you're the agent in charge."

They turned around and opened their eyes as wide as they could go. "Gio, I don't know what our mission is. That can only mean one thing."

"What?"

"Our first mission is to find out what our mission is."

"Sounds reasonable."

They beamed. "You look great. Just like a princess."

"A foreign princess?"

"Yeah. You might need to work on your accent. Maybe stumble on the big words a bit more. I love you a whole lot, you know that?"

"Even when I'm a princess?"

"Even so." Their hand crawled along the bench, inching closer to mine. "Hey, so, can I, like, kiss you and stuff?"

"I don't know about stuff, not in public. But you can definitely kiss me."

"Won't that smudge you?"

"Maybe, but it'll be worth it."

They threw themself at me with gay abandon, stopped an inch away, and parked their lips on mine with the precision of docking space crafts. When they pulled back, they looked puzzled.

"It tastes weird. I thought it'd taste like cherry or something."

"It's lipstick. It tastes like lipstick."

"But it's red! It ought to taste like cherry, or what's the point?" They frowned. "Do you think Ms. Anzengruber would do me up too, one day?"

"Almost certainly. She seems to like this kind of thing. Why, would you like to be a princess?"

"Oh hell, no! Then I'd have to sit straight and behave! But I'd like to *look* like one, for a bit." Their brain skipped to a new track, which brought them a grin. "Hey, do you wanna hit the town? Ms. Anzengruber said there's a bookshop and a museum and stuff."

"Yeah. I'd like to see the ocean, too. I've never seen it."

"What? You've never seen the—" They leapt off the bench and dragged me upright. "Come on! You have to see it! You have to see it *now!*"

We charged around at Frankie-speed all morning. They kept seeing things in the distance that we just had to check out, and dragged me along with them. The only reason I didn't keel over was that every time we got there, wherever "there" was, they had to stop and kiss me for a while. It probably didn't do my make-up much good, but it made me inordinately happy.

When my stomach started growling, they put their hand against it. "Gio, we have to get some food into you, stat. Now, do you remember our mission?"

"What? Oh, yeah."

"I know you don't like spending money, but we are spies and you're being a princess and we need to get food and we need to stay in character."

"Is that going to be a problem?"

"I hope not. Thing is, when princesses get their lunch, they don't just look for the cheapest item on the menu and buy that, even if they hate it. Or get something nice and hate it anyway because it's costing money. They get what they want, and they enjoy it. Do you think you can do that? Just for today? Because we're spies?"

They looked so earnest that I had to say yes and mean it.

We found a coffee shop that sold books, or a bookshop that sold coffee. Either way, it was just our kind of place, or the kind of place we'd choose if we were the sort of people who can afford to go to places. It was relatively quiet, the food was lovely, and I was having a good time, until I looked up and caught an eyeful of Frankie, so beautiful they were resplendent, smiling down at me. Well, they might have been smiling at the cookies in front of us, but the result was the same: something inside me froze up and I couldn't eat anymore.

It took them two nanoseconds to work out that something was up with me. They leaned across the table and whispered, "Gio, if you don't like that, I'll eat it for you."

"No. That's not it."

"I know. Are you OK?"

"Never better. It's just... I was thinking that one day, maybe it could be like this for us, but for real."

"What? You want to be a princess full-time?"

"Not that. But I'd like us to go out, together, going to bookshops and having coffee and cookies and enjoying it. For real. Not just because we're spies for the day."

They grabbed my hand. "Gio, that's the thing: this is real, right now. We're doing it. That means that we can do it. One day we'll be able to do it all the time. Well, as much as we want, anyway. Won't that be glorious?"

"You really think that? That we can do it?"

"Of course! That's what we're working for, aren't we? Well, that's why I'm working."

"So when we grow up we can have cookies?"

"Not just that. That'd be silly. So we can have the smallest house that will accommodate all your books and all my music."

"Why the smallest?"

They leaned towards me and let it all out. "So it won't cost too much, and we won't be worried about money all the time. It'll be for living in, not for show, anyway. Pretty, because you like pretty things, but not so much that you'd worry about me breaking stuff when I get carried away. It'll be warm in the winter and cool in the summer, but not too cool, because then you'd get cold. And we'll have flowers outside, all around, so when you come home you'll see them and be happy. I'll put lights in the windows in the winter, even when it's not Christmas, so you have something pretty to look at until the flowers come back. And the kitchen will be little, so you won't have to walk a mile every time you're cooking dinner like you do now, and the table will be right by the window so you will have breakfast in the sun. And the living room will face west, so you will sit on the couch and have the sun set outside your window, just for you. And the bedroom will be too small and you'll always complain that you don't have enough closet space, but actually the problem will be that I'm messy." They frowned. "I will always be messy. I'm sorry. I can't help it, even when I really try. But I'll make it up to you in other ways, so maybe you won't mind it so much. I'll get Ben to teach me to bake and wake you up on Sundays with fresh bread and cakes, and I'll never, ever play music you don't like when you're around. And I'll always put your books back in the right place, and I'll try really hard not to spill coffee on them. And I will love you so much, Gio. Every. Damn. Day."

A drop fell on my hand, and I realized that I was crying. "You've been thinking about this."

They shrugged. "Yeah. All the time. It makes me happy."

"But what about you?"

"What about me?"

"Everything you just said was all about me. What about you? What do you want?"

They looked at me in utter confusion. "That's what I want. I want to live with you. Don't you know that?"

"Yeah, but... What about everything else?"

They shook their head. "There isn't anything else. Well, I mean, I'd like to keep my guitar, but I'd play it in the bedroom when you're home. And I'd like to have a stereo."

"That's all you want? A stereo?"

They nodded. "Yeah. I'd like a decent one, with an equalizer and speakers that don't rattle. Maybe a little boom box for the kitchen, too, if we can stretch to that, but it doesn't really matter. I just want to be home waiting for you, knowing that you'll be coming back. And, when I'm out, I want to be thinking about getting back home, knowing that you'll be there waiting for me. Gio, if you keep crying like that, you're going to end up looking like a panda."

I picked up a napkin and dabbed at my eyes. "I'm not a very good princess, am I?"

"Princesses cry. But I'm not sure why you're crying now. We don't have to have a small house, you know? I just thought that it would be the least stress and the most comfort."

"That's not it. It all sounds wonderful. Better than wonderful. But what if we can't get it?"

They shrugged. "Then we'll get something else. If it all goes to shit, we can get a van like Uncle Marin's, live in the back of it, and wash dishes for a living."

"Winter would suck."

"We'd move south for the winter and north for the summer, so you're never too hot or too cold. We could chase the fall and the spring. You like them best, anyway." They grabbed my hand. "If I had all the money in the world, I'd get a motorhome and drive you around so you'd never have to see the winter again unless you really want to."

"Love, you just said you'd live in a van if you were poor. Now you want to live in a van if you get rich. What gives?"

They shrugged. "Bigger van. Better parking."

"That's all money means to you?"

"No. If we get really loaded, I assume you'd start buying hardbacks. I would really like CDs rather than tapes, but, you know, I can do without. It makes no odds unless we have a good stereo, anyway."

"Why do you even want a house?"

"I don't. I want a home, and you like books. Books and vans don't mix all that well."

My eyes started to leak all over the place. "It's all about me, again. And you make it sound easy."

"Easy? No. But it will be wonderful." They dropped their eyes to the table and started to pick up stray grains of sugar. "Gio, there's something I've been meaning to talk to you about, but I don't know how."

"Short words and simple sentences, ideally. What's up?"

They took a big breath and flung their question at me. "Would you still love me if I was a plumber?"

"What?"

"I've been really enjoying working with Uncle Marin. I like doing things with my hands. I've never actually done anything before. I was thinking that I could carry on working for him, when the term starts. The money is not fantastic, but I'm picking stuff up pretty quickly, and I thought... Hear me out, OK? Before you tell me that I'm full of shit."

"Frankie, I've not said a word."

"I know. It's just.... I thought maybe I could work full-time, or near enough, and study part-time. I'd take as many classes as I could, obviously, but this way I could keep earning and learning, and if shit hits the fan, I'd have something I could do to keep us going. I like that feeling. It makes me feel like life won't just drown me, you know?"

"I think I do. But is that what you want to do? Plumbing?"

They blushed. "I'd like to think about it, with you. You're so much better than me at thinking things through. I like the idea of it, at least for now, but it would mean that we couldn't work together anymore. I'd tell you that you wouldn't have to work at all if I'm working full-time, but then you'd just yell at me."

"I wouldn't yell, but I might use some stern words."

"Right. So I won't suggest that. But I like working with you. I like doing everything with you. And, if I go part-time, I couldn't graduate at the same time as you, but I can't do that anyway unless you decide to wait for me. I don't know how that would work out."

They looked at me, their enormous eyes full of hope, fear, and trust, and something inside me broke. I'd been so far away, thinking about the two of us in our little home, tripping over books and sitting in the sunshine, that I'd forgotten about our actual lives: college, work, money, Jacob.

I'd forgotten it all for the whole day. I'd flittered about as if we didn't have a care in the world, as if we were free, but this wasn't our real life. In a couple of hours we would have to climb into Ms. Anzengruber's car and let it take us home, back to all the crap of the world. I started to shake and just couldn't stop. The contrast between Frankie's dream and our reality was just too damn big.

Frankie stared at me, horrified. "Gio, I won't do it if you don't think it's a good idea. You know I won't. That's why I talk to you: you tell me when I'm full of shit."

"No. It's not that. It's just... It was such a good dream, Frankie. About the house and the flowers. But that's all it is: a dream."

"It isn't! If we work towards it, it's a plan!" They scooped up both my hands. "Wouldn't you like that? A little home, just for the two of us?"

"In what country?"

"I don't care."

"You should. In less than three years my visa will expire."

"If you want to stay, you'll get another one."

"What if I can't?"

"Then we'll go somewhere else."

"And your degree?"

"I'll study somewhere else, or do something else. I'll be a plumber. I'll wash dishes. I'll find something."

"Where? In Canada? I would still need a visa. You'd need one to come home with me. You won't get that for washing dishes."

"We'll work something out."

"And what if we can't?"

"We will, Gio! I promise—"

"Don't! Don't make promises you can't keep. You can't make this happen. You can try, but that's all you can do. It's out of your control."

That was when something broke inside them. I could see it through the open windows of their eyes. They had genuinely believed in their dream, held onto it, not just because it was beautiful, but because to them it was real. I had just turned something they cherished, one of the things that kept their inner light on, into a corpse. Worse than that, I couldn't undo what I'd just done. I couldn't tell them that I believed in their vision, that I harbored any concrete hope that we would realize it. They would know that I was lying.

I sat on my chair, across the ruins of our lunch, our day, and Frankie's dream, frantically scrabbling for something I could do or say to make it all better. I couldn't come up with anything good, so I gave them what I had.

"I love you."

"I know, but—"

"No buts. I love you."

They smiled a brave little smile. "OK. Would you like a cup of tea?"

"Why?"

"Tea always makes you feel better. And you've lost a lot of liquids, what with all the crying. I'm so sorry."

"Don't be. I'm sorry. And thank you, but no, I don't want any tea. What I'd really like is to go somewhere where I can hug the shit out of you."

"You're still a princess. You could hug me here."

"I don't feel like a princess anymore. I feel soggy."

"You still look like a princess. Lemme go pay."

They leapt out of their chair and squeezed my shoulder on the way to the till. I dabbed at my face with our napkins, but I didn't know if I was making things better or worse, so I gave it up and focused on stopping my eyes from acting up. When they came back, I had gotten myself back together as much as I could.

"Do I look a mess?"

"No. You look beautiful." They wrapped an arm around my waist and escorted me out. They still looked stricken, as if they were recovering from bad news or a kick in the guts. I didn't like that, so I tried to fix it.

"Frankie, what do you know about princesses?"

They shook their head. "Not much. Hereditary position, though you can marry into it. Crowns, tiaras, and thrones. Fancy hats seem to be involved, for some reason."

"Do you think princesses wash?"

"Yes. A lot, I would imagine. In those big baths with the lion's feet, and a ton of bubbles. They probably have someone to scrub their backs, too."

"Have you ever heard of a princess taking a shit outside?"

"What? No! I mean, I don't follow celebrity gossip, but... No."

"There you go. That's the answer to your question."

They looked at me in utter confusion. "What was my question, again?"

"Whether I'd still love you if you were a plumber. Princesses love indoor plumbing. They're famous for it."

"Yeah, but they probably also like clean dishes, and they don't necessarily bunk up with the kitchen staff."

""That's beside the point."

"Alright. What is the point?"

"That I love you. You wash dishes now, and I love you."

"Yeah, but my socioeconomic potential—"

I stopped to look at them. "Love, aside from the fact that you'd probably make more as a plumber than as a sociologist, do you really think I care?"

Their voice came out as a squeak. "No? But when you graduate—"

"I'll still be me. I didn't get with you because of your socioeconomic potential. I love you, and I want you to do what makes you happy."

"That's easy. I want to do what makes us both happy."

"What about you? What about what you want?"

"I just want to be happy. That means that I want to be with you, and that I want you to be happy. Then I'll be happy, too."

"That's how it works?"

They nodded. "Yeah. For me, anyway. Gio, you're the one with the top grades, the scholarships, and the future. I just want to be happy, and you make me happy now. I don't need a future. I have a present."

I wrapped my arms around their neck. They hugged me and murmured in my hair. They weren't making any sense, just talking gibberish about the many kinds of perfection I apparently embodied. I didn't believe a word of it but I knew that they did, so it all hit me anyway.

We found a bench out of the way and spent the rest of the day hugging. Frankie chattered in that broken-dam way of theirs, going on about everything and nothing: the cool stuff they were doing at work, the music I should check out, the pretty things we'd seen that day, and how they were going to learn to make soup so they could feed me come winter. Every now and then, though, they'd stop all of a sudden, as if their stream of consciousness had hit a dam. After a while, I worked out that they were stopping themself every time they strayed towards the future. I didn't know if they were doing so to protect their dreams from me or me from them, but it made me unbearably sad, either way. My best cure for sadness was kissing them, and they didn't seem to mind, so I did that a whole lot.

By the time we had to meet up with Ms. Anzengruber, I was pretty sure that there wasn't a shred of make-up left on my face. I didn't care, though, and neither did Frankie, so it was alright.

5. THE MESS INSIDE

The postcard arrived on Tuesday. I picked it up with a huge bunch of mail from our postbox, while Frankie raced off to the shower. I was flicking through a pile of envelopes for Ms. Anzengruber, in the unlikely case that one of them may be for us, when I spotted a picture of a lighthouse. It was addressed to me. The message on the back said "Here's looking at you, kid." It was signed with an X in lieu of a signature.

At first I thought it may be from Ben, but he wasn't anywhere near the seaside, and the handwriting didn't look right. I stared at it, uncomprehending. Nobody else had my address, apart from the university, and they sure as hell didn't go around sending cryptic postcards. When it finally clicked, I had to sit down before I fell down.

It was a photo of the Castine lighthouse. Jacob. It had to be him. He'd followed us, or had us watched. I'd not seen him for a couple of days, and I had genuinely hoped that he'd had enough of us. Had he been watching us all day that Sunday? Had he watched us kiss? Had he seen me cry? Had he been listening to Frankie pouring their heart out? How far was he willing to go?

When Frankie bounded out of the shower, I'd barely gotten myself back together. I was trying to calm the fuck down, but my brain kept running through a million scenarios at breakneck speed. What the postcard meant, what Jacob might and might not do, what I could and couldn't do, his most likely reactions to my actions, whether I could actually do anything at all that wouldn't just make things worse. My brain weasels were running around screeching their hearts out, and the loudest screeches were about how I needed to stay calm, to keep it together, to act normal.

I tried my best, but I failed. Frankie spotted that I was unhinged in seconds, and proceeded to grill me. They just wouldn't drop it, which made me feel more panicked, which made them more frantic to know what was up with me. I was just about to totally lose it and scream at them, when my head decided to save me by giving me a splitting headache. Frankie went into nurse mode, and I spent the rest of the evening with my head on their lap, sipping tea, while they watched TV with the volume turned down way low. Even that didn't manage to stop my brain weasels from running around, but it calmed them down enough to let me go to sleep.

I woke up because my heart was thumping so hard against my ribcage that I could feel myself rattle. When my ears came online, screams filled them. That made my brain shut down completely, so that I couldn't work out where or when I was: all I knew was that grown-ups were fighting and the world was about to come to an end. I only came back to myself when the noise finally stopped. I peered out from under my blanket to check if it was safe, and found Frankie doing precisely the same. Their eyes were brown and full of terror, but they still flashed me a tiny smile.

"You're alright. I think it's over."

I crawled closer to them. "What is going on?"

"Not sure. Ms. Anzengruber and Uncle Marin just started screaming – well, Uncle Marin did. I figured the long pauses where her telling him whatever at her own volume. I was hoping you'd sleep through it."

"Not bloody likely. What do you think happened?"

"I don't know."

Steps thumped down our stairs, and the front door slammed shut. I had the presence of mind to turn the circle off, and was rewarded by hearing Marin's truck screech out of our driveway. When it was over, I found myself squashed against Frankie, wrapped so tightly in their arms that I could hardly breathe. I couldn't remember how I got there.

They sighed into my hair. "Do you think this is it?"

"The fight? I hope so."

"No, I mean them. Together."

"I don't know. He sounded pretty pissed, but he always sounds pissed."

"I couldn't hear her at all. I hope she's alright."

That sent a chill down my spine. "She must be. She wouldn't let him... Do you think we should go check on her?"

"I don't know. Do you think she'd want us to?"

"I don't know. Frankie, I don't like this."

"Me neither." They rested their cheek on my head and sighed. "Hey, do you think I still have a job?"

"What? Why wouldn't you?"

"I dunno. I think Uncle Marin only hired me to look good for Ms. Anzengruber. It's not as if he wants me around. I'm mostly dead weight."

"What? You're not!"

"You don't hear the way he talks to me sometimes." Their voice was so small that I barely heard it over the sound of the blood rising to my head.

"You're right: I haven't heard that. If I ever do, I'll kick his ass."

They snorted. "You probably would. I hope I still have a job, Gio. I don't know what I'd do if I don't. It's too late to find something else for the summer."

"You'd have to wait till the start of term, and we'd go back to working at the commons. Money would be tight, and I know that bussing tables isn't your vocation, but you'd be fine. And we'd get to work together."

"Right." They nodded. "I can do that. Would you be alright with that?"

"Why wouldn't I?"

"I dunno. It's just... I thought I was getting somewhere. Like I'd gotten a toehold on life."

Something about the vulnerability in their voice got to me. They were clearly worried, and I didn't have the mental space to deal with it. Knowing that scared me, because I was letting them down, yet again, and they were bound to be disappointed or pissed off at me. Jumping on top of my original panic, that new fear grew so fast and so large that it converted into anger before I had a chance to even think about it. I told myself that I was being unfair, but a little voice inside me insisted that I wasn't: I'd woken up in a panic, and instead of helping me calm down, Frankie was whining at me about bullshit. I had an urge to snap at them, but I knew that it would have only made things worse.

I took a deep breath, unclenched my teeth, and tried to make my voice sound level. "Come on. It's not going to happen. If it does, there's fuck-all we can do about it. Let's get some sleep, alright?"

"But... OK. Sure."

They rearranged themself so I could nestle next to them: my head on their shoulder, one leg over theirs, and my hand over their heart. It was my favorite position in the world, but it felt oddly uncomfortable. They felt rigid and distant, almost absent, as if they'd gone off somewhere and left their body behind as a favor to me. That sensation scared me so much that I got angry all over again – at myself, at them, at bloody Marin and his bloody temper, at everyone and everything. Wave after wave of anger washed over me. By the time I was calm enough to fall asleep, Frankie was already snoring.

The following morning, they woke up before me and didn't bother to wake me. When I opened my eyes, I found them sitting up, staring at our wall as if the scuffs in the paint were transmitting some kind of arcane knowledge.

"What's the time?"

They flinched, turned, and half-smiled at me. "Oh. Hi. It's early."

"Why are you awake?"

"Sorry. Did I wake you up?"

"No, you didn't. Why you didn't wake me was going to be my next question, not that you answered the last one."

I must have said that a bit sharply, because their smile disappeared.

"Sorry. I couldn't sleep not knowing if I needed to wake up for work or not, so I woke up super early. Does that make sense?"

"Not much, no."

That made them blush, and my heart broke. They were so beautiful bathed in the morning sunlight that I could hardly bear it. I slid closer to them and wrapped my arms around their waist. They hugged me back, but that was it: they didn't slip back under the covers, they didn't run their hands on my skin, and they didn't seem to even consider the possibility of anything else, anything more, happening between us.

I didn't feel rejected; not right away, anyway. It wasn't as if we jumped into each other at every available opportunity. We kind of did, though, and having them ignore the chance of a roll before breakfast was both odd and oddly hurtful. I didn't say anything because I would have rather removed one of my kidneys than nagged them into sex, and I hoped that my proximity would be enough to get them in the mood. Alas, it wasn't: they stayed as close to me as two people could be without interlocking body parts, but they were present in body only, their mind clearly elsewhere. As for the location of their heart, I couldn't begin to fathom it. After they got up, they went through their morning preparations on autopilot. They didn't snap out of it until a discordant honking made them jump.

"Do you think this is Uncle Marin?"

"Sounds like his van, and nobody else is enough of an asshole to make this kind of racket this early in the day."

They beamed. "Then I might still have a job!" They jumped up, ran around the table, kissed the living shit out of me, and rushed out. Five seconds later, they rushed back in to pick up their bag. I got another kiss into the bargain, so I really didn't mind.

I stayed in the garage waiting for Ms. Anzengruber to drive me to work. I could have gone back to our room, but I felt too agitated to relax, or even to read. I was sure that she was OK. She was the strongest, most resourceful person I'd ever met. She wouldn't let an asshole do anything bad to her. Marin was much bigger than her and had a lousy temper, but there was no way anything bad could have possibly happened. We would have heard it. I was sure of that, just as I was sure that she wouldn't have let it happen. I kept telling myself how very sure I was, but my stomach called bullshit on that, tied itself into a series of knots, and proceeded to make me regret eating breakfast.

When I heard Ms. Anzengruber's steps coming down the stairs, I felt so relieved that I thought my heart would explode. I picked up my bag and ran out to see her. I wanted to hug her, pick her up, and jump up and down in sheer joy. I wasn't going to, obviously, because it would have been grossly inappropriate, but I really wanted to. Then I saw her face, and my blood froze.

Ms. Anzengruber wasn't unemotional, I knew that. She had a heart the size of a continent and a whole bunch of feelings, but she always kept herself together. She never, ever lost her cool – not when her house was a charred mess, not when she randomly adopted me out of the snow, not even when she came to rescue us out of Ben's wardrobe. She was so steadfast, so balanced, that I thought of her as a constellation in my sky; I could look at her and know that some things in my world were constant.

That had been true the night before, anyway; everything looked different in the bright morning light. She looked different: small, weak, tentative, awkward. I still wanted to hug her, but just so I could protect her from the world.

She looked up at me and gave me a resigned smile. "It's fine, Gio. Everything is fine."

My hands wanted to grab her, to make sure that she was OK, that she was real, so I shoved them in my pockets. "Are you sure?"

She patted my arm. "The universe is unfolding as it should."

"That doesn't mean that things don't suck."

"No. That's true." She sighed. "Come on. It's going to be a long day."

We were halfway down to the library when she spoke again. "You don't have to take sides."

"What?"

"Between Marin and me. You do not have to take sides; in fact, I'd much prefer it if you didn't. We are adults, and we're not going to start a feud just because things did not work out between us."

I tried to think of a sensible response. All I could come up with was a weak, "OK."

"And, whatever happens, my home is your home as long as you need it. That includes Frankie and Ben, obviously. I don't want you to be worried about that."

"To be honest, I wasn't."

She flicked me a glance. "And now?"

"And now that you mentioned it, I kinda am."

Her face did a weird thing then: her mouth started laughing, but her eyes looked like they wanted to cry. I wasn't sure what was going on and I was a bit spooked by it, so I tried not to do anything at all. Whatever it was, it seemed to do her some good: when it passed, she looked a little bit better.

We had a reasonable morning at work, even though Ms. Anzengruber looked exhausted and was snappier than usual. I tried to keep an eye on her while getting on with my work and keeping another eye out for Jacob. It didn't work terribly well, but it kept me busy enough to keep my anxiety under control.

I was trying to work out what to do at the end of my shift, whether to 'port to Frankie or stay at the library to make sure that Ms. Anzengruber was OK, when it became apparent that I'd been agonizing over nothing: Frankie came charging towards me, their hair streaming behind them and a panicked look on their face. Judging by their panting, they'd been running at full tilt for a while.

They stopped right in front of me, their face crimson, and gasped words at me. "Gio. Circles. Down. Now!"

"What?"

"The circle. Around the library. And the other one. Take them down!"

"Why?"

"Just do it!"

I went into my head to the place where circles happened, and took them both down. I nodded at Frankie, who took a giant gulp of air and drooped against a shelf.

"This is bad. Really bad. Uncle Marin is fuming."

"What? Why?"

They grabbed my hand. Their breathing had gone nearly back to normal, but they still looked agitated. "The circles stop gods, yeah? They're as solid to them as a wall. Can you imagine if one of them tried to drive through a circle? Circle is solid, so's the car seat, bang! Or rather, squash."

"But that couldn't happen! The gods see circles or feel them or something, don't they? Marin can. And it's not as if the place is crawling with damn gods! Is it?"

"No, but apparently there are demigods all over the place. The descendants of gods, you know? Zeus being a golden shower, or whatever they get up to. Some of the demigods won't be able to see the circles, but they might still be stopped by them. Or, like, only part of them might get through. Kinda like pushing them through a sieve."

"Shit." I let myself drop to the floor. "I could have killed somebody."

Frankie dropped next to me. "It's OK. We didn't know. We can explain that to him. It's just... He's not in a great mood today. He dumped Ms. Anzengruber, or she dumped him. I can't quite work it out."

"What? Why?"

"He didn't say. He's just... Well, he acts like he's angry, but he isn't. I can tell that his anger is bullshit, but I don't know what he's actually feeling. Hurt, I guess, but it's all coming out as angry."

"That figures. It's not your fault."

"I know that, but it doesn't help." They sniffed. "Do you want me to talk to him? Tell him that I explained to you about the circles?"

I took a good look at them. They looked determined and eager to help, but they also looked terrified. I shook my head. "No. I'll talk to him."

"Are you sure?"

"Yeah. My shift is nearly over, anyway."

"Is it OK if I come with you?"

"If you want to."

"Yeah. I don't want you to do it on your own. Not unless you want to."

They helped me up and carried on helping me until the end of my shift. We walked out of the library side by side and found Marin leaning against the wall near the entrance. When he looked at us, I nearly shat a brick: for the first time since I'd met him, I couldn't read his expression. He looked pissed off, but he also looked all kinds of other stuff. Tired, mostly; more tired than I'd ever seen anyone in my whole life.

Frankie's hand tightened around mine. I gave their hand a squeeze, let it go, and marched on, even though my stomach wanted to head in the opposite direction. Marin didn't say anything until we were standing right in front of him. When he finally spoke, his voice was so deep that it did strange things to my intestines.

"Has the kid explained it to you?"

"Yes. I'm sorry, I really am. I didn't know! I didn't think about it!"

"It's always do first, think later with your people, isn't it?"

"I never meant to—"

"I'm sure you didn't. Let me tell you a secret: most of the time, what you mean doesn't mean shit. It's what you do that matters. You've got yourself a new toy, something that makes you feel special, and of course you can't help fucking around with it. You don't know what you're doing, you haven't thought about the consequences, but you're used to playing with fire and getting away with it. Let me tell you: one of these days, you're going to hurt somebody. You're going to hurt them so much that they may never recover. But who cares, as long as you're having fun?"

Frankie's hand tightened around mine. "Please, don't be like that. Gio didn't mean it."

"Yeah, right: let's spare her feelings, because that's what matters right now. Don't you get it? She could have killed someone today. Eventually, playing with magic will probably kill her. She'll fuck something up and that'll be the end of her."

Frankie spluttered, "But you taught us how to put up circles! The one around the house—"

"The fucking thing was supposed to be up for a day at most. I should have made her take it down, but nobody ever comes down there. The chances of one of my people finding it were so slim, and she's so fucking paranoid... But putting one where everyone can see it? If she doesn't end up killing some poor bastard, she'll end up killing you."

"What? Why me?"

"One of my people will notice what she's doing, notice you, and bump you off." He sighed, and his shoulders slumped. "Kid, I don't know. I just don't know. I knew you two were messed up, but I thought you could keep your shit together. Clearly, I was wrong. There is no helping you. I'm done. You're on your own."

Blood was rushing to my head, making it really hard for me to think. I didn't know how to feel, so I felt a bit of everything: anger, fear, shame, and everything else in between. Frankie didn't look much better. They were staring at Marin, limp and expressionless. When they finally spoke, their voice was barely audible.

"Uncle—"

Marin growled, "I'm not your uncle. I'm your employer."

"Alright. Why me? Why would your people want to kill me?"

"Your power, kid. If anyone else had a power like that, I'd take them out myself." He lifted his paw-like hand and thumped Frankie twice on the shoulder, nearly making their legs buckle. "Do you want a lift home?"

Frankie blinked. "What?"

"Do you want me to drive the two of you home?"

"Huh. Eh. No, thank you. We'll walk."

"Alright. I'll see you tomorrow." He turned around and limped off.

We watched him go. I couldn't have done anything else: my legs felt like concrete, and a storm was raging in my head.

Frankie snapped out of it first. They turned me around to face them and hugged me until I relaxed.

"You're alright, Gio."

"He didn't mean it?"

"Nah, he meant every word. But you're still alright."

"I don't feel it."

"Join the club." They pulled away from me and stared right into my eyes. "Will you tell me something?"

"Probably. What?"

"Why did you do it?"

"I didn't know that—"

"I know. That's not what I meant. We've known how to make circles for months, and we spend most of our waking hours in the library during term time. Why now?"

The last of my nerve left me and I started shuddering. This was the conversation I didn't want to have with them, the conversation I couldn't have without our entire world collapsing. I couldn't lie to them, I couldn't tell them the truth, and I couldn't think of a third option, so I just gave up and let myself fall apart. Frankie caught me and held me close to them. They murmured into my ear that I was alright, that we were alright, that they were sorry. Hearing their apology made me pull myself together.

I pushed them away from me, grabbed their arms, and tried to sound authoritative. "Don't be sorry! You didn't do anything!"

"But—"

"No! I did it. It's my fault. Even Marin knows that! I'll talk to him when he's calmed down, alright? I know you don't want us to fall out."

A muscle jumped in their jaw. "Everything is going to shit, isn't it? First they split up, and now this, and..." They trailed off and stroked my face.

"And what?"

"And something is wrong with you, something bad enough that you've gone off to hide under the porch."

"What?"

"That thing you do when things get too bad. You carry on with everything you need to do, but you're not really here; a part of you is hiding under the porch, like a sick animal waiting to get better or die. And it's the most important part of you for me, so, yannow, I really wish you didn't. I mean, I love your body, and I am totally in awe of the sharp bits of your mind. You get so much shit done that I can't believe it, even when it's happening right under my nose. But it's the rest of you that, I don't know, makes me feel so much about you. The bit that doesn't do anything, that just is... I miss that bit. But it's not up to me, I know that. I just wish I knew why it's happening. Don't worry: you don't have to tell me. I know that you'd have told me already if you wanted me to know. But it makes me feel so fucking useless." They sighed. "I feel like I've been punished –

not by you! By life, or something. Everything looked like it was going so well, and now everything is falling apart bit by bit, and I feel like I should have seen it coming, like I should have known that I didn't deserve it."

"It isn't falling apart! We're together, and we've got a home, and—"

They locked eyes with me. "We're together? Even when you're under the porch?"

"Of course. I love you, even when my brain is full of rats."

They stroked the hair off my forehead and kissed it. "Your brain is beautiful. Every part of you is beautiful."

"My brain misfires, though. You know that."

"Yeah, but it's still beautiful. I love you so fucking much."

"I love you, too. Do you want to go home?"

Their bottom lip wobbled. "I don't know. Does Ms. Anzengruber want me around? You know, after the thing with Marin."

"Of course she does! She gave me a whole speech about how her home is our home, no matter what."

Their smile was so dazzling that it made my knees go weak. "Alright. Let's go home."

We got through the rest of the week without any further mishaps. I was wound tighter than ever - there was still no sign of Jacob and I spent way too much time wondering what that meant – but I managed to keep myself relatively together. I just pushed my emotional dial down until my anxiety was tolerable. I felt zombified, but it got me through the day.

Frankie didn't seem to notice. They weren't there to notice: their body was there, but their mind kept wandering off, I didn't know where to. It was as if their focus was a lighthouse: its light was dazzling when it was on me, on us, on the present moment, but an instant later it was gone. A few minutes later it would be back, and then gone again; it came and went time and time again, all day long. I didn't think it was something they were doing consciously. I wasn't even too sure that they were aware of it. I could have asked them what was wrong with them, but I was too scared to; there were so many things they could be unhappy about, and I couldn't fix a single one of them. Having them so distant and distracted was a relief, in a way: if they didn't notice me, they couldn't notice how messed up I was. It wasn't a great way to be, but it made things manageable.

At the end of each day, when we found ourselves in our bed, in each other's arms, I felt so good, so safe, so loved, that I wanted to kick my ass for being such a whiny brat: I had it better than I had any right to. I fell asleep rocked by Frankie's breathing, feeling their heartbeat against the palm of my hand, and there was no better feeling. But then morning would come and remind me of how comprehensively fucked our life was.

Things didn't magically improve during the weekend. Frankie and I had two whole days with nothing to do but enjoy each other's company – the rarest of treats, and the sweetest – but we were too wound up to enjoy ourselves. I was relatively OK at home, even without my circle, but the mere thought of going out with Frankie terrified me. I was sure that Jacob was waiting for the right moment to spring out at us and totally ruin my life. Frankie, on the other hand, couldn't bear to be in the house. Maybe the sunshine called out to them, maybe I was just not good enough company; either way, they were so twitchy that they couldn't stay still, twitchy enough to test my patience, while I tested theirs with my reluctance to abandon our lair. By the end of the weekend, we'd pissed each other off more than I ever thought possible, and were both so upset at having upset each other that we ended up being extra clingy. When we finally gave up on the day being any good and turned in, I felt as if we were taking refuge on a life raft; while we were in our bed everything was OK, but the world beyond was too tempestuous for me to bear. I didn't even want to think about all the monsters out there.

All in all, I was actually relieved when Monday came and got us back into the semblance of a groove. Frankie didn't look too happy to be going to work, and Marin's truculent expression when he picked them up gave me a good idea of why that might be, but I thought that a change of scenery would still do them good. Ms. Anzengruber wasn't precisely cheerful when she drove me to work, but she was so self-controlled that I couldn't discern how she was doing. It was hilarious, really: Marin's moods upset Frankie because he made no efforts to control them, while Ms. Anzengruber's worried me because she was so buttoned up that I had no idea how she felt.

I was musing about that irony when my pervdar pinged and my heart sank. I turned around, and spotted Jacob sitting at our favorite table. He was wearing a man's face, again, and looked breathtakingly attractive, if one liked jocks. Unfortunately, I did. Fortunately, knowing that Jacob was hiding behind that chiseled jaw and spectacular shoulders made the whole package about as appealing as a maggot-filled donut.

As soon as he sensed my eyes on him, he looked up from his book and grinned. I froze my face into a non-response, which seemed the only safe response I could choose. His response to my non-response was an increase in the width and fierceness of his grin. My stomach filled with lead and sank to the bottom of my abdomen, a movement that my bladder did not appreciate – well, either that, or I was about to piss myself just because a guy had smiled at me from across the room. I was being totally ridiculous, and I needed to get my shit together with desperate urgency, so I spent a few minutes yelling at myself. That didn't make me feel any better, but it made me act better, so I classed it as sort of a win.

I spent the whole damn shift with Jacob tagging me. He followed me around everywhere I went, browsing the stacks with apparent fascination. Every so often, he'd come up to me with a book and a question. There was no consistency to the materials he dug up, but the questions were always on the same theme: abnormal sexuality. That he managed to find a way to crowbar that topic into our conversation while wielding books on utterly unrelated subject ought to have impressed me, but I was a bit too busy being terrified and grossed out.

At the end of my shift, I found a spot on the floor where Ms. Anzengruber could see me, put my schoolbag under my knees, closed my eyes, and tried to disappear into the wall behind me. Jacob sat himself where he could get a good view of me, but left me otherwise alone. Even so, waiting until the end of Ms. Anzengruber's shift was torture. There was no way in hell I was going to walk across a semi-deserted campus with Jacob on my tail, though, and I wasn't going to 'port to Frankie after everything Marin said about my use of magic, so I stayed put.

Frankie had quite a bit to say on the subject when I got home, and none of that was good. They'd been expecting me at lunch. Yes, my reluctance to 'port made perfect sense, but I had legs and I could have used them. They were annoyed and disappointed, and they had a right to be. When I finally told them the only thing I could think of, that I desperately wanted to walk to them but I just couldn't, they switched to being angry at themself and worried about me. They asked me a million and one questions about what was wrong with me, until dodging them gave me a violent headache. I spent the rest of the evening with my head on their lap and my eyes closed. I was supposed to be resting my brain, but I couldn't stop groping for a way out of the hole I'd put us in. I wanted to transport us to our old life, to the time when we could escape from all our worries just by jumping into each other's arms, but I'd lost my way there and I couldn't see another one.

When we finally went to bed, the touch of Frankie's skin against mine made my flesh crawl. That shocked me so much that it took me a couple of seconds to work out what the fuck was going on. I couldn't stop thinking about the hungry look in Jacob's eyes while he was asking me all those questions. I didn't want him to intrude into our intimate moments, but my brain kept bringing him up.

Things came to an ugly halt when Frankie kissed behind my ear, and I couldn't stifle a shudder. They pulled away from me and stared right into my eyes. "What's wrong?"

I nearly blurted out a "nothing" before I remembered whom I was talking to. "I feel bad about myself. About my body."

"What? Why?"

"It's just... I'm so fucking queer, Frankie."

They looked stunned. "Yeah. So am I. Is that a problem?"

"For some people, it is."

"We've never been those people, though. We've never cared. I mean, beyond avoiding stuff in public that could get our heads kicked in."

"I know. I just feel icky, you know?"

They stuck their chin up in the air. "Do you feel icky, or do you feel that we are icky together?"

"Don't ask me that. Please."

Their bottom lip wobbled for an instant, and they were up. They put on their shorts with their back turned to me, and handed me one of their shirts without looking round. When we were both dressed, they climbed back into bed, but they didn't touch me.

"Is this alright?"

"No. It's not. I miss you."

"Gio, I'm a foot away."

"Exactly."

My head was hurting like blazes again, and I just couldn't hold the tears in. Frankie moved towards me inch by inch, asking me if it was alright all the way. When we were finally hugging, I still didn't feel half as close to them as I had the night before.

Jacob came to see me every day that week. He put on a new face every day, but he played the same game: tagging along with me, asking me inappropriate questions, looking about to pounce every time we were alone, pulling back with an amused grin as soon as anyone came into view. Nothing bad actually happened: I was physically unharmed, and that was all that mattered. I kept telling myself that, but it didn't do any good. By the end of the week, I was beyond frazzled. So much of my mental capacity was sucked up by acting as if nothing was the matter that I didn't have enough left for the rest of the stuff I had to do.

I knew I wasn't good company for Frankie, who was getting sadder and twitchier by the day. I also knew that I was slower than usual at work; I kept fucking shit up, so I had to check and recheck everything I did. The simplest task took me forever to complete and drained more energy than I had to spare. I thought I was doing alright, though; or, rather, that nobody gave enough of a fuck about me to notice that I was not doing alright at all. The only person who was remotely interested in me was Ms. Anzengruber, and she had left me alone all week. I knew that she wasn't that impressed by my personal and professional performance, but her only reaction was a tiny little crease that occasionally appeared between her eyebrows when I fucked up more than was reasonable.

She knew me well enough to know that I was a waste of space, so I'd hoped that she might just file this period under that same heading and forget about it, particularly as she had her own Marin-flavored shit to deal with. I should have remembered that fate always pissed on my hopes.

The shit hit the fan on Friday. I ought to have felt proud of myself, because Jacob had dropped the game before I did. Halfway through my shift, he'd tipped his hat to me with a winning grin and left the building. I'd still spent the rest of my shift looking out for him, expecting him to come at me out of nowhere, but he didn't. By the end of it, I felt more tired and wired than I did when he was around. I'd just found a spot where I could close myself off from the world and weather the rest of Ms. Anzengruber's shift, when she appeared at my elbow.

"Dear, may I ask you a question?"

"Of course."

"Have you done something to upset a fraternity member? And I don't mean intentionally, though I'm sure that's a possibility."

Ice started to trickle down my veins. "What?" No!"

She smirked. "But you have upset someone. Were that not the case, you would have asked me why I'm asking."

That was it: she'd find out about Jacob, and then she'd tell Frankie, and then my whole life would implode. I had to stop this, and fast.

I ignored the lump in my throat and tried to speak authoritatively. "I really don't want to talk about it. Sorry."

She spoke coolly, but not unkindly. "You are starting to sound like Frankie."

"I still have a long way to go. I've only apologized once."

"I was referring to your open reluctance to discuss your situation. They have been obviously upset of late, and they've been very clear about their disinclination to talk to me about it. I had assumed that it was something to do with their uncle. Having just spent a week watching you getting harassed by a pack of jocks, I am not so sure."

"Frankie doesn't know anything about this. You can't tell them."

That little crease in her forehead came up. "I can, actually, but I won't do it without your permission. However, I have to say that I'm summarily unimpressed by how you're handling the situation."

That dig pissed me off, most likely because it was not uncalled for. "I'm fine. Nothing happened. I don't want Frankie to worry about this."

She shook her head. "I am not entirely sure that you really understand how and why Frankie worries about things."

"Maybe not, but they're my partner, and what goes on between us is nobody else's business." The words were out of my mouth before I could stop them.

I looked up at Ms. Anzengruber. Her expression had gone completely blank. I was just about to blurt out the biggest apology of my entire life, when she waved it away.

"Gio, you routinely forget that I'm not just your landlady."

My stomach cramped. "I know. You're my supervisor. I know I've been slow, but—"

She cut me off. "No. That's not it. I am your friend, I care about you, and it would be swell if that occasionally counted for something." She turned on her heels and marched off.

The wave of shame that washed over me drained what was left of my energy. I closed my eyes, slumped in my chair, and did my best to convince myself that I didn't exist. Maybe, if I thought hard enough, I could fade away. Maybe it would have worked better if I stopped thinking altogether, but I knew that there was no chance of that.

When a hand landed on my shoulder, my body snapped before I had a chance to think or look, and I narrowly avoided elbowing Frankie in the balls.

They jumped a foot back. "Whoa. I'm sorry."

I told my heart to return to its normal location. "Sorry. Got startled. What are you doing here?"

"We finished early. I came to see if you wanted a lift home. You looked really tired this morning, and you didn't show at lunch again, and... Anyway, I thought you might want to head back straight away, put on a movie, maybe catch a nap."

"Oh. Yes, please." As I got up, they took a step back from me, keeping their distance. I had no idea if they were doing it for my benefit or because they were concerned about their personal safety, but it made me feel like a piece of shit regardless.

I dragged myself over to Ms. Anzengruber's desk. "Frankie is here. I'm gonna get a lift back with them, if that's OK."

She rolled her eyes. "Of course it is." She looked up at Frankie and frowned. "Just drive carefully. You look exhausted."

Frankie shrugged. "Oh, I'm not driving. Uncle—" They swallowed the end of that sentence. "We'll be fine. We'll see you at home."

Her voice dropped below zero. "Is your uncle driving you back?"

Frankie squeaked a feeble, "Yes."

"And why didn't he come in with you?"

"He, huh, I, we, I mean, we weren't sure it was a good idea."

"This is absolutely ridiculous."

"Yeah, I mean, I don't know, so, huh, we're going to go now."

She crossed her arms and stared at them. "No."

"What?"

"Marin can come in here and get you. This has gone on long enough."

Frankie and I looked at each other. They looked as confused as I felt.

I raised my hand up before I knew what I was doing. "Huh—"

"If you need the potty, dear, you may go without my permission. Otherwise, you're going to stay right here until that mulish excuse for a man comes for you. If the worst comes to the worst and he leaves you here, I'll drive you home via the pizza place. That ought to be a fair deal."

Frankie raised their hand. "Could we, like, get donuts instead?"

"Yes. Now settle down and be quiet. This could take a while."

She went back to her work, cool as a cucumber, while we loitered by the front desk. I had never felt that uncomfortable in that building, not even on my very first day. Frankie was twitching so much they looked about to explode. I wanted to hug them, but there were too many people about, so I shoulder-bumped them instead.

"Are you alright?"

"No. Uncle Marin is going to kill me."

"He's not. He knows what Ms. Anzengruber is like."

"I hope you're right. You know, I was of the impression that people got to a certain age and started acting all adult and shit as some kind of natural process. I thought that was what growing up was all about. Now I'm starting to think that I've been sold a bridge. They're more messed up than we are, and that's saying something."

"Shit. Look."

Marin was peering through the front door. He spotted us and gesticulated at us to get out. Frankie shook their head and pointed at Ms. Anzengruber over their shoulder. When Marin saw her, his face went rigid. I thought he was going to just fuck off and leave us there, but he braced himself and walked in.

He looked tired, and he dragged his bad leg behind him as if it was really bothering him. When he got near us, he gave Frankie such a dirty look that they cringed. They were about to launch into an apology, but Marin shook his head at them and walked straight up to Ms. Anzengruber.

"Cynthia. It's nice to see you."

She stared up at him, her arms crossed. "Is it?"

"Yes," he sighed. "I've missed you."

She blinked. "You have?"

He tensed up for a moment and I thought he was going to flip out, but he slumped instead. "Yes. Of course I have. I wish I found it harder to believe that you didn't know that already."

She nearly smiled then. That made him nearly smile, which made her nearly smile a little bit more, and on and on it went until I figured that we were stuck in a weird version of one of Zeno's paradoxes: their smiles would increase in smaller and smaller increments forever, without ever actually reaching the status of a full, honest smile.

Marin broke first; maybe his face just wasn't used to stretching in that direction, or maybe he'd just had enough of that game. Either way, he let his face drop back to its normal, miserable configuration.

"Cynthia, I was right and you were wrong, for which I'm eternally sorry. I mean it. Let me make it up to you."

She blinked a few times, and then started giggling – a tinkling, joyous sound more appropriate to a girl of seven than a librarian in her forties.

The visible bits of Marin's face went puce. "Are you laughing at me?"

"Absolutely." She stretched her hand out to him, and he took it.

They were still holding hands across the desk, gazing soulfully into each other's eyes, when Frankie tugged at my sleeve. When I looked at them, they nodded towards the back of the library. We crept away as quietly as we could, but we could have probably marched off to the sound of bagpipes without those two noticing.

When we got to the side exit, Frankie dragged me up the stairs. I was a bit surprised, but I didn't mind. I loved that staircase: it was the first place where we made out. Sure enough, they walked up five steps, stopped, and proceeded to kiss the living shit out of me.

When we resurfaced, their smile made me smile. "You look so happy."

"One thing down, Gio. It was just a blip."

"You'll need to elaborate on that."

They wound a hand in my hair and kissed it. "They're back together. They just hit a rocky patch, and now they're back together. It wasn't broken: it was just a bit fucked up."

"That's what it looks like."

"And he's going to be in a good mood, again—"

"When was he ever in a good mood?"

"Alright. He's going to be in a less rancid mood, so work won't be a total nightmare, and your class will start soon so your work won't be a nightmare, either, and everything is going to be alright again. Isn't it?"

I froze. I couldn't say yes, because I knew that we had problems we'd not even begun to deal with, but I couldn't say no without breaking Frankie's heart. There was only one thing I could say, so I said it.

"You deserve so much better than what you've been getting."

They cupped my face in their hands. "Nonsense. I've got you. I don't deserve you, and there's nothing better."

We kissed a little bit more, and then we made our way home with our hands touching. It felt just like the old days, until we crossed the bridge. Frankie wanted to take our shortcut down to the railway line, as we always did, but I didn't feel safe out there, not even with them, so I asked them if we could walk by the store.

"Why?"

I desperately searched my brain for a good reason, and, miraculously, I found one. "To get ice cream."

"Right now? I really want to kiss you, and I can't kiss you on the street."

"Huh. Alright. I wasn't going to eat it, anyway. I was going to put it there." I pointed a finger at their solar plexus. "Other places, too. But I guess we could kiss instead."

After they'd picked their jaw off the floor, they grabbed my hand and pulled me towards the town. "Store. Now!"

They would have ran all the way home if I'd let them, but I didn't fancy giving myself an asthma attack. I had other plans for the evening. When I reminded them of that, they were happy enough to dawdle with me. All in all, we had as good a walk home as anyone could possibly have. It was only when they stood on our porch and put their hand in their pocket to extract our key that our bubble burst. They froze, their expression a mask of horror, and let off a string of expletives.

"Fuck! Shit! Fuck!"

"What is it?"

They took their hand out of their pocket. "Uncle Marin's van key. This is it: he's going to kill me."

"He's not."

"Of course he is! If he's walking here—"

"He won't be. He'll have to get a lift with Ms. Anzengruber."

Their expression drifted from horror to wonder. "Oh. Yeah."

"If you're lucky, he might believe you did it on purpose."

"Jesus, Gio! I hope he doesn't! That'd be wrong on so many levels!"

"Alright. Just give him his key, tell him you're sorry, and come back quick so I can eat ice cream from every conceivable part of your body."

They blushed. "Can you be more specific?"

"Nope. But I'm willing to show you."

We retreated to the garage to kiss and cuddle on the couch, because there was no way in hell we could have gone to our room and not gotten into each other. Even so, by the time our front door opened, Frankie was lost in the moment. The sound of voices in the hallway made them freeze mid-kiss. After taking a deep breath, they went out with their jaw set and the van key in their hand. When they came back, only moments later, the van key was still in their hand and they looked concussed.

"Love, what happened?"

"He said I should go pick it up from campus as soon as possible, because it's safer here, but that I should keep the key and take you out somewhere nice. They were hugging, Gio. They looked so happy. It was kinda creepy."

"I thought you liked them being together."

"I do! Sometimes I just find it hard to think about what that actually means." They looked at me looking at them, and blushed. "Hey, do you want to go somewhere nice?"

"Absolutely."

Their face fell. "Sure. Right. Do I need to change?"

"No. But you'll need to take your clothes off."

I was still not used to Saturday mornings. During term time, Saturday was a day like any other. We went to work, we did as much schoolwork as we could, and then we collapsed in a heap. It didn't feel like part of the weekend; it felt like our last chance to get our affairs in order so we could spend our Sunday Morning together without feeling panicked or guilty. Now we had no school and no work, but Saturdays still didn't feel the same as Sundays. They were still my second favorite day of the week, though;

waking up with Frankie in my bed, knowing that we didn't have to get up unless we wanted to, was pretty much the best way to start any day.

That Saturday was no exception. I'd woken up very groggy, probably because we'd been up extremely late the night before, and the first thing I'd managed to focus on was Frankie's ass. They were sleeping on their belly, which they hardly ever did, and my hand had ended up resting on one of their ass cheeks. It was a *good* ass cheek: soft and hard at the same time, pleasantly rounded, and just a little bit fuzzy, like a peach. I didn't want to wake them up, but I really wanted to check if the other cheek was as good, so I slid my hand over, as slowly and gently as I could. They let off a soft moan, so I stopped. Then their breathing changed, and my heart sunk: I'd woken them up, after all.

I stayed very quiet and still, hoping that they'd find their way back into slumber, but they turned around and mumbled, "You missed a bit."

"I beg your pardon?"

"Left and right. You missed a bit."

"Love, experience has taught me that your ass only has two cheeks."

"Didn't say nothing 'bout cheeks." They sighed and lifted their knee up, until it was resting on my thigh.

"Huh. Are you thinking what I'm thinking?"

Their hand slid down and rested against my crotch. "I'm not thinking."

"Alright, then."

Things had just started to get to the point when I wasn't thinking, either, when screams tore through the air. When they stopped and my brain cut in again, I found myself in Frankie's arms. They were wrapped all around me, protecting me as much as they could, even though they looked terrified.

I stroked their face. "Are you alright?"

"Yeah. No. I guess they've fallen out again.

"I guess. I didn't hear him leave."

"He hasn't. Unless she chucked him out the window."

"We would have heard the splat. Maybe he opened a portal?"

"Fuck!" They sat bolt upright. "His van is still on campus! I've gotta go get it." They jumped out of bed and went hunting for their clothes.

When I got up, they frowned. "You don't have to come."

"I don't wanna stay here if they're fighting."

"They won't hurt you."

"I know. I just... I don't wanna stay here."

"I'm going to be getting there as fast as I can."

"I'll bring my inhaler."

They snorted. "That'd be a first. Come on."

We didn't run to campus, largely because neither of us was fit enough. We walked as fast as we could, though, and I was breathing hard by the time we got to the van. Then we had a moment of panic, because Frankie couldn't find the van key. They'd stopped swearing at the top of their voice and were just about to head back home to get it when they found it, right in the pocket where it was supposed to be.

By then, they were so wound up that I wasn't sure they ought to be driving, but I couldn't drive at all, so we didn't have much of a choice. We got home safely, left the key on the bottom step of Ms. Anzengruber's stairs, and retreated to the garage for breakfast.

The screaming cut in again while we were finishing our coffee. By the time we had cleared up, it had stopped. We had just settled back into bed when it cut in again. We got up and were about to go sit outside, because we just couldn't bear it, when it stopped. It did that all day long. It never lasted long enough for us to actually get our ass in gear and leave the house, and it was a duet, so we didn't have to worry about Ms. Anzengruber's welfare, but it was damn unpleasant.

By evening, Frankie and I were both so drained that we didn't feel like cooking, so we raided Ben's shelf and stole a can of soup. We had just snuggled on the couch, with warm food in our bellies and the prospect of a long, relaxing evening ahead of us, when the screaming started again.

Frankie closed their eyes and head-butted the cushion. "I should have seen it coming."

"You know, I'm starting to feel better when they scream."

"Say what?"

"The rest of the time I'm waiting for them to start screaming, and that's more stressful."

"You've got a point. Hey, do you want to go somewhere? Uncle Marin's key is still there."

"Like where?"

"Anywhere. Just out. I don't care if we just drive around for a bit."

"Yeah. Alright. Are you going to ask Marin if that's OK?"

"Yeah. He might have changed his mind. I don't want to piss him off."

"I think it's a bit late for that."

We waited for them to stop screaming, then gave them ten minutes to simmer down. That turned out to be a tactical error: Frankie was tiptoeing up the stairs when they started screaming again. Rather than waiting for the end of that episode and trying again, we went for a walk. We didn't go far, just down to the river and back up again, but the evening was beautiful and the town was peaceful. Walking past the liquor store gave me a pang, because I could have really done with a drink, but there wasn't a damn thing we could do about it, so we just ambled home. When we got there, our peace shattered. We could hear them from the fucking porch.

I rested my head against the door. "I can't believe they're at it again."

"Maybe they never stopped."

"If that's the case, they oughta go pro."

"You're not wrong. Hey, I have an idea." They grabbed my hand and pulled me down the side of the house and across the yard. When they headed into the woods, I slammed my brakes on.

"Frankie? What the hell?"

"We can go hide in the kids' house. There's cushions in there, and comics and stuff."

"Have you been smuggling stuff out for them?"

"Obviously. Come on!"

I liked racing Frankie through the woods. It was the only race I had a chance of winning: I was smaller than them, so I could sneak through gaps they didn't even see. I got there only a few moments before them, but it was enough to give me a chance to see what was out there, turn around, and stop them.

"Don't go in there!"

They craned their neck trying to look past me. "What? Why?"

"I don't know. It looks bad. Like something bad has happened."

"Like what?"

"Like something really bad. The place is trashed and everything is covered in—" I couldn't finish the sentence. I was shaking so hard my teeth were chattering. I tried to stop myself, but I just couldn't.

Frankie went cold and rigid. "Gio, you stay here."

"I don't want you to look at that. You love the kids."

"You love them just as much. You just can't stand them." They sighed. "Come on. Let's go together."

We inched towards the kids' house. It had never been a beautiful or well-built structure, purely because Ben and Frankie had to make do with whatever materials they could scrounge, but it had been homely. Anything Frankie or Ben put their hands to felt homely. Now it was a mess. It looked like someone had gone around it and ripped off or kicked through everything they could reach. And then there was the red stuff – crimson smears and splashes covering every surface.

I started shaking again and Frankie hugged me. "It's not blood, Gio. It's meant to look like it, but it's not blood."

"How do you know?"

"The ants."

I took a closer look, even though I really didn't want to, and Frankie was right: the place was crawling with ants. They were clustering around the bigger splashes – which, now that I looked at them properly, were way too red to be actual blood.

Frankie poked a finger into a little pool of red and held it up to their nose. "This is gonna piss you off."

"What is it?"

"Cherry syrup. It smells like it, anyway. I really don't want to taste it." They straightened up and looked at me. "Someone thought they were being funny, I guess. Kids, probably. Assholes, definitely."

"But what about the kids? Where are they?"

"Hold on."

They crawled inside the house and pulled up the spattered cushions that had once made a cozy nest in the corner. Underneath them was a wooden board. They prized that up and uncovered a large plastic bucket buried in the ground. It was empty.

They looked up at me with a smile. "They left, Gio. They're alright. They took their backpacks."

"Their what?"

They blushed. "I was at the thrift store with Ben a while back—"

"To drop off Ms. Anzengruber's stuff?"

"Yeah, but we never got around to that. Anyway, they had these teeny backpacks, for toddlers or something, and I thought it'd be good for the kids to have little bags for their special things, you know, the things they wouldn't want to leave behind if they had to leave in a hurry."

"Huh. Love, did you have a backpack with your special things stashed somewhere when you were a kid?"

They blushed. "Yeah. You?"

"Yup. I kept it hidden on top of my wardrobe for three years or so. I never had the guts to leave, though."

"How old were you?"

"Eleven. And I tell you, I didn't know how to pack back then."

"Gio, that's not fair! You were just a kid! And it takes more than guts to leave home at that age."

"Like what?"

"Like a shitton of desperation. It's dangerous out there." They shook themself off. "Anyway, I just wanted the kids to have that option, you know? For their peace of mind."

I harbored some doubts as to whose peace of mind was at play here, but I kept them to myself.

Frankie carried on. "Plus the backpacks were really cute. They had faces on them. One of them was a monkey. And they were cheap, I swear."

"You're a sweetheart. I love you so much."

They crawled out of the house, got up, and hugged me. "What are we going to do?"

"Not much we can do. When the kids come back, we'll have to make them a new place."

Their eyes widened. "*When* they come back? Not *if*?"

"No. *When*. We'll have to find them somewhere safer to live. Somewhere vandals can't get to."

"Like the house?" They were staring at me, holding their breath.

"Maybe. But we'll have to talk to Ms. Anzengruber about it. No more sneaking around."

They beamed at me. "For real?"

"Yes. And we'll have to clear up this mess, I guess."

They slumped. "Do I need to ring Ben?"

"No. There's nothing he can do, and it would worry him. We'll tell him when he comes back. Tell you what: how about you put a message out for the kids, so they know to come to the house when they come back?"

They blushed. "You know about the hole in the tree?"

"I know now. I figured you must have a system."

"But why?"

"Because you're a sweetheart, and a secret agent, and I love you. Come on. Let's go home. We can deal with this another day. Or, like, never."

We held hands all the way back, even though it made squeezing through the trees really difficult. When we got home, the screaming had stopped.

Frankie looked up at the house. "Do you think it's over?"

I couldn't say anything nice, so I stayed quiet. They sighed, and we walked in together. We didn't let go of each other all evening.

I didn't think about a possible connection between the kids' house and Jacob until much later. The thought came to me in the middle of the night, and woke me with a start. I wanted to throw myself at Frankie, to hold them, to be held by them, but they were asleep and I didn't want to wake them, so I kept myself still and quiet and watched the night fade into day.

Sunday morning with Marin in the house meant no portals. I wasn't about to open one right under his nose, particularly as our relationship was still on very shaky ground after the circle debacle. It didn't matter, anyway, because Frankie and I could celebrate our Sunday Morning anywhere, as long as we were together. We thought so, anyway; when the screaming from upstairs shook us out of a perfectly good post-coitus cuddle, we realized how wrong we'd been.

It was a rehash of the previous day: brief moments of furious fighting broke the peace into chunks so small that they were worthless. I kept trying to tune it all out, but all I could do was tune myself down. I could bear it, but purely because I wasn't really there to notice it.

Frankie couldn't even do that. They just got more and more agitated, each fight building up on the stress of the fight before until they were as tight as a guitar string. About halfway through the morning, they finally snapped. They got up to go to the bathroom, and the screaming started while they were out. Ten minutes later, they'd still not come back, so I went looking for them. I found them in the cupboard under the stairs, sat on the floor, bouncing a tennis ball against the dryer.

"Are you alright?"

"No. I just don't want to hear it anymore."

I sat down next to them. "I'm sorry."

"You're not the one shouting." They caught the ball and squeezed it between their hands. "I don't get it. Why do they stay together if they fight all the time?"

"They didn't use to fight."

"Now they do. Why doesn't he just fuck off?"

"I don't think she wants him to. She seemed pretty happy to see him on Friday."

"Yeah, and they've not stopped screaming since. Why don't they just split up again?"

"People stay together even when they fight. Happens all the time."

"I wish they fucking didn't." They looked at me, their enormous eyes exuding righteous indignation. "I wish they would love each other nicely or leave each other alone. This is horrid."

"Maybe they're hoping they'll get through it. We argue sometime, and we get through it."

"We don't just scream at each other, Gio! And anyway, I think it's horrid when we argue, too. I hate this. I hate it so much. And I know you hate it too; you just handle it better."

"I'm used to it."

A wave of naked hurt swept the indignation from their eyes. "I'm sorry."

"It's not your fault!"

"Marin is my uncle. He's in your life because of me."

"Ms. Anzengruber is... I don't know what she is. But she is in your life because of me."

"Exactly. You bring all the good shit, and I bring all the bad."

"That's absurd, as well as grossly incorrect."

"Maybe. It feels like that, though."

They started to bounce the ball again. After a few throws, it got stuck between the dryer and the washer. Instead of getting it out, they pushed their hands hard against their temples.

"Gio, do you wanna go out? I don't care where. I just can't stay here."

"For a walk?"

"No. We can't walk far enough."

They got up, stepped over me, and walked over to Ms. Anzengruber's stairs. They bellowed, "Uncle Marin!"

Ms. Anzengruber's door opened and Marin bellowed back, "What?"

"Can I take your van for the day?"

"Do whatever the hell you want, but stop bloody screaming!"

When I got into the hallway, I found them by the door, twitching maniacally and clutching the van key as if they were about to stab it into the wall. They'd only marginally calmed down when we set off. By the time we got to Old Town, their shoulders had stopped hugging their ears. I thought they were starting to calm down, but then they spotted a restaurant just off the road, and turned into its car park so suddenly that my head smacked the side window.

They turned to me. "Sorry. Do you mind?"

"You wanna go eat?"

"Maybe? Not really. I just want to go and sit in there for a bit. They have something you're really going to like."

"I'm not hungry."

"You don't have to be. And it won't cost much."

I didn't feel like going in there, same as I didn't feel like going into any place with people in it, ever, but Frankie looked so sad and worked up that I couldn't say no. We walked in almost holding hands, and they made sure that we got a table stashed relatively out of the way, so it wasn't so bad.

When our food arrived, they looked anxious. "What do you think?"

"They're milkshakes."

They nodded. "Yup."

"But they've got purple balls floating in them."

"That'd be the blueberries. Try it. If you don't like it, I'll eat my hat."

I was just about to tell them that they weren't wearing a hat, when the milkshake hit my tongue. "Holy shit! Is this even legal?"

They smirked. "Told you."

"How do you know about this place?"

Their smirk dissolved. "My dad took me here, and my mom. Last year, after they'd dropped me off. Nowhere on campus was good enough, you know? They didn't like the food here, either. I can't even remember what I ate. I was a bit distracted. But I remembered the milkshakes."

"Were you scared when you got here?"

They nodded. "Terrified. Everything was falling apart. I just couldn't hold it together anymore. It did fall apart, I guess."

"But then you put it back together. Well, some of it. Some things can't be fixed, love."

They stared out the window for a million years, hardly touching their drink, until I reminded them. Then they guzzled it down in no time flat, without tasting it, and we were up and out in moments.

When we got back to the van, they turned to look at me. "Do you ever wanna just drive off and keep on driving?"

"I can't drive, love. But yes, probably."

"We can't though, can we?"

"Not really. It will be alright. They'll fucking settle down, or break up, or get sore throats."

"I've gotta work with him tomorrow, and I don't think I can. I mean, I will, because I have to, but I don't think I can."

"I'm sorry. Getting a job with him seemed like a good idea at the time."

"Carve that on my tombstone, will you?"

They put their hand in their front pocket, frowned, tried the other front pocket, blanched, and then proceeded to inspect each and every pocket they had, including some that turned out to be purely decorative.

"Gio, I don't have the key. Did I give it to you?"

"No. Look, you can't have lost it."

"But I don't have it!"

"That's not what I mean. We literally just walked from here to the restaurant and back. If it's not on the floor between here and there, it must be on our seat, or under it."

They rushed to the restaurant. Two minutes later, they stumbled out. "I couldn't find it. They'd not found it, either. It's not there."

My gullet started to fill with blueberry-flavored bile, but I made myself push it back down. "We'll be alright. How far are we from home?"

"I don't know. Five miles? Ten? It's a fucking hike."

"Alright. If we ring Ms. Anzengruber—"

"I can't tell her! She'll tell Uncle Marin!"

"You'll have to tell Marin, love. He'll find out, won't he? He'll need to get a spare from home, assuming he's got one."

They slumped. "He's gonna rip my head off and piss down the hole."

"He won't. Do you want me to ring him?"

"Nah. It'll only make it worse in the long run." They took a deep breath, kissed my forehead, and strode back to the restaurant.

Five seconds later, they were back out.

"What happened? Did you find it?"

They lifted their hand up. "Yup."

"Where was it?"

"Pocket. I don't want to talk about it."

They looked so miserable that I really wasn't tempted to bother them. We drove all the way back without saying anything.

When we got home, the house was quiet. Ms. Anzengruber and Marin were sitting on the upstairs deck, drinking and chatting quietly. They were quiet all evening, but that brought me no peace. I kept waiting for the screaming to start again.

The week that followed wasn't one of the worst ones of my life, not even close, but my life had been such a train wreck that that wasn't saying much.

Jacob returned on Monday. He walked into the library right behind us and stuck to me all week, occasionally asking me prurient questions about my body's ins and outs and what Frankie did with them. Ms. Anzengruber clearly noticed him, although she couldn't know that she was noticing the same person wearing different faces. She gave me a few funny looks, but she didn't say anything. She wasn't quite herself, which wasn't surprising as the Shouting Olympics were still going on all evening long. They never woke us up again, but they still made our life miserable.

Frankie was suffering more than I was. They hated leaving the house to go to work, but they also hated coming back from work. No part of their life gave them any comfort anymore; I could see it in their eyes. They were forcing themself to walk back into situations they found deeply upsetting, and they hated themself for it. The only silver lining in the entire situation was that they didn't seem to hate me, but I wondered how long that would last. The current state of their life wasn't my fault, but it was partly my responsibility. I'd been with them when their life was changing, and I'd helped them make a whole bunch of decisions that had turned out bad. It was only a matter of time before they realized that and told me where to go, I was sure of it.

The fact that I couldn't be there for them didn't help. I was handling the situation the only way I knew how, by focusing on what I had to do and obliterating how I felt about it. It made it possible for me to function, but it also made me terrible company. It was a race, really: would Frankie break up with me because I'd fucked up their whole life, or because I was a shitty partner? Or would they find out about Jacob and dump me because of that? Our relationship had been the one thing in my life that gave me solace, the only thing I'd ever had that was both stable and good. Now I could find no comfort in it. Even stressed out and cranky, Frankie was still the most wonderful human being I'd ever met, probably the most wonderful human being who ever lived, but I couldn't even look at them without hearing the clock ticking on us.

I was a total mess, worse than they'd ever seen me, and that terrified me, even though I wasn't sure that they could notice it. Their focus was still fluctuating wildly, to the point that I might have worried about them if I had any scope for extra worry. Their absent-mindedness suited me fine, anyway. I didn't want them to look at me too closely, in case they found me wanting. I didn't trust my face not to betray me, not to broadcast the knot of fear that was chewing at my insides.

Every now and then, though, they'd fall right out of the daydreams that consumed them and into our shared present. When that happened, I was so conflicted about my feelings that I didn't know what to do with myself, so I tended not to do anything; it seemed the only way to avoid fucking things up. I hoped that what they experienced was a comfortable silence rather than the frozen, wordless dread that clawed at me, but I wasn't sure. And anyway, it didn't always work.

When they got back from work on Friday, they were wholly present. They were so switched on, in fact, that they scared me a little. I did my best not to shy away from their gaze, but it was hard. I was worried about them noticing how fucked up I was, so I decided to try something else: I dragged them to the couch and sat myself on their lap. They looked more puzzled than pleased, so I decided to try harder. I buried my face in their neck, and I was just about to slip my hands south of their waist when they caught them.

"Gio, I appreciate you trying, but you're really not into this."

My stomach sank. "I like touching you."

"I know you do, and I'm really glad about that, but you don't feel like it right now, so I'd rather you didn't. I'm sorry." They wrapped their arms around me and rocked me until I'd calmed down. When I'd stopped snotting up their shoulder, they brushed the hair off my face. "Gio, do you remember that Sunday in Castine?"

I stifled a shudder. "Yeah. It feels like years ago."

"It feels like a different life. But we had a good time, didn't we? Away from here, by the sea."

"Yeah. It was pretty great."

"Yeah. So, I thought maybe I'd like to go home, one of these weekends."

I hadn't seen that coming, and I wasn't in a good frame of mind, so I totally failed to modulate my response. "Are you kidding? After what happened last time?"

"Not to my parents'. To Saint John. Most of my friends are there, and I still remember some of their phone numbers. Even if nobody wants to see me, I thought it could be a nice trip. I could show you all the nice spots—"

"Me? You wanna take me?"

"Yeah. Of course I wanna take you. I thought we could spend a fun couple of days. It wouldn't cost much. I can take Uncle Marin's van—"

"You asked him already?"

"Yeah. Is that a problem?"

"You asked him before asking me."

They blushed. "I thought I'd ask him first, to make sure that we could do it. I thought you might like the idea. How did I fuck up?"

"You didn't."

"OK, you mean that, but something is clearly wrong. What's up?"

"Nothing."

They winced. "Gio, why are you doing this? If you tell me what you don't like about it, we can plan a way to make it right."

They sounded so concerned, so caring, so reasonable, that my heart melted. They also sounded determined to work it all out, though, to quiz me about it until they got an answer they could work with, and I couldn't let them do that. I couldn't bear the thought of being all the way out there, so far away from home, at Jacob's mercy, but I couldn't talk to them about it. If I told them a lie, they'd know. If I told them the truth, I'd lose them. Every option I had was a bad one, and all my fears combined into a storm that raged inside my brain, so I could hardly think. I buried my face in their shoulder and tried to disappear.

"What is it, Gio? Just tell me."

I took a deep breath and emerged into the light. "I think you should go.

See your friends. You'll enjoy it. I wouldn't."

"I would never ask you to come if I didn't think you'd like it. We can afford it now, and we have the time. Come fall, we're going to be buried in work. And it's not that far away. If you wanted to scram, I'd have you home in three hours, no questions asked."

"No. I don't want to go."

They bit their lip. "Alright. If you change your mind, just tell me, OK? Or if you'd be up to at least talking about it."

"You should go. Don't make it my fault if you don't see your friends."

They leaned back from me, their face expressionless. "Alright. I'll think about it."

They were so fucking transparent that I could hear all the words they were keeping back. They didn't want to go without me, but they didn't want to pressure me into going, or even into talking about going, so they were stuck. I'd gotten them stuck, and they weren't even giving themself permission to be cross about that.

We turned in shortly after that. The silence between us had become oppressive. They were clearly miserable, and going to bed didn't cheer them up. Even though they lay right next to me, I felt lonely, disconnected from them. The air between us was full of the ghosts of unsaid words.

One of the glorious things about Frankie was that they didn't overthink everything like I did. That very Saturday, they woke up at an ungodly hour, found me already awake, and came right out with it.

"I'm going to Saint John. Today. I don't want to, but I will. It's not fair me asking you to do things just because I want to do them. And maybe if I do this trip right, next time you'll trust me enough to come with me."

"Frankie, it's not about that!"

"Alright. Whatever it is, I hope it goes away. I'll be back tonight."

We argued about that, but not for very long. They just weren't going to be away from me overnight, and that was all there was to it. Having sorted that out, they kissed me rather chastely, got dressed with their back turned to me, and left the house without having any breakfast.

I closed my eyes and followed them in my mind. I could feel them moving away from me: down the hallway, down the driveway, and then up the road. Every bit of distance they put between us filled me with dread.

All of a sudden, I felt them speed away from me. They must have reached the end of town. I panicked and wrapped my mental tentacle even tighter around them. Then they went too far, and something inside me tore up. It was a physical sensation, as real as snagging a piece of cloth on a fence and feeling it rip, but it was inside me, in my skull. An axe made of pure, blinding light descended on my forehead, and I was pain.

I was still in bed, and couldn't get up. I didn't even consider it. I knew that Ms. Anzengruber and her medicine cabinet were out there, only feet away from me, but there was nothing I could do to reach them. Time passed, raking its claws on the inside of my skull with agonizing slowness. Each passing second gave me a new wound, until I hurt so much that I gave up trying to resist the pain. I let myself fall right into it and let it consume me.

I must have blacked out or fallen asleep, because a string of muttered curses woke me up. A hand landed on my forehead, as gentle as a butterfly. I recognized it, even through the scorching pain. It didn't make the pain go away, but it made it matter less, and that was nearly as good.

"Frankie." Talking really hurt, the words booming and scraping inside my head, but saying their name felt good.

"What happened?"

"Headache. Bad."

"Does it hurt when you open your eyes?"

I tried that. The dim light of evening drove spears through my eyeballs. I shut my eyes against that, and tried to nod. That set the jumble of rocks and metal in my forehead tumbling down and made me groan.

"Jesus, Gio. Have you taken anything for it?"

"No."

"Alright. I've got you. I won't be a moment."

They stroked my cheek, their fingers as light as feathers. It still hurt, but it felt so good that I didn't care. Endless moments later, I felt the bed sag.

"Take this. Please. It will help."

I swallowed a couple of pills, followed by a swig of something repugnant and warm. Frankie laid me down again and sat next to me, their hand on my temple. Slowly but surely, it seemed to suck all the pain away, until all there was left was the knot of agony where my forehead had torn. I tried opening my eyes. Focusing them hurt way too much, but seeing Frankie's blurry profile in my sky was enough.

They murmured, "Hey."

"Hey, you."

"Are you feeling better?"

"Yeah. Still hurts, though."

"Where?"

I picked up their hand and placed their index over the tear in my forehead. They stroked it, slowly and gently, and each stroke rubbed away some of the pain. The relief was so much that I attempted a smile.

"Thank you."

"*De rien.* I didn't know you got migraines."

"Neither did I. First one."

"What happened?"

"I fucked up. I tried to follow you in my head and broke something."

Their hand froze in place. "This is my fault? Because I left you?"

"No. I told you, I tried to do magic, or whatever, and hurt myself. Not your fault."

"But it wouldn't have happened if I stayed here."

"You can't be with me all the time."

They sighed and started stroking my head again.

"Thank you. That feels really good. Did you have a good day?"

"Yeah. The driving kinda sucked, but I got there. I missed you."

"What did you do?"

"I drove all the way home and found that it's not home anymore, but that's OK. Everything looks the same, but it all feels different."

"Different how?"

"Like it belongs to someone else's life. Familiar and alien, all at the same time. When I think of myself there, I can't imagine me here, and vice versa."

"But it was good?"

"Yeah. I got to see Charlie. It was great. I didn't know how it would go at first, because we've not spoken in so long, and, like, I thought I was a boy when I knew him, but it was great. We just started out where we left off, kinda. I guess we know each other well enough to do that. It was as if I'd never left, only I did, so we had a lot to talk about." They wound a strand of my hair around their finger. "I talked about you a lot. I hope that's alright. You're the greatest thing ever, so I kinda had to."

"What did you tell him?"

"That you're wonderful. That I lucked out somehow, and ended up living with you, and you make me so happy I can hardly believe it. That you put up with me and all my crap."

I tried to sit up, but it hurt too much so I contented myself with frowning up at them. "I don't put up with you! I love you!"

"The two are not mutually exclusive. With me, they kinda have to go in tandem." Their voice dropped. "Charlie would like to meet you."

"Did he ask why I'd not come?"

"No. Probably figured you were just giving me space. It was OK, Gio. It wasn't weird." They said it in a tone that let me know that it definitely wasn't weird, but it just as definitely was something equally unpleasant.

"You wanted me to come."

"Yes. But not if you didn't want to." Their hand clenched on my shoulder. "Maybe we can do a few short trips, Gio. So I can show you that it's OK. That you can trust me."

"I do trust you! That isn't the issue!" I said that too loudly and sent a reverberation through the holes in my head.

Frankie saw me flinch and went straight back into nurse mode. "Sorry. I didn't mean to wind you up. It doesn't matter. Just try and relax, OK?"

A wave of anger surged through me: anger at myself, at them, at their friend Charlie, and at the world. I wanted to destroy everything to take it all apart and reconfigure it in a way that didn't suck. Maybe that was what Frankie had felt back in March, that day when they nearly broke reality. I wanted to ask them about it, but my head was filling up with a pink, soft fuzz, so I let myself fall into it instead.

When I woke up, I wasn't hurting anymore. The memory of pain was there, and my head felt brittle, like an egg shell, but I could focus my eyes, move my head, and even think. I decided to use said abilities, and immediately regretted it: the first thing I noticed was that Frankie wasn't there. They weren't in my bed, they weren't in my room, and they weren't anywhere to be seen.

The thought of panicking about their absence scared me; I would probably give myself another migraine. The thought of feeling my way to them scared me even more, and so did 'porting. The safest option was using my body, pathetic as it was, and going to look for them.

I staggered down the hallway, calling out feebly, and the door of the cupboard under the stairs opened up.

"Hey."

"Hey, you." I tottered over and sat down next to them. "What are you doing?"

They closed the door. "Nothing. Just sitting."

"I mean, why are you in here?"

"I like it here. It's quiet."

"Why aren't you in bed with me?"

They folded their knees up and wrapped their arms around them. "I fucked up, Gio. I fucked up big time. I woke up, and I could hear them moving upstairs, and you know how they've been, so I went up and all I did was ask them if they could be a little bit quiet, because you had a bad migraine yesterday and you needed your rest, and Ms. Anzengruber just looked at me like I'd sprouted horns, and I thought Uncle Marin was going to shout at me or throw me out the window or something, but he just picked up his bag and left. Ms. Anzengruber is going to hate me forever."

"She's not! Did she even say anything?"

"No. She said that it was OK. But it isn't. I can't do anything right."

"Love, that's not true."

"It is, though. Whether I go or stay, people around me just get hurt."

I couldn't talk any sense into them, so I gave up. I sat next to them until I needed a piss, and then went to have my breakfast. They came out before I had finished eating, but they were so mentally absent all day that I wondered where they'd left their head, or their heart.

Marin picked Frankie up on Monday morning as if nothing had happened. I didn't know how to feel about that: should I be relieved, because Frankie still had a job? Pissed off at Marin's inconsistency? I could not understand how he could bellow at Frankie one moment, and give him a lift the next. What would be worse for Frankie, unemployment and penury or putting up with Marin's moods?

I knew that that whole train of thought was a waste of time and effort, because no part of that was up to me; Marin's van turned up, Frankie got into it, and that was all there was to it. They didn't look happy, though, and I was finding it harder and harder to remember how their happiness had looked and felt.

I thought about them all day long. A chunk of my brain kept showing me photos of how they'd looked when I first met them, when we first kissed, when we first moved in together, and comparing them with the way they looked now. That comparison was neither flattering nor reassuring. Between worrying about them, keeping an eye out for Jacob, who was nowhere to be seen, and doing my job, my brain felt overcrowded and underpowered, and my shift seemed to last forever.

When Ms. Anzengruber drove us back from work, we found Frankie sitting on the patio steps. They were so wired that they were visibly twitching, as if their muscles were misfiring. When they saw us, it took their face a couple of goes to arrange itself into something like a smile.

My stomach sank. Something bad must have happened. Maybe Marin had fired them – but no, that made no sense. If they had finished work early, for whatever reason, they would have found me and told me straightaway. Maybe they'd seen Jacob. Maybe that was why I'd not seen him: he'd been hassling Frankie instead. This was bound to be it: Frankie knew everything, and our hours together were numbered.

I felt dizzy and nauseous, but I managed to step out of the car without falling over. Frankie looked up at me, their eyes vacant with fear and the grotesque caricature of a smile plastered to their face. They got up when Ms. Anzengruber walked over to them and greeted her so formally that they sounded Victorian. She looked a bit puzzled, but she didn't say anything. As soon as she'd walked in, they rushed over to me.

"Gio, I'm so sorry. I didn't mean to, I swear."

"You didn't mean to what?"

They swallowed. "I lost my key. I don't know how the fuck I could have lost it because I always keep it in the same pocket, you know I do, but I realized it wasn't there at lunch and I looked everywhere and I couldn't find it. I checked all my pockets and literally turned my bag inside out, and I looked all inside the van, and there was no way I could have left it at work, but I went back anyway, and then I didn't have anywhere else to look so I figured I'd just wait for you, and... Gio, what am I going to do? Ms. Anzengruber is going to kill me!"

All the tension I was harboring left me, and took my patience with it. "For fuck's sake, Frankie! You just gave me a heart attack! I thought something bad had happened!"

They went from looking frantic to looking hurt and frantic. "But this *is* bad! People could find it and get in!"

"Unless you left it in the bloody door, which I know you didn't, that's not likely. It doesn't have an address on it, does it?"

They blinked a few time. "No. I guess not. But Ms. Anzengruber—"

"She knows you. She must have known that this was bound to happen, sooner or later."

They froze for an instant. When they got unstuck, then their bottom lip wobbled and they let off a weak chuckle. "Yeah. I guess you're right. I try to be careful, but..." Their voice trailed off.

I took their hand and pulled them inside. "Come on. You're being silly."

They came along with me, and they were polite and attentive all evening, but they were so subdued that it felt as if their personality had shrunk in the wash. I didn't feel great about it, and I wondered time and time again whether it was my fault, whether I'd grossly underestimated how big a deal losing that fucking key was to them. Had I known what was to come, I would have worried less. The week that followed gave me ample opportunities to perfect my response to such an eventuality.

On Tuesday, Frankie lost their bank card. They looked everywhere for it, with no success, until they were in a total panic. It was only when they'd managed to calm down enough to tell me about it and we retraced their steps that they realized what had happened: they had gone to get some money out of the ATM, and they couldn't remember taking the card out. Getting it back should have been just a matter of asking the bank for it, but we couldn't do that, because the bank was already shut. Frankie didn't get a chance to go in until lunchtime on Wednesday, by which time they were so keyed up with the stress of waiting that they got a serious telling off from Marin for not concentrating at work.

Marin's mood only marginally dented their joy and relief, though. They came bounding up to me at the library, waving their bank card in the air and grinning wildly. Seeing them that happy almost cut through the fog of fear I'd been swimming through. Jacob wasn't around, so we hid behind a quiet stack for a bit of a kiss and a cuddle, and things felt almost normal.

Five minutes later, they tried to buy us cookies and realized that they were $50 short. They'd picked up their card, gone to the ATM, and had been so focused on retrieving their card that they'd left their rent money behind. They trudged back to the bank, their tail between their legs, and they were told that they couldn't get their money back until the machine was emptied and checked. When they related that to me, they were so down about it that I didn't know whether to cry or yell at them. Seeing them so forlorn was heartbreaking, but I had enough going on without having to deal with them freaking out over nothing. I couldn't tell them that, though, so I tried to act normal. I must have been bad at it, because it didn't seem to work. Even dinner failed to cheer them up: they kept spacing out and hardly touched their food. I tried not to snap at them, but it got harder with every passing minute. I settled for parking them in front of the TV for the evening and hiding behind a book I couldn't read.

They set off for work on Thursday utterly determined to keep track of their shit. They were so focused on that that they didn't even notice how wound up I was. I'd not seen Jacob for days, and I was so busy obsessing about what he might or might not be doing that I could hardly think. They kissed me a perfunctory goodbye, performed a pocket check that looked so much like the sign of the cross that it gave me flashbacks, and fucked off to work with gritted teeth.

By lunchtime, they had lost their wallet. It didn't stay lost for long: a member of staff spotted it in a trash can later on that day, emptied of all valuables, and handed it in at the campus police station. Frankie's student card and bank card were also missing.

By the time they told me the whole story, they had already done everything they could do to fix the situation. Marin had advanced them their wages, so they had plenty of cash to see them through, and a new bank card and student card were on their way. They were going to have to pay for the student card, but they were earning enough for that not to be a real problem. They were still sorry, and still totally mystified at how it could have possibly happened because they had been so fucking careful and paid so much attention that they'd given themself a headache. They'd checked their bag half a million times, and they'd made sure that their jacket pockets were always closed, and there was just no way they could have possibly lost anything, but they still had, and it made no sense. I knew that because they told me time and time again, in increasingly distressed tones, until I broke down, threw my arms around them, and kissed them into silence.

When I let go of them, a few minutes later, they were considerably calmer. They were still not quite right, though: their eyes were solid brown, and a trace of sadness lingered at the corners of their mouth.

I stroked their cheek, trying to rearrange their mouth into the shape I loved so well. Every time I let go, it fell back out of shape. I poked it a few times before they caught my hand in theirs.

"Wenchlad, what the hell are you doing to me?"

"Trying to make you smile."

Their breath caught. I looked up from their mouth until my eyes found theirs. Their eyes were still brown, but a bright green circle was expanding around their pupils, blossoming like a flower.

I let myself stare deep into their eyes and told them my biggest truth. "You're so beautiful I don't know how my heart can bear it."

The green circle burst outward, filling their eyes, making them so bright that I thought I might fall inside them and never come out. Their nose saved me from that fate: it poked mine and made me blink.

They smiled at me. "Hey."

"Hey, you."

"I wish I was more like you. You're so fucking strong."

"Are you shitting me?"

"Nope." They cupped a hand over my cheek and stroked my face with their thumb. "When you're under pressure you just get harder, sharper, more focused. Everything kind of disappears for you apart from what you have to do, and you do whatever it takes to get that done. It's impressive to watch. Scary, like, but impressive."

"Why is it scary?"

"Because I never know how far you're gonna go before you stop. I mean, you've made yourself sick before, working too hard and not resting enough. You don't eat enough, either." They sighed. "When we get out of here, I'm going to make sure that you get soup every day. Cookies, too."

"Soup and cookies: the two food groups."

"Don't be silly. There's three, obviously."

"Toasted cheese sandwiches?"

"I was thinking coffee, but you're right: four food groups." They let their hand slide down to my neck. "You distracted me again. You do that a lot. When you want me to drop something, you distract me. It never fails."

"Frankie, I..." I didn't know what to say, so I nearly kissed them, and realized that I would only have been proving them right.

"It's OK. I know I'm easily distracted. That's what I meant, before: under pressure, you get all focused and determined. I just scatter. My brain feels like a flock of birds."

"Graceful? So naturally synchronized that it looks unnatural?"

"Nah. Bad comparison." They pulled me closer to them and sighed into my hair. "I wish you could trust me more, but I don't blame you. I don't trust me, either."

I told them that that wasn't true, that I loved them, how much they meant to me, but their head had gone off somewhere, and I couldn't quite reach them. I did my best: I put their favorite cartoons on, made the best dinner I could rustle up with the ingredients we had, and held them whenever my hands weren't busy, but they didn't come back all night.

Frankie still looked upset when we woke up on Friday, so I decided that it was imperative for me to find a way to cheer them up. I thought about it over breakfast, and by the time we headed to work, I had it all planned out. I would ask Ms. Anzengruber to take me to the store so I could get us something special to eat – which, given the shit we lived on, wasn't going to be much of a struggle. I would cook Frankie a lovely dinner, put some candles on the table, borrow Ben's lava lamp, and generally make sure that the place looked less like a shithole than it normally did. Time was going to be tight, but I thought I could do it. Frankie wouldn't mind dinner being a little bit late, anyway, not if I was all dressed up and the place looked swanky when they rolled in.

I walked into work with a picture in my head: Frankie's face when they walked into our garage to find that I'd made a date for us, how their eyes would widen and glow while their smile slowly blossomed, their happiness trailing behind their wonder. It would be their best face ever, and I couldn't wait to see it.

Then I turned a corner, spotted Jacob sitting primly in a chair, waiting for me with a grin on his face, and something broke in my head.

I did what I had to do: I worked, I kept myself safe, I finished my shift, I got home. I couldn't bear to walk into the garage, because the picture of the dream I'd had about a date with Frankie was still too sharp and painful, so I went straight to our room. I lay down on the bed, trying to think of nothing, but it was no good: The pressure built higher and higher in my body and in my head, until I just couldn't take it anymore. I got up, took out my backpack, and started packing. I knew that it made no sense, that I wasn't going anywhere, that there was nowhere for me to go. I kept screaming at myself that I'd lost it, that I needed to calm down, that I was being stupid, but it did no good. A chunk of my brain had hijacked my body and didn't give a damn about the reality of my situation: it was gonna get the fuck out, and that was it.

I'd loaded and unloaded my backpack somewhere between a dozen and a million times when Frankie walked in. I'd lost all track of time so I wasn't expecting them, and the door opening made me turn and freeze like a rabbit in the headlights.

They bounced into our bedroom, and then they saw me. Their wild, lopsided grin slipped down their face.

"What are you doing?"

"Nothing. I just... I don't know." I was suddenly dizzy, and would have fallen over if they hadn't caught me. I realized that my breathing was so fast and so shallow that no air was getting in, so I tried to slow it down. I tried to hug Frankie, to soak in the feeling of their body against mine, but they pushed me off.

"What's happening? Where are you going?"

"Nowhere. I'm not going anywhere."

"But you're packing your bag."

They stared at me for a few seconds, then walked over to the wardrobe. They moved their laundry pile from their corner and dug up a drawstring bag. It looked like the bags people used for their toiletries back in the dorm, but it had a picture of Animal from the Muppets on it.

They gave the bag a squeeze, as if checking its contents, and then they sat on the bed, the bag on their lap. "Gio, if you want to go, we go."

"Frankie, we have nowhere to go *to*."

"I know. I don't care. If you want to go, we go. Just don't leave me behind." Their eyes were so dark and empty that they looked like tunnels.

I wanted to hug them, but I didn't want to spook them even more, so I just sat next to them and kept my voice as calm and low as I could. "I wasn't really going. I just... I just lost it. Everything is just too much. I wasn't going to leave you."

They shook their head. "You packed your bag. Not mine."

"I just lost it for a minute. I'm not doing so great at the moment."

They nodded. "Yeah. I know. Would you like a cup of tea?"

"Maybe later." I let my hand slip towards theirs. They didn't flinch, so I left it there. "Love, what's in the bag?"

"Just my stuff. My passport and photos and my bunny and stuff."

"Your bunny?"

They nodded again.

"Can I see it?"

Their bottom lip wobbled, but they stuck their hand in their bag and extracted a stuffed bunny; or, rather, a bunny that, once upon a time, had been stuffed. What fur was left on it was mostly beige.

"My aunt brought it back from England so my dad had to let me keep it, and then when they were clearing my toys out because I was too old for them they put it in the bin because it was too ugly to give away so I just fished it back out and washed it and hid it and kept it ever since."

"You never showed it to me before."

"It's silly. I shouldn't have it. Do you need a break from me?"

"What?"

Their eyes bore into mine. "You said everything is just too much. I'm part of everything. Do you need a break from me?"

"No!"

"Don't say it without thinking about it. Would it be easier on you if you didn't have to worry about me? About us?"

I tried to breathe and think at the same time. I didn't seem to be able to, so I focused on thinking. That didn't work either, so I just said the only thing I could think of. "I love you."

"I love you, too. I love you more than anything, and I want us to be together properly. I want it to be good for both of us. So, if you need a break, we can take a break."

"You want to sleep with other people?"

"No! I just want us to be good with each other. It could be like a holiday, you know? A break from me, so you can get better. I'll be here when you come back."

"Is this what you want?"

They shook their head. "No. Not even close. But I want us to stay together. If that means taking a break now, I can do that. I'll be good. I won't be on your case and I'll work really hard on getting my shit together. I can move into the garage if you want."

"No! I don't want you to move!"

"OK. So I can stay here, like now, but I'll be off your case. I promise. You won't have to worry about me, and you'll get better, and then things will be good again. And Ben will come back, and the kids, and Ms. Anzengruber and Uncle Marin will get on again, and, and—" Something caught in their throat and they ran out of air and words.

I let myself slide sideways, until my shoulder was resting against theirs. They let me do that, but they didn't touch me. They just clutched their bunny harder. The silence built up between us, until I felt like I was never going to speak again, like the worst possible present had us in its jaws and would tear us to pieces if we dared to move.

Frankie saved me from that. They nodded to themself, put their bunny back in their bag, put the bag back into the wardrobe, and turned around to look at me. Their eyes weren't bottomless pits anymore, but they were solid brown, and their smile looked like hard work.

"Would you like me to cook dinner? So you can rest?"

"You never cook dinner."

Their smile wobbled, but they caught it before it fell. "I know. About time I started. If you can live with my cooking, that is."

"Is that what you want?"

Their expression went through a myriad changes before settling on calm determination. "Come on. Let's go eat."

We had a quiet evening together. Frankie was courteous, attentive, and wholly present, sort of: it felt as their dials had been turned down to about half way. They were focused on the present moment, on our shared reality, but they felt faded, washed out like their bunny. I was glad to have them there, though, and they were glad to have me there; I knew that, because they told me several times, in a quiet, formal tone. I missed their energy, but I did enjoy the calm. It felt like lotion on a burn.

Then the time came to go to bed, and everything got awkward. I had half thought that their suggestion of having a break was just something they'd said in the spur of the moment, but they clearly meant it. They changed in the bathroom, and came back wearing their robe and PJs. I'd not seen them since our first night together, and the combination of that memory and our present was such a kick in the guts that I had to get out of the room not to show Frankie how upset I was. I came back dressed for bed, too, and we lay side by side without touching. It was companionable, but it was so far removed from what I wanted that it made me shudder.

They looked away from their book to frown at me. "Are you cold?"

"No. I'm exhausted." It wasn't a lie; it just wasn't the whole truth, or the most important part of it.

"I'm sorry." They put their book on the floor, switched off our fairy lights, and turned to smile at me. "Good night." Their smile had none of its customary dazzle, and I had the horrible feeling that it wasn't just because of the encroaching darkness.

They fell asleep a foot away from me, their head on their pillow, their body arranged on their side of the new, invisible line that dissected our bed. I stifled the urge to grasp at them, to pull them close to me, and watched them drift off to sleep.

That night, I woke up gasping for air, still caught up in my dream. Frankie had come up to me, a bleeding hole in their chest, a still-beating heart in their hand, and a faint smile on their face.

"Take it, Gio. I don't want it anymore. It hurts, and it was always yours, anyway."

"No!" I wanted to tell them to put it back in, to heal themself, but I couldn't get any air in and it was too late, anyway: when I rejected their offering, they stopped smiling, looked at their hands, and let them drift apart. The heart slipped out of their limp fingers. It kept falling, going further and further into the abyss under our feet. The further the heart fell, the paler Frankie became, until they were as white as snow.

Their last words were "I'm sorry, Gio. I'm so sorry." I read them on their lips, because they could no longer speak. And, just like that, they were gone, floating limply away from me.

That was when I woke up, soaked in sweat, screaming a silent scream. When the horror in my head finally cleared, I looked for them. They were next to me, looking too pale and too limp, just like in my dream. I was shaking them before I could stop myself. When they woke up, I was so happy that I started crying. Then I saw them properly, and my cries turned into howls.

They sat up and wrapped their arms around me, trying to calm me down. "Gio, it's OK. You had a nightmare."

"No. Your eyes!"

They pulled away from me. "My eyes are fine. Look."

I looked, and what I saw made me shudder. Their eyes were moss green and earth brown, without a trace of the light that had always shone out of them. They looked as dead as stones.

"You have your mother's eyes."

They flinched. "Yes. I grew up hearing that. Come on, Gio. Let's try and get some sleep. Tomorrow is going to start way too soon."

We lay down next to each other without touching. That nearly set me off crying again, but I managed to stop myself. I wanted them to get their rest. They weren't falling asleep, though: they lay too rigid, too still. I left them alone for a while, hoping that they would relax, until I just couldn't bear it anymore.

"Where are you?"

"Right here." They stretched a hand out to grab mine, but it felt perfunctory: Little Soldier Boy Frankie attending to their duty.

"What's wrong?"

Their hand convulsed around mine. "Do you really wanna know?"

"That's a trick question."

"No tricks. I can tell you or keep it to myself, but I won't tell you a lie."

"Tell me? If you want to."

I felt their nod. "I used to make you happy. I used to make you feel safe. You used to look at me and brighten up, like I was someone special."

"You are!"

"I'm some kind of special, but that's not what I mean. Every time you looked at me, you made me feel that I was enough, even better than enough. I never felt like that before I met you. It felt so good. Isn't it selfish, that I used to take so much pride in the way you looked at me? I'm sure that's a bad thing, and it's not as if I ever did anything to deserve it."

I tried to disagree with them, but they spoke over me.

"It doesn't matter anyway. It's gone."

"Frankie, I love you!"

"I know. Thank you. But I don't make you happy anymore. I don't make you feel safe. You look at me and you're just as scared as the rest of the time. More, perhaps. I can't tell. I can't read you anymore. I don't think you want me to."

I couldn't disagree with anything they were saying, because none of it was untrue. It was all fucked up, all wound up the wrong way, but it was technically true. I tried talking around it instead.

"Dealing with my anxiety is not your job. You're not a security blanket."

"What is my job, then?"

"You don't have to have a job. You're not performing a role for me."

"If I don't make your life better, why am I in it at all? What's the point?"

"But you do! You're everything to me! I love you more than I've ever loved anyone!"

They shuddered. "See, that's true, too. I just wish it was enough."

"Why isn't it?"

Their voice dropped to a whisper. "Because I'm selfish. I miss the way you made me feel because of the way I made you feel. But if it's enough for you, then it's enough. I'm sorry. I'll get over it."

I wanted to scream at them that I didn't want them to get over that or anything else, that I wanted us to travel back in time and find ourselves again, but I checked myself. I didn't want to make things worse. They were bad enough.

They gave my hand a squeeze and put it down next to me, tenderly, carefully, and inexorably. "Thank you. I'm sorry for keeping you up so late, or so early, but thank you."

"For what?"

"For listening. It's nice talking like this, in the dark. It's easier. The words are still heavy, but they don't feel so sharp, and it makes me feel like you care."

"I do care!"

"I should thank you for that, too. I don't thank you enough. It's been a wonderful year, Gio. Just wonderful. Every bit of it."

"It's not over yet!"

"I know. Thanksgiving is months away. I just thought I'd tell you now, because I feel it, and if... I just wanted you to know. The part of the year we've had has been the best part of my life, and that's all thanks to you."

"It's been my best year, too."

"I'm glad we got to have that together. I really am, Gio."

They let off a huge sigh and their body became fractionally less rigid, as if they'd put a weight down. I was still wondering what that weight was, whether they'd managed to find a scrap of memory of the way things used to be and hold it in their heart, or they'd just put it all to bed, accepted that that was then and this was now, when their breathing changed and they were gone from me, taking refuge in the arms of Morpheus. I tried to match their breathing, to follow them in their slumber, but I couldn't find my way to them.

6. THERE WILL BE NO DIVORCE

Frankie had been right, more or less; being on a break was restful. It sucked, but it was definitely restful. Frankie was still in my life, still around the house most of the time, but they always seemed to be doing something. It was like having a really good roommate who wasn't a really close friend; there was no friction between us, but our lives ran on two separate tracks.

I hated that, but it made life easier. I didn't have to worry about controlling my every move and my every mood to stop them from upsetting Frankie. I could hide away from them and let myself fall apart, knowing that they'd still be there when I pulled myself back together. That reassurance calmed me down enough to enable me to manage my day-to-day existence. I didn't care about anything much, not even about Jacob's shenanigans. Nothing mattered, so I just put a foot in front of the other and got on with what I had to do.

We still slept together and woke up together, and we still ate together. The rest of the time, we did our own thing. It took me a week to get used to that, to turn that pain into an ache – ever-present, but survivable. Our first weekend was the hardest. We both drooped around the house and around each other, neither of us able or willing to use their new "freedom" for anything constructive. On Monday, Frankie bounced back, though; they took the bit between their teeth and threw themself into their week with a frantic energy I could barely comprehend. I didn't feel up to emulating them, but I had to, so I did.

By the end of the second week, being on a break was our new normal. Things could have been so much worse. I could have lost Frankie altogether, after all, instead of just losing a part of what we had.

I chanted that to myself on repeat all of Saturday, while Frankie flitted in and out of the house. I had no idea what they were doing, and I wasn't too sure that they knew, either, but it involved never being in the same room as me for more than a quarter of an hour. When I realized that I was chasing them around the place, I planted myself on the couch and made myself stay there. They had a right to their own space, and the garage felt gloomier than ever, which suited my mood.

They turned up in the evening, a faint smile tacked to their face, and offered to cook dinner. We were just finishing it off when our front door slammed open. My heart hit my tonsils and I found myself clutching at my throat, like a heroine in a cheap movie.

Frankie dragged themself out of whatever rabbit hole they had fallen into and frowned. "What was that?"

I didn't get a chance to answer. The garage door burst open and Ben stumbled in, a case of booze under one arm and a huge smile on his face. I'd never been that relieved to see him in my entire life, but I still found it hard to smile back. I was too busy trying to catch my breath.

Frankie snapped into action way faster than me. They got up, walked up to Ben, and stuck their hand out to him. "Welcome back. We weren't expecting you. It's great to see you. Have you eaten?"

Ben looked at Frankie's hand in utter confusion while his smile slipped down his face. "Huh. I've had lunch. I could eat. I brought beer."

Frankie retracted their hand without missing a beat. "Great. I can fix you up some light refreshments, if you want. Gio?"

I managed to find my tongue. "I'm alright. Thank you."

While Frankie rummaged in the kitchen, Ben walked over and sat down. "I wanted to surprise you."

"You did. How is your sister?"

"Better now. She's well enough that I'm in her way, so I thought I'd come back before she kicked me out."

Ben was regaling me with tales of his sister and her brood when Frankie returned with snacks. They helped themself to one of Ben's beers and sat in an attitude of polite attention. They spoke when spoken to, interjected the appropriate sounds and gestures to show that they were listening and interested, and generally behaved in a manner perfectly suited to a well-programmed robot. I fumbled frantically, trying to keep up with the conversation, as always. When Ben had finished telling us about his adventures, Frankie asked him if he wanted to play Magic. I could have kissed them for that: it meant an end to complicated conversation, particularly if Ben kept drinking.

The evening drew towards its end without any major mishaps. Social-interaction-wise, I didn't feel that I'd acquitted myself terribly well, but I didn't think Ben had noticed. He was used to me being a weirdo, anyway. I still retired to my bower as soon as I could do so without raising suspicion. I was honestly glad to see Ben, and I told him as much, but I knew that I could enjoy his presence best when I wasn't in his company. It was weird, even for me, but that was how it was.

Frankie got up to wish me goodnight. They even kissed my cheek. Then they sat back down at their game, and I dragged myself off to bed.

The knock on the door felt like a punch in the gut. Things were heinously bad between us, but if Frankie really thought that they needed to knock before entering our bedroom, then we were fucked beyond redemption. We were standing over the corpse of our relationship, neither of us willing to bury the thing. I sure as hell wasn't. I would rather bury myself, alive or dead. Dead was preferable.

I thought about not saying anything and seeing what they'd do. They couldn't just stay out there; that would have been too absurd for words. It wasn't impossible, though, and that possibility terrified me. If we started sleeping apart, that'd be another nail in that coffin, or in my heart.

I pulled myself together and managed to deliver a "Come in" that sounded only mildly strangulated. I tried to make up for that by not looking up when they walked in. I buried my nose in my book, to show that everything was cool. I was cool. We were cool. Things between us were so cool that I could feel icicles perforating my heart, but this was just our new normal, and I was going to be cool about that.

My performance may have worked, if I'd aimed it at the right person.

"What is, huh, going on?"

I looked up. Ben was standing just inside the door, looking dazed and confused. For the first time in my life, I wasn't glad to see him. I knew what he wanted to talk about. I also knew that I didn't want to. I decided to stick to my current strategy, and spew shit that was true without being in any way pertinent.

"We told you. Frankie's learning to be a plumber. Ms. Anzengruber and Marin have decided to re-enact 'Much Ado About Nothing' without the costumes. I am learning the Dewey and looking forward to digging holes in the dirt. The raccoons have gone AWOL. Given the chaotic nature of things around here, I can't blame them."

I had hoped that my cunning misdirection would put him off, or that he'd get the hint and fuck off, but I should have known better. He was too smart to fall for the former, and probably too baked for the latter. Instead, he walked in and leaned against the wardrobe, the confusion in his eyes mingling with fear.

"That's not what I meant. Frankie is in the garage."

"I know."

"And you're here."

"I'm aware of that, too."

"But, like, they're out there."

"They're playing guitar. They do that most evenings."

"On their own?" Ben closed his eyes and scrunched up his whole face.

When he unscrunched it, the fear had overtaken the confusion in his eyes. "You two don't hang out anymore? But you still live together? But you're not, like, together?"

The fact that he'd put it into words filled me with rage. Didn't he understand that he'd just made it all real?

"Why the fuck are you asking me? They are the one out there."

"But—"

"They're choosing to be out there. Nobody's making them. If this is what they want, I'm not going to try and stop them."

He walked over and loomed over me. I looked up at him and regretted it, because his eyes were burning with rage. In the context of his face, of everything I knew about him, they looked unnatural and terrifying.

"You think this is what they want? Where is your head at?"

"It's not as if I'm telling them not to be with me. It's their choice."

"You're full of shit. Go out there, right now, and look at them. Fucking look, man. Then tell me if you really think this is something they want."

He was twice the size of me, he was angry, but I didn't give a fuck: what he was saying was hurting me, so I hurt him right back.

"You're going to try and tell me how to run my relationship now? Based on what: your extensive practical experience?"

Instead of exploding, he deflated. "Of course not! What the fuck do I know about relationships? I'm just telling you, something is wrong with them, and something is clearly wrong with you if you haven't spotted it." He closed his eyes. When he opened them again, they were even redder. "I've not been gone two months. When I left, Frankie was bouncing off the walls and the two of you were... You know how you were. And now you're in here and they're out there, looking like a five-year-old whose dog just died." He frowned, and I could see an idea taking shape behind his eyes. "No. They look like a five-year-old dog whose owner just died. That's how they love you. It's not people love, it's dog love. They don't want anything from you; they'd just rather be together than apart. And now that's gone, and they can't deal with it."

"I'm still here!"

"Yes, and they're out there. That's got to hurt them double, to miss you when you're still here. You've got to fix it. They sure can't."

I squeaked through the knot in my throat, "Why do you think I can?"

He sagged. "I don't know. You always fix everything." He sighed and shook his head. "It's just... Watching you two love each other has been the most beautiful part of my life. Don't give up on it just 'cause it got hard."

I blinked back weeks of tears. "I don't know what to do. I don't have a fucking clue."

He shrugged. "You always made shit up as you went along, and it always worked."

"It's not working now. I've tried to think of a way through this, and—"

"God, don't do that! Like, seriously, don't. Man, you're one of my favorite people, but your head is totally full of shit."

"Thank you?"

He frowned. "Sorry? But your heart is true, or something. Don't do what you think is right. Do the right thing."

"That makes no fucking sense."

"Yeah. That's what I'm trying to say. Look, if you'd tried to think your way into going out with Frankie, you wouldn't be here now. You'd have taken a look at them and talked yourself out of it. I don't know where you'd be, but you wouldn't be here. None of us would be here." He rubbed his face and emerged blinking. "Man, I've got to have a smoke. This has been too much. You want some?"

"No, thank you."

"Alright." He nodded, gestured a vague greeting, and stumbled off.

I lay there for a while, thinking about what Ben had said, about how things were between me and Frankie, and mostly about sticking a kitchen knife right through my ribcage. It would have hurt less than what I was feeling, and it would have been over quicker.

The sound of Ben's feet stomping to his bedroom roused me, and then the squeaking started. He hadn't closed the door properly on his way out, and it was slowly opening itself, like it always did. The hallway outside was pitch black. Darkness oozed out of it, radiating grotesque tendrils that threatened to envelope me. Somewhere out there was Frankie. I could feel them. If I let myself, I could be with them.

No, I couldn't: I could be near them, maybe, but not with them. I'd fucked that up, and there was no coming back.

I could be near them, though. I knew that I would feel worse, because every scrap of joy would be balanced out by the unbearable pain of being cut off from them, cut off from us, but at least I could see them. I needed to get them to come to bed, anyway. It was late.

I got up and nearly fell over. The pain in my chest made it hard for me to get any air in, so I was horribly dizzy. I thought about 'porting to them, but I was afraid that I'd give myself a migraine if I could, and twice as scared to find out that I couldn't. I didn't need to 'port, anyway: I could make it to the garage. If I didn't, I would be no worse off collapsed on the floor than I was alone in our bed.

I stumbled down the hallway, holding on to the wall, until I got to the garage door. I stood in front of it for a million years or so. I could hear the faint plinking of Frankie's guitar. They were fingerpicking rather than strumming; maybe they were just trying to be quiet because it was so late, but it sounded beautiful. It sounded mournful, too, and way too close to how I was feeling. I stood and I listened, even though it hurt. It took me a while to realize that I knew the song. "Famous Blue Raincoat." Leonard Cohen. Frankie was playing Leonard motherfucking Cohen, alone, in the garage, at night.

Ben was right. The world was broken, and I needed to fix it.

I opened the door a crack. They didn't see me. I wasn't sure if they could see anything at all. Their eyes were half open and unfocused, and their eyelashes cast long shadows over their cheeks. They were unnaturally pale and thin, way thinner than I remembered them. I hadn't been paying attention. I had been so busy trying not to have them look at me that I had not been looking at them.

I swallowed the lump in my throat to get a breath in, and kept watching them. They were sitting all hunched up, in an odd posture I had not noticed before, but wasn't new: it had become their normal way of sitting at some point during the last few weeks. They looked as if they were wrapped around a pain, as if they were nursing a chest wound. The way they were holding their guitar hadn't changed, though. It sat in their hands like a part of them, as if it was the most natural thing in the world that strings would start where their fingers ended. Their guitar *was* a part of them: it was the organ through which they could express how they felt.

When they started singing, my heart broke. They just murmured the lyrics, but it sounded so beautiful and so mournful that it drove a spear through my chest. I found myself slightly hunched too, wrapped around a pain of my own. For an instant, I wondered if they felt as bad as I did, but of course they didn't. They always felt more than me. They could reach highs in their joy that I could not even dream of; their lows must be heart-rending. Yet here they were, turning a pain I could barely comprehend into something beautiful.

When they got to the last verse, the grief in their voice grabbed me by the throat, and I finally lost it. A minute quantity of the pain I'd been feeling came out of my mouth in a strangled wail, and made them jump.

They turned around and looked up at me, their face unguarded. Emotions shot across their eyes like comets: joy, terror, longing, loss, and pain. The pain was so big that it buried them all, like a fucking meteorite, and Frankie buried the pain; they hunched a little lower and schooled their face back to that vague politeness it had been wearing ever since I'd fucked us up.

When they spoke, their voice was only slightly choked. "I'm sorry. Did I wake you up?"

I thought of all the right things to say; all the rational ways in which I could answer their question. I contemplated them for a moment, and decided that rationality could go fuck itself. Frankie was hurting, and so was I. It was high time we faced that. I forced air into my lungs and let rip.

"I can never go to sleep when you're not with me. All I do is lie there and wish I was dead, until I pass out."

Their pain resurfaced for an instant, but they blinked it back down. "I'm sorry. I thought you wanted some space."

"No. It's been killing me. Frankie, there is something I have to tell you. I should have told you ages ago."

They flinched and curled in on themself, as if I'd stabbed them in the chest. "Gio, if you're trying not to hurt my feelings—" Their eyelashes fluttered wildly. "If it's over, just tell me. I'm sorry. It's just... I'll never be able to call it. I know it's not fair on you. You do enough for me, and you have enough to deal with, and to put this on you... But I can't do it."

"I don't want to call it! Everything I've said and done was because I didn't want us to be over!"

They looked up at me, eyes filled with desperation. "I don't get it. What do you want, then?"

"Right now, I want you to come to bed with me."

They flinched. "Gio, I don't think I can... I can't. I'm sorry."

It took me a second to work out what they were on about. "That's not what I mean. I don't want you to have sex with me."

They reeled as if I'd slapped them. "Sorry. Of course you don't. I shouldn't have presumed."

I prayed for the ground to open up and swallow me, but it didn't. It probably didn't have any use for me. I couldn't blame it.

I closed my eyes and tried to think my way through the mess we were in. Nothing came up; just an endless stream of things I could say that may have this or that effect, that may lead the conversation in this or that direction. There were too many factors to take into account, and every strategy seemed too damn risky. When I opened my eyes again, the pain in Frankie's eyes drove all thoughts out of my head, leaving a clear realization in its wake. What had fucked us up wasn't Jacob: it was the game of half-truths I'd tried to play with Frankie. From that moment on, I would tell them the truth, the whole truth, and nothing but the truth, and if any gods were listening they could help me or fuck right off.

I wrapped my arms around myself so I wouldn't fall apart, and tried to keep my voice steady. "I love you. I want to be with you. I miss you so much it's killing me. I want you to come to bed with me because I want to tell you everything that's been going on, and because I want to feel close to you. I can't even imagine having sex with you right now because I'm hurting so fucking much that I don't think I could go through with it."

They looked up at me, gasping. "I don't get it. I thought you didn't want me around so much."

"I wanted you around. I always want you around; my life isn't worth living without you in it. There was something I didn't want you to know, and the only way I could keep it from you was to distance myself a little."

Their eyes darkened. "A little?"

"I aimed for a little. I missed. It seemed like a good idea at the time, and it wasn't. It was the worst idea I've ever had." I took a deep breath and let it out. "Jacob has been threatening me. He's been coming to the library and... He says stuff. None of it is nice stuff."

Their jaw dropped slowly, while a myriad of emotions cascaded behind their eyes. "Why didn't you tell me?"

"I didn't want you to find out. He's threatening me to get to you. I thought that if you knew what he was doing, you'd dump me to keep me safe. You always look after me."

They looked at me so blankly and for so long that I wanted to shake them, but I stopped myself. When they finally spoke, their voice was eerily flat. "Jacob has been threatening you? This is why you have been so wound up? Putting up circles everywhere and not wanting to go anywhere? Getting all those headaches?"

"Yes."

"And you kept it from me so I wouldn't break up with you?"

"Yes."

"That's what it was, all along?"

"Yes." I took a step towards them. "I was afraid that you would leave me. I'm afraid of that all the time."

They stuck their chin up in the air. "I was afraid that you'd already left."

I threw myself at them. They gripped me so tight it hurt, but I didn't care. Feeling them close to me was all that mattered.

After a while, they spoke into my hair. "So you still love me?"

"Of course I love you, you dodo."

"And you still wanna be with me?"

I nodded. We were wrapped so close that I knew they could feel it, but it didn't seem like enough. "Yes. I want to be with you all the time. Frankie, I miss you when you're in the toilet."

They snorted. "You would not like to be in there when I'm taking a shit. You really wouldn't."

"I'd take my chances."

"You'd need to take a gas mask."

We stayed up way too late that night. Neither of us wanted to let go of the other long enough for us to get to bed. We were also still extremely wound up, so we drank what was left of Ben's booze in a pathetic attempt at chilling out. It didn't work terribly well, but it did help us get out of the garage, because Frankie really needed a piss. I followed them into the bathroom. I didn't watch; I just stood behind them, hugging their back. It took them a while to get started, and they giggled so much through it that I had some concerns about their aim, but they managed alright in the end.

Once we finally stumbled into bed, we didn't fall asleep. We were both exhausted and we both needed to rest, but sleep just wouldn't come. At irregular intervals, Frankie would shudder and ask me, "Gio, what the fuck are we going to do?"

I had no useful answer to give them, so I always told them the same thing: "I don't know, but I hope that we'll do it together."

When I woke up in the morning and saw their face on my pillow, so close that I couldn't quite focus on it, my heart skipped a beat. We were together, really together. I'd fucked up royally and nearly destroyed us, but that was in the past: we'd straightened things out, and now we could pick up the threads of our life and carry on. We still had to deal with the whole Jacob thing, but that seemed like a minor issue now that I had my Frankie back.

That illusion shattered when they woke up. I was looking forward to watching them look at me, to see that blossoming of joy that was better than any sunrise. Instead, their eyes just opened, like regular human eyes, and my stomach sank in response.

They managed a tiny smile. "Hey. Why so gloomy?"

"It feels like a gloomy kind of morning. Sorry."

"I am so fucking tired." They closed their eyes and sagged back on the pillow.

"I'm sorry. I kept you up late."

"That's two apologies in two sentences. It ought to be illegal."

I barely stifled a third apology. They chortled, but there seemed to be very little joy in it.

I couldn't bear to be so close to them and feel so far away. It had been bad enough when things were fucked up, but I'd genuinely thought I'd fixed everything. I clearly hadn't, and witnessing that just hurt too fucking much. I was up and out of bed before I'd had a chance to think about it.

"Coffee?"

They squinted up at me. "Yes. Please. Thank you."

I threw some clothes on, trying not to cry, and stumbled over to the garage. It was just as well that I was decent, because Ben was already up and baking. I'd forgotten that he'd come back.

He turned around sluggishly, looking bleary-eyed. "What the fuck are you doing here?"

"I live here. And a good morning to you, too."

"Yeah, but, it's Sunday morning. Why are you out here?"

I was too upset and too tired to dodge that question. "Because there's no point in being in there, alright? Look, I tried. We had a long talk."

"I figured. You also had all my beer."

"We did. Sorry. I'll pay for it."

"No worries. You alright?"

"Yes. No. You were right and I was wrong."

"That's a first. "

"I tried to fix it. I couldn't. They're still... whatever you want to call it."

"But you talked, right? And..." He blushed fiercely.

My face blushed in response. "We're still sharing a room. I just thought... You know how they bounce back from pretty much anything? I thought they'd bounce back from this."

"But this isn't just anything. This is a huge deal."

"When their parents cut them off, they got over that in no time."

"They had longer to get used to that. I mean, it's not like they were getting on. And, like, they really love you, you know? When you're not there, they talk about you a lot. It's kind of annoying. I mean, I know you, and then I have to listen to how wonderful you are, and I do get it, but... Anyway. They might need a bit of time to come round."

"But it only took saying the wrong thing to fuck it all up. Why can't I just say the right thing and unfuck it?"

Ben squinted. "Are you seriously asking me that?"

"Not really. But I wish it worked like that."

He raised his arm up to slap or stroke my shoulder, but something stopped him. He scratched his head instead. "Do you want me to try and cheer you up?"

"I don't know. Can you?"

"You get to, like, court them. You didn't really do that the first time round. You just kinda fell into each other."

"You make it sound like an accident."

"It was cute. But it wasn't, like, your traditional courtship. Now you get to do all that."

"Fantastic. Thank you for that. Nothing like a bout of raging anxiety to brighten up my morning."

He snorted. "Anxiety? Man, you don't get it, do you? They're gonna say yes. They already have. You just have to, like, walk them to the yes, or something."

"When have you ever seen Frankie walking anywhere?"

He shrugged. "That should just make it faster."

That appeared to be the sum total of Ben's wisdom on the subject, because he finished off his baking and went off to get baked. I returned to my quarters with two coffees, fresh bread still hot from the oven, and a generous portion of Ben's sister no-cook strawberry jam. If that didn't get me back in Frankie's good graces, then nothing could.

I found them sprawled on the grass just outside our patio. They'd thrown up an arm to shield their eyes from the sun, and the breeze was tickling their curls. They were so pretty that they took my breath away, so I stopped and stared.

I thought I had been ninja-like in my snooping, but I was wrong. After a few moments, they sighed without looking at me.

"Hey."

"Hey, you."

"Whatcha looking at me for?"

"Because you're the most beautiful person in the world, and every time I'm reminded that you exist, that you're really real, I can't quite believe it."

They blushed. "Wenchlad, if I didn't know that you believe every word of that, I'd call bullshit. As it is, I'm tempted to check your temperature."

"Feel free." I walked over, put our breakfast tray next to them, and sat down. "Go on. Check it."

"You're quite absurd, you know that?" They uncovered their eyes, sat up, and rested the back of their fingers on my forehead. After a moment, they let their hand fall to the ground. "You feel just fine. Must be a software problem."

I tried to smile at that, but I couldn't. I thought of all the other ways our exchange could have gone, of how it would have gone only a few weeks ago, of how one type of touching would have led to another, and those contemplations didn't leave much room for joy.

Their eyes narrowed. "What is it?"

"I miss the days when you couldn't touch me without getting into me."

"I'm sorry. It's just... Touching you hurts."

"What?"

They looked straight at me, their eyes full of courage, fear, and unshed tears. "It feels good for a moment, and then I think that it might be the last time, that I might lose this. That hurts."

"But it's not going to happen. We're alright."

"I know." They blinked. "Well, I think I know. But, when we're not properly together, I say goodbye to you every moment of every day. In my heart, like. Jesus, that sounds so dramatic. I love you, you know?"

"I know. I love you, too. I can't tell you how much. I never meant to–"

"I know you didn't. In my head, I understand it. I think I'd be angry at you if I wasn't so damn happy, you know? But that's not even it. It's just... I want to touch you because it feels so good, but the memories get in the way. It's like wanting to go near a stove, because it's warm and you're freezing cold, but then you remember getting burnt – you remember it in your body, I mean. Your body replays the whole thing again, and it feels just as real as when it happened. So you reach out, but then you stop yourself, and every part of it hurts, and you're still cold." They let their eyelashes drop down and half-cover their eyes. "Is that what it's like for you? When you want to do something, but a part of you dreads it?"

"I don't know. Maybe. I think it's easier for me. Your heart is so much bigger than mine. All your feelings are dialed up to max."

Their bottom lip quivered. "I'm sorry."

"I'm not. I'm sorry it's hurting you, but I love the way you are. Love, I want to fix this. I want it more than I want anything else in the world."

"Gio, in the context of everything that's going on in our life—"

"It's the most important thing. For me, anyway."

They blinked. "You mean that."

"Yes. Of course I do."

They picked up their coffee and spoke into it. "Gio, I miss us, the way we used to be. I've never had anything like that, not in my whole life."

I felt tears pushing at my eyes. "Me neither. It was the best thing ever."

"Yeah. It was."

We sat next to each other and picked at our food until I couldn't take it anymore and broke the silence.

"Every time you use the past tense to talk about us, it kills me."

"I think you started it."

"I know. It just doesn't hurt as much when I do it. When you do it, it feels like a death sentence. Do you remember when we got married?"

They snorted. "What do you think?"

"I got away with just standing there and not doing anything."

"That's because we didn't really get married. I hadn't even asked you."

"You asked me afterwards."

"It doesn't work like that, and anyway you never said yes."

"I never said no, either."

"You never said anything. You didn't get a chance to. It's not binding."

"Does it bind you?"

They locked eyes with me. "Yes. Absolutely."

"There you go. It binds me, too."

"But—"

"No buts! Anyway, back then, I never got to say anything. You did all the work. So here is my vow to you: I will never, ever lie to you again. Or hide anything. Not even when it really sucks."

"That's going to be hard."

"I know. Chances are that it'll be hard for both of us. But I think that's what we need. No barriers. No hiding."

"No boundaries. No embarrassing secrets. No privacy."

"I'm good with that, if you are."

"What if it doesn't work out?"

"What if it does?"

A smile crossed their face like a shooting star, dazzling and gone all too quickly. They stared out towards the trees at the end of our yard for a while. When they wrapped their arms around their knees, I knew that some serious shit was heading my way.

"Gio, I was thinking about forgiving you. I know I shouldn't get distracted like that, that we have way more important things to think about, but I can't drop it. It's too important to me. I understand what you were trying to do and why. I know you didn't mean to hurt me. I know that you hurt yourself, too. I know that it's partly my fault—"

"It isn't! You didn't do anything!"

"Precisely. I should have done something. It might not have made things any better, but at least I could have told myself that I tried. Anyway, I know that the right thing to do when people wrong you by mistake and they're genuinely sorry is to forgive them. But I just can't, Gio. I really want to, and I can't." A muscle started twitching in their jaw.

"I want to believe that you made a mistake, you learnt from it, and you won't do the same thing again. That's what people are supposed to do, right? But that's never how it's been in my life. What I know, what I've seen, is that people do the same shitty stuff again and again and again. Even when they're sorry, really sorry, it's like they can't help themselves. So there's what I've been told to believe, and there's what I know, and the two things don't match."

"But I did learn from this! I might fuck up again, I almost certainly will, but I'll never fuck up like this again. Not if I can help it."

"I know. That's not even it, though. When I first met you, I thought you were wonderful. You're clever, you're funny, you're so fucking beautiful it hurts, and you're kind. There were things about you that made me angry, but never angry at you. You got hurt way back when, and that wasn't fair, and the fact that you're still dealing with the fallout makes it exponentially more unfair. You make me wanna slay dragons. I never, ever want anything or anyone to hurt you. But you hurt me, and you saw that you were hurting me, and you just fucking doubled down on it, and I really can't get that. I never thought you could hurt me. I knew that you cared about me, and I figured you'd care for me, too. And you have: you've been looking after me from the first day you met me. But now I know that you can hurt me, because you have. That's never gonna go away. Even if I forgive it, I won't forget it."

Their words tore my insides into chunks. I took as big a breath as I could manage and croaked, "Is there anything I can do or say—"

"No. That's not even the problem." They turned around to face me, their eyes wide open and lost. "I know that plenty of people would just shrug it off and carry on as normal, but I can't. And a whole load of people would tell you to fuck off and not give you a second chance, but even if I thought it was the right thing to do, which I don't, I couldn't do that, either. I love you too damn much, and the thought of being without you hurts more than all of the hurts I've ever had put together. I mean it, Gio. For real. That's why this whole thing fucked me up so much."

"I get it. I'm so sorry."

"It's not your fault. I mean, it is, kinda, but you never meant for it to go like that. I know that. But the thing is, it doesn't matter whether I forgive you or not, whether I can trust you or not. I want to be with you regardless, because being without you is hell. That's what scares me. I was thinking about what I'd do if you hurt me again, and the truth is that I'd let you. I'd cling on to you, because I can't do anything else. I'd like to think that if you started being mean on purpose I'd learn to let you go, but

I'm not sure I would. And I know that if things between us just went to shit, I could be really unhappy and I'd hold on to us anyway. That's what scares me: the way I love you. I know that you don't love me like that."

"I love you more than I've ever loved anyone else!"

"I know. But if things went bad between us and you didn't think they could be fixed, you'd call it. And if I ever hurt you on purpose, you'd call it on the spot. You're way stronger than me."

"The hell I am!"

"You are. You could break up with me and take it. I couldn't. So that's where I am, Gio. I'm scared of you, I'm scared of myself, and I'm fucking terrified that you're gonna dump me over this."

"Over what? Loving me? Wanting to be with me?"

"Needing you. I'm sorry, I really am, but I can't love you any other way."

They let their head rest on their knees and stared at the ground between us. The shadows under their eyes and their cheekbones made them look gaunt, desperate, and beautiful. I understood what they meant about being willing to slay dragons for me: I would have killed anyone, including myself, to spare them their suffering. I couldn't jump into a time machine to undo it all, but I could try to find our spawn point. I could move us forward by going backwards.

I took a deep breath and went for it. "Do you remember when we used to be just friends?"

They blinked. "Yeah. But I still liked you. I mean, I would have been more than happy to be friends, but, you know, you're fucking gorgeous."

"Can you try and park that, for a second? I need you to focus on the bit when we were just friends."

They nodded. "Alright. What about it?"

"That person you were friends with never hurt you, did they?"

"Nope. And they helped me out a hell of a lot."

"Did you trust them to watch out for you?"

"Yeah! I mean, I was pretty lost back then. I needed to make some big decisions and I didn't know how. They were there for me. They were great." They flicked a smile at me. "I never thanked them enough."

"I'm sure you did. So, could you trust them to help you make other big decisions? For instance, about your relationships?"

Their eyes widened. "That never came up. I was painfully single. But yeah, I guess. I mean, I'm pretty sure that if they saw me fuck anything up, they'd speak up. They could be pretty vocal about that kind of thing."

"Huh. I don't know if I like them. They sound a bit overbearing."

"No! That's not it at all! They were marvelous, Gio. You were marvelous. You *are*... Fuck! Sorry. You know what I mean, right?"

"I think so. So, how about this: if I see you in a bad relationship, I will tell you. Even if you're going to hate me for it. Even if that relationship is with me. How does that sound?"

They stared at me in fear and confusion. "We're going back to being just friends?"

"Not unless that's what you want. What I'm saying is that I'm not going to stop being your friend just because we're, you know, other stuff, too. I can't promise you that I won't fuck up again, but I promise you that if I see you fuck up, if I see you staying in a bad place when you ought to get out, I will tell you, however much it costs."

Their eyelashes fluttered. "Thank you. It means a lot to me."

"I mean it."

"I know." They let off a huge sigh and turned to me. "Gio, do you remember that day when we were spies?"

"Yeah. It seems like a million years ago."

"It does. Do you think we could have a way for me to call on my friend Gio when I need to talk to them? Not that I don't wanna talk to you, but sometimes I need *that* Gio."

"We can give it a go. How do we do it?"

They chewed their bottom lip. "If I just ask you to speak to my friend Gio, would that work?"

"We'll have to try it out. You wanna give it a go now?"

They blushed. "If it's alright with you. Do you think it's silly?"

"Totally. And, therefore, perfectly in keeping with the rest of our lives."

"Alright. How do we do it?"

"We're doing it now, you dodo."

They turned to look at me, their eyes enormous. "Gio? Is that you?"

"No, it's the fucking Queen of Sheba."

They threw their arms around me. "I've missed you so fucking much."

"Alright, but no need to crush me. What's up?"

They locked eyes with me. "Gio, a whole lot has happened." They unleashed a torrent of words about how they met this person, and how wonderful they were, and how they started to go out with them, and how great that was, and how they thought that it was all going to be wonderful forever, and how they got a home together, and how fucking fantastic that was, and how they were looking forward to things being even more fantastic, and how everything just went totally to shit all of a sudden, and how cut up about it they were, and how they finally found out why, and how cut up they were about *that*, and how they didn't know what to do about it all. Then they sat back and looked at me with their anime eyes wide open and expectant, as if they truly believed that I could contribute something useful.

I was reeling under the onslaught of their feelings, which took up a large chunk of my processing power. The rest of me was torn: I felt terribly guilty, because I was the one who'd put them through it all, but also unfairly accused, because I hadn't meant to do any of that. A third part of me just felt fucking angry because Frankie was hurting. Frankie was hurting because they'd been hurt. Someone had hurt Frankie, and that was all kinds of fucked up.

I let that feeling sit with me until I could articulate it. Even then, I had to do so through gritted teeth.

"You want my honest opinion?"

"Yes. Please."

"Alright, then. I don't like this person. I don't think they're good for you and they're sure as hell not good enough for you."

"No, that's not right! They're wonderful!"

"They don't sound it. They sound like hard work. You can do better."

"I couldn't! They're pretty fucking perfect when they're on form."

"Yeah, but how often is that?"

They frowned. "Look, there was a ton of mitigating circumstances. And anyway, I don't want to do better. I want to be with them. I love them."

"Alright. So, if this was up to me, which it isn't, I'd find a way to make sure that you can stay in the relationship, but it won't fuck you over again."

"Alright! How does that work?"

"Mostly it doesn't. You kind of end up half in and half out, and it sucks for all concerned."

They winced. "Right. I don't think I want to do that. Sorry."

"I don't blame you. And you definitely want to stay with this person?"

"Yes. But I don't want to shortchange them."

"I beg your pardon?"

"That's what worries me the most. I don't want to get hurt, but I don't want to give them less than I used to just because we had a few issues. That wouldn't be fair."

They looked so earnest that something inside me snapped. Whatever it was, it took my filters with it. I took a deep breath and let rip a diatribe of unprecedented proportions. I let everything out: how shitty a thing their partner had done, how careless, clueless, or callous they must have been for not fixing it as soon as it had started to impact Frankie, and how

Frankie needed to have their brain checked if they thought that *they* needed to worry about how *their* hurt may affect their partner, *who was the one who'd hurt them in the first place*. It took a while. It was only when I'd finished, my throat raw from screeching and my soul hollow after releasing more rage than I thought myself capable of containing, that I realized that I'd been railing against Frankie staying with me.

I looked at them. They looked concussed. I wasn't surprised, but I was sorry, so I told them.

They shook themself off. "It's OK. Gio, can I ask you something?"

"Sure."

"Will you still be my friend, even if it turns out that I kinda suck at relationships? I mean, I really wanna fix the situation, but maybe I won't be able to, and you seem to have some very strong feelings about it—"

"No. I have some very strong feelings about *you*. You should always only have the best of everything."

"Why?"

"Because you're the best person in the world, and I love you."

They threw themself at me, sending our crockery flying and squashing me hard enough to make me squeak, and spoke into my hair. "I love you, too. I love you so fucking much."

"Who are you talking to?"

"You!"

That didn't quite answer my question, but I let it go. Feeling them next to me like that, with no barriers between us, felt too fucking good for me to question it.

After they let go of me, we lay next to each other on the grass. We stayed there all morning, talking about everything and nothing. Frankie's inner light shone strong and bright. Then the breeze picked up and made me shiver. And, just like that, everything got fucked up again.

Frankie didn't want me to catch cold, so we retreated to our bedroom. With the curtains open, lying on our bed was almost like lying outside, but it was clearly enough of a change to send Frankie reeling off into a rabbit hole in their brain that sapped all the joy out of them.

They still lay next to me, but they were clearly struggling with being there, clearly performing a duty that, although not wholly unpleasant, was causing them more worry than enjoyment. I lay next to them, without touching them, feeling infinitely colder than I had outside.

After a few minutes of stilted conversation and awkward silences, I gave up. "Frankie, we can be friends in here, too."

"When we're in bed, we're generally more than friends."

"So what? We've never played by the fucking rules. If we're going to start now, I'd like us to at least pick rules that make us happy."

Their voice dwindled to a whisper. "Do you think things are ever going to go back to the way they used to be?"

"No. They'll go forward to a new way of being. I'm going to work damn hard to make sure that it's a good one, for both of us."

I felt them relax. "You don't know how good that makes me feel. If you're taking care of that, it's as good as done."

Their hand crept towards mine. Mine crept in the opposite direction, until our fingers touched. We lay like that for an eon or so, until they rolled over to stare at me with a grave expression.

"Gio, do you wanna cuddle?"

"With you? Literally always."

"Why the fuck aren't you doing it, then?"

"I don't know. You always started it."

"First of all, I never did. Either you fucking jumped me or you were so damn beautiful at me that I had to be near you."

"How can one be beautiful *at* someone?"

"No fucking clue, but you can, and you do. Secondly, why the fuck is this my job? What are we, binary or something?"

"No. But as you're the injured party—"

"And making me feel like you don't even wanna touch me is going to make me less injured? You really haven't thought this through, have you?"

"I guess not. I just wasn't sure if it was OK with you."

They took a deep breath. "Gio, this is important: you've got to learn to use your words. I can't read your mind. I can barely read my own."

"Alright. Would it be OK if I snuggled up to you?"

"Yes. It would be very OK. But..." Their face spasmed. "I'm not sure I'm up to doing anything else. There's still a giant heap of shit between us. Until that's clear, I don't think I'm up to having sex with you. I want to make love with you, or nothing. And I'm not up to that. Not yet."

I tried to school my face into neutrality while searching for the right words. I didn't get a chance to, because Frankie snapped.

"No! Don't fucking hide! This is a big deal for me, too. Talk to me!"

"OK. When you said that you don't want to have sex with me, I felt awful. When you said that you want to make love to me—"

"*With* you. It's got to be mutual."

"With me, yes. That felt like the best thing ever. When you said that we can't, I felt horrible again. I'm sad that we can't have that yet, but I get it."

"And you're cool with waiting?"

"Of course. You waited for me."

"Hardly. And anyway, what are we doing, relationship accountancy?"

"No. I just want this to be right for both of us, same as you do. I'm not a complete asshole. I know it's hard to remember, given the way I carry on."

They nodded. "Alright, then. You wanna hug?"

I didn't get a chance to move closer to them: as soon as the words were out of their mouth, I found myself pressed against them. I nearly knocked out their front teeth in the process, but that didn't seem to bother them.

"Gio, did you just 'port?"

"I think so. I'm not sure."

"But that's great! And your head doesn't hurt? You're OK?"

I looked into their eyes, only inches away from mine, and my mouth dried up. I barely managed to croak a, "Yeah, I'm fine," before my throat closed up.

"You don't sound it."

"I'm OK. It's just... It's so great to be next to you like this."

They snickered. "Like what? We're barely touching."

"Alright, then. How about this?"

I slipped my arms around their waist. They took a deep breath. When they let it go, they let themself relax into me. Their body felt familiar and unfamiliar at the same time; it smelled like them, but it felt broader, harder, more angular. I ran a hand up the side of their chest.

"You've been working way too hard."

"Not really. But as I hadn't been working at all before, maybe it made a difference."

"It definitely did." I ran my hand down their back. It felt so good that I forgot to stop when I reached their ass, and I found myself cupping it. When I realized what I was doing, I yanked my hand off. "Sorry."

They sighed in my hair. "Nah. It's alright."

I let my hand go roaming again. The contours of their body were just different enough to make it a real exploration. They were also different enough to be concerning.

"I've not been feeding you enough."

"I've not been hungry."

"Well, you've gotta eat." I ran my hand up their chest. "I can feel all your ribs."

"You don't like that?"

"Not as much as I'd like you to be healthy."

"I am. Look: I have muscles."

They lifted up an arm and flexed it. I couldn't see what they wanted me to see through their shirt, so I gave it a prod. "Yeah. That's a muscle alright."

"I got it just for you. I hope you're impressed."

"You know me: I'm all about brawn. I'm practically bowled over."

"Good thing you're already lying down, hey?"

"Yeah. Much safer."

I slipped my hand off their arm and onto their chest. It felt harder than I remembered it, but it was just as warm, just as comforting. Their heart beat in there, the heart I'd hurt so badly.

I had an urge to kiss it better, so I did. They tensed up in response, so I stopped.

"Is that alright?"

"Yeah. It feels good." They lifted a hand to cup my face. I turned and kissed their palm a few times, then moved on to kissing the mount of Venus at the base of their thumb.

"Your hands are all muscly, too."

When they didn't answer, I looked at them and nearly shat a brick. They looked pained, their eyes squeezed shut under a creased brow.

"What is it? What's wrong?"

They took their hand off my face and held it up in the air, as if they didn't know what to do with it. "You know when I said all that stuff about us making love or having sex? I wasn't just saying it. I thought about it long and hard, and I really believe it."

"Yes. I get that."

"But I'd not taken all relevant factors into consideration."

"Like what?"

"Like the fact that you're the most beautiful person I've ever met, and you're hot, and you're willing to be in my bed."

"It's my bed, too."

"That you're willing to have me in your bed, then."

"And that's a problem?"

"No. The problem is that I really don't want us to be just having sex, and I'm pretty sure I'm not up to making love yet, but, right now, I just want to be inside you."

"Inside me?"

They nodded.

"Inside where?"

"Anywhere. Everywhere. Wherever you'll have me. If you'll have me."

I snaked my arms around their neck and put my lips to theirs. They kissed me tenderly until I took their bottom lip between my teeth. Three seconds later, our clothes were scattered all around our room and we were doing a lot more than kissing.

I was not totally into it. I had missed their body as much as the rest of them, but they were right: the ton of unresolved shit between us wasn't as easy to cast aside as our clothes. I still wanted this, though, and I knew that I could make it work. I'd spent many a happy hour working out exactly where their buttons were and how to push them. It didn't take me too long to have them lost in the fever of the fuck, gone where the concerns of our life couldn't reach them. I was having a good enough time, too, even though my head wasn't quite right. Then I realized that they were saying "God" and "Gio" interchangeably and in the exact same tone, and the fuck swept me away.

We didn't emerge from our room until Frankie's stomach started growling. When we did, we found Ben in the garage, sitting in front of the TV, enjoying his lunch. Frankie sprawled next to him while I went off to get us some food. All the way through my foraging, I could feel eyes on my back. It made it hard for me to concentrate, because all I wanted to do was drag Frankie back to our room and our bed. They were hungry, though, and I could stand wanting them for a little bit longer, now that I knew that I could have them later. Feeding them was top priority. All the same, I found myself doing things a bit more slowly than normal and paying more attention to how I looked than to what I was doing. I resolved to apologize to Frankie at the earliest occasion: apparently, what they'd said about me trying to be beautiful at them wasn't wholly incorrect. When I turned around, though, all those considerations disappeared. Frankie wasn't looking at me; they were too busy scowling at the ceiling. The eyes I'd felt on me were Ben's.

We locked eyes for a moment, blushed in perfect synchrony, and looked away. I managed to carry the food over to the couch without dropping anything, but it was a struggle.

When I sat next to Frankie, all I wanted them to do was to reassure me that everything was normal, or as normal as we could make it. Instead they grabbed my hand, gazed into my eyes, and sunk every hope I had for a nice, quiet day.

"Gio, we've got to tell Ben."

Ben shook himself off. "Tell me what?"

Frankie looked a question at me. I nodded, though all I wanted to do was run away. They nodded back, took a big breath, and let it all out.

"Gio picked up a stalker. It's my fault, in a way. Do you remember my Uncle Jacob? The one who sent the raccoons?"

They told Ben the whole story, exactly as I'd told it to them. I was enormously grateful not to have to go through the whole thing all over again and stunned by the level of detail they got into. They remembered every single little thing I'd told them. Knowing that they didn't just care in theory, that they actually dedicated their time and attention to me and my problems, made my heart swell up so much that I thought it might explode.

Frankie read something in my eyes and sighed. "Gio, this isn't the time. This is important. How the fuck am I supposed to go to work tomorrow without knowing if you'll be safe?"

"It's been fine so far. Nothing really happened."

"It's *not* fine. Just because he hasn't hurt you, it doesn't make it fine. We need to do something. I just don't know what the fuck we can do."

Ben rumbled, "What are your options?"

"The only thing I can think of in the short term is telling Uncle Marin and Ms. Anzengruber. She could keep an eye on Gio, and he might be able to get some of his people to help us."

I piped up. "Ms. Anzengruber is already keeping an eye on me. Two eyes, in fact, and sometimes it feels like more. I don't want her to get even more paranoid about my safety. She's been threatening to drag me to a self-defense class."

Frankie winced. "You know, if the prospect didn't terrify you so much, I'd be tempted to tell you that you'd deserve that. As things are, I'm sorry about it, but I'm still furious at you for not telling me what was going on."

I sneaked my hand in theirs. "I know. I'm sorry."

"Are you sorry enough to agree that your strategy up to this point has been appalling?"

"I didn't get hurt!"

Ben cleared his throat. "Frankie's right. You totally failed to make use of your resources."

"What resources? I'm a weed! I can't make circles! What else can I do?"

He squinted at me. "Ask us for help."

"You were all the way up north!"

"My sister has a phone. Seriously, I know you're smart, but sometimes it's hard to remember that."

The shame hit me like a truck, but Frankie was there to hug me.

"That was before, Gio. Now we're gonna make new plans. Together."

"Plans to do what? I mean, what's our actual goal?"

"To keep you safe. To make you feel safe, too. I'm really not happy with some asshole terrorizing you."

"I'm terrorized most of the time. I'm self-terrorizing, really."

They scowled. "Gio, don't make light. It's not cool."

"Alright! I just don't see what we can do, the three of us against a god."

Frankie erupted. "Jesus Christ on a pogo stick, Gio! There's five of us! We need to tell the grown-ups! And one of them is a god, and the other one is a motherfucking librarian!" They stopped, blinked, and peered into my eyes. "What exactly is the problem? I know why you didn't want to tell me, but why don't you want to tell them?"

I had to stop and think. I knew that I really, really didn't want to tell them, that the mere thought of it put a huge knot in my stomach, but I'd not stopped to think why. "I just don't think it would do any good."

Frankie's eyes bore into mine. "Why?"

"They'll be angry at me."

"Why?"

"Because I'd not told them sooner. Because I'm causing them trouble."

"We can't go back in time. But how are you causing trouble? You're wholly innocent."

"I'd be taking up their time. It's my problem. It's bad enough that I can't fix it, but if I start spreading it around—"

"What exactly do you think is going to happen if we tell them?"

Thinking about it filled my insides with ice. "Marin will just yell at me because I can't deal with my own shit. Ms. Anzengruber will hate me."

"She won't hate you!"

"Alright, but she'll be disappointed. And what if she decides to kick us out? She might not want me around with Jacob on my tail. Maybe she would have tolerated a regular stalker, but a god? And what if I have to give up work, too? I'm putting everyone in danger just by being there." I started to shake and couldn't stop. "We won't have a home, and—"

Frankie grabbed my shoulders. "Gio. Stop. She's not like that. She's not going to turn on you because you have a problem, particularly when that problem is not your fault."

"You say that, but you can't be sure."

"I can, because I know her, and I know that she's not an asshole. It would take a giant, flaming asshole to react like that. Decent people don't punish the people they love because they have a problem. They help them out. People who love people want to help the people they love, because they love them. Jesus, that's not English. But do you get it?"

I only realized that I was crying when they started wiping the tears off my face. I took three long breaths to calm myself down. "I get it. But can we try to sort this out ourselves? And tell them if we can't?"

They bit their lip. "I don't like it. I want you as safe as you can be. It's bad enough that I'm putting you through this—"

"You're not. Jacob is."

"Alright." All the energy drained out of them, living them limp. "I can't make you tell them, and I won't tell them if you don't want me to, but I don't like it, and I would like to discuss this further when you feel better. Is that OK?"

"Yes. Of course. I'm sorry."

Seeing them upset made it harder for me not to cry, which upset them more. We were setting off on a spiral that might have sucked us in forever, when Ben cleared his throat.

"Was that it?"

Frankie looked at him over my head. "Say what?"

"So far, your only new tactic consists of not doing the one thing you think you really ought to do. I mean, I don't know much about strategy—"

"You play 'Axis & Allies' once a week."

"Yeah, but that's just a game."

"It still makes you the most qualified person here. My brain doesn't do higher thinking, and Gio... Gio gets wound up. You're our best strategist."

I started giggling. "Help me, Ben Kenobi! You're my only hope!"

Frankie sighed and rested their hand on my head. "Do you see what I mean? We need you, man. If you've got any ideas, tell us."

Ben sighed. "Alright. Lemme see if I got this right."

And he launched on a point-by-point analysis of my situation that was so comprehensive and systematic that Frankie got out their notebook and started taking notes.

As Ben pointed out, we were operating under a number of assumptions, the main one being that Jacob wouldn't do anything drastic in public. As that was supported by evidence, Ben and Frankie decided that the best short-term course of action was for me to be under supervision at all times. I initially baulked at that, because I didn't want to take up their time, but that made Frankie freak out so comprehensively that I withdrew my objections. Once we got over that, my babysitting rota wasn't too hard to arrange. Ben would come with me to the library in the morning and hang around until the end of my shift. Then he'd walk me over to where Frankie was working, so we could all have lunch together. After that, I had two options. If Frankie was working in an area open to the public, I could stay with them until the end of their shift. If not, I could head back home or to the library with Ben. Going anywhere else increased my risk and the trouble I'd put Ben through, so I didn't even consider it.

Ben and Frankie debated at length over which place was safest, the library or our home. I could put a circle around the house, but getting here on foot meant walking through some isolated areas, where Ben's presence may not be enough of a deterrent. Staying at the library eliminated that risk, but left me more exposed. Ben offered to drive me back in his truck, but Frankie and I both vetoed that. We'd take our chances with deranged gods over Ben getting pulled over in an illegal vehicle.

If I stayed on campus, Frankie would take me home at the end of their shift, so they could spend the evening with me and hold me all night. The latter promise made Ben gag, but I was overjoyed. They said it like they meant it.

All in all, it was business as usual for Frankie and me; we always spent as much time together as we could. The weirdest thing about it all was that Ben agreed to his part in it. I was going to be taking up most of his day, but he insisted that he didn't mind.

"I can start working on my classes."

"Ben, I have never seen you open a book during a holiday."

He frowned at me. "Yeah, but, I'm a grad student now. And I'll have to actually work during term time. It's all good."

I couldn't change his mind, so I gave up trying. By then we were all hungry again, so we ate. Then we drank, listened to music, and played cards. Frankie rested his knee against mine all the way through. It was almost like the good old days. Frankie looked haggard, I was burning with stress, and Ben kept looking at me weird, but it was such an improvement compared to the previous weeks that I wanted to fall to my knees and kiss the ground in thanks. Our floor wasn't all that clean, though, and the guys might have thought that I'd finally lost it, so I didn't. I did get down on my knees later, when Frankie and I retired to our room, but the circumstances were different and I got no complaints.

Although conceptually repugnant to me, my babysitting rota turned out to be just wonderful. I was still concerned about taking too much of everyone's time and energy, but they clearly didn't mind, and having them keep an eye on me made me feel so much better that I couldn't even find the words to express it. Instead of feeling hounded and forlorn, I felt protected. It was a new feeling for me, one I really, really liked. The fact that Jacob was still out there was on my mind, but it didn't seem as big a deal as the fact that I wasn't alone, that people actually cared for me, even though I needed more than I could give.

The fact that one of those people was Frankie made it even more wonderful. Everything they did with or for me was special. Now they were taking care of me while we were trying to rebuild our relationship, and getting that volume of love and attention from them was almost too much for me to bear. The way they were doing it made it even more touching.

They were still terrified: by the intensity of their feelings for me, by the pain they had experienced, and by the pain I could yet cause them. The first time they'd fallen for me, they had no idea how far that fall would take them, how their entire existence would become all about our relationship. Now they were walking back into that situation knowing just how much it would affect them, and how much it would wreck them if it all went to shit. They knew just how much I could hurt them. That didn't stop them, though; it didn't stop them wanting to be with me, and it didn't stop them telling me all about it.

Sometimes they talked to me as their partner, and sometimes they called on their friend Gio. Either way, they opened their heart and mind to me and let me see all of them, including the bits they didn't like and the bits they thought I would not like. Their misgivings, their fears, their urge to pull back from me, to find some kind of balance, to corral their love so it wouldn't consume them: everything was laid bare for me to see. That was the root of their terror: that I would see them, judge them, and reject them. The fact that they wouldn't let their terror stop them revealed the depth of their bravery, as well as the intensity of their love. They thought themself weak. I did my best to explain to them that the opposite was true, that their willingness to embrace their vulnerability and to follow their heart was the biggest strength I knew.

Every single time I said that, or something like that – every single time I told them that I liked any part of them, in any way – they would look at me and melt. They had no words to express what they thought and felt, but the naked joy in their eyes was more than enough.

I couldn't be with them like they were with me. I wanted to, but I couldn't – not yet, anyway. I just didn't have the guts. There were parts of me I still kept hidden, and not just from them. I just wasn't ready to think about them too closely, to pick at scabs over wounds that were not quite healed. I would tell them that, and every time they'd take it at face value, same as they'd take anything we said to each other, and respond in the only way they knew, by throwing their love at me. They loved all of me, just the way I was. They loved me because of the way I was. They loved me all the way, and there was no bigger feeling.

The first time they'd said it to me, half asleep and tangled in my arms, it had made me chuckle.

"But it's true, Gio! I love you, all the bits."

"Do you mean that all of you loves me, or that you love all of me?"

"Yes."

And that was it. They were falling head over heels, again, and they were happy with it, even though they knew how risky it all was.

I wasn't doing much better. Falling in love with them the first time had been the biggest experience of my life, but I'd gone through it alone. Back then, I didn't have anyone to talk to about it. Hell, I struggled to even think about it; it was too delicious a dream for me to let myself indulge in it, because I knew how much waking up would hurt. This time, it was totally different. We were falling in love with each other all over again, *and* we had each other to talk to about it. I could tell Frankie how I felt about them, because they were my best friend in the whole world. They would feel joy on my behalf, and joy of their own, because they were loved. They could tell me about their feelings, and I'd feel joy for their joy, and for my own joy returned to me. On and on it went, and our joy was amplified until it was overwhelming. My feelings would get so big that my body and soul would resonate with them, so big that I thought they would dissolve me, but it was OK: Frankie was with me. Nothing bad could happen while Frankie was with me.

7. SPILLING TOWARDS ALPHA

The day my course started, Ben walked me to school. That conclusively proved to me that our household had reached a new, unprecedented level of weird; the last time anyone had walked me to school I was eight years old. There was no way around it, though, because Frankie had to go to work and I couldn't be left unattended. I wasn't sure that Ben could do much to protect me against an ill-intentioned god, but I knew that both he and Frankie would freak out if I mentioned that, so I kept my reservations to myself. It felt good having him with me, anyway; it might not have made me safer, but it made me happier.

It seemed to make Ben happier, too – from what I could tell, anyway, which wasn't much. I'd accepted months before that I couldn't reliably read him. If Ben could look totally chilled out while planning to wander off into a magical wilderness without supplies, knowing full well that it amounted to a suicide, then he could look happy about walking me to school when he would have rather stayed in bed.

He did look happy, though. He looked proud, too, and way more alert than usual. We chatted all the way over to campus and I was having a great time, until I realized with a pang that I'd not missed him while he'd been away. I'd had a lot on my plate, granted, but that didn't seem enough of an excuse. He was a great guy and a fantastic friend, but I forgot all about him as soon as he was out of sight. I wondered if that would have happened had Frankie not been there for me. I doubted it. I'd liked Ben a whole lot before Frankie appeared in my life. I'd even begun to wonder whether I was doing more than liking him. Now that I had Frankie, though, I didn't seem to need anyone else. It worked, kinda, but it was probably unhealthy.

Ben tugged at my arm and shook me out of my daze. We were standing in front of my classroom. I didn't know how long we'd been there.

He looked down at me. "Are you OK?"

"Yes. Sorry. Just thinking."

"I'm going to sit right across the hall. You'll be alright."

"I know. Thank you." I had a sudden urge to hug him, so I shoved my hands in my pockets. "You don't have to do this."

"I know. I'm doing it 'cause I want to. See you at lunch."

He turned around and lumbered off. I stared at his retreating back for longer than was good for me, and then I walked into class.

When I got out for lunch, Ben was waiting for me in the hallway.

"How long have you got?"

"Only a half hour, but we get to go home early."

He frowned. "So you can't have lunch with Frankie?"

"No, but it's alright. I don't want you running back and forth all over campus for nothing."

"You seeing Frankie isn't nothing."

"I know, but... You wanna sit outside?"

"Sure."

We found a quiet spot under a tree and opened our lunch bags. When we were done eating, he lay down on the grass, and I dropped the news.

"So, this class... It's not classroom-based."

"I kinda figured. Not much soil to be found there, is there?"

"Not so much. We're going to be bringing samples back, though."

He squinted. "That's cool? I think?"

"You don't. If it's not unreal, you think it's dead boring."

"Not true! My dad is... was a farmer. So's my brother-in-law . Soil is important."

"But it's boring?"

He shrugged. "Yeah. Kinda. But if you like it..."

"I'm not sure I do, but I need to take this class. Anyway, on Mondays and Fridays we are going to be in here, poking at samples. The rest of the week, we are going on field trips."

He lifted himself up on one arm. "What?"

"I thought we'd be digging around on campus, but we can't. We have to go to where the soil types are."

"Is your teacher gonna drive you?"

"Nope. They seem to assume that everyone can get transport."

"Alright. So I'll drive you."

"You can't. Your truck is gruesomely illegal. It's all sorted, anyway: one of the guys is going to give me a lift."

His face turned into a mask of disbelief. "No way, man! You can't just go off into the woods with some guy!"

"I have to. I can't take you with me. I'll be alright. My whole class is going to be there."

"But what if Jacob... What if this guy... I don't like it!"

I did my best to sound more comfortable than I felt. "It's the easiest way to deal with the issue. He's going to pick me up from the top of the road. He said he could pick me up from home, but that didn't feel right."

Ben growled, "It's not even a quarter of a mile. It wouldn't have taken him a minute."

"I know, but it'd be out of his way. I don't know. It just felt wrong."

"This whole thing feels wrong."

"It's not ideal, but that's how it is. And I will need you to help me sell it to Frankie."

He flinched. "What? No way!"

"They're gonna freak out. They'd have me locked in a vault if they could."

"Not true. They know you'd hate it. They just want you to be safe."

"I want to be safe, too, but I have to take this class. I can't graduate without it. It will be alright. I'm used to hitching rides."

Ben let himself drop to the ground and mumbled, "Yeah, that makes it so much better."

"You wouldn't be half as worried if it was Frankie doing it."

"Damn right, I wouldn't."

"Why?"

"I don't know. It's just different."

"Because I'm weak and feeble?"

"No. That's definitely not it."

"What is it, then?"

His response was a shrug, and he hardly spoke after that. He didn't seem pissed off, though; he walked me back to my classroom, waited for me until my class ended, and walked with me to find Frankie.

They were so overjoyed to see me that they acted as if I was a conquering hero returning from a month-long mission rather than a twerp who'd just finished a half day in school. When they were done hugging and kissing me, they hugged Ben, too. He looked as if he didn't know how to feel about it, but he hugged them back.

Frankie's ebullient mood evaporated when I told them about my class.

"Are you shitting me? You're seriously thinking about getting in some rando's car and going off into the woods with him?"

Ben mumbled, "That's what I said."

I tried to sound a lot calmer than I actually felt. "Look, I have to. That's how this class works, and I have to take it."

"So take it next year! This thing with Jacob won't last forever."

"They don't offer it every year."

"Yeah, but they've gotta offer it often enough for people to graduate."

"Most people take four years, though."

They froze for a moment, then sagged. "Right. And you won't be here that long."

I grabbed the front of their shirt and pulled them down so we were nose to nose. "And I might not be in school by then, but I'm sure as hell going to be where you are. You got that?"

Their shock melted into a stupendously goofy smile. "Loud and clear."

"Right. So for the next three weeks, I'm going to spend three days a week digging holes in the woods. Nine days in total. 72 hours, tops. In the grand scheme of things, it's nothing."

"If Jacob hurts you, I'll have to kill him. And then I'll probably kill myself." They spoke in a calm, dispassionate tone, but I knew that they meant it.

"I know. I promise you, I'll be OK. I'll be around people at all times. It won't be the same as having Ben with me, but it's the best I can do."

They picked up my hand. "Gio, if this guy who's giving you lifts hurts you, I'm going to want to kill him, too."

"I know, but you're worrying over nothing. It wouldn't be safe for him to try anything. Everyone knows I'll be in his car. And if he so much as touches me, I'll report him."

"You would?"

"Yes. He's probably not into queer weirdos, anyway, and I made damn sure that he knew that I have a boyfriend—"

They glared at me. "I'm your boyfriend now?"

"For the purpose of this exercise, yes. It makes you a valid impediment. A lot of guys respect territory more than they respect consent."

Their face fell. "I guess you're not totally new to this kind of concern."

"Not totally, no. It's going to be OK. I'm going to make damn sure it is."

"I trust you. It's the rest of the world I'm not so sure about."

I hadn't lied to Frankie and Ben: I was used to getting lifts from people I barely knew, or didn't know at all. I'd started hitchhiking because it was the only way I had to get around. After a while, I'd realized that, for someone like me, hitching was safer than public transport. Yes, I was stuck in a confined space with a stranger, but it was a stranger I'd picked, who had at least one hand busy. On a train, I had no control at all over who got on. After a couple of eventful trips, when I found myself stuck on a moving train, alone, faced with a group of people who didn't mean me any good and no bystander willing to help, I'd decided to take my chances on the road.

I must have lost my nerve since, because I found the thought of waiting for a near-stranger on a street corner really uncomfortable. I didn't mind it half as much as Frankie did, but I didn't like it at all. It put another knot in my stomach, and I felt that I was already at top capacity in that respect. I didn't want to alarm Frankie unduly, though, so I managed to hold myself together until they were off to work, and then I let myself fall apart. I grabbed my coffee, retreated to the couch, burrowed under Frankie's crochet project, and turned into a sniveling heap of snot.

I was still under there when Ben peered through the garage door. He looked rougher than I'd ever seen him, as if he'd spent the night on a giant bender before crawling home through several hedges, and maybe a ditch. His hair fell all over the place in tangled strands, his eyes were red-rimmed, and his whole face had an unfocused, half-baked quality – which, oddly enough, I'd never seen on him, even when he was totally baked.

I wiped the worst of the snot off my face and peered out of my security blanket. "Are you alright?"

"Yeah," he grunted. "You?"

"Yeah."

"We're terrible liars, aren't we?"

"We don't get enough of a chance to practice. Frankie's fault."

He shuffled over and sat next to me. "I've been thinking. How are you going to know if the right guy is picking you up?"

"Say what?"

"Jacob can shape-shift, right? So, like, how are you gonna know if the right guy is in the car?"

My brain ran through that scenario without me having any say on the matter. When it was done, I shook my head. "Nah. I'd know."

"But how?"

"The way Jacob looks at me, even when he's not looking at me."

"I don't get that."

I looked up at Ben. I had to, because his head was at least half a foot higher than mine when we were sitting down. His chest was as deep as my shoulders were broad. He was the sweetest guy on the planet and a really good listener. He'd been my first friend on this continent, and he'd probably be my last if shit really hit the fan. He really cared about me and he never dismissed anything I told him, even when it didn't make any sense to him. I still didn't think I had the slightest chance to make him understand how things were for me, but I gave it my best shot.

"When people see you as prey, it feels different. For me, anyway. I pick up on that. I probably get false positives, but I don't care. Every time I've ignored that feeling, something bad happened, so now I listen to it. I'll be alright."

He frowned. "I still don't get it."

"I know."

"But I believe you."

"Thank you."

"It's fucked up, isn't it? All of it."

"It's the way it is."

"Yeah, but it shouldn't be that way. Are you totally sure about this?"

"Yes. If I get any kind of bad feeling when I look at the guy in the car, I won't get in. I promise."

"Alright. I'll walk you up the road."

"You don't have to."

"I'm not doing it for you. Or for Frankie." He got up, waited for me to pick up my gear, and shambled all the way up the hill with me.

We didn't have to wait long. When Ben saw the car, he muttered, "That piece of shit is way worse than my truck."

"It is, but I believe it's legal. Even if it isn't, none of us will get into trouble for it being on the road."

"Your priorities are all over the place."

"Do you want to have that conversation where I tell you what I think about your financial priorities?"

"I'll pass. I remember the last one. Is he dropping you home?"

"I don't know."

Ben's hand landed on my shoulder. "Gio. Make him drop you home."

"Alright! I will!"

I managed to greet my schoolmate without choking on my own tongue. I was sure that he expected me to make conversation, like normal people did, but my brain just wouldn't get in gear. Ben had stayed on the street corner, watching us drive away. I could see him in the mirror, getting smaller and smaller as my heart sank.

Getting dropped back at the house turned out to be the easiest thing in the world – in fact, I would have had to argue my way out of it, because my ride insisted. I still felt supremely uncomfortable at having him find out where I lived, but I knew that it had nothing to do with my pervdar and everything to do with my brain being full of festering shit.

As soon as the car stopped, I wanted to rush out of it and into my home, but I made myself say thank you and goodbye. It all came out stilted and excessively formal, and my ride gave me one of those looks that made me want to disappear into the ground, never to be seen again. As there wasn't a fucking thing I could do about it, I just added it to the pile of things I could torture myself with later.

As soon as I stood on home ground, the weight that had been crushing my windpipe and chest dissipated. The weirdest thing about it was that I'd not even noticed it being there, but its disappearance felt so good that I wanted to cry. I told myself not to be ridiculous and limited myself to patting the house to say thank you. I patted the porch banister, the front door, the wall of the hallway, and the door to the garage. Ben wasn't in there, which didn't surprise me. It was too beautiful a day to stay hidden in a room with no windows. His door was open, but he wasn't in there, either, so I carried on walking to my room. He was in there, and so was Frankie. They were sitting by the patio door, talking quietly. I couldn't hear what they were saying, but it must have been quite engrossing as they didn't even hear me come in.

I stood and watched them, while my heart swelled up. I could have stayed there forever, watching my two favorite people framed in sunlight, but Ben said something funny and got me caught out. Frankie laughed so hard that they fell backwards and spotted me.

"Gio? Gio!"

I expected them to be happy to see me back and safe, but I was wrong. Ben stood up, mumbled something incomprehensible, and disappeared off towards his smoking spot. Frankie got up to give me a hug, but they kept looking at me as if I were a piece of unexploded ordnance likely to go off at no notice.

"Love, is something wrong?"

"No. I just wasn't expecting you back yet. So, huh, how was your day?"

"I got in the guy's car and realized that I couldn't remember his name. It kinda went downhill from there."

They snorted. "You didn't ask him?"

"I couldn't! I was already in his car! And he wanted to make small talk, so it was kind of harrowing. But hey, I didn't get killed or anything, so it's all good."

"Your standards are somewhat concerning, you know that?"

"Sorry." I tried to wrap my arm around them, but they went rigid. "Do you want me to clear off for a bit? You look busy."

The shook their head. "Nah. You need to see this."

They sat back down on the doorstep and I sat next to them. Their hand reached out towards my leg and hovered there for a few seconds before retreating into their pocket. Whatever was up with them, it was serious.

They fixed their eyes on the horizon and cleared their throat. "You know how Ben has taken a bunch of philosophy classes?"

"We haven't really talked about it, but I guessed as much, what with him being a philosophy minor." A thought between a hope and a worry gripped me. "Are you thinking about changing majors again?"

They chortled. "You wish."

"Actually, I don't. I always thought philosophy was a giant snoozefest."

"What? But it involves big books and long words!"

"Yeah. I just can't really understand why I should care about what some dead white guy thought just because a bunch of other dead white guys liked it. I prefer to do my own thinking. Pre-masticated concepts are icky."

They turned around and beamed at me. "You're such an anarchist!"

"Too right."

"So you wouldn't prefer it if I took philosophy instead of sociology?"

"I didn't say that."

"You can be a real asshole, you know?" Their smile started to fade. "Anyway, Ben has read a lot of stuff about ethics, and why are you rolling your eyes?"

"No reason."

They winced. "You little liar. Don't do that to me! It's not funny!"

"Then why are you smiling?"

"Because I'm here with you."

They said it so artlessly that I wanted to jump on them and kiss them for a million years, but I didn't want to interrupt them, so I just smiled.

They smiled back, but their eyes were still brown. "Anyway, I've been talking to Ben about my powers. He thinks they're not inherently evil."

"Of course they're not! It'd be like saying that a knife is evil! Evil isn't in things, it's in what you do with them. I could have told you that!"

"Actually, you probably couldn't have. I mean, you could have, but I don't know if I could have heard you. I know you're biased. You love me too much."

"Would you like me to cut down?"

"No! But I needed an unbiased opinion, and I couldn't get it from you. You're still the best thing that's ever happened to me. That's rather the point. Kinda."

"Love, I'm lost. What is the point?"

They took a deep breath and turned back to stare at nothing. "Ben agrees with you. Hell, he even used the metaphor about knives. Then he quoted about twelve dead white dudes to prove his point, and would have probably quoted more if I'd not asked him to stop. The general consensus seems to be that the issue isn't what I've got, it's what I do with it."

"Great! So you feel a bit better about it?"

"No. Of all the people I know, I'm the last one who should have been given the nuclear codes. I have no impulse control – and no, I don't want to discuss that. But I think that the whole issue is moot."

"Moot? If you feel bad about something that is a part of you, how can that be moot?"

"Because I don't like what I've got, but we might need it."

"We might? Me and you?"

"Mostly me. I might need it to protect you. Don't yell at me, alright?"

"I've not said a thing! But you don't need to protect me."

"I don't need to protect you because you need protecting. I need to protect you because I don't know what I'd do if I lost you. It scares me so much I can't even think about it. And I need to know that I can protect you because the thought of having to stand by and do nothing while something bad happens to you just makes me feel... I don't have the words for that. How would you feel if you couldn't protect me?"

"But I can't!"

"Nonsense. You do it all the time. You're doing it now. Anyway, that's what I came up with, and Ben didn't disagree, and neither of us was sure what you'd make of it, but we both decided that worrying about that wasn't a priority at the moment, so here we are."

They stared at me with a question in their eyes. Unfortunately, I had no idea what it was.

"Love, I'm still lost."

"Alright. Watch this."

They turned towards the end of the yard, took a deep breath, and became more real than the reality around us. My senses couldn't quite parse what was going on and kept screaming at me to stop trying, but I was too spooked to listen. Frankie looked too vivid, the contrast and sharpness of their features whacked up so high that my eyes could hardly stand it. It was a lot like the way they'd looked and felt in Jacob's circle, all those months ago. I was just about to totally lose my shit and have a panic attack, when I heard a faint puffing sound, and they went back to normal.

They turned to face me. "What do you think?"

"About what?"

"Gio! Are you kidding me? I just blew that up!"

"Blew what up?"

"Oh, for the love of... Come on!"

They stood up, pulled me upright, and dragged me to the end of the yard. Just in front of the tree line was a line of little stones – pebbles from the driveway, most likely – spaced about three feet apart. That was weird, but not that weird. What was weirder was Frankie pointing at a spot about three feet from the last stone.

"Do you see?"

"No. What am I supposed to see?"

"Look properly!"

I started to bend down to take a closer look when they tugged at my sleeve and shook their head.

"No. Look!" They waved their arms around them in a circle, and I realized what my problem was: I'd been looking for something in front of me, while I should have been looking for something all around me. We were standing in some kind of circle; the ground around us was sprinkled with something greyish.

I bent down to touch it. "Dust?"

"Yeah. That's what you get when you make a stone take itself apart, apparently."

I looked up at them. "You did that?"

"Yeah. I can do metal and stone. Stones are easiest. They just go POOF! Wood is hard, or not hard enough, or something. I thought I'd get splinters, but I get soup."

"Soup?"

"Yeah. Kinda. It goes all slushy."

"Are you compromising the integrity of the cell walls?"

They gasped. "I don't know! Don't tell me what I'm doing! It doesn't work when I think!"

"What?"

"It only works if I do it without really thinking about what I'm doing. Don't say it!"

"Say what?"

"That I never think about what I'm doing."

"I wasn't going to say that! And you're learning to blow stuff up so you can protect me?"

"Yeah. I've been trying different ways. If I break it into shards instead of pulverizing it, it travels further and it's got more oomph."

"Love, how is this going to protect me?"

They bit their bottom lip. "I dunno. Maybe I can blow Jacob's buttons up or something. I know. It's stupid."

They turned to walk away, but I grabbed them.

"No, it's not. It's the nicest thing anyone has ever done for me."

"What?"

"You're doing something you hate, something that scares you, so you can protect me. You're lovely."

They stuck their chin up in the air. "You don't think I'm a freak of nature and a danger to myself and others?"

"Nah. I think you are the kindest, bravest, most wonderful person who ever walked the earth, and I love you so fucking much I can hardly bear it."

They closed their eyes and let off a huge sigh. I stood up with the intention of just giving them a hug, nothing special, but I felt them shuddering in my arms and I just lost it. I found myself trying to kiss them and to tell them how wonderful they were at the same time, which didn't really work, so I ended up fudging the whole thing and screaming, "Only one mouth, dammit!"

They giggled. "I beg your pardon?"

"I need two mouths for this!"

They slipped their hands down my back, all the way to my ass. "You know, I'm perfectly happy with what you've got and what you do with it, but I've occasionally found myself wishing that—"

"Cut it out, you pervert. This isn't the time."

"Huh. What is this the time for?"

"Blowing shit up. Show me what you got, hotshot."

I thought it may take me some time to get used to Frankie's new ability, but it didn't; it fell into the giant pile of weird shit that always to happen to and around us and get lost in there. Gods roamed the earth, people worked magic, I could sort of teleport, my partner was a walking polygraph, and now they could blow shit up by just thinking about it, provided that they didn't think about it too much. In the grand scheme of things, it just didn't seem a big deal.

It took Frankie a lot longer to get used to me being OK with it. They kept expecting me to freak out and leave them, and I just could not convince them that it was never going to happen. I was used to living with negativity and paranoia, but only the ones in my own head. Coming from Frankie, they freaked me out on a regular basis. The fact that I was freaking out about that just confirmed Frankie's anxiety, and round and round we went, winding each other up in the worst possible manner until someone – Ben, usually – stepped between us and stopped us.

Ben was an absolute angel about everything. He babysat me, he talked Frankie down, he cooked dinner for us most nights, and he was generally wonderful without apparently realizing it. None of that surprised me, because I knew that he was a great guy, but I kept catching myself looking at him, wondering why he was so giving and how long it'd be before he had enough of our bullshit. I was really thankful, but I also felt terrible: I knew that I was taking up an unfair share of his time and energy, and not giving him back enough of mine. Things were uneven between us and I hated that, but I also hated the thought of diverting any of the time and energy I spent on Frankie on anyone else. I was, as usual, a selfish asshole, and Ben's selflessness highlighted it just enough to make me resentful, which made me feel even worse about everything.

All and still, we were managing. I'd not seen Jacob at all since Ben's return, which made me wonder if Ben was some kind of good-luck charm. I knew that it was bullshit, that Jacob was probably off doing whatever the fuck trickster gods did with their summer and would turn up whenever it was convenient for him, but I still felt better for having Ben around.

After two weeks, I'd gotten so used to our new routine that I had almost stopped feeling bad about it. I even stopped counting every minute of Ben's life that I was taking up. I had grown so comfortable that I was complacent. I should have known that it was going to cost me.

On the Friday of the second week of my course, I managed to forget about my personal problems long enough to start worrying about my coursework. I had only a week to go before my exam, and I didn't feel that I was making any headway. I was normally pretty good at cramming stuff into my brain, and even better at regurgitating it on demand, but this course was different: I actually had to know how to do a thing, and it was a thing I had no aptitude for. I liked it when things were black or white, either/or, and soil taxonomy didn't fit that bill. There were too many variables, too many options, and too many ways of getting things wrong. I knew that I was not doing great, and I was feeling pretty despondent about it. When I got stuck on my last set of samples, the only thing that stopped me from crying was that I was in public.

I spent forever and a day trying to work out why nothing was working out. By the time I realized that my problem was that I was looking at the samples in the wrong order, it was nearly five and everyone else had cleared off. Everyone but Ben, anyway: he was waiting across the hall for me like a faithful hound. Hell, he even seemed genuinely happy to see me. That made me feel all choked up, and I decided that the best way to unchoke myself, show Ben how grateful I was, and generally cheer up the entire household, was to stop by the liquor store to get some beers. Alas, I was so lost in my fuzzy feelings that I momentarily forgot that stores require payments in exchange for goods. I had no cash about my person, obviously, and I couldn't use my card because I was under age. Ben had no money at all. Neither of us minded taking a detour via the bank, though, so it wasn't much of a problem.

I liked walking around with Ben. The evening was perfect – just warm enough for me to be comfortable, but cool enough for him not to melt. A gentle breeze rustled the trees as we walked, and the sunlight felt like a blessing. I could have ambled around the town forever, but Frankie was waiting for me at home.

I only realized how late we were, and how inconsiderate of us that was, when I opened our front door to find Frankie and Ms. Anzengruber standing in the hallway, looking frantic. I started to apologize, but Frankie cut me off.

"Ben, you have to go home. You have to go now."

"What happened?"

"Your sister. She rang, tons of times. Your brother-in-law is missing. They've looked everywhere, and they can't find him, and she was crying so much! You have to go home!"

Ben looked at them for a minute without moving a muscle, then bolted towards his room. He came out moments later, cramming clothes into his backpack. He hugged Ms. Anzengruber, squeezed Frankie, and rushed out the door without even looking at me. I stood there like a spare part, while the blood drained out of me.

Frankie had the presence of mind to wait until Ms. Anzengruber was out of the way and the garage door was shut behind us before turning on me. When they did, the anger in their eyes made me stagger back.

"What the fuck, Gio? You should have been back ages ago! I was terrified!"

"School kind of dragged and then..." I lifted up the beer.

"Are you fucking serious? Did you stop and think for a goddamn moment about how worried I might be? Is this whole thing a fucking game to you?"

"We're not that late!"

"You've been home before me all week!"

"Yes, but that was because I finished early!"

"And how the fuck was I supposed to know that today would be different? You didn't tell me!"

"I couldn't! I didn't know!"

"And then you just stopped for booze?"

"I thought you might like some! I thought the three of us could sit in the sun and enjoy it and celebrate and—" and I dissolved into tears. The contrast between what I'd looked forward to and what I was getting was just too much.

Frankie stopped yelling, but they were clearly still furious. They were breathing hard, and their fists were bunched tight. I was less scared of that than of the way they were looking at me. Something about it sent all my brain weasels scattering, leaving me alone to face a volcano of rage that I couldn't avoid or survive.

I managed to make my lips move, but no sound came out. "I'm sorry."

"I know that! But it doesn't help! I wanted so bad to come out and look for you, but I knew that then I wouldn't know if you'd come back and we'd just end up chasing each other around in circles. And then Ben's sister rang, and she was in a state and I didn't know what to tell her because I was in a state, too, but I couldn't tell her that, but I couldn't lie to her either, and... Fuck, Gio. How could you?"

"Sorry. I'm so sorry."

"I know! I'm sorry, too!"

They took a step towards me. I stepped back without thinking about it, and they froze, their rage all but gone. "Gio, I wasn't gonna hurt you."

"I know." I said that, and I meant it, but when they took another step forward my feet still moved back. "I'm sorry."

They looked like they wanted to walk towards me again, but thought better of it and went to sit on the couch instead. "Look, it doesn't matter. I was just worried, and I couldn't even freak out because Ms. Anzengruber doesn't know about Jacob, and then Ben's sister... I'm sorry. I didn't mean it." They winced.

"You did. You never say anything you don't mean. I'm a stupid asshole."

"You're not! I lose track of time all the time, and you don't call me names."

"Yeah, but—"

"But what?" Their rage was coming back. "When I do something like this, it's alright because it's me doing it? Riddle me this: am I a piece of shit because I do it, or am I such a piece of shit that you have to let me off for doing it? It's gotta be one or the other."

"It doesn't! I don't think about you like that!"

"But when you do the exact same thing that I do all the fucking time, you call yourself horrible names."

"It's different!"

"Because you're better than me."

"No!" I searched around my brain for the right thing to tell them, the thing that would make it all unhappen, the thing that would rewind us to when they didn't hate me, when everything wasn't an unmitigated disaster, but all I could find were fear and jagged corners. The beer slipped out of my hand and hit the floor, and then my ass hit the floor, too, and I was crying so hard I couldn't see, and arms were around me and that felt so good and so scary that I was crying even harder.

When it all stopped, about a million years later, I found myself sitting on the floor, feeling like I'd just gone down a stretch of rapids without a kayak. Frankie was sitting next to me – or their body was, anyway. They looked vacant and battered, like an abandoned building.

I stretched out a hand and rested it on their shoulder. They shuddered.

"Hey."

"Hey, you.

"Gio, I'm so sorry. I really didn't mean to... But it doesn't matter. I did it anyway. That's what matters."

"What? You didn't do anything. I'm the one who fucked up."

"Nah. You were five minutes late, and I fucking unloaded on you."

"I was way later than that, and you were upset. You had a right to be."

"Not like that. I'm just like my dad, ain't I?"

"What? No, you're not!"

"Right. At least he's got a proper job. My mom never worked a day in her life. I can't even look after you."

"Looking after me isn't your responsibility!"

"Just as well. I'd only fuck it up, like I fuck up everything else. I put you in danger, and now I've done this. I'm not good for you. I'm no good."

"You didn't do anything! I'm OK!"

"You didn't see your face, Gio. I saw it. I'll never forget it. I'd rather rip out my own eyes than let myself forget it."

I could feel them spinning away, sinking into a dark vortex, and I didn't know how to pull them out of it. I tried to recall the other times things could have gone bad between us and didn't, to remember exactly what I did to put things right, and it hit me: I hadn't done a damn thing. Ben always fixed things for me. Frankie was the person I loved the most in the whole world, and I could only have a functional relationship with them if Ben was around to referee it. I couldn't do right: not by Frankie, not by me, and not by Ben. I was going to lose them, both of them.

I was thinking myself into a storm, so I let my body do its own thing. It sidled next to Frankie, wrapped its arms around their waist, rested its head on their shoulder, and proceeded to soak their shirt in a flood of tears.

They turned around, their eyes brown and desperate. "I'm sorry. Do you want me to go?"

"Go where?"

"I don't know. Just away from you."

I tried to say "No," but my voice failed me, so I gripped their clothes as hard as I could to stop them from slipping away. After a million years, they sighed and stroked my face.

"We're a mess, aren't we?"

I nodded.

"Do you want a beer?"

"I thought I'd smashed them."

"Nah. They look alright." They stretched just enough to reach the bottles, but I still panicked and held them tighter. When they sat back, two bottles in their hand, they sighed. "Gio, I can't open them one-handed."

"Too bad. I'm not letting you go."

"You can't just hold onto me forever."

"Watch me."

They snuffled, and I couldn't tell if they were trying to suck back tears or almost laughing. "Now you're just being silly."

"Yup. Frankie, can we rewind this and do it again, but better?"

"We could hardly do it worse. Well, no. I could have hit you, I guess."

"No. You couldn't have. You're not like that."

"You thought I was gonna."

"I didn't. I was just... I don't like that kind of thing."

"Me neither. It was awful. I never, ever wanna do it again."

"Me neither."

"Alright. So how about this: we go and sit on the couch, and we drink the beer you brought home, which I never thanked you for—"

"It made me late."

"It made you kind. And we put on a really sad movie, so you can cry the tears you've got left and I can pretend that I think it's just because you're a sweetheart, and not because I'm a monster—"

"You're not!"

"I made you cry."

"I made you yell."

"I want to kiss it all away."

"Huh. Do I get to tell you when to stop?"

"No. You'd cheat and have me kiss you forever."

It took us a while to make it to the couch, because I was being ridiculous and I just couldn't bear to let go of them. We lay there for ages, wrapped around each other, and I would have stayed like that all night, but Frankie insisted on getting up.

"Gio, you need a cup of tea. You have a headache."

"How do you know?"

"Your forehead is all scrunched up. I won't be a moment."

"You'll be several moments, unless you're making cold tea."

"How about this: we both get up, you get yourself all snuggled up in bed, and I bring you your tea. Then we can be horizontal *and* naked."

"We could just get naked here."

"No blanket, no pillows, and no cup of tea. No deal."

"You're a meanie."

Their voice dropped to a whisper. "I know. I'm trying to make it right."

"I didn't mean it like that!"

"I know that, too."

They disentangled themself from me and stumbled off to the kitchen. At some point during the evening's clusterfuck, they'd lost all their energy. Now they moved as if their limbs were too heavy. Watching them struggle, I felt like a heel: I was being useless while they took care of me, yet again, and the only reason I needed to be taken care of was that I was a thoughtless, spineless excuse for a person.

They turned around and half-smiled at me. "If you don't hurry up, I'm going to beat you to bed. Go on. I'll be there in no time."

I suddenly realized that they really wanted me to go. Maybe they didn't even realize it, but they needed some time and space without my bullshit, a chance to feel and act out whatever was going on inside them without having to worry about its impact on me. I felt awful for taking so long to work that out, and even worse because I had created that need and stopped them from voicing it. They were always putting me first, even when it hurt them, and it hurt them way too often.

Those cheery thoughts put a lump in my throat and sand in my eyes. I knew that I had to do something or I was going to start crying all over again, so I got up, gave Frankie a quick squeeze, and retreated to our bedroom. At the speed at which they were moving, I might have the chance to pull myself together before they came in.

I took my clothes off and put one of their t-shirts on. I knew that it wasn't what they'd suggested, but I felt cold and lonely, and wrapping myself in their smell felt really good. I lay on our bed, desperately wracking my brain for something I could do to make things better. Our room was too small, and the décor could be charitably described as "shabby Spartan." The light trickling in through the patio door was too dim. Our main light was too bright. Our fairy lights had blown a bulb, and we'd not dug up a replacement yet. The more I looked at what Frankie was going to come back to, the worse I felt. In a fit of despondency, I did something I'd not done in weeks: I opened our portal. When I saw what lay beyond it, I sank down on our bed and marveled.

Our glade was bathed in moonlight. It streamed in through the tree canopy and covered the ground in shimmering kisses. The moon itself was just out of sight, but so bright that no stars were visible. Maybe there were no stars in that sky; we'd never been across at night, so I couldn't be sure. Maybe the moon wasn't the same moon, either. I couldn't tell without looking.

I got out of bed and threw Frankie's robe on. I was just about to open the door when they walked in.

"What? You opened up the portal?"

"Yeah. I thought it may be pretty, but I didn't think it'd be this pretty."

"It's never been night out there before."

"We've never opened it at night."

"True, but we've gone through at all kinds of time and it's always been early morning."

"How did you figure that out?"

"The sun has always been in the same position, and it just feels like morning. Like the world is new, you know? Untarnished."

"Well, it's definitely nighttime now, and it's beautiful."

"Hold on. Something about it isn't right."

"What? You don't like it?"

"That's not it. It just doesn't feel right. Is your circle on?"

I tried to look for the circle in my head, and I couldn't get a read on it. "I can't tell. It feels like it's there, but not quite." I turned the door handle.

"Gio, don't go out there."

That riled me. "I just want to check out the moon. I'm just going to stick my head out the door. I won't even walk out."

"Gio, I don't think—

8. Thanks For The Dress

I couldn't see, because it was dark, but I knew the smell. I stretched my hand out and felt clothes. Some were soft, some were itchy. Then I heard noise: people screaming and breaking things. The noise was loud, and it made my chest hurt. I closed my eyes to make it go away.

Something bumped my feet. I opened my eyes and I saw a man sitting across from me. He wasn't old-old, like my mom, but he was old. He was very pretty. His hair was curly, like the angels'. His smile was like the angels', too.

He smiled at me. "Hey."

"You can't be here. I'll get in trouble."

He shook his head. "I don't think anyone else can see me. Just you."

"Oh. OK, then."

"You're not worried about that?"

"No. Are you an angel?"

"No. Definitely not." He rubbed my foot with his foot. "Where are we?"

"The wardrobe."

"Why?"

I pointed at the door. "They're fighting."

He frowned. "So you hide in the wardrobe?"

"Yes."

"What happens if you go out?"

"I can't go out. They're fighting."

He smiled, but he looked sad. "I don't think they're going to stop."

"They always stop."

"Not this time. You have to get out."

"No!" I didn't like him anymore. He was not nice. He was pushy, like the boys in school.

"This isn't real. It's a dream, kinda. You have to get out."

"When they stop fighting."

He said a bad word, then he closed his eyes and pressed his hands hard against his head. He stayed like that for a bit. I watched him, because it was better than listening to the screaming outside.

When he opened his eyes, they were really bright. "Do you trust me?"

I hated it when grown-ups did that. Saying yes was a lie. That was bad. Saying no was rude. That was bad, too. I stayed quiet. That was rude, but not as rude.

He rubbed his face. "OK. You know when you go with the angels?"

I closed my eyes. Going with the angels was my secret. Nobody knew about that.

"Gio?" He stroked my foot with his foot again. He was nice *and* pushy. It was weird. "Could you go with the angels now? Please?"

He sounded sad, and going with the angels was nice, so I did.

I was sitting in a wardrobe. It stank of mothballs and cologne, and it was cramped as hell. That was largely because Frankie was in there with me, their legs tangled with mine. One of their feet was halfway up my ass. A little kid with straight hair and the most feral expression I'd ever seen on a human was sitting between me and the door.

"Frankie? What the fuck is going on?"

The kid gasped and looked shocked.

Frankie beamed at me and grabbed my hand. "I thought I'd lost you!" They looked both happy and sad, with a side dish of terrified.

"That doesn't answer my question."

"We're in the shit. Don't panic, though: we're mostly safe. We're not really here – well, we are, kinda. It's complicated. You know our portals?"

"Of course I do!"

"They're not actually doors into Faerie, or whatever. Well, they are, but not really."

"Frankie, I know you're trying to help, but you're not."

They sighed. "OK. They are openings into our projection of what Faerie is like. Uncle Marin called them 'tourist traps.' If you know how to get past them, you can get out of the other side. Most people never work out that there is another side. Their expectations are met, so they stay put."

"Other side? Into where?"

"He didn't say. Where his people are from, I guess. Assuming that they're all from the same place."

I stopped and tried to think. It was hard, because my brain weasels were racing at top speed, but I tried as hard as I could. "OK. So that's why Ben's portal took us to a gingerbread house?"

"Yeah. If we'd gone a bit further, we would have probably found three little pigs and a bridge with a troll under it. He was obsessed with fairy tales way before he became obsessed with fantasy. They're baked into his subconscious."

"And my portal?"

They smiled. "And your portal is like you: full of wonders beyond description."

"And my portal is straight out of a medieval bestiary."

"That too. But it *is* wonderful."

"That still doesn't explain why we're here." I dropped my voice. "And who the kid is."

"That's you, kinda. Someone messed with your portal, Gio. They set up a trap on the other side. You're in one of your memories."

"But I don't remember it!"

"That doesn't make it any less real. You got caught in it, and you're going to be stuck in it until you get out. Your body is still in our room." Their voice grew husky. "You look like you're in a coma. I tried so hard to wake you up, but I couldn't, so I called Ms. Anzengruber, and she called Uncle Marin. He can't get you out, either. All he's doing is talking crap about direct interventions and summoning a council, and nobody's doing a damn thing. It's fucking scary, Gio: you're breathing, but that's about it. So I came after you."

"How the fuck did you get in here?"

They shrugged. "You know how I can see cracks and shit? Turns out that I can break into places, even when they're not actual places."

"You broke into my brain, or something?"

"Something. I'm not sure. I just went for it."

"And Marin let you do it?"

"Nah. He just got so wound up that he forgot I was there, like he does, so I came here."

"So I'm stuck in a simulation—"

"Not quite. This is all real, in a way. It's real in your head."

"OK. I'm stuck in my own head, and you decided to wade in with me?"

They nodded. "Yeah. Of course."

"But why? If it's a trap—"

They squeezed my hand. "Don't worry about me. If I can break out of here as easily as I broke in. I could break us both out of here – I could literally break whatever this 'here' is – but there's no knowing what it would do to you."

"Because we're in my head?"

"Yeah. It could bust you out, or, like, break your brain. Or worse."

I swallowed the lump in my throat. "Well, then we're truly fucked."

The kid gasped again. I was about to bark something sharp, but I stopped myself. There was enough fear in that wardrobe already.

I closed my eyes to think, then opened them again because I just couldn't bear not to see Frankie. "So I need to find the way out of this?"

"Yeah."

"What happens if I just bust out of the wardrobe?"

"Dunno. It's not my memory. You need to consult the local expert." They pointed at the kid with their chin.

I fucking hated talking to kids. They were as alien as dogs, with an unfathomable view of the world, but they had none of the charms of the average puppy. I liked no part of our situation, though. It wasn't just the eeriness of the concept, the thought of my body out there somewhere, with no mind to guide it. Something about being in that fucking wardrobe was pouring ice into my veins. If talking to a kid was the price of getting out, I was willing to pay it.

I took a deep breath and tried to translate my question into language it may comprehend. "Why don't you just get out?"

The kid scowled ferociously at me and clamped its mouth shut.

I took a couple of deep breaths to stop myself from screaming, then tried again. "If you go out, what will happen?"

The kid folded its legs up and wrapped its spindly arms around itself. From a cuter, chubbier kid, that gesture may have looked cute. This kid was so angular and hostile that it looked like an insect folding itself up, ready to strike. It made me want to be as far from it as possible.

I looked at Frankie and shrugged. They shook their head at me and smiled at the kid.

"What Gio is trying to find out—"

The kid snapped. "I'm Gio!"

"She's Gio, too. You both are. He's you, all grown up."

The kid glowered. "When I grow up, I'm ugly?"

"No! When you grow up, you're the most beautiful person in the world, and I love you very much!"

"Why? You're pretty."

"Thank you. You're pretty, too. I think you are, anyway. And that's not what love is all about. You're kind, you're clever, and you take care of me." Their voice dropped to a murmur. "You take care of everybody. You take care of yourself the least, but you're getting better at it."

"My mom doesn't think I'm pretty."

Frankie's jaw tightened. "Then your mom is—" They stopped themself and took a couple of deep breaths. "Your mom doesn't see you right. Maybe she needs glasses. And it doesn't matter, anyway: she doesn't have to think you're pretty. Plenty of other people do."

The kid wrapped itself even tighter. "And she doesn't think I'm kind."

Frankie stretched a hand out to touch the kid's hand, but it flinched, so they pulled back. "You are. You are the kindest person I've ever met. And it's hard for you, because you're clever and you see people as they really are, so you don't like them that much. But you try to be kind to everyone who doesn't deserve unkindness. If they do, that's a whole other story.

You're kind of terrifying when you get angry. But you're fair."

The kid dropped its chin between its knees. "Getting angry is bad."

Frankie frowned. "I don't like it. But sometimes people do things that deserve our anger. And sometimes we just get angry, anyway. It doesn't mean we have to act it out."

"No. That's wrong. Getting angry is bad."

Frankie tilted their head. "Is that why you're here? You got angry?"

The kid wrapped itself so tightly that I feared it might implode. "I got mad and did a bad thing, and now everyone is mad."

"Wait. Them being angry is your fault?"

The kid went rigid for an instant, then nodded.

Frankie stared into space, their mouth agape. When they spoke, they sounded as if they were fishing their words slowly and laboriously from a deep well. "So when you get angry, it's bad, and your fault. But when they get angry, it's also your fault? That's not right."

The kid growled, "It is!"

"No. It doesn't make sense. Either getting angry is bad for everyone, or for nobody. You can't have two different rules. What are you supposed to do when you get angry?"

"Count to ten."

"And if that doesn't work?"

"Count to ten again."

Frankie mumbled under their breath, "I guess this test isn't going to be multiple choice." They pulled their mouth this way and that, deep in thought. "OK. What must you not do when you're angry?"

"Scream or say bad words or break things."

"And what are they doing?"

The kid sunk into itself. "Screaming and breaking things."

"So they are being bad."

No!" the kid screeched. "It's my fault! I made them mad!"

"You made them angry by getting angry? What made you angry?"

The kid ducked its chin between its knees again. "I was writing my name. I couldn't get it right. The lines were wobbly."

Frankie snorted. "What? How old are you?"

"Four. I'll be five next year."

"At your age, I was still sticking crayons up my nose! Writing is hard!"

The kid shrugged. "I couldn't stop until I did it right. And I tried, but the lines were wobbly, so I got mad."

"And did what?"

The kid whispered into its knees. "I threw the pencil."

"What, like, at somebody?"

"No! Away."

"That's it? You threw a pencil? That's what started all this? Dude, I threw a book at a wall so hard I made a dent in it a few weeks ago!"

The kid's eyes widened. "What happened?"

Frankie shrugged. "I felt pretty bad about it. Then I told Gio, not you, Big Gio here, and he made me a cup of tea. Then I had to go and tell Ms. Anzengruber, because it's her house and her wall. Gio would have done it for me, but that wouldn't have been fair. Ms. Anzengruber asked me if I was OK and said that maybe I needed a break. I said I'd pay to fix it. She told me not to worry, but I'll get it fixed anyway. I want to."

"She didn't get mad?"

"No. She's very kind. Almost as kind as Gio. And she knew that I hadn't meant to do it and that I was really sorry."

The kid stared at them for a while, then shook its head. "No. That's not right. If you get mad, you're bad, and then everyone gets mad, and it's your fault."

Frankie pulled their knees up to their chin. "Gio, that way you are responsible for everyone's feelings and everyone's behavior. That's not right. And anyway, you just threw a pencil. They've been screaming for a long time, and it doesn't sound like they are even trying to calm down. They are not counting to ten."

The kid looked confused. "I made them mad."

Frankie tilted their head. "Is that why you're in here? Because when you're around, they get angry?"

The kid glowered at them for a few seconds before shrugging.

"And if you stay in here, they will eventually get over it and stop screaming? But if you go out, they'll stay angry?"

The kid shrugged again.

Frankie's hand found my ankle and grabbed it tight. They took a deep breath and locked eyes with the kid. "Do you believe me? Do you believe that if I tell you something, it's because I think it's true?"

The kid stared at them for eons before nodding.

Frankie took a deep breath. "I've lived with you for half a year now, and that's a pretty long time. You're my best friend and I love you. Sometimes I get angry. At you, at something you do, or at something else entirely when you're around. But I would never, ever make you responsible for my anger. My feelings are my own, and it's up to me to manage them. And you live with me, and I know I can be really annoying at times, even though I really don't want to be. I'm messy, I lose stuff all the time, and I don't know how to do anything. I make your life chaotic. But you never, ever take it out on me. We talk about it and we try to fix it so it doesn't happen again, because we love each other and we want each other to be happy." They winced. "And also because neither of us likes raised voices. We both hate them, really. But that's what people do when they love each other: they manage their own feelings and they try to get along. That's what we try to do, anyway. And I really, really like it. It's one of my favorite things about our life together. That, and—" They blushed. "Never mind. Look, I'm sorry that you're in here having to listen to all that out there. I really am. I wish I could whisk you away and take you to our house. I can't, and that makes me really sad. Angry, too. Frustrated, like you were when you threw that pencil. But I really, really need you to understand that it's not your fault. You don't control other people's feelings. You're only responsible for your own, and for how you express them. And I promise you, one day you won't have to put up with any of this crap. One day you'll make a home around yourself, and that home will be peaceful. No shouting. No breaking stuff, unless it's an accident. And if people do something bad, they'll be able to put it right. It's going to be a long time coming, but I promise you, it's worth it. I've lived there for six months, and I hope I can live there forever."

The kids' bottom lip wobbled. "How long?"

Frankie flinched. "Fifteen years. And a whole load of crap is going to happen to you before you get there. But every day of our life together is so wonderful that it's totally worth the wait. I think it is, anyway."

"And now?"

Frankie blinked. Their eyes were awfully wet. "And now, you just need to remember that not everything is your fault, no matter what everyone says. That you making a small mistake doesn't justify someone making a bigger one."

"If I go out, they'll keep shouting."

Frankie shrugged. "Maybe. But whether you're in here or out there, their shouting is not your fault. It's something they are choosing to do. You don't control everyone else, Gio. Only yourself."

9. YOUNG CAESAR 2000

I was lying on my bed, in my bedroom, staring at the ceiling. If I squinted, the stain from the flood upstairs looked like the map of Australia. If I squinted more, I could make it look like almost anything: a coiled dragon, a mangled heart, or a spaceship that could beam me out of here. I focused and unfocused my eyes, trying to find a picture that may make the noise outside disappear, but I couldn't. My mom was wailing and my grandma was screaming, as usual. Their Greek chorus was occasionally interrupted by his baritone, but that never lasted long. They always shouted him down. They could shout anyone down.

When I spotted the guy sitting at the foot of my bed, looking at the wall as if trying to read it, I had no idea how long he'd been there. I was seeing things again; fucking great. One of these days, I'd slip and they'd find out about it. Then they'd ship me off to a hospital, and I'd never see daylight again.

Not much of a change, then. Maybe I'd be better off there. Maybe the meds would feel nice. Maybe they had a library.

The guy turned to look at me. He was really, really pretty, so pretty that I wanted to look at him forever, but I didn't want him to see me – not just to spot me staring at him, but to see me at all. His brown eyes were huge. His hair was brown, too, and stuck out in curls all over the place. It made him look untidy. His clothes looked like they'd never seen an iron. I imagined what my mom would say if I tried to leave the house looking like that, and that nearly made me smile. As if that'd make any difference.

The guy took a deep breath and murmured, "Do you know what dissociating means?"

"The fuck is that to you?"

He frowned. He still looked pretty. "I need you to dissociate right now, if you can. Go with the angels. Whatever you call it."

"You can fuck off. You don't tell me what to do."

He closed his eyes. "No. I don't. Ever. I am asking you, as a favor, if you would do that for me."

"I don't even fucking know you."

"But I know you." He leaned forward and eyeballed me so hard that I felt like he was drilling into my brain. "Every time you get in the car with your mom, you fantasize about getting in an accident, something that would give you the chance to jump out before the car got totaled and went up in flames. That way you could disappear, because they wouldn't look for you. They'd just assume you'd burned to death, and you could be free.

It wouldn't work, by the way, not unless the car got hit by a truck carrying nukes or something, because burnt corpses don't just evaporate, but that's a whole other story."

I was sitting on a bed, staring at myself. My hair was short, barely grazing my ears, and it looked thin and unhealthy. I looked thin and unhealthy. I looked frozen, too, like a rabbit in the headlights.

Frankie was sitting next to me. I leaned into them, because the horror in my eyes – my other eyes – was threatening to send me into a panic.

"Hey. What the fuck is going on?"

They found my hand and gripped it. "Do you remember what I told you about memory traps?"

My brain readjusted. "Now that you mention it, yes."

"Any idea where we are?"

"My mom's house." I looked around. "I have my own room, so I'm at least twelve. No stereo, so I'm not fourteen yet."

Frankie turned to stare at me. "You didn't have a stereo until you were fourteen?"

"Nah. No reason to: my mom had a radio."

"But you fucking hate the radio! You only listen to weird shit no station would ever play! You have a whole tape of songs about dying of dust pneumonia, for fuck's sake!"

"I didn't even know any of that existed until I went to boarding school. I was only allowed to listen to classical music. Other types of music are inferior and would pollute my ears."

Frankie blanched. "Jesus. I'm so sorry."

"You didn't do it."

Teenage Me was thawing out, if I could call it that. The frozen look was being replaced by a closed-in, reptilian, hostile stare. No wonder nobody liked me: I was a fear-biter.

I smiled at me, or tried to. "What's going on?"

"Am I dead?"

"What? No. Why?"

"I only see dead people, and you look like me, but old."

"I'm twenty, you little fuck!"

The reptilian stare didn't waver. "Yeah. That's what I said. Old."

I was just about to flip my lid when Frankie started guffawing. "This is the best thing ever! A battle of wits and sarcasm against the one opponent who's got a fair chance! My money's on the kid, though. You mellowed out in your old age."

"Don't you dare side against me!"

They wrapped their arm around my shoulders and kissed my cheek. "That's a meaningless injunction, under the circumstances."

The kid lost that shuttered look for a split second, as if under the layers of hostility there lay an actual human being. "You two are together?"

Frankie nodded. "Yeah! We've been living together for six months! And it's great!"

The kid turned towards me, looking supremely unimpressed. "No way you're me. My mom wouldn't let me live with a guy. Or anyone else. This," pointing at the noise through the wall, "Is because I wanted to go out. Not anywhere in particular, just out. For a walk."

"My mom doesn't know anything about me living with Frankie. I've not told her. I'm not planning to, either. No part of my life is her business. And if I told her, she'd only make a scene, pretend that she's ill, and try and get me to go home. So I don't tell her anything anymore."

"Doesn't she ask about it?"

"She doesn't have my number. She wrote to the university a couple of times. I threw the letters away without reading them. I knew exactly what they were going to say, anyway."

"That's a rotten thing to do."

I felt Frankie tensing up. They didn't respond well to people talking sharply at me. I put a hand on their knee to calm them down, and did my best to keep my voice steady.

"Plenty of people would say that. I think that, often enough. But I've tried everything else, for years, and nothing worked. She doesn't listen. She doesn't change."

The kid glowered at me. "She's ill."

"She is, but not the way she thinks she is, and definitely not the way she wants you to think she is. She has a thing called a personality disorder. Her doctor wants her to see a specialist for it, but she's not interested. It doesn't bother her. She's happy being unhappy, and making everyone around her unhappy, too."

"She can't help it."

I shrugged. "Maybe you're right. Maybe she couldn't, even if she tried. But that doesn't make it any easier on everyone else. It doesn't make it any easier on you."

"I'm alright."

I reached underneath the mattress and pulled out the utility knife I knew would be there. "You're not alright. You feel like shit, like you're about to crack. You *are* about to crack: you'll crack several times, in several ways, before you find a way to stop it from happening. But you will

172

get better. Right now, you feel like you have to perform all the time, to be the person she needs you to be, and that person gets more and more different from the real you with every passing day. That person is too small: you don't fit in it, and you're getting crushed. And it's not going to get better, not until you give up and leave."

"I can't just run away. The police would be after me. I couldn't live like that."

"You could, but you don't want to. I don't blame you. When you're older, you'll find a way to walk away. I know. I did it."

The kid sneered. "It won't make any difference. She won't leave me alone. She needs me. She doesn't have anyone else."

"That's because nobody else puts up with her crap for any length of time. How haven't you figured that out?"

"Shut up! She's my mom!"

"She is. And she has a personality disorder, and doesn't want to change, and you will never, ever be able to live with her and stay sane. It takes two people to compromise, and she doesn't want to. All you can do is give in until she gets everything she wants, because she'll never settle for less. And it will do neither of you any good: try as you might, you can't be the person she wants you to be. And it's totally fucked up of her to ask that of you. You don't breed children so you can shape them to be your emotional supports. That's not parenting: it's abuse."

The kid growled. "Don't talk about my mom like that!"

"OK. I won't. Look, I'm not saying that she's a bad person. I'm saying that she's doing bad things, because she's sick, and that if you try to make yourself into the person she wants you to be, you'll get sick, too. You'll get so sick that you'll end up doing bad things, really bad things, to yourself and to others, just to release the pressure. And it won't work: it'll just give you other problems and a guilty conscience."

The kid turned away from me and stared at the wall. I felt like I'd been turned off. There was a monsoon of words tumbling around my brain, words I wanted to say to try and make this right, words I wanted to wail at the stars, but there was no point: nobody was listening. Nobody ever listened.

I was spiraling off to a dark place when Frankie caught me. They leaned against me, resting their forehead against my temple, and whispered in my ear. "You never told me any of that. Not the details, anyway. I know you had problems with your mom. I didn't know she was ill like that, or that you'd cut her off."

"I didn't. Not really. I just ghosted, I guess. I don't like to talk about it. I don't like to think about it. It feels wrong."

They pulled away from me. "If what you said is right, it's the only thing you could have done."

I nodded. "I think so. I honestly do. But I don't feel so. I feel terrible about it."

"Why?"

"I wish I had a normal family, like normal people. You know, somewhere to go back home to."

Their eyes darkened. "Yeah. I get that."

"I know. But it's different for you. You had no choice. I feel like I had the chance to choose between myself and her, and I chose myself, and that's selfish."

Frankie sighed into my hair. "Gio, if you had to choose between being with me and being yourself, what would you choose?"

"What? That's not even a question!"

"Why?"

"I couldn't be with you without being myself. There wouldn't be a me to be with you. And you'd see right through it, and you'd hate it."

"Why?"

I pushed them off me so I could look at them. "Because you can spot lies. You know that. If I pretended to be someone else, you'd see it and you couldn't stand it."

"Why?"

"Frankie, you get worked up if I have a headache and I don't tell you. I don't think you'd like it if I created a whole persona to try and make you happy."

"Why?"

I loved them dearly, but I was already wound up, and four "whys" in a row was pushing the limits of my tolerance. "Because you'd find it creepy as fuck! Fake and unreal. And because you love me, and you want me to be happy. You've said it enough times, and you've shown it even more often. If I made myself unhappy in order to make you happy, that'd make you unhappy. Why are you even asking this?"

They stared at me with a question in their eyes. It took me a while to work out what it was.

"That's completely different. You're my partner. She's my mom."

"Isn't parental love supposed to be unconditional?"

"Have you ever seen that in real life? I haven't."

"Ben's parents—"

"Ben's dad fucking killed himself when Ben was still in shock over his mom's death. I would not hail him as an example of selfless parenting."

Frankie reeled. "Shit. I never thought about it like that."

"That's because you're unnaturally kind, and you understand pain. Don't get me wrong: I love you for it. But you justify Ben's dad's suicide because you know that he was grieving and frightened. You don't even think about what he did to Ben."

Frankie took a deep breath and hugged me. "You think that Ben's dad let Ben down by not prioritizing Ben's needs over his own, despite the pain he was in?"

"Yes. Sorry. I know it's harsh, but Ben was his kid, for fuck's sake."

"He's an adult."

"He was still his kid."

They stroked my face. "Let me see if I got this right. Ben's dad let Ben down by acting on his own grief instead of looking after his kid. But you let your mom down by not letting her completely obliterate your personality so she could have a lifelong mental illness buddy? What gives, Gio? Why is there always one rule for you, and one for the rest of the world?"

A million answers tumbled around my brain, clashing against each other. They spun around so fast that I didn't get a chance to look at any of them properly, but it didn't matter; the real answer sat in the middle of that maelstrom, clear as day and ugly as sin. I thought about putting it into words, and the thought sickened me.

Frankie was looking at me, though. I didn't have to talk to them about this, but, if I didn't, that'd be a barrier between us. I didn't want that.

I took a deep breath, locked eyes with them, and told them the truth. "Because that's how I got brought up: thinking that we were special and better, and anything we did that didn't tally with the rest of the world was just a sign of how special and better we were. Because my family was run like a sect, with its own set of beliefs, rules, and fail-safes against wrongthink. Because I was raised to be a victim, a tool, and even though I got out of it physically and rationally, emotionally I'm still there. I feel the way I've been programmed to feel. And it's all kinds of fucked up."

A muscle twitched in their jaw. "I hate that. Can I help you with it?"

"Yes. You can help a lot. You can tell me when I'm letting that bullshit lead me by the nose. And you can put up with me until I figure it out."

They shook their head. "No. I can't put up with you. I love you, fucked-up programming and all."

"But you'd like me to fix it."

"Yeah. Because I think it'd make you happier and healthier. But I want you to do it for you, not for me."

"I'd like to do it for us."

"Works for me. I love you so much. You're so fucking brave."

I was about to throw myself at them and kiss the living crap out of them when I remembered where we were, and with whom. I glanced at the top of the bed. The kid was watching us with a stare so blank that it looked like a death mask.

I tried to put it all into words that would make sense, but I couldn't think of any, so I stole some instead. "Heinlein said that 'Love is that condition in which the happiness of another person is essential to your own.' Frankie and I love each other. Sometimes it gets hard to tell when our individual happiness starts and ends, because they are so intertwined, and maybe that's a bit messed up, but we couldn't be happy in the knowledge of the other's unhappiness. Love wants you to live and grow, to be happy and healthy, to be the best version of yourself you could be, according to your own standards. Anything that doesn't want that isn't love. It may call itself that, but it's lying. And self-love is the same: it's about respecting your own feelings, making sure that they're being taken into account by yourself, if by nobody else. Love that demands that you forsake self-love isn't real love, either. I don't really know. I can't work it out for myself, half the time. But I know that I love Frankie, and that Frankie loves me, and that what we have is what love should be, what love really is."

Frankie squeezed me and leaned into me. My heart was melting, but I managed to keep talking.

"Frankie taught me that, even though nobody had taught them. I think they just had it in themself. And they've taught me a way to look at things, to work out whether they are OK or not. They are my litmus test for the behaviors I tolerate. If something is wrong when it's done to them, then it's wrong when it's done to me, too. I have to think like that, because I don't feel like that, yet, but it gets easier every day. I'll get there one day. I hope you do, too."

10. WHOLE WIDE WORLD

I was staring at the ceiling, a searing pain inside me. I felt his weight before I saw him, and I ran from him. I ran from it all. I was out of my body and out of that room so fast that I slammed right into Frankie.

"Get out of here! Don't look!"

They didn't budge. "What? Why?"

"I don't want you to look! I don't want you to see me like that!"

They looked over my shoulder and froze. "What the fuck?"

I pushed them out of the door and around the corner, but it was too late. They'd seen too much already. I could tell by their expression.

"Frankie, it's alright."

They stared at me blankly. "It's not. That guy is hurting you."

"He's not doing it on purpose."

"What? Gio, he's fucking hurting you! You're crying!"

"I know! But it's not like that."

"Like what?"

"I started it. I came over here. I got into bed with him. I wanted to."

"And then what?"

"It just went wrong, OK? He didn't mean it like that."

They started to shiver. "Like what, Gio? Like a rape? Because that's what it looks like."

"Don't say that!"

"Why? Because it's ugly?" They bunched up their fists. "Gio, a guy is raping you next door, and instead of getting you out of there, you're here defending him. What the fuck?"

I tried to sound calm, to talk some calm into them, even though I felt none myself. "I tried to get out, alright? He's too big, and the way he's got me... If I fight, it just hurts worse. But it wasn't meant to be like that."

"I don't give a fuck. I want to go and kick him into a pulp."

"That's not what happened. You weren't there. You cannot get me out of here like that."

Their shivering turned into shudders. "This is too much, Gio. You can't ask me to grin and bear it."

"It's over soon. And he's not hurting me on purpose."

They erupted. "Will you fucking stop saying that? He shouldn't be hurting you at all!"

They looked so bereft that I threw myself at them. I wanted to hug them, to comfort them, but they wouldn't let me. They held me off, gently but firmly.

"No. Don't make this about me. It's fucked up, Gio, and you know it. If you won't let me do anything about it, at least call it by its name."

"What good would that do?"

"What good does lying about it do? What would you do if it was me in there, getting hurt like that?"

I didn't have to think about it. "I'd kill that bastard."

"He's twice your size."

"I'd still try."

They gripped my shoulders. "Why?"

I tried to squirm away from their stare, but I couldn't. "Because nobody hurts you like that and gets away with it."

"Like what?" They stared at me, their eyes demanding an answer from me.

I couldn't give it to them. They let go of me and leaned against the wall. They slammed their head backwards into it a couple of times before I put my hand against their head. Then they closed their eyes, slipped to the floor, and sat there with their arms wrapped around their knees.

I'd not lied to them. It was over soon, though nowhere near soon enough. I watched myself stumble into the bathroom. I knew that I was going to get straight into the shower to wash it all away, and I knew that there was no point in stopping myself. I wasn't going to go to the police with this. It was my word against his. Plenty of people knew we had a thing. I started it. I'd agreed to come here. I couldn't lie about that. And if the police took me seriously, they'd tell my mom, and I couldn't have that. I was under age. She would pull me out of school, lock me in my room, and throw away the key. By the time I turned 18 and got out, I would have lost my scholarship, and I'd have nowhere to go and no prospects.

The police wouldn't take me seriously, anyway. Nobody would. They never did. It didn't matter, anyway. It had been over so quickly. It was just a thing that happened, just a shitty ten minutes of my life. It wasn't a big deal.

I looked at Frankie sitting on the floor, the very picture of anguish, and thought about what I'd do if this had happened to them. I wouldn't kill the guy. I'd want to, but I wouldn't do it, even if I had the opportunity. It would land us in a world of shit and it wouldn't really help Frankie. It particularly wouldn't help them if they thought that the whole shitshow was partly their fault.

I squatted down in front of them and kissed their forehead. "Don't worry. I've got this."

They looked up at me, their eyes enormous and wet. "What happened wasn't right. And nothing you said about it was right."

"I know."

"You do?"

"Yeah. I told you. I've got this."

They started to get up, but I pushed them down. "Can you wait here? Or go home and wait for me? I'm going to have a chat with me, and I'm probably not in a mood to see a strange guy right now."

They flinched.

I kissed them again. "It's not your fault. You're alright. It's just—"

"I get it." They nodded. "I'll be here when you want me."

"I want you all the time, love."

Their face scrunched itself up. "Right now, I can't figure out why."

I gave them a last kiss and got up.

I walked into the bathroom and saw myself sitting on the edge of the bathtub. It was like looking in a mirror, mostly. I'd not changed much in three years. My ribs didn't threaten to break through my skin anymore, my hair had grown a few inches, and I didn't look so lost. I hoped I didn't, anyway.

I'd expected my other me to freak out, but I didn't. Maybe I'd just burnt out that circuit. There was no nice way of saying what I needed to say, so I just let rip.

"You think this is your fault, but that's because you don't know shit. You don't get to hear about consent until you get to university, and by then you've built such a cathedral of excuses to cover this up that you can't put two and two together. This was a rape. I know you don't want it to be, but it was. It became a rape the moment you told him to stop and he didn't. Nothing else matters. You know this, even though you won't admit it to yourself. You wouldn't stand for anyone you love getting treated like this, and you wouldn't stand for them blaming themselves, either. The guy didn't make a mistake: he fucking raped you. If he doesn't realize that, that doesn't make it any better. Don't make excuses for him. Look after yourself; your body will heal itself soon enough, but your head and your heart will need help. Let yourself take it. You don't know this yet, but you're a person, too. Don't treat yourself worse than you would treat someone you love."

I watched the words pummel me and I felt like an asshole. Frankie would have done this so much better. They would have found the right words, and the right tone.

11. IT FROZE ME

I was in our glade, alone. It was still shimmering with moonlight. A swarm of hummingflies had alighted on a tree and was filling the night with a soft, rustling sound. Nothing else stirred, not even the breeze. In my entire life, I'd never been anywhere half as peaceful.

I braced myself for the next round of shit, but there was nobody else: just me and Frankie, their face as pale as the moonlight, their eyes as glowing. They looked somber, but I expected that, after all we'd been through. Behind them I could see our portal, kinda. The door to our room was there, clear as anything, but the curtains were drawn so I couldn't see inside. Still, I knew that our room lay just through it. All we needed to do was walk a few paces and we would be home, safe, and together.

"Frankie, is this it? It's over?"

"I think so."

I turned to run into their arms, but their expression stopped me. "What's wrong?"

"It's just..." They swallowed and stared at the ground. "That was a lot to take in."

"I know. I'm sorry."

"I can't just forget about it."

"Neither can I. But it's just shit that happened."

They shook their head. "It isn't, though. That's the issue, isn't it? If you were over it all, that whole thing wouldn't have worked. You wouldn't have gotten stuck in those memories."

"I got through it, though. I'm here now."

"Did you? Really?" They looked up at me, their eyes glowing green. "If I ask you a question, will you tell me the truth?"

"Yes. You know that."

"When we do it, do you ever think about him?"

They didn't need to explain what they meant: I got it. I hadn't expected them to ask something like that, but they had a right to.

I swallowed the lump in my throat and tried to speak normally. "Yes. But not like that. My brain just throws it up sometimes, you know? It doesn't mean anything."

They scowled. "Of course it means something. It means that I'm making love to you, and you're off somewhere else, thinking about... Fuck. Why do you do it?"

"Because I like it!"

"No. That's not what I meant. Why do you do it *to me*? Why do you put me in that position? I don't want to be that guy."

"You're not! It's nothing like that! You know that!"

"But it could be, couldn't it?" Their eyes slid off my face and started darting all over the place. "The mechanics are the same."

"The mechanics are not the issue here. Frankie, if I didn't want to make love to you a certain way, I'd tell you, and you'd stop. That's all there is to it. I'd do the same with you. We'd both do that with anyone and everyone, because we're not rapists. There is nothing wrong with what we're doing."

"You say that, but..." They sagged and dropped their eyes to the floor. "Gio, when I got with you, I knew that I was taking on a lot. But I didn't know how much."

My heart sank. It left a hole in my chest as big as the moon, and as cold as its light. "Taking on a lot?"

"Yes." They fixed their eyes on me. Even through the pain, I admired them for that: this was going to get ugly, but they were going to face it head on. "I can't do this anymore, Gio. It's just too much."

I felt the words as much as I heard them. They hit me right in the chest and shredded my insides. Even though I'd expected to hear them from the day our thing became more than a friendship, they still destroyed me. I had to handle this right, though. I had to keep myself together, for both of us. It was the only way I could rescue anything out of the situation.

It took me a couple of goes to make my throat work, but I managed to speak almost normally. "Is this something we're going to talk about, or is this it?"

They sneered. "I can't talk to you about it. You know that. You're way smarter than me. You'd talk me round to giving it another try. You needed to get out of those memory traps, right? Well, I need to get out of here, out of this. I have to look after myself."

That felt like a slap, and a slap I didn't deserve. "I've looked after you, too. We've looked after each other."

"I know. We tried. We gave it our best, but it's just not working. Or rather, it is working: it's all work, Gio. Every bit of it. It's relentless. And now I can't even make love to you without thinking about you—"

I cut them off. "Don't say it."

They snorted. "Do you see? You tell me that you're over it, but I can't even talk about it without you going off. How am I supposed to ever touch you again?"

My hands were shaking. I couldn't stop them, so I stuck them in my pockets to hold them still, and I found it: the utility knife I'd taken from my old bedroom was still in there. My hand recoiled from it at first, but I forced it to get back in there. The knife fit easily in my hand. I knew the shape of it so well. I knew what it could do: I could use it to let out some of the pain I was feeling. All I needed to do was push the catch and slide it open. I wouldn't even have to take it out; I could cut right through my pocket. It would be a new scar, a new pain, but it would hurt so much less than what Frankie was telling me right now.

I let my thumb rest on the slider and spoke through the ice in my veins. "If that's how you feel about it, you shouldn't touch me. Not until we've sorted this out."

They scoffed. "There you go again, pretending to be reasonable about it. You don't mean a word you're saying, do you?"

"I don't lie to you. You know that."

"Maybe not, but you lie to yourself all the fucking time. You're going to walk back into my house, and act like you've heard me and you've accepted what I'm saying, but then you're going to carry on as if I'd never said a damn thing. You'll look at me the same, talk to me the same. Our lives will be the same. They will still run in parallel. They will still be shitty, pathetic lives, the only difference being that we won't have each other. And in a day or in a week you'll catch me when I'm feeling sorry for myself, or for you, and you'll crawl back into my life, back into my bed, as if this wasn't still standing between us, as if this wasn't going to stand between us as long as we live. And we'll both pretend that it's OK, pretend that we can be normal, but it isn't and we can't. It's all fucked up, Gio. We can't be near each other anymore."

So I was going to lose them altogether: not just as a partner, but as a friend. Hearing that ought to have hurt, but it didn't. It didn't hurt me any worse than I was hurting already, anyway. For a moment I spaced out trying to figure out why: was it because the worst had already happened, and anything else just didn't seem to matter? Was it because they'd ripped my heart out, and I just couldn't feel anything anymore?

I got knocked out of my musings by their yelling. "Are you even listening to me?"

"Yes. I am."

"Whatever," they sputtered. "It makes no difference, anyway. I can't get away from you. You can fucking teleport to wherever I am, whenever you want. Do you realize how fucking creepy that is?"

"Frankie, I'm not going to fucking stalk you!"

"You're sure about that?"

"Of course I am!"

"You're not going to be tempted, when you're alone at night, wherever the fuck you end up? You're not going to want to check in on me, to see if I'm OK? If I'm alone?"

I thought about them lying in someone else's arms, their curls spilled all over someone else's pillow, purring in delight at someone else's lovemaking, and my heart imploded. I gritted my teeth. "Yes. I'll be tempted. But I won't do it. If I have to quit you, I'll quit you."

Their eyes bore into mine. "You talk about me as if I were a drug."

"You are, in a way, but it doesn't matter. If you want me out of your life, I'll get out of it."

They crossed their arms over their chest. "Prove it, then."

"How the fuck can I prove that I won't do something in the future?"

"Stay here."

"I beg your pardon?"

They shrugged. "You like it here. You like it way better than back home. You've said that plenty of times. So let me go, and stay here. Close that fucking portal and let me get on with my life."

That didn't make any sense. Everything they'd said up to this point had made sense, even though it really hurt, but this didn't. "Frankie, Earth is big. I think there's enough room for the both of us."

They smirked. "Sure. You can teleport to wherever the fuck I am whenever the fuck you want, but Earth is big. Sure thing. You know what? It doesn't matter. Do whatever the fuck you want, like you always do. Go through. I'll stay here. Get Marin to seal it up tight when you're on the other side, and have a nice life."

"That's ridiculous! You have a life out there!"

They eyeballed me, their mouth misshapen by fury. "I do. A life I want to live without you, but you won't let me. If you had a shred of decency..."

They carried on screaming, but I'd stop listening.

I knew that I didn't know much about anything. I was bad at navigating life, I didn't understand people, and I barely knew myself. But there was one thing I knew for sure: Frankie did not do emotional blackmail. They never had, and they never would. They'd grown up with it and they despised it with every fiber of their being. They'd rather smack me in the face; it'd be more honest, and cleaner.

I turned my feelings down and made myself think. Frankie's entire performance didn't quite fit. Even at their most distraught, I'd never seen them lash out at anyone like that. I'd never seen them throw ultimatums around. They'd never been resentful of my past lovers, even the ones I had a lot of fun with. While what they were saying made some sense, it didn't make sense coming from them. And, throughout their little diatribe, they'd not said sorry, not even once.

I looked into their eyes. They were still glowing green. That clinched it.

I forced my face into stillness while I thought the situation through. There were three main possibilities: I was stuck in a made-up reality, and no part of this was real; that really was Frankie, and they'd been spelled into acting completely out of character; or that was someone else, pretending to be Frankie.

I was almost sure that Jacob was behind this. He could be the guy pretending to be Frankie: he could look like anyone he wanted, and he was the sort who might enjoy watching me crumble. My pervdar ought to have picked up on that, but I was all over the place, so maybe it had gone offline. My brain definitely had. It didn't matter, anyway: I would have bet my life that I was dealing with Jacob, but I wasn't willing to bet Frankie's. I needed to get out of here without hurting them. I needed to try and get them out of here, too; if they were Frankie and they'd been spelled into actually believing the crap they were spewing, they would need help from someone who knew how to fix that kind of shit. Marin might be able to do that, or he might know someone who did. I sure as fuck didn't.

They were still spewing venom at me, charging back and forth around the glade in fury and disgust. Every now and then they'd step between me and the portal. They were either standing between here and my home, or they were my home. Only one way to find out.

The next time they stepped in front of the portal, I 'ported to them. I tried to, anyway.

12. BLUEBERRY FROST

I was in our bedroom, lying on the floor. My head was resting in Frankie's lap. I looked up at them and tried to make sense of what I was seeing, but I couldn't, and it wasn't just because their features were upside down. They were wearing an expression that didn't fit their face, as if it was taking them every ounce of strength not to cry. Uncle Marin and Ms. Anzengruber were standing over us. Marin was talking to Frankie, or *at* them: they were clearly in no fit state to talk, but that asshole just couldn't leave them the fuck alone. Ms. Anzengruber was stroking his arm, but he wasn't paying any attention to her.

Under normal circumstances, that scene would have upset me, I was sure of it. I looked all around inside myself for the appropriate sad feeling, but I just couldn't find it. I was all out of sad, but I had a lot of angry, so that was what I felt instead: an all-encompassing anger – no, a rage – filling me up, taking me over. It was red, hot, loud, and strong. Much stronger than me. Bigger, too.

"Frankie?"

They looked down at me through red-rimmed eyes as if I were some kind of divine apparition. "Gio! I waited for you, and then that place just disappeared around me, and I ended up back here, but you didn't come! I couldn't find you anywhere!"

"I'm alright. I need to talk to you." I sat up, even though it made me want to throw up, and nodded to Marin and Ms. Anzengruber. "I'm fine now. Thank you. You will have to excuse us."

Marin put his hands on his hips. "Listen now—"

"No. I need to talk to Frankie. In private. *You will have to excuse us.*"

Marin took in a breath to fuel his next rant, while Ms. Anzengruber tugged at his sleeve and murmured at him. Neither of them moved a fucking inch. Alright, then.

I took a deep breath, and when I spoke my voice rattled the rafters. *"Get out of my room. Now."*

Marin slid backwards. He didn't walk backwards; he slid along the floor, as if a current was sweeping him away. In the blink of an eye, he was out the door. Ms. Anzengruber stood frozen in place for a few seconds before shaking herself off and walking unsteadily out the door. She pulled it shut behind her with a fearful glance at us. I filed that among the things I'd have to worry about later, and slapped a circle of protection around the room. I knew that I couldn't, not without actually drawing a circle, but I didn't care about the rules anymore, so I did it anyway. I felt the circle snap around us, leaving just me and Frankie in our room, in our home, safe and alone together.

Frankie was still staring at me, their huge eyes marred by unshed tears. "Gio, what the fuck did you just do?"

"Don't worry about it. We can deal with that later. Frankie, I love you very much. You know that, right?"

Their bottom lip trembled. "Yes. But?"

"But I have to tell you something and you're not going to like it."

"You're breaking up with me. Of course you are. This is all my fault."

"No! This isn't your fault, and I'm not breaking up with you." I leaned close to them and did my level best to look straight at them. "Sometimes, when we're making love, I think about that guy. I don't want to. I just get flashbacks. I can't do anything about it."

Their eyes opened and released a flood of tears. "Gio, I never... I'm so sorry! Is it something I do? I don't want to... You've got to tell me what it is! I don't want it to be like that! Not ever! I'm so sorry!"

I threw myself at them and hugged them. "You're alright. We're alright. I'm sorry. I had to tell you. I had to see what you'd say."

They disentangled themself from me with a horrified expression. "What? But it's true! You didn't make that up!"

"No! I wouldn't do something like that. I just had to check that you were you. Frankie, when I got out of that place, I got waylaid."

I told them about the glade, and "our" conversation. Then I told them the whole thing again, because they asked me to. They wanted to know everything their lookalike had said to me, in detail.

By the time I was done, their tears had dried up, and they were so angry that they'd gone cold.

"That's it. I'm going to kill that fucker."

"Please, don't. I don't need this right now. I need you to calm down."

"I'm calm."

"No, you're not. Your eyes are fucking glowing. Frankie, I need you not to flip out and do magic right now."

"Why not? You just did." Their voice resonated oddly, as if it was developing its own echo.

"Because you're not thinking straight. And, before you scream at me, neither am I. But you can't just have a go at Jacob."

Every trace of Frankie's supernatural bullshit vanished and was replaced with pure rage. "He fucking kidnapped you! He put you through hell! He tried to split us up! And you want me to sit here, being calm?"

"No. I want you not to do anything that's going to make things worse. I want you to help me think of a way out, because not a single one of my ideas has fucking worked, and I'm getting desperate. And I want you to fucking hold me, because I just can't deal with this anymore. Too much, Frankie. It's just too fucking much."

Their arms were around me in nanoseconds. As they held me, they murmured into my hair, "I'm sorry. Just tell me what to do, Gio, because I have to do something. I can't just let this carry on."

My body was shaking and I couldn't stop it. "I don't know. I just don't know. I don't even know what the hell he wants anymore, whether he is still after you or he's just enjoying fucking with us so much that he just won't quit. We have to stop him, Frankie. We can't let this get any worse."

They let their head lean against mine. "Can it? What could he have done that would have been worse than this?"

"He could have done it to you."

They started shuddering and their eyes unleashed a flood. They tried to move away from me, but I didn't let them.

"You're OK, love. It's OK."

"It's not. Don't look at me."

"Don't be silly. I've cried in front of you a million times. And don't try and tell me that it's different, because it really isn't."

They sucked up a ton of snot. "Of course it is. You're braver than me."

"Bullshit. Let it flow, love. It'll make you feel better."

"When?" they wailed.

"When it's over."

They rubbed their eyes. It was pointless, because they were still streaming, but I guess it gave their hands something to do. "I don't want Uncle Marin to see me like this."

"He won't. I'll talk to him."

"I should be doing that. I should be looking after you."

"What the hell do you think you're doing right now?"

"He'll want to know about that magic shit you just pulled."

"I'm sure he will, but I don't have anything to say about it. I'll tell them I had a pre-made circle or something."

"You didn't?"

"Nope."

"How did you do that, then?"

"I don't know. And, right now, I don't care. I'm going to go and tell them that I'm not well and I don't want to talk to them, and then I'm going to come back here and I'm going to hug you until you force me to let you go."

They wiped their face with their sleeve. "Then you'll be here for the rest of your remaining days."

"Suits me fine. Though I suspect you'll need a toilet break, by and by."

They shrugged. "I can piss out the patio door."

"Can you shit out of there, too?"

"Give me a couple of hours and I'll give it a go."

I kissed their forehead and went out the door. I apologized to Ms. Anzengruber and told Marin that we could talk in the morning, or never. Then I walked back into my room and spent the whole night making good on my promise to Frankie.

13. TALLAHASSEE

Frankie and I spent all night holding each other, and not just because it was pleasant. The events of the last few weeks had frazzled us and the previous day's little adventure had finally tipped us both over the edge. We were both trying to keep our shit together and failing. Every now and then, one of us would lose it and flip out completely. Frankie kept exploding in a righteous rage. They were totally justified, I knew it, but I just couldn't let them indulge in it. I couldn't risk them doing something hasty and getting in the shit for it.

My reactions were infinitely less appropriate, and totally inconsistent. I oscillated between being overwhelmed by abject panic, being incapable of feeling or thinking anything at all, and revisiting one of the feelings that my little trip down Memory Lane had kicked up. I was a total mess, and I knew that my emotional instability was feeding Frankie's, but I couldn't do a damn thing about it. We couldn't calm ourselves down, so we focused on comforting each other instead, on letting our bodies and our voices communicate a sense of safety we didn't really feel. It mostly worked; we made it through the night together and without doing anything rash, but we didn't get any damn sleep.

When dawn jabbed her fingertips of rose into our eyeballs, we were both exhausted. I knew that I ought to get up and face the day ahead, but I just couldn't. All I wanted to do was hide under our blanket with Frankie and pretend that the world outside didn't exist, that it had disappeared overnight and left us alone and safe. I knew that it was bullshit, but it was bullshit so comforting that I let myself fall for it. I should have known that it was a mistake. By the time my bladder forced me to get up, the world had moved on without us.

We found the note on the garage door when we ventured out for food. "Please, come upstairs. We need to talk. It's urgent."

Frankie literally growled when they read it. "That's it. I'm going to tell Uncle Marin to fuck off, and I shall mean it."

"This isn't from him. It's from Ms. Anzengruber."

"How do you know?"

"I recognize her handwriting, and she didn't actually get into our house to put it up. Marin would have barged into our bedroom and stapled it to our foreheads."

"I'm still going to tell him to fuck off."

"Love, I don't think we can afford to do that. I hate to say it, but you were right. I think he wants to help us, and we probably need him."

Frankie's face sunk. "You're right. I can't protect you. That's painfully obvious. Gio, you should consider—"

"No!"

"You won't even listen to me?"

"Not when you're talking trash! I'm not leaving you!"

They sagged. "Fine. Then we better see what Uncle Marin can suggest, because I'm all out of ideas."

I made myself climb up the stairs, and they dragged themself up behind me. When we got to the door, I checked on them. They looked fucking awful, but determined. When I hesitated, they shook their head.

"I am not going to tell you what to do, but I'm going to ask Uncle Marin for help. For me, if not for you. I can't live like this."

They sounded so desperate that I swallowed my misgivings and knocked on Ms. Anzengruber's door. I knew exactly what was going to happen: Marin would bellow at us, I'd bellow back, Ms. Anzengruber would pat our arms to calm us down, and Frankie would be in the middle of it all, getting walloped by everyone's emotions. Eventually, if we were lucky, something may actually get done. We had to go through it, though, because Frankie wanted to. I owed them that much.

When Marin opened the door, looking grave but calm, I started to get the inkling that my predictions were way out of whack. Ms. Anzengruber was nowhere in sight. He directed us towards the couch, as if we'd forgotten where it was located, and we all sat down. When he spoke, his voice was eerily quiet.

"Gio, Cynthia would like to talk to you. She wants to talk to both of you, but not right now. She's not well."

My stomach clenched. "What's wrong?"

"What do you think? She saw you in a coma. She didn't know if you were going to make it. She found out that you've been in serious danger for weeks and neither of you saw fit to tell her about it. She watched you work magic right under her nose. She's an open-minded woman, and she's used to kids fucking up, but—"

"Is she going to throw us out?"

He growled, "No! She wants to make sure that you're alright! She wants to talk sense into you, which is a pointless waste of her time as you're clearly a total idiot. I'd thought better of you, I don't know why. Worse than that, she wants me to make you safe."

Frankie straightened up. "Can you do that?"

"Yes and no. I can't do it on my own."

"But you can get us help?"

"Possibly. My people have rules about this kind of thing. By reporting the situation—"

"Do it."

I grabbed their hand. "Shouldn't we discuss this? And we should definitely find out what may happen if we go for it."

"Should we? What are we going to do, Gio, wait for the next instalment? This is way out of control. If Uncle Marin can fix it, let him."

"I want to know—"

"I want to know you're safe. How do you not get that?" They were panting hard, as if they'd run a marathon.

"Look, I'm not saying no, OK? I just think we need to find out more about it before we go ahead with it."

They erupted. "What's the point? We have no alternative!"

I was trying to calm down enough to answer them without screaming in their face when Ms. Anzengruber's voice crept down the hallway.

"Gio?"

Marin grumbled, "Now you woke her up. Go see her."

I didn't want to leave Frankie like that, all wrapped up in their anger and fear, but they nodded at me to go. Judging by the set of their jaw, there was no talking to them for a bit, anyway.

I tiptoed into her bedroom. I'd only been in there once since we had cleared it out after the fire, and that seemed a million years ago. I knew she'd bought stuff to decorate it since, because Frankie had helped her carry it upstairs. I had wasted a bit of time fantasizing about what it might look like. Ms. Anzengruber was like a dragon, fierce and powerful, but she was also neat and graceful. She liked peace, quiet, and order, but she also liked to blast Black Sabbath as loud as her car stereo would allow. At work, she cut an imposing figure, which was quite a feat as she was tiny. At home, she'd taken the three of us in like a mother hen. She was one of my favorite people in the whole world, but I couldn't quite fathom her. Whenever I thought about her inner sanctum, my brain threw out a jumble of conflicting images – satin, polished oak, metals – and I could never settle on anything. I had forgotten the most important thing about her: she never failed to surprise me.

The curtains were drawn, but that didn't make the room gloomy. I didn't think anything could achieve that. She'd painted the walls a pale green, like the color of buds in the spring. All the woodwork was white.

The curtains and comforter were patterned with tiny flowers and leaves. A big bunch of flowers sat on a chest of drawers. It all combined to make the room beautiful, fresh, relaxing, cute, and profoundly unlike what I'd pictured.

That was weird enough, but there was more. Frankie and I were both conflicted about Ms. Anzengruber's relationship with Marin. We didn't talk about it much, mostly because it gave us a serious case of the creeps, but we generally pretended that the two of them were friends. Friends who occasionally screamed the house down. Friends who spent almost every night together, but that was just what good friends did. We spent most of our evenings with Ben, after all, and it didn't mean anything.

I had to abandon that illusion, because Ms. Anzengruber's bedroom was obviously *their* bedroom, and half the room was unequivocally *his*. Her clothes were out of sight, while his were thrown over and under a chair. Her nightstand held one book and her glasses, while his was heaped with weeks' worth of the crap one finds in one's pockets at the end of the day. Above her nightstand hung a bunch of framed cross-stitch pictures of tiny animals wearing Victorian clothing, while his side of the wall was bare. They lived together, same as Frankie and I, but they had clearly found a way to do so without compromising. Maybe that was the compromise: that they'd let each other make themselves at home, even though their idea of what "home" looked like was completely different. Maybe their idea of home was a place where people could be themselves.

Thinking that put a lump in my throat. Spotting Ms. Anzengruber's face, nearly as pale as her pillow, made the lump treble in size.

"I'm so sorry."

She stirred. "What are you sorry about, dear?"

"Everything."

"A fine sentiment, but not terribly informative."

"I'm sorry things got out of hand like that. I didn't mean to worry you."

"I'm assuming this is why you didn't tell me what was going on."

"Yes. Though there were other reasons, too. I was trying to keep Frankie out of it. I don't know what I was thinking."

"I'm not sure that you were thinking at all. You're much smarter than that, and I've never doubted your instinct for self-preservation."

I forced the words out of my throat. "Do you think you can forgive me?"

"I already have. I am still extremely angry at you, and I still want to let you know exactly what I think of your actions, but I'm too tired to do it right now. Have you spoken to Marin about it yet?"

"Kinda. Frankie wants to get him to ask his people for help."

"And you?"

"And I'd like to know what that's going to cost us before we go for it."

Her voice dropped to a whisper. "Because, naturally, there would be a cost. Gio, I wish I could meet your parents."

That surprised me so much that it made my head spin. "I only have the one, and I don't think you two would get on."

"Getting on with them was not the purpose behind my wish. Let Marin help. He is going frantic with worry. He believes he is to blame for this."

"What? Why?"

"Because, like most of us, he'd rather feel guilty than powerless. He would prefer it if this was something he has done and he can undo, rather than admit that there are forces at play utterly outside of his control. I would probably find it excruciatingly annoying, were I not so prone to doing the exact same thing." She sighed. "Let him help you, if he can. I would ask you to do it for me, but I'm sure you've had enough of that kind of request to last you a lifetime. Let him help you, because it's the smart thing to do. Unless you have other options."

"Nah. We're all out."

"There you go." She sunk into her pillow. "Now, if you don't mind, I am going to have a rest. But, before you go, let me make something very clear: if you ever do anything like this again, I will personally make sure that the rest of your life is a living hell."

I knew she meant it, and that was terrifying, but I also thought I knew *why* she meant it, and that made me feel so good that I felt bad. My insides were getting all mixed up again, and I felt suddenly exhausted.

"Thank you."

She snorted. "You are very welcome."

I was halfway through the door when she piped up.

"Gio? How are you feeling?"

"OK, I think. I'm not sure."

As I said it, I realized that I meant it. I was tired, scared, and worried, but all those feelings felt far away. My head felt oddly empty and my body oddly light. That got me even more confused, so I walked out of her bedroom feeling mildly seasick.

Frankie looked up at me with a beatific expression. It shouldn't have terrified me, but it did.

"What's going on?"

"It doesn't matter, Gio. We don't have to argue. We don't have to do a damn thing. He's already done it."

"Say what?"

"Uncle Marin. He's already told his people. There's nothing we can do about it. Whatever is going to happen is going to happen."

"Huh." I looked at Marin. He looked distinctly uncomfortable, but defiant. I briefly considered having an argument with him, but I didn't have the energy. I turned back to Frankie. "You want pancakes?"

"Yeah. What are we celebrating?"

"The fact that we can have pancakes."

"Sounds good to me."

We walked downstairs with our arms linked, even though the staircase was way too narrow. When we got to the garage, we found ourselves in one of those rare moments of perfect synchrony, when it felt as if we were one person with two bodies, working towards a single goal with no need for words. It usually only happened when we were having sex, so it felt really special. We made pancakes together, ate them sitting side by side in companionable silence, and then plopped ourselves on the couch.

With my belly full and my head resting on Frankie's shoulder, I was perfectly comfortable, but something was missing.

I sighed, "It's sunny outside."

Frankie rested their head on mine. "It'd be sunny in here if I opened the doors."

"There's a metric ton of crap in front of them."

"I could shift it."

"That's a damn fine idea, but it involves getting up. Give me five minutes, alright?" I slid sideways, nestled my head on their lap, and closed my eyes for a moment.

When I opened them again, it took me a moment to work out what I was seeing – or, rather, why I couldn't see a damn thing. "Why is it so dark?"

Frankie stroked my hair and murmured, "Because it's very late."

"What?"

"You've had a long nap. It's past your bedtime."

"Why didn't you wake me up?"

"Because you were asleep, silly."

"And you've been there all the while?"

"Yup. I wouldn't have missed it for the world. You're beautiful when you sleep. And I got to watch all kinds of crap without you complaining." They bent down to kiss my forehead. "Would you like something to eat before we go to bed?"

"I have no idea."

They dragged me upright, made me eat a sandwich, and walked me to our bedroom via the toilet. I felt light and heavy, alert and disconnected, rested and tired. More than anything, I felt still, as if the part of my brain that normally dealt with most of my thoughts and worries had gone offline. It wasn't unpleasant, but it was weird. I didn't have the capacity to worry about that, though.

Frankie and I lay on our bed, wrapped around each other. I wished for the moon to rise, so I could see them properly. I took a deep breath, so I could fill my nostrils with their smell, and closed my eyes.

When I opened them again, the sunlight made me blink.

"Don't tell me. I fell asleep again?"

Frankie put their book down and smiled at me, more dazzling than any sunrise. "Yup. You slept like a log. A beautiful log."

"I love you. Hey, is it Sunday?"

"Yup. Sunday morning. You know what that means?" They slipped under the covers, right next to me.

"Yeah." I nuzzled their neck. "You taste so good." I closed my eyes, so I could focus on the feeling of their skin against mine.

When I opened them again, Frankie was sitting up next to me, writing furiously in their notebook.

"Whatcha doing?"

They turned and smiled. "Hey. Welcome back. There's a milkshake on your nightstand."

"Why?"

"Because you need liquids and nutrients. Up you get. Drink up."

I was halfway through the glass when a thought lit up my head. "Do you think I'm a bad person for cutting my mom off?"

They blinked. "What? No. From everything you've said, she didn't give you any other options. She doesn't sound like the kind of person who understands boundaries."

"But she tried to be a good mom. I was drowning in toys. And she only hit me once in my entire life."

They took the glass from my hands. "Wenchlad, that's quite a salad you're tossing. Buying you toys doesn't make her a good mom, and not hitting your kids is a pretty low bar for good parenting."

"Most of the kids got hit where I grew up."

Their eyes darkened. "Yeah. There's a load of that around. But it's not enough to make your mom a good parent."

"But your dad..."

A muscle jumped in their jaw. "My dad has anger management issues. It seems to run in the family."

"You're not like that."

"I get angry way more than I'd like."

"Exactly. And you don't use that as an excuse to take it out on people."

They blinked. "No. But it still scares the fuck out of me."

"That's because you're wonderful. I'm so glad you love me."

A really goofy smile spread on their face. "I'm glad I love you, too. And I'm really glad you love me back."

"This is so nice. Being with you is the best thing ever." I snuggled down next to them, resting my head on their lap. They stroked my hair.

I blinked. The room was bathed in a pale glow. "What time is it?"

"Dinner time. Do you need a pee?"

"Yeah." I sat up, wobbling a little.

Frankie put their arm behind my back. "How are you feeling?"

"My head is full of whispers."

"Is that a bad thing?"

"I don't know, but it's a thing."

They escorted me to the bathroom. After doing what I needed to do, I washed my face. Looking up into the mirror, I got stuck.

"I look weird. Don't you think I look weird?"

They wrapped themselves against my back and kissed my cheek. "No. I think you look beautiful. But I might be biased, because I love you."

"You do, don't you? Even after all that's happened."

They nodded. "Yeah. I just hope it stops happening."

"No, I don't mean that. I mean what happened before. To me."

Their breath caught. "I love you. I hate some of the things that happened to you, but you're the best person who ever lived. That's why I want to be with you forever and ever."

"I wish I could make it all unhappen."

"I don't. I thought I did, but then you wouldn't be you."

"But I could be better."

"No. You couldn't. There's nothing better than you. You know what I really, really want? A chance to be bored with you. I mean, not bored *at* you; just to be together, me and you, having a chance to be bored."

I looked at their eyes in the mirror, and I felt as if I could see all the way into their soul. They weren't trying to hide anything, and everything about them was beautiful. The tears started dropping out of my eyes before I could stop them.

"You really love me."

"Of course I do. You're really lovely." They let off a huge sigh. "Come on, Homeslice. This is super extra nice, but we really need to get some food into you before I get distracted."

"Homeslice?"

"Yeah. I can't call you Wenchlad forever."

"Why not?"

"It scares the tourists."

They made me eat a sandwich. I found it hard to chew, because they were so fucking radiant that all I wanted to do was look at them. They didn't seem to mind, although they blushed a lot. When I was done eating, they escorted me back to our bedroom, where I put my foot down.

"Frankie, I flatly refused to lie down."

They raised an eyebrow at me. "Was that pun intentional?"

"What pun?"

"Thank the gods! I thought I might have to dump you. Why can't you just make yourself comfy?"

"I don't want to go back to sleep."

"Why not?"

"Because you're unbelievably pretty, and I want to look at you."

They blushed again. "How about this: we go to bed, and you can look at me, but if you feel sleepy you can just close your eyes and see what happens. I'll be here when you wake up."

"You will?"

"Absolutely. I love you a whole lot. Are you feeling alright?"

"Yeah. I love you so fucking much."

They ran a finger along my cheek. "I have an idea. Get into bed quick, and I'll show you."

"Where are you going?"

"Garage. Won't be a minute."

I started counting. They raced out the room and were back before I got to forty. After I snuggled next to them, they showed me a book.

"Here you go. I bet you haven't read this."

"Winnie-the-Pooh? From the cartoon?"

They gasped. "You poor, deprived child! Prepare to be astonished."

They rested a hand on my shoulder, cleared their throat, and started reading aloud, quietly but clearly. About a minute into it, I was entranced. They must have noticed, because they stopped.

"You like it?"

"Yes! Can you read some more? Pretty please?"

"Yes, if you close your eyes. You'll picture it better."

"But I won't be able to look at you."

"You can look at me later. Go on."

I closed my eyes. I knew what they were trying to do, but it wasn't going to work: I'd had tons of sleep, and I wanted to hear the story.

When I opened my eyes again, the room was bright. Frankie was sitting up, sipping a hot drink and reading. They were so focused on their book that they didn't notice that I was awake until I snuggled up to them.

They stroked the hair off my face. "Hey."

"Hey, you. We must stop meeting like this."

"I don't think so. Meeting like this is one of my favorite things."

"What time is it?"

"Time we got some breakfast. You hardly ate yesterday."

"No, seriously."

"I'm not sure. About mid-morning."

I sat up so fast I made myself dizzy. "What? But today is Monday! I have school! You have work!"

They rubbed my back. "Nah. I got up, told Marin I wasn't going in, and came back to bed. And you were in no fit state to go to class. You needed to rest. You've been through a lot."

"I feel fine!"

"You slept two days and two nights almost continuously, and the alarm clock didn't wake you up. You needed to rest, and I needed to watch you resting." Their voice quivered towards the end of that sentence.

I slid closer to them and hugged them. "I get that. But–"

"No buts, please. I think we need a day off. Don't you?"

"Maybe. But—"

They gave me A Look, so I swallowed the rest of the sentence. As a reward, they gave me a kiss.

"What do you want first? Food, shower, sex?"

"What if I want all three?"

"At the same time? Doable, but tricky, and potentially very messy."

I tried to get up and managed it on the second try. Frankie half hugged me and half held me up. When they were confident that I was stable, they gave me a long, slow kiss.

"How are you feeling?"

I ran a quick internal scan. "Empty. Still. My bladder is about to burst."

"I'd call that full, not empty."

"Empty head. Full bladder."

"Huh. We should probably turn that around."

"You want to fill my head with pee?"

"Not quite that. Come on, Homeslice. Pee, food, and then we'll see."

After I'd taken the longest pee of my life, they sat me down at our table and started bustling around our kitchen. They were so beautiful that I couldn't stop looking at them. Every time they caught my eye, they'd smile and blush, and that made them look even more beautiful. It was only when they'd put a heap of toast and eggs under my nose that I realized that I was ravenous. The more I ate, the happier they looked, so I filled myself right up. I washed it all down with a cup of the best coffee anyone had ever had: it was the cheapest instant coffee we could find, but it had been made by Frankie.

When I put my cup down, they picked up my hand and weaved their fingers into mine. "How are you doing?"

"OK, I think. I think I needed to just switch off for a while. Give my brain time to install some updates, or something."

"Are you going to be OK catching up with school?"

"I think so. Maybe I'll go in this afternoon."

They glared at me. "Maybe you won't."

"Maybe you're right."

"I'm really sorry all of that happened. You know that, right?"

"Yes. I know that better than I know most things. But it's alright now. It's over."

"Marin still hasn't heard back."

"Either he will, or he won't. We'll deal with that when it happens. We've dealt with everything else."

They squeezed my hand. "What's up with you? You're being awfully optimistic for a Monday."

"I feel good, love. I think I really needed a rest."

"No shit. I've been telling you that for months."

"Yeah, well, there never seemed to be time for it."

They locked eyes with me and spoke slowly, enunciating every syllable. "Gio, when you're running around so much that you can't find the time to take a break, that's one of those things we call 'clues.'"

"Oh, yeah?"

"Yeah. It should inform you as to your need for a fucking break."

"Nah, that can't be right. Next thing, you'll be telling me that I need to eat when I'm hungry, or some suchlike shit."

"Now that you mention it—"

"Alright. I give up. Maybe you're a little bit right, OK? I don't know what it is, but right now I feel as if I could walk out of here and straight into a normal life. Does that make any sense?"

"I think so." They rubbed my fingers with their thumb. "I'm sorry."

"Why?"

"Because our life isn't anything like normal."

"That's not what I meant, but yes, it's not. But we can be normal within it. Healthy. Sane. Happy, even."

"I'm not sure how normal happiness is. It seems rare enough."

I pulled their hand towards me and kissed it. "Stop arguing. I feel good, Frankie. Like I'm balancing on something solid, instead of struggling to stay upright on a unicycle."

They took a deep breath. "OK. That's a big deal. And it's a new thing?"

"Yes. I never felt this way before. I didn't think I could."

They smiled, but their eyes tightened at the edges in that expression I'd learned to read as abject fear. "I'm glad for you. I really am."

"But?"

Their fear went up a notch. "No. No buts. I'm happy for you. I'll do my best not to fuck it up, OK? My absolute best."

"Love, what are you on about?"

"It's just... I don't feel like that. I still feel fucked up, and our life still seems fucked up, but you are feeling good and I don't want to fuck that up for you. I'll do my best. I promise you that."

I got up, walked around the table, and pulled them up so I could hug them. They hugged me back, but they were rigid, vibrating faintly with barely-contained tension.

"Frankie, you've got that all wrong. You're not part of the problem: you're the best part of the solution. You're the main reason I feel good. I know that. I wish you knew it, too."

They shuddered a couple of times. "I just want everything to be perfect for you."

"I don't. Perfection is so hard to get that it fucks up everything else in the process. Good enough is good enough."

A little smile crept on their lips. "And I'm good enough for you?"

"No. You're more than I could ever deserve. You're my moon and stars. You make the world better just by being in it. And I love you."

"You say that as if it were a secondary thing."

"It is, kinda. You'd be just as wonderful regardless."

They smiled and blushed. A few moments later, they melted into me. "I'm so glad you feel better. So glad. I'm sorry I need so much from you—"

"What? Where the hell is that coming from? You've been looking after me for days, while I've been Sleeping Beautying!"

"Oddly enough, you don't take much looking after while you sleep."

"And I'm sure that listening to me snore for two days must have been fascinating to you, and that you had nothing better to do."

"Yeah. Absolutely every part of that is entirely correct. You still don't get me, do you?"

"Nope. But I've got you, and that's good enough for me. Wanna go to bed?"

They frowned. "Are you feeling tired again?"

"Not in the least."

They bit their bottom lip. "Are you saying what I think you're saying?"

"You'll have to find out."

We were basking in the glow of each other's love when the front door opened. We weren't expecting anyone, so we both went rigid. Frankie jumped out of bed first. Instead of putting clothes on, they picked up a crowbar from under our bed. It was an addition to our home décor I was unfamiliar with.

"Frankie, what the hell? What are you doing?"

They stood by the door. "Stay behind me. If things go screwy, open the portal, get the fuck out, and shut it behind you."

"No way. If things go screwy, I'm staying with you."

They turned around to glare at me. "Which part of staying safe is causing you problems?"

"The part where I stay safe when you're not." I threw on their t-shirt and picked up the most threatening item I could see. I wasn't too sure about the martial applications of a large hardback, but I'd give it all I had.

Heavy steps came down the hallway, closer and closer to our room. When they stopped, Frankie braced themself and yanked our door open.

A horrified scream tore the silence. "Jesus!"

"Ben?"

I walked towards the door and, sure enough, Ben was standing in the middle of the hallway, clutching at his chest and staring at the ceiling.

"Holy shit, Frankie! I'm glad to see you, but I wish I wasn't seeing so much of you."

"What?"

"Put some fucking clothes on, man!"

"Oh, that. Sorry. I thought we were having a break-in."

"And what were you going to do, beat them to death with your dick? Why are you even here? Shouldn't you be at work? What's going on?"

"We've had a few minor issues." They stepped back into our room and we threw our clothes on while they gave Ben a quick summary of the last few days' adventures. When we were dressed, Frankie opened the door.

Ben stood in the middle of the hallway, looking stunned. "I wasn't here."

Frankie rolled their eyes. "Of course you weren't. You needed to be home. How's your sister?"

Ben winced. "Pregnant."

"What? But didn't she have a baby like two minutes ago?"

"Two months, but yes."

"Haven't they discovered condoms yet in Aroostook County?"

Ben glared at them. "We do. However, as my sister had her tubes tied after her last cesarean, she didn't deem them a necessity."

Frankie blushed. "Oh. Shit. Sorry."

"Yes. It was all a bit of a surprise for them. James took it badly."

"Is he OK?"

"Yes. He just went off because he was freaking out, and he didn't come back when he was supposed to. They found him in his truck, sleeping it off. My sister may have stopped yelling at him by now. We both respond badly to sudden disappearances, you know? Family history and shit."

Frankie's shoulders slumped. "Yeah. Shit. What are they going to do?"

"I don't know," sighed Ben. "It's not safe for her to have more babies, hence the whole tube-tying business. James is very sorry about, you know, everything. But they'll be alright. They've been together forever. They'll work something out."

"What are you going to do?"

"Nothing much I can do. They've asked if I can go visit before term starts so they can have some time without the kids. I said I'd have to see if I can. You know, with the shit going on here—"

"You still have to take care of your family."

"But—"

"No! Priorities, man!"

Ben glanced at me with an odd expression, then shrugged. "Alright. What are you going to do?"

"About Jacob? Nothing much we can do. We're waiting to see what Uncle Marin's lot come up with."

"Do you mind doing that with your clothes on?"

"I'll do my best."

We went forth to the garage. Ben cooked lunch, we ate together, and then Frankie and Ben fought a vicious duel to gain control of the VCR –

best of three on a twenty-sided dice. Ben won two out of three throws, but he lost overall on points, and he felt the unfairness so keenly that he ended up picking 'Amélie,' which was what Frankie had wanted to watch in the first place. Frankie, in turn, had only picked that because they were trying to cheer me up. I was still feeling way too spacey to watch anything at all, let alone a movie with subtitles, so this sequence of misdirected selflessness resulted in the three of us sitting in front of something none of us wanted to watch. It was ludicrous, but it still made me feel all squiggly inside, because it reminded me that I was surrounded by the sweetest people on earth. We were a bunch of fuck-ups, but we tried to be good to each other, and that mattered. We were also slow to learn: we were about to repeat the whole absurd procedure to pick something to watch before dinner, when a knock on the garage door made us all jump.

Seeing Marin dithering in our open doorway told me everything I needed to know. He never stood on ceremony; if he wasn't barging in and growling at us, something was definitely up.

Frankie jumped up, so tense that they were literally vibrating. "Have you heard? Are they going to do something?"

"I don't know yet, but they want to talk to you."

"Who's 'they'?"

Marin rolled his eyes. "Does it matter?"

"Yes."

"Some of my people—"

"How many?"

Marin's eyes narrowed. "Seven is the usual number. Anything else you need to know?"

Frankie turned to look at me. I tried to smile up at them, but the prospect of what lay ahead had put a huge knot in my stomach. They seemed to look right through me, and their tension went up another notch.

When they turned to speak to Marin, their voice was low and cold. "This isn't going to work. We've been having a pretty bad time lately and Gio doesn't like talking to a bunch of people. You know that."

"I don't like it either, OK?" growled Marin. "I'd hoped that it wouldn't come to this. But it has, and now we have to deal with it."

Frankie clamped their mouth shut and thought for a few moments. "What if we don't go?"

"Then they'll come to their own conclusions without hearing your side of the story."

"Is Jacob going to be there?"

"Probably." Marin took a long, hard look at us and sighed. "Look, I know you won't like it, but that doesn't change how things are. We need to go, and we have to go *now*."

I could see Frankie racking their brains, desperately searching for a solution. "Could you talk for us?"

Marin's brows unbunched for an instant, then knotted up tighter than ever. "Let's get one thing straight: when we get there, you will behave yourself. You will speak if you're spoken to, politely and concisely, but otherwise you will keep your damn mouth shut."

Something snapped inside me. I stood up and took a couple of steps towards Marin, even though I didn't want to be anywhere near him. "Don't talk to Frankie like that."

Marin stepped in and walked over to us, his eyes burning with fury. "I'll talk to both of you any way I want, and you will fucking listen, if you know what's good for you."

"You know what would be good for us? The lot of you leaving us alone. We didn't ask for any of this, so how about you get off our backs?"

He lifted his hand as if he was going to poke me in the chest, but stopped himself at the last moment. "Don't tempt me." He wheeled around and stomped off.

Frankie let off a huge sigh and grabbed my hand. "Alright. Looks like we have to do this. I know you're not going to like it, but when it's over, it'll be over, know what I mean?"

"Not really."

"It's just something we have to do, Gio. We do it, and then it's done. Then we'll be able to come back here and really relax. Won't that be nice?"

The lump in my throat was too big for me to speak, so I nodded.

They nodded back. "OK. Let's go."

Ben stood up, looking more uncertain and unsteady than usual. When he spoke, his voice quavered. "Can I come?"

Frankie shook their head. "It's probably best if you don't, but thanks."

"It's just... Every time I leave you two, something bad happens."

Frankie chortled. "Come on, man! You've never been superstitious."

"You're heading off to talk to a bunch of gods. Superstition seems appropriate."

"We'll be alright," I told him. Frankie and Ben both looked at me in shock. "We will be. This can't be worse than what we've already gone through, and we coped with that. Don't worry about me. I'll be fine."

My confidence was genuine, for a change, but it didn't do much to calm Ben down, so it took us an age to say our goodbyes. Marin didn't come back to yell at us, which worried me more than anything else. He just waited for us in his van, like a normal person. He didn't even yell at us when we finally got in; he just started the engine and set off down the road. It took me no time at all to realize where he was taking us. After all, I went there almost every day.

"Are we meeting on campus?"

Marin grunted an assent.

"Where?"

"Theatre."

"What? Why?"

"Because that's the place they picked."

There didn't seem to be any point in trying to talk to him, because he clearly wasn't in the mood, so I decided to put my time to good use. I snuck an arm around Frankie's waist and put my hand into their pocket. They leaned into me and kissed my hair.

"Hey."

"Hey, you. Can I ask you a question?"

They kissed me again. "You just did."

"Very funny. I just need to know one thing: is there any way this thing can go that would end up with us not being together?"

"What? No!"

"Don't just say that. I need you to think about it."

"OK." They unfocused their eyes. When they refocused them, they shook their head at me. "No. Not if it's up to me, anyway. And for you?"

"No way. I told you what my priorities are."

"And that hasn't changed?"

"Nope."

"Good."

They heaved a huge sigh, grabbed my free hand, and held it all the way there. They let go just long enough to get out of the van, and then they stretched their hand out to mine.

I looked around. The campus was quiet, but it wasn't empty. "Are you sure about this?"

"Positive. What's the worst that can happen?"

I put my hand in theirs. "I'll write you a list later."

We followed Marin down to the pavilion. I'd been there before, just once. It was a tiny open stage theatre, the kind of intimate space where the spectators sitting up front had to be careful not to trip up the performers. It didn't strike me as a suitable place for a quiet chat, though, particularly given the number of empty classrooms we could have used instead.

I leaned to whisper in Frankie's ear, "Marin's lot must like drama."

"I guess. I don't know. Gio, I have a bad feeling about this."

"Why?"

"Not sure. It just seems that they ought to have come to us. We're the injured party."

"Huh. I don't think I want a bunch of gods around the house."

"Me neither, but if they didn't even offer, that's off."

"But you'd go to the police station to make a report."

They shook their head. "Never of my own free will. Maybe that's why I don't like this. I have a history with law enforcement, you know?"

We turned a corner, and spotted them straightaway. It would have been hard for us not to. People wearing matching black bomber jackets, sunglasses, and ear pieces weren't all that common on campus. People thusly attired and over six and a half foot tall, even less so. Two of them were lurking between us and the theatre. I did my level best not to cower and scurry past them, but it was hard.

Frankie murmured, "OK, now I'm getting flashbacks."

"I thought the police in Canada wore red jackets."

"Only n TV, and no, not that. Of watching 'Men in Black.' First movie I watched in French. I couldn't understand a damn thing."

"That seems oddly appropriate."

One of the tall people was leaning casually against the wall by the theatre door. She raised a hand when Marin got about five feet away, and he stopped immediately. It was right at that moment that I realized that we really were in the shit. I held Frankie's hand as tight as I could. I wanted to pull them away from this, to run off with them until we were safe, but I knew that it was only half a fantasy: a complete escape story had to include what you ran away from and what you ended up running *to*. And if you didn't write the whole story right, you might never get the chance to tell it to anyone. I couldn't think of anywhere we could go and be safe, and that realization filled my bones with lead. When the tall woman waved us in, Frankie and I looked at each other, shrugged, and followed Marin into the dragon's maw.

The theatre was dimly lit, with the only decent light shining on three chairs in the middle of the stage. We didn't need to ask who those chairs were for; we just took our seats. Even with Frankie and Marin flanking me, I couldn't have been more uncomfortable than sitting there on display. Outside the circle of bright light that was already giving me a headache, the theatre was cloaked in darkness, and in that darkness lurked more of those tall, black-dressed goons. I counted four before my pervdar pinged and diverted my attention to a group of people sitting directly across from us, on the third row.

Jacob was there, staring straight at me, a grin splitting his face in half. He was wearing an older version of his Sexy Frankie face for the occasion – late thirties to early forties, his dark curls trimmed just short enough to look respectable but still long enough to give him a carefree, rakish air, a dash of grey at his temples, and laughter lines framing his dazzling green eyes. My heart did a somersault; this was a Frankie I'd not met yet, a Frankie I would only get to meet if we made it that far. Looking at the slump of Marin's shoulders and at the expressions of the people assembled in front of us, it didn't seem all that likely.

Then it hit me: there were seven people sitting in front of us, like Marin told us to expect, and Jacob was one of those seven. He didn't look uncomfortable or concerned, either; he was chatting and laughing with the two sitting on either side of him. This wasn't an investigation; it was a trial, and we were the defendants.

I turned to look at Frankie, wondering if they'd worked out what was going on and how they were going to take it. They looked back at me with an expression I'd never seen on their face but I recognized: they were studiously calm and utterly shuttered, as if what was going on had only the most peripheral bearing on their life. They knew exactly the kind of trouble we were in, and they were going to handle it like a fucking pro.

A flash of love and pride for them washed through me; I thought I knew them, but they could still surprise me. I let myself indulge in my feelings for a count of ten, and then I shut them down. We had a job to do, and we had to do it well.

The woman sitting in the middle of the row cleared her throat, and silence filled the room. She looked us over as if we were something she found stuck at the bottom of her shoe. When she was done demonstrating how repulsive and insignificant we were, she asked Marin, "Which is which?"

"That is my godchild. This one," his hand fell on my shoulder and stayed there, "is their consort."

The woman's nose twitched. "Did you have to bring them both?"

"They are both involved in this situation."

"We're aware of that. Are they the only mortals involved in the security breach?"

"No. There is my consort."

The woman raised an eyebrow. "You have a mortal consort?"

"Yes." He kept his voice low and steady, but he dropped that short word from a great height, and with great effect. It left no room whatsoever for any further snooty comments on the subject.

The woman swallowed whatever she was going to say and moved on. "That's it? Three mortals?"

"Are you classifying my consort as a security breach?"

The woman blinked. "Are you saying I shouldn't?"

"I am merely asking you if that is the case. If it is, I look forward to receiving the board's advice as to how to conduct a long-term cohabitation and sexual relationship with a mortal without breaching security."

I nearly swallowed my own tongue. Marin was the most private person I'd ever met. We practically lived with the guy, and he still bit our heads off if we so much as mentioned his relationship with Ms. Anzengruber. Yet here he was, openly talking about the fact that he was banging her in front of a whole panel. I was totally flummoxed, until I realized that he'd managed to circumnavigate the woman's question. Ben was definitely involved in the security breach, but Marin had not squealed on him, and he'd managed to do so without lying. Frankie and I weren't the only pros in that ring.

The woman looked momentarily torn between embarrassment and vexation, and settled for going cold and businesslike. "There remains the matter of these two mortals."

"They are my consort's family. My family, now. The breach is in-house."

Frankie's breath caught for a few moments. I looked at them out of the corner of my eye. Their face remained impassive, but this was something we were going to have to talk about at some point.

The woman rolled her eyes. "Noted. So, why are you wasting our time?"

Frankie's whole body tensed up. I thought they were going to flip out, but they took two deep breaths and settled themself.

Marin nodded towards me. "A direct intervention was carried out against my consort's stepchild, who is also my godchild's consort."

Jacob leaned towards the woman with a broad smile. "Can I take this?"

The woman nodded.

Jacob turned to Marin and grinned. "Leaving aside the issue of where one should draw the line between 'in-house' and 'incest,' Frankie is my godchild as much as he is yours."

"That has no bearing on the direct intervention. You interfered with my family. This is a gross breach of protocol."

Jacob groaned, "I think we can spare the board a petty squabble over which of us is more closely related to these mortals. I have as much right to involve myself in my godchild's life as you."

"It was their consort you attacked."

"Attacked?" Jacob clutched at a string of imaginary pearls. "How very melodramatic. I can assure you that if I'd decided to harm your godson's consort, she would not be sitting here, taking up my evening."

"Godchild. Not godson."

Jacob sneered. "Whatever. The point is that nothing I did was against policy or custom. You would know that, if you remembered who you are."

Marin thundered, "What am I supposed to have forgotten?"

"That we are gods. You might have decided to dedicate your existence to unclogging toilets and consorting with mortals, but some of us still remember our rights and duties. My godson's consort was quested and tested; what could be more acceptable than that? Furthermore, the direct intervention, as you call it, took place after the security breach. Therefore, your objection is ludicrous, and this meeting is a waste of the board's time."

He leaned back with a grin. Marin turned to the woman, his face blank. He looked as solid as a mountain, and just as likely to back down.

She shrugged. "Unless you have any additional evidence, I will have to agree with Jacob. You may request to have this put to a vote, but—"

"I don't care about the board's opinion on what happened. That is in the past. I want Jacob to stop interfering with my family."

Jacob chortled, "It's my family, too. Isn't this nice? We're relatives!"

The woman raised a hand, and Jacob shut up instantly. She turned to Marin. "The board does not interfere in the internal affairs of members. You know this. Our remit is limited to ensuring that those affairs are conducted in private."

Marin shook his head. "I can assure you, if Jacob's interference continues, our privacy will be a long-forgotten dream."

Jacob stood up. "Is that a threat?"

"No." He flashed a smiled. "I don't make threats."

While they stared at each other, a movement at the edge of my vision caught my eye. Frankie was raising their hand.

The woman had seen him, too. She squinted at him. "What is it?"

"Hi. I don't really understand how your system works, in fact I didn't even know that you had a system until we got here, but I don't get this. You're not going to do anything?"

The woman shook her head. "There is nothing to do. Nothing untoward happened."

"My consort, Marin's nephew, was abducted and tortured."

Jacob started chortling. Two seconds later, he was guffawing. "Abducted? Tortured? That's ridiculous!"

Frankie kept their voice calm, even though their fists were bunched. "Are you denying that you did it?"

"I don't have to. But, just for you, I will explain. Mortals are sometimes chosen to undergo quests and tests. Lucky mortals, I should say: those who pull through are richly rewarded for their efforts. In the olden days, those quests could be deadly. These days, standards have fallen perilously low. If I have erred, it was in making your consort's test so safe for her."

"Gio could have been stuck there forever."

"Yes, but that would not have harmed her in the least."

"That's ridiculous! It's like saying that jail isn't a punishment!"

"Jail? She had the key. All she had to do was let herself out. That was the whole point: it was a journey of self-discovery and self-liberation."

Frankie shook their head. "You're talking about it like it was some kind of therapy, but it can't be. Gio didn't consent to it."

Jacob snorted. "Consent? Child, mortal consent is irrelevant. More than that, it's a joke, a made-up concept used by the weak to defend their right to weakness. A wolf doesn't ask for a sheep's consent."

"But you're not a wolf. That's not what you said, anyway: way you talk about it, you fancy yourself a shepherd."

Jacob grinned. "A shepherd doesn't ask for consent from his flock, either. We are gods. We will do with you as we please. To believe otherwise is the ultimate foolishness."

Frankie nodded. "That's good to know. So, this is it?"

Jacob's eyes narrowed. "I didn't say that."

"That's cool, because I wasn't really asking you." They turned to the woman. "What happens now?"

For the first time since we met her, she looked like she was having an emotion that wasn't nausea. She looked embarrassed. "We are assigning a Guardian to you."

"I beg your pardon?"

She waved at one of the people in black, lurking in the shadows. "A Guardian. She will investigate the scope of the safety breach."

"I thought you said there wasn't a breach because we're all family."

"There is no security breach. The safety breach is another matter, still to be investigated."

They leaned back in their chair. "Oh. This is about me, isn't it?"

She nodded. "We need to ascertain that your powers do not present an excessive risk. Your godparents' opinions are not consistent. The Guardian will observe you and report her findings to the board."

"Huh. Well, that's something. How long for?"

"As long as it takes."

"Starting now?"

"Yes."

"What happens if we don't go along with this?"

The woman gestured, and a tall, slender woman dressed all in black walked out of the darkness and stood at the edge of our circle. She reached down to a short holster attached to her belt, the kind some cops use to carry a folding baton, and proceeded to extract a four-foot sword out of it. It was a bit like a magician extracting a rabbit out of a hat, except that it was terrifying.

Frankie blinked. "Oh. Wow. That's pretty cool."

The guardian flicked the sword forward, and flames issued out of its whole length.

While I caught my breath, Frankie sighed. "Alright. Point taken. Can we go now? Gio has school tomorrow."

The woman up in the seats looked flummoxed for an instant. Frankie could have that effect on people, and I loved it every time it happened.

She pulled herself together and put her authoritative face back on. "Do we need to impress upon you the seriousness of this situation?"

"Nah. The sword kinda did that for you."

They let themself go blank and motionless, and another surge of pride for them coursed through me. I allowed myself a small smile. I didn't think that it could make things any worse for us, anyway. I had to struggle to keep the smile on when I caught Jacob's expression, but I wasn't going to let him know how much he scared me. A storm of fear and anger was brewing up in my guts, but this wasn't the place to let it out.

The seven gods got up and walked off, and we did the same. Just getting off the stage made me feel better, even though I still felt utterly awful. Marin led us towards the exit, where one of the goons stopped us with a gesture. Marin looked tempted to pop him one, but Frankie grabbed his arm and led him a few feet away, to one of the darker spots. When we were relatively out of sight and sound, they allowed their mask to fall.

Their eyes were full of dread, but they still looked after me first. They grabbed my hand. "Are you alright?"

"Yes. But I won't be for long."

"I really wish I could hug you. We'll be home soon." They looked up at Marin. "What the fuck are those people? The tall ones, I mean."

"Angels. Guardian angels."

"What? Shit. I thought they'd be, dunno, friendlier. Cuddlier."

"Lucifer was an angel."

"In half his statues, he just looks like a cutie. And I could never quite understand what he actually did wrong."

"That's classified. Anyway, angels are agents tasked with carrying out the will of the gods, whatever that will is. It's not a cuddly kind of job, kid. Haven't you read the Bible?"

"Nah. I've had it read to me, but I think they picked the nicer bits." They swallowed. "Uncle Marin, I'm sorry. I really am."

Marin sputtered, "What? Kid, this was my idea."

"Not about that. I've always thought you were kind of an asshole. I never realized how much better you are than the people you come from. That matters, you know? To us, anyway. But I've never cut you any slack. So I'm sorry."

"Kid, I..."

Marin choked up. He shook his head and thumped Frankie's shoulder in lieu of saying the gods only knew what, and then there was no time for chatting, because the Guardian was upon us.

I couldn't conclusively say that she was looming; I always thought of that as a deliberate pose on someone's part, and too much of her face was covered by her sunglasses for me to read her. But she was tall, uncannily fit, and felt like a cop, so I was intimidated just by having her near us.

Frankie was no happier than me, I could tell, but they were infinitely kinder, so they smiled up at her. "Hi. I'm Frankie. This is Gio. What's your name?"

"We don't have one." I'd expected her to sound like a robot, but her voice turned out to be perfectly normal. That made it eerier, somehow.

Frankie's smile wavered. "What can we call you? Assuming that we can call you."

"I am your Guardian."

Their shoulders sagged a little. "Guardian it is. Let me know if that changes, alright?"

The van only had three seats and the Guardian needed all the leg room we could give her, so Frankie and I squeezed in the back. I didn't mind; that way, I could hug them. I didn't let go of them until we got home. I don't know what did it, whether it was the fresh air hitting my face or watching the Guardian walk towards my home, my sanctuary, but something snapped inside me, and I couldn't take anything anymore.

I stormed into the house, right past Ben and Ms. Anzengruber, who were hanging around the hallway. They tried to stop me, but I shrugged them off me and went straight to our room. I slammed the door shut, but it just bounced open again. I was just about to kick the shit out of it when Frankie walked in and shut it gently behind them.

"Gio, you have to calm down."

"Are you insane?"

"Probably, but you still have to calm down."

They stretched out their arm to grab mine, but I shrugged them off. I was too angry to stay still, too angry to be pacified, too angry to put up with another second of this bullshit. I paced and paced around our room, because it was either that or kicking the walls down. Our fucking room was so fucking small that I had to keep turning around, so I made myself dizzy and had to sit down.

They sat down next to me. I looked at them looking at me, and couldn't understand how a single human being could be so forlorn and so determined at the same time. If I tried that, my heart would explode.

"Frankie, this is fuckery of the highest order."

"It's not so bad. At least—"

"Not so bad?" I was up again, and yelling at them even though I knew that they were the last person who deserved it. "They're on his side! They know what he's been doing, and they're on his side, and now they dare to treat you like this, and you think it's not so bad?"

"Look, it's not as if I'm happy with it, but you're going to be safe. While the Guardian is keeping an eye on me, she's gonna keep an eye on you, too. Jacob won't dare try anything. I know it's not ideal, but it's a step up."

"No. It's not. It's unfair, and I won't stand for it."

They grabbed my hand and stared at it. "Whatcha gonna do, Gio? We are kinda powerless here."

"I've been powerless all my life! I've had enough of it! It's like being back in school, for fuck's sake! Stuck between a psychotic asshole and a whole fucking institution that has all the power, that could fix everything, but just doesn't give a fuck! All they care about is covering their own backs! I've had years of it! I've had enough!"

"I'm so sorry. This is all my fault."

"It's not! You're the best thing in my life! Will you fucking get that?"

I threw myself at them. They wrapped their arms around me and nuzzled my neck, murmuring things that, on any other occasion, would have melted me. I was just too pissed off to snap out of it, though. My brain kept going around in circles, about Jacob, bullies, institutional unfairness, and how the characters in the story changed, but the story stayed the same. When they let go of me, I was still breathing hard.

"Gio, I have to go next door. We left Ben out there with her. It's not right."

"Alright. I'm coming with you."

"Are you sure? I mean, you look a bit agitated."

"Oh, I'm agitated alright. But I'm not leaving you out there with her."

"Sure. But can you, you know, try and be civil? I'd really like not to die."

The blood that had been thumping in my head rushed from it so quickly that it left me dizzy. "Shit. Right. Oh, Frankie..."

"You're alright. We'll be alright. Let's just go out there and get this sorted out. Just pretend she's my aunt or something."

"Why your aunt?"

"Only relative of mine you don't wanna stab. Come on." They got up, put their hand out to me, and escorted me out.

Everyone was still standing around in the hallway. I felt a twinge of glee because this fucking farce was making everyone uncomfortable, not just the two of us. That made me feel like a total asshole, but by then it didn't matter: my good will and dubious social skills were not needed, because Frankie was already working their magic.

Everyone made such a fuss about Frankie's ability to break shit. That obsession made them miss out on what Frankie was really good at: making people comfortable. They could negotiate the most perilous social waters and make sure that everyone felt as OK as they could. Maybe it wasn't as earth-shattering as their other powers were, but it was a wonder to behold. This occasion was no exception. Even though they were exhausted and stressed to the point of panic, in under two minutes they had pacified Marin and Ms. Anzengruber and sent them on their way, managed to get Ben to relax enough to breathe, and ushered the Guardian around our home as if they were welcoming an honored guest.

"This is our kitchen and our living room. It's a garage, really, but it works out. Sorry about the lights; they are a bit hard on the eyeballs, but you get used to them. Maybe one day we'll get windows. You can help yourself to our stuff if you're hungry, but if you cook you have to make sure that you turn the stove off at the wall switch. Ms. Anzengruber asked us to. There was a fire here a while ago. It's all fixed now, but she worries, and I can't blame her because I forget stuff all the time. Never the stove, though. Gio doesn't let me. So, yeah, everything on the bottom two shelves of the fridge is ours, and you're welcome to it, but, like, if you leave us enough bread to make sandwiches for work that'd be helpful, because otherwise we can't eat. Will you be coming to work with me?"

"Yes."

They shuddered, but only a little. "Alright. We'll make three packed lunches, then. Are you OK with peanut butter? If you're not, we can get cheese. We normally have some, but we're out. Gio makes a mean cheese sandwich. We eat a lot of cheese. Sorry."

She took off her sunglasses. Her eyes were clear blue, just like Ben's, and had that half-confused cast that Ben's eyes wore almost permanently. "Why are you sorry?"

"Well, we're really not set up for guests. We weren't expecting this, you know?" They let off a nervous giggle and ran a hand through their hair. "We really weren't. Anyway, we don't have a spare bed, but the couch is really comfy. Gio and I fall asleep there all the time. It might be a bit short for you, though. I'm sorry. The bed in our room is bigger, but we need somewhere to sleep, too. Gio has got school, so she's got to get her rest. This whole thing has already been quite, well, disruptive."

"It's not a problem. I don't sleep."

They blinked. "Oh. Right. So, yeah, just make yourself at home, I guess. Don't sit on Gio's chair – I mean, you can if you really want to, but it breaks really easily and it'd probably be too small for you, anyway. You don't sleep?"

"No."

"Huh. I guess that makes sense." Their smile dropped a couple of notches before they noticed and bolstered it up. It looked strained as hell, but they were trying. "There's a ton of books if you want to read. Just help yourself. And, huh, our bedroom has a door onto the patio. I hope that's alright. I'm not planning to abscond."

"That won't be a problem."

"Because you trust me, or because you'd just catch me?"

"The latter."

They bit their bottom lip and nodded. "Alright. Good to know. So, it's getting late, and Gio has school tomorrow, and he really needs to be rested for that because she missed today, and we're all a bit riled, frankly, so we need to chill out. Is it OK if we stay out here? We can take the TV into our room, but it's a bit of a mission and we have to put it on the floor, so we can't really watch it properly. But if you'd prefer us to clear out..."

"Not a problem."

"Right. Great." They turned to Ben and me. "Alright. Who's doing what?" When neither of us reacted, they sighed. "Ben, you're on food. I'll do the drinks. Gio, can you pick a video for us? Meet you at the couch when we're done. Go!"

Frankie set out a chair near our couch for the Guardian and chatted with her for a few moments before coming back to the kitchen to do their bit. Ben was working hard on a heap of ramen and eggs and muttering about how he couldn't trust the two of us to keep a fridge stocked. My brain was still misfiring badly, so I couldn't even begin to think about entertainment for the evening. What the fuck could we watch to calm down while a supernatural law enforcement officer was sitting in a corner of our room waiting for Frankie to put a foot wrong?

I twitched by the fridge, getting in everyone's way and coming up with nothing, until I tuned into what Frankie was singing under their breath: "She'll see me when I'm sleeping, she'll know when I'm awake..." That gave me an idea. It wasn't a great idea, but it was the only one I had, so I went with it.

By the time Frankie and Ben had our dinner ready, I was all set up. We had a bit of a tussle at the couch: I normally sat in the middle, but I wasn't going to have Frankie sitting next to *her*, so I swapped seats with them. We ate our dinner, drank our tea, and then Frankie cleared up our crockery. On the way back, they stopped at the light switch and smiled at the Guardian.

"Do you mind if I turn the lights off? It's a bit more relaxing that way."

The Guardian blinked for the first time that evening. "No. Of course."

"If you want to read, just say."

They put the fairy lights on, flicked the main lights off, and promptly whacked themself on the coffee table on the way to the TV. They sat down next to me, rubbing their shin, as the video came on.

"'The Grinch'? Gio, it's July!"

"August. And you've been singing Christmas carols all evening."

"I have? I'm sorry."

"Don't be. Do you mind?"

"Not a bit. Ben?"

He shook his head. "Nah, I'm good. What's on after it?"

I shrugged. "It's a mystery. Knowing Ms. Anzengruber, it's gonna be really good or really weird."

Frankie squished right up against me and picked up their crochet. Having them snuggled next to me under the fairy lights should have made me feel all warm and cozy, but I just couldn't forget about the six-and-a-half foot of Guardian looming on my other side. I didn't know how badly we had to fuck up for Frankie to be in trouble, but we had a tendency to fuck up quite a bit. We usually didn't mean to, but I wasn't sure that that would matter to her, or her employers. Thinking about that made me shiver, and that pulled Frankie out of the movie. One moment they were crocheting furiously and mouthing along with the lyrics, which they evidently knew by heart, and the next they were hugging me.

"Are you cold?"

"No. Maybe. A little bit."

"Do you want me to get you a blanket?"

"No. I don't want you to get up. You're snuggly."

They picked up their crochet and spread it over my legs. "Here. I hope you're not getting ill."

"I can't get ill until my class is over."

"Yes, Gio: that's totally how it works."

I snuggled up a bit closer to them. They turned to kiss me, and went rigid instead, looking over my shoulder. I could imagine the Guardian behind me, perched on our too-small chair, watching over the Doom of Humankind while they sang along to a kid's movie and crocheted a blanket for their partner. The whole scene was so incongruous that my nerves gave up, and I started giggling. That pulled Ben out of the movie, too, and the moment was shattered.

We sat there pretending to watch the movie until it was over, and then we turned in. In the hallway, Ben looked like he wanted to say something; whatever it was, he took it to bed instead. Frankie made sure that the Guardian had cushions and a blanket, and even brought her our flashlight in case she wanted to read. When they got back to our room, I was already in bed. I had tried really hard to calm down, partly because I was exhausted but largely because I knew that they really wanted me to, but I wasn't doing very well. When they slipped under the cover next to me and hugged me, I did my level best to relax enough to give them a proper hug back, but I wasn't terribly successful. They didn't seem to mind, though: they just sighed and kissed my nose.

"Gio, I'm so sorry."

"Of course you are. You shouldn't be, though."

"I'm sorry about that, too. And I wish I could tell you that everything is going to be alright."

"Let me guess: but you can't, and you're sorry about that."

"You know me too well. You can't sleep, can you?"

"Nope. But if you go to sleep, I'll do my best to follow you."

"Let's race each other. First one asleep wins." They arranged themself against my back. "You know, I hate spooning you. Always have."

"Say what?"

"I want to be both sides of you and I want you both sides of me, but I always have to pick instead, and that sucks."

"We'll just have to set up a quota system. We can rotate every five minutes, or something."

"But I want both, Gio. At the same time. So we need at least two of you and two of me. And even then, one of us each won't be getting enough."

"Huh. That's a bit trickier, then. I'll see what I can do."

"If you could find a way to at least replicate yourself, that'd be great."

"I wasn't planning on it, but I'll consider it."

They went quiet then, but I knew that they weren't falling asleep. Their breathing didn't change, and they were stiff as a board. After five minutes of that, I turned around and kissed them.

"Do you want to talk about it?"

"It's just... It's too weird, Gio. The contrast."

"Between what?"

"Some bits of our life are so fucking normal, you know? How you brush your teeth, the way you snore when you sleep on your face—"

"I don't snore!"

"You do. You sound like a tiny piglet. It's cuter than words. Anyway, that's not my point. So much of our life is so very mundane, you know? And then there's all the supernatural stuff that's snuck in on us, and it's gotten so weird that I can't understand how we got here. When I first found out about it, I thought it was exciting, but now it's just surreal, and it's consuming our whole life. I keep thinking about where we went wrong, where we could have stopped, or taken a different turn—"

"You're not going to try to fix that, are you? With your powers?"

"No. I've learnt that lesson. But I feel like we're not us anymore. Everything is too weird for us to be us. I mean, we're pretty competent as total fuck-ups go, but we just can't play them at their game and hope to win. We're like balls in a pinball machine: the best we can hope for is to keep bouncing from one thing to another. I really don't like that."

"Me neither."

They turned around and squished their back into me. "I'm sorry."

"Naturally." I tried to relax into them and go to sleep, but my brain just wouldn't switch off. I was debating whether I could get more rest if I just gave up on sleep and concentrated on being still and quiet when it hit me. "Frankie, I've been a total idiot."

"Don't call yourself names! What is it?"

"I've been going about this all wrong. I've treated this whole debacle like something special—"

"Gio, there's an angel with a fiery sword in our living room—"

"No, not that: the Jacob thing."

"Having a god stalk you isn't special?"

"Not really. He's a god: big whoop. That just means that he's more powerful than me, and most people are. Bullies always are. Or they think they are, anyway. Most of the time, they only are if you play their game by their rules."

"Alright. So he's a bully. What are you gonna do? You can't meet him on the playground at recess and slug it out."

"Nah. He's a god. He'd total me."

"He could total you anyway. No offense, but he's twice your size."

"Most people are, which is why that kind of thing has never been my style. Have you ever been bullied in school?"

They snorted. "Are you kidding? Of course I have. I got with my first boyfriend at four."

"What the hell were you doing with a boyfriend at that age?"

They let off a dreamy sigh. "We held hands until they stopped us. We kissed in the playhouse a couple of times. Mostly I gave him my coloring books to try and make him like me, but I don't think he was ever really into me. Anyway, of course I got bullied. Nowhere near as much as a bunch of other people, but yeah. Didn't you?"

"Not really."

They squinted. "Again, no offense, but how? You stand out."

"I only stand out when people actually look at me, and most don't. When someone noticed me, I made picking on me not worth the hassle. You had to, in my school. It wasn't safe not to. A kid in the class below me got held out of a third story window by his ankles."

They turned over and hugged me. "What! Why?"

"Second best student in the school. The seniors didn't like that."

"Jesus. What happened to the best student?"

I smiled. "They moved to America, met the most beautiful person in the world, and are trying really fucking hard to live happily ever after."

"Oh. Shit. Of course. Gio, that sounds awful!"

"It was alright. You just had to know how to navigate it. It wasn't so bad. It can be pretty hard to get a rise out of me, and I get a bit vexed when I'm pushed."

They mumbled something about rabies under their breath.

"What?"

"I plead the fifth. So, basically, you ignored them or flipped out?"

"Yes and no. Most of the time, it never went beyond a lot of mouthing off. They'd say something bad, and I'd laugh it off or I'd say something infinitely worse, so they'd give up. They wanted me to be scared and humiliated, and I don't do well at either. I mean, when I deal with people who're not assholes, that's scary, and when I fuck that up, that's humiliating. But dealing with assholes is different."

"Yes. It's dangerous."

"Sometimes, but I know what I'm dealing with. There is nothing to worry about."

"Apart from being made to eat your own teeth?"

"Yeah, well, but that's not half as scary as embarrassing yourself in front of people you like."

"Gio, I really love you, but your priorities are way out of whack."

"Maybe, but that's how they are. Anyway, it generally didn't go physical. When it did, I didn't treat it as a fight. It wasn't, really, because fights are mutual, and I just wanted to be left alone. So I treated it as an assault, and went all out. They didn't want to play like that. Hell, maybe I just freaked everyone out a bit too much. Guys and girls tend to bully their own, by their own rules. Maybe I was just too alien."

They stroked my face. "It sounds pretty hardcore."

"It wasn't that bad, and I had bigger fish to fry. Anyway, if Jacob laid a finger on you, I would have no qualms about cutting it off at the neck."

"Isn't that a bit excessive?"

"No. The power imbalance is too damn great. I can't just hurt him a little bit and expect that to stop him."

"Homeslice, you're blithely ignoring the simplest solution."

"What?"

"Me." Their arms convulsed around me. "I could take him out. Or, like, change him so he wouldn't want to hurt you ever again."

"No. That is out of the question."

"Gio, let me fix this. It's all my fault."

I pushed them away from me so I could look at them. "No, it isn't. You didn't start it, and we're in this together. You better get that into your head, or I'll keep screaming it at you until it sinks in."

"But—"

"No! You didn't do anything to call this upon us. Not a damn thing. It's totally, utterly, and completely Jacob's fault."

"Alright. Even if I accept that—"

"Frankie, I'm going to scream at you."

"Alright! So Jacob is the problem. But he's *our* problem, not yours. Why are you taking me out of the equation? I'm our best weapon."

"You. Are not. A weapon!"

Their bottom lip quivered. "You're willfully ignoring reality."

"No. Frankie, you got told that you've got the power to hurt and control people, and you've been scared shitless of using it by accident ever since. You know how rare that makes you?"

"No, and neither do you. It's not as if you've run a fucking survey."

"I haven't, but I know people. Plenty of people would have enjoyed that feeling of power. You don't."

"Of course I don't! I'm a fucking liability!"

"You're not. You're you. Love, what would it do to you if you ever hurt anyone like that?"

Their eyes strayed off my face, avoiding my gaze. "I would feel very bad about it, alright? But if it's to protect you–"

"In the heat of the moment, you'd do it, and you'd pay for it later. We both would. But the moment isn't hot. And anyway, if you used your power against Jacob, that'd prove the Guardian and her lot right. We'd have to deal with all of that."

"But you're in danger! That's all that matters!"

"No. That's all that matters *to you*. To me, a whole load of other stuff matters, too. You are right on top of that list."

They stuck their chin up in the air. "What comes second?"

"We do. The two of us, staying together."

That was too much for them. They squeezed me so hard that I couldn't breathe. I squeezed them back and patted all the bits of them I could reach, but it still took me an age and a half to calm them down.

When they finally let go, they seemed a lot more serene. I felt more serene, too, but in a different way: they were ready to carry on with our life, while I was ready to smash everything up.

I brushed the hair off their face and tried to smile at them.

"Love, you know that movie with the swords and stuff?"

"Yes, Gio. Of course I do."

"That one with the guy who can't die, and Sean Connery, and the bad guy being super evil, and the inevitable gratuitous rape?"

They winced. "Do you mean 'Highlander'?"

"I dunno. There were kilts, I think, and they ran around cutting people's heads off and having orgasms or something."

"Yeah. Definitely 'Highlander'."

"You know when Sean spouts all that hifalutin bullshit about how to fight a monster?"

"Not a monster: a savage." They pulled back from me and put on a serious face. "'How do you fight such a savage? With heart, faith and steel. In the end there can be only one.' It's one of the most famous quotes of our generation, Gio. How is it that you can quote from the Kalevala but you don't know that?"

"Because I don't care. There's not a single part of that movie that doesn't rub me the wrong way. Heart and steel? Look at how that turned out for them. I'd fight him with guns, nets, and a combine harvester. I'd throw bricks at him from a fifth floor. I'd—"

"Alright, I get the point. You're not a fan of duels."

"Not against overwhelming odds. Actually, just no. I don't want to be a hero, and I find pain painful. The only sensible way to fight a monster is to catch them by surprise, to hurt them worse than they thought you ever could before they've had a chance to realize what's going on. And you chuck all of your resources at them, you skew the balance of power until it's in your favor. You go all in, get the job done, and go home."

"By that logic, you should let me liquefy Jacob."

"Nah. He's not a monster: he's a fucking bully. He thinks he can use his magic against us, and that we can't fight back."

"Yeah. He's right, isn't he?"

"Nope. We can't fight back and win if we play their game by their rules. And that, love of my life, is where they've all fucked up. They neglected to consider one of my favorite things about us."

"And that is?"

"We might go along with the rules for convenience' sake, but we never actually follow them."

14. GRENDEL'S MOTHER

My life had never been entirely normal. My life with Frankie and Ben, even less so. It was wonderful and wonder-filled, but it wasn't normal. We were all used to that and generally swung with the punches, purely because it was a hell of a lot more comfortable than catching one of them in the guts. All and still, I just couldn't get used to sharing our home with a fucking angel.

She was a good guest, as uninvited guests go. She was always with us, because she had to be, but she was quiet and neat, and she mostly left us alone. She spent most of her time hidden behind a book, only peering out when she had to do something or go somewhere. It was a behavior we could all relate to, except that she didn't seem to give a damn about what the book was. Our garage was still the repository of a ton of Ms. Anzengruber's junk, including a bunch of books she didn't want but couldn't quite bear to part with. We'd walk in there and find the Guardian reading a third-rate fantasy novel, a treatise on medieval pharmacology, a children's atlas of the universe, or an old catechism, apparently enjoying each and every one of them just as much. She'd greet us with perfect courtesy, exchange whatever pleasantries she deemed sufficient, and then return to her book. Frankie swore that they once got up for a glass of water and found her reading their crochet pattern.

That oddity aside, she didn't give us much cause to complain. Had she not been there to scrutinize Frankie, I might have tolerated her presence. Alas, she was, and I could neither forget nor forgive that.

I did my level best to be civil, I really did. Every now and then I'd catch a look from Frankie that suggested that I could have done better, but they never actually said anything, so I chose to ignore it. Ms. Anzengruber wasn't doing much better; although she was always courteous, her courtesy had to squeeze out from behind gritted teeth. She was at least as offended on Frankie's behalf as I was, but didn't have the advantage of years of social incompetence to help her modulate her responses. Marin was even worse: his speech had devolved into a combination of monosyllables interspersed with grunts and growls. How Frankie put up with him for eight hours a day was beyond me.

The Guardian didn't seem to mind our behavior, much as she didn't seem to mind what she read. Whatever we threw at her, she responded with the same precise, unwavering courtesy. I was willing to bet that she would have responded in the exact same way had we sworn at her, or declared our undying love. She was unflappable, which brought into sharp relief how much she made us all flap.

Ben was the worst affected. He was normally so chilled out that he was borderline catatonic, but the Guardian had wound him up to the point that he was nearly as twitchy as Frankie. At first, I thought that he was really freaked out about having the police around the house. None of us liked that, but Frankie and I were juvenile offenders currently acting almost legally, while Ben was a good kid from a good family whose current lifestyle involved the daily consumption of a stupendous amount of drugs. He didn't want to do something illegal right under the nose of the law, so he stayed straight for two whole days before the sweating, shaking, and cramps finally got to him, and he caved. Thankfully, the Guardian either didn't notice or didn't care. Unfortunately, returning his brain to its normal chemistry didn't return Ben's behavior back to normal.

I broached the subject with Frankie the night I'd finished my course. We were in our bed, whispering conspiratorially even though the Guardian was in the garage. If she could hear us from all the way over there, she could hear us whisper, so it made no sense, but it made me feel better.

"Frankie, I'm telling you: there's something wrong with Ben. Seriously wrong. Half the time, it's like he's not even there; his body is present, but his head is somewhere else entirely. The rest of the time, he's so focused on the Guardian that he's got no idea what the hell is going on."

"Yeah. I know."

"I told him to go home, that now that my course is over I can just stay at home, or tag along with you at work, but he won't. I don't get it. He's so wound up he can hardly think, but he won't go away."

"Well, yeah. Of course."

I pulled back from them. "OK, since you're apparently the resident smartass, how about you tell me while I shouldn't worry about this?"

"Maybe you should worry. I don't know." They sighed and stroked my face. "Gio, Ben has a crush on the Guardian."

"He *what*?"

"You heard me. I'm sure it's not going to go anywhere. I mean, Jesus, I hope it doesn't: angels don't date, do they?"

"Not that I know of. And neither does Ben."

"He has dated."

"One girl, twice. And we all know how that went."

"He was a bit fucked up back then, and his taste has improved since."

"You call the Guardian an improvement?"

"No. She's just a blip. She's tall, beautiful, svelte, and so competent that she's literally awesome. She's the closest thing to an elf he's ever met or likely to meet. She has a real sword. Of course he has a crush on her. Who wouldn't?"

"Me. I wouldn't."

"Well, yeah. Your taste is peccable."

"You know what that means, right?"

"Yeah. It means that you're happy to engage in lewd and lascivious acts with me. I'm glad of it, I tell you. Anyway, Ben has a crush on her, so he's terrified of her but wants to be around her, all at the same time. And that's on top of the other thing."

"What other thing?"

"The usual thing."

"What usual thing? Oh, Christ. You're not revisiting your delusion about Ben having a crush on me, are you?"

"I know this thing with the Guardian is just a blip, so I'm not worried. But Ben doesn't yet, so he's confused and upset. He feels like a traitor."

"Frankie, you're making no sense at all."

They kissed my nose. "And that surprises you? Anyway, Ben will be OK, by and by. We will all be OK. We just have to wait. This too shall pass."

So we waited, because we had to. That didn't make the waiting any easier.

Day after day, I woke up to find Frankie already awake, staring into space, wondering if that was going to be the day they fucked up and paid for it. They tried so hard to reassure me, to convince me that it was all good, that the important thing was that I was safe, but I couldn't buy into that. They'd kiss me goodbye on their way to work with a smile that tried to convey how perfectly peachy everything was, while their eyes screamed in terror. Every single time, I thought that I couldn't go through with it. I did, though: I watched them climb into Marin's van with the Guardian and let them go, not knowing if I'd ever see them again. In the afternoon, when I rushed into their arms, I still couldn't feel safe. We spent our evenings doing our best to comfort each other, even though we couldn't comfort ourselves, not while the Guardian was hovering at the edge of our vision. Yet we carried on as if nothing was the matter. The world kept ticking on, and we had to tick along with it, as if our troubles were wholly insignificant. It was surreal, really, or obscene. I would have called it unbearable, except that we were bearing it.

It seemed to go on forever, and we couldn't see an end to it. When it finally started ending, we didn't even realize it.

Ben moved the first piece. One week after the end of my course, he relented and agreed to go home for a spell. His sister needed him, so he had to go, but he was so conflicted that it took forever to get him to actually leave. In the end, it was Frankie who managed to say the right thing to get into his truck. I wasn't surprised, because Frankie was better at people than the lot of us put together. I was mightily peeved, though, because they wouldn't tell me what they had told him.

"Sorry, but it was between me and Ben."

"But—"

"I love you, and I don't keep secrets from you. You know that. This is just not your business. Not yet, anyway."

"But—"

"If I told you, it would upset Ben. Do you want me to do that?"

"Of course I don't!"

"There you go. You'll be alright."

They wrapped their arm over my shoulders, which nearly made things better. They were whispering sweet nothings into my ear while walking me back into the house, when we almost walked into Ms. Anzengruber, who came charging out, looking extremely agitated.

"Where the hell is Ben going?"

Frankie blinked. "Home. His sister—"

"Damn! Well, that's torn it."

"Torn what?"

"It doesn't matter. It's just..." She sighed. "Your uncle and I were going to go away for the weekend. You might have noticed that things have been somewhat tempestuous between us."

Frankie and I both froze. There was probably an answer to that kind of statement that didn't make people flip out, but I sure as hell couldn't divine it. By the look of them, neither could Frankie.

Ms. Anzengruber didn't seem to mind; she just rolled her eyes and carried on. "Having that— Having your guardian around the house hasn't improved matters. We had planned to spend the weekend in Kennebunkport."

"Kennebuttwhat?"

She sighed again. "It's a coastal town, about two and a half hours south. There's a resort. With a pool. And a spa."

Frankie's arm dropped off my shoulder as their jaw hit the deck. "You were going to take *my uncle* to a *spa*?!"

Ms. Anzengruber glared at them. "Actually, he was going to take me. It doesn't matter. We can go another time."

I took a step forward. "No. You should go."

"Out of the question. With Ben being away—"

"We can manage. We'll be safe. The Guardian will make sure of that."

"Gio, we can't just leave you here alone with her."

"You have to. The alternative is having us spend the weekend thinking about how you're having a crap time because you think we can't manage. Believe me, that would be infinitely worse for us. Things are bad enough without us feeling that we're ruining your life, too."

She locked eyes with me. "You are being overly dramatic. It's just a weekend at a spa."

"Yeah. And I know what I'd give to do something like that with Frankie. Maybe we will, one day. Maybe we'll find a place that would take us. But you can go now, and you should. Tomorrow isn't a given. You know that."

"Gio—"

"Don't fight it. You know I've already won this one."

For a moment she looked as if she was about to throw something at me, and then she started cackling. "You did. But if something happens to you while we're away—"

"It will be our responsibility. We're adults."

She turned on her heels and marched indoors, but I could still hear her muttering, "Saying that doesn't make it a fact."

I had to yank Frankie to make them move. "Come on. We can't stay here all day."

"Gio, did all that just happen?"

"Me winning a word fight with Ms. Anzengruber? Yeah."

"Not just that. The bit about her and Uncle Marin at a spa."

"Yup. Weirder things have happened, love."

"Have they? I must have missed them."

"You know what that means?"

"That some poor bastards are going to have their holiday ruined. Can you imagine Uncle Marin chilling by the pool? Getting massages?"

"I'd rather not. I'd have to bleach my brain. But do you know what else that means?"

"That we'll be home alone? If we can discount the Guardian."

"Precisely. I intend to do my damn best to forget that she exists."

"How are you going to do that? She's always around."

"She doesn't follow us into bed."

"Yeah, but we can't just stay in bed for two days!" They stopped. "Wait. We can, can't we?"

"Yup. Bit of a waste of sunshine, but—"

"We can keep the curtains open."

"What if someone sees us?"

They scooped me up and marched down the hallway. "Then they'll learn a thing or three. Come on, Wenchlad."

"I'm back to being a Wenchlad now?"

"For what I have in mind, you better."

"What about dinner?"

"You can eat it off me."

"I was planning to make pasta."

They stopped, turned around, and walked back to the garage. "Alright. This is how this is gonna go. We're going to have pasta first, because your pasta is the absolute best, and then we're going to have hour after hour of unbridled sex."

"Are you sure you don't mean bloated sex?"

"That, too." They kissed my nose and opened the garage door.

The Guardian looked up from her book just long enough to nod at us. If she thought anything of the fact that Frankie was carting me around like a sack of potatoes, she kept it to herself.

Frankie wiggled their eyebrows at me, walked me over to the table, and plonked me right on it. "Tell me what you need, your majesty. I am at your bidding."

"'Your majesty'?"

They knelt at my feet. "I can't make prince or princess work out. I can't pick one, and they won't blend. Princecess? I am bereft and ashamed."

"Cease thy prattling! Go forth, and put a pan of water on the stove."

They sprang into action while I tried to stop my head from spinning. Living with Frankie was never boring, which was great, but it could be enormously discombobulating.

I grabbed a glass of milk, walked over to the Guardian, and did my bit for the smooth running of our household.

"Ben won't be here tonight. He's gone home. I'm going to cook dinner. It won't be as good. Sorry. Is pasta OK with you?"

She closed her book – a carpentry manual, of all things – and rested it on her knee. "No, thank you. I'm leaving."

Milk spurted out of my nose. "I beg your pardon?"

"I've completed my assignment. My presence is no longer required."

Frankie appeared next to me. "And your judgment?"

She smiled for the first time since we'd met her. "What do you think?"

They grabbed my hand. "I don't know. That's why I'm asking."

"You're fine. There was never any doubt."

Frankie covered their face with their hand and shuddered. When they emerged, they looked grave. "Are you sure? Are you absolutely sure?

You've only been here ten days."

I grabbed their arm. "Frankie, the Guardian said—"

"I know what she said. I just want her to be sure that she's got it right. This is important, Gio."

I hissed, "Yes, it is. So shut up and let her go."

"No. I have to be sure."

"You never will be." She got up and put her hands on their shoulders – another first. I'd never seen her touch anyone. "Good people always worry about whether they're good enough."

"So I'll never know if I'm safe to be around?"

"Most likely. Which means that you'll always do your best to act virtuously, because you don't trust yourself. I have no concerns about you. I've known that since my first evening here."

While Frankie wilted with relief, I exploded.

"Why didn't you fucking tell us, then? I was worried sick!"

She let go of them and turned towards me. "You shouldn't have been. You know that they're a fundamentally good person."

"Of course I fucking do! What I didn't know is whether you—" I managed to catch myself, and turned the rest of the sentence into a wail of incoherent rage. It was safer than verbalizing my thoughts on the subject.

She stared at me, utterly unmoved. "I couldn't let you know. Frankie doesn't lie."

"What the fuck does that have to do with anything?"

"My assignment was to stay here until Frankie's status was clarified."

"Precisely! You could have fucked right off and left us alone!"

Frankie wrapped an arm around me. "Gio, you need to calm down."

"The fuck I do! She could have told you, and you wouldn't have been so scared!"

"No. I would have been just as scared."

"What the fuck are you on about?"

"Jacob." They turned me around so they could look into my eyes. "Gio, the Guardian stayed here so she could look after us, and she couldn't tell us that because it would have been bloody obvious, because I'm shit at lying. I love you, but you have to calm the fuck down, because we need to listen to what she has to tell us. Alright?"

I felt so angry, relieved, and embarrassed that I couldn't speak. Two nanoseconds later, my eyes were swimming in tears.

Frankie hugged me. "I know. Me too. Let's just get through this, and we can go to bed, alright?"

I nodded into their shoulder. "Yes."

"Good." They stroked my back and spoke over my head. "How bad is it?"

"I'm not sure," murmured the Guardian, "But it isn't good. Jacob is not going to appreciate you reporting him to the authorities."

"But we didn't! Uncle Marin did! Jesus, this is just like school, isn't it?"

"The worst situations in life often are. I thought that was the point."

"What? I... don't think that's the case. School isn't designed to immunize children against life's horrors."

"Huh. I guess it's fortuitous that it does, then."

"Yeah. Maybe. So now Jacob is going to come at us twice as hard because we tattled on him? And you won't help? We're screwed."

She shrugged. "That depends on who gets to make the first move."

"What first move?"

"The one Gio spent the last ten days planning."

I went rigid in Frankie's arms. We'd been so careful not to say anything when she could hear us. What else had she heard?

Frankie shook their head. "That's not a plan. It's a pipe dream."

She laughed. "Then your dreams are far less pleasant than mine. Here is the situation as I see it: I will be leaving you as soon as this conversation is over. I will not report back until Monday. I will make that report directly to my supervisor and do my best to ensure that you-know-who doesn't hear about it, but you cannot rely on that to keep you safe. As you know, he has friends in high places. You have two days to make a decision and act on it. If I may give you a piece of advice, make sure that you do decide. Do not let yourselves do nothing out of inertia: make a decision and embrace its consequences."

"Will that make us more likely to succeed?"

"No. But it may make you feel better about failing. Now, if you have no further questions, I will be off."

Frankie stammered, "Actually, I mean, if it's not a problem..." They tapped their shoulder.

"What?"

"The, you know, the wings. Could you? Show us?"

"Oh. Yes."

She took off her jacket, revealing a spectacular pair of shoulders, and extended a pair of wings easily as wide as she was tall. I had expected them to be black, like her hair, but they were a rich, milky cream, with golden highlights and fine black details on the primary feathers. As six-foot-wide wings went, they were very understated.

Frankie picked their jaw up off the floor. "Wow. Just wow. Do you mind if I, huh, you know."

"Touch them? Go ahead." She extended a wing towards them.

"Wow. OK." They stretched an arm out tentatively until they could reach. "They are so soft."

"Thank you. I try to take good care of them."

"And do they, you know, work?"

"Yes. Would you like me to show you?"

"Yes! But, like, won't people see you?"

"No. We have our ways, and your people are remarkably impervious to seeing what they believe is impossible." She folded her wings against her back. "If you have no further questions, I will take my leave."

Frankie scrunched their face up. "I'm sure I'll think of a million things the moment you're out the door. Gio?"

I was still catching up with the conversation, so I shook my head, sure that I would regret that later.

She nodded at us. "Fine. Just one more thing." She stared at me. "My people are very rule-bound. That is in our nature. You despise us for it."

"I don't!"

"You do. That is in your nature. But it made you oblivious to one factor: I may be rule-bound, but I also make the rules."

"What? What does that even mean?"

She smiled. "Think of it as a koan. A present from a friend you never realized you had." She wrapped her jacket around her waist. "It is time."

Frankie and I stood side by side on our porch, holding hands, and watched her fly away. Frankie's jaw was hanging about level with their knees, but I couldn't blame them. When she finally turned into a speck high up in the sky, they shook themself off.

"Well, that would be cool. Having wings like that, I mean."

"It sure would."

"But not cool enough to make me want to be an angel."

"You're pretty enough, but I don't think you'd enjoy it."

They sighed. "You're going to go for it, aren't you?"

"I think we should. Don't you?"

"I don't know. It's pretty high-risk, isn't it?"

"Not really, and inaction is pretty high-risk, too. Love, this is our chance. There's not going to be anyone to stop us."

"There's not going to be anyone to help us, either."

"So what? They haven't helped us up to now."

Their face fell. "Gio, I'm really not sure. The more I think about it—"

"Don't, then. Look, the Guardian is gone. Nobody is going to help us. What else can we do? I can't just sit and wait for the next installment of what Jacob considers fun. I have to do something."

"Right." They grabbed my hands and squeezed them. "Would you like some dinner before we go for it? The pasta has probably turned to glue, but we can rustle something up. You'll need your strength."

"If I eat, I will need a sick bag."

They nodded. "OK. I'll pack some snacks, just in case. I won't be long."

They walked into the garage, while I sat down in our room. I needed to relax and focus, to steady my breathing and my mind. By the time they came over, I was as close to calm as I could be.

They sat on the bed next to me. "Ready?"

"I think so."

"Let's do it."

We got up, picked up our gear, and stepped out on the patio hand-in-hand. Frankie locked up behind us, which put a lump in my throat: I didn't know if they were securing our home while we popped out, or making sure that Ms. Anzengruber's house didn't get trashed if we never came back at all. I didn't ask them, because I wasn't sure if I wanted to know, so we walked into the woods in companionable silence.

We didn't have to get far before we found a spot we were happy with. I could have done the whole thing at the house, but I didn't want to, and Frankie agreed. We didn't want what we were about to do contaminating our home.

I drew a circle on the ground while Frankie stood guard, holding our makeshift portal. When I was done, they helped me put it up; it wasn't heavy, but it was wobbly, and I just couldn't get it to stand up on my own. When we finally had it upright, they sighed.

"Homeslice, we should have tried harder. Two bits of dowel and a broom handle tied together with a zip tie do not a portal make."

"You and your high standards. It's perfectly functional, and I think the holly lends it quite a festive air."

"You still haven't explained to me how holly counts as a thorn."

"Back home, it's the same word for thorn and spine."

"Yes. But in English, it's not, and you of all people should know that."

"Don't remind me! Then I won't know, and then it will work."

They shook their head. "I am a bad influence on you."

"Always. That's why I keep you around."

"But this looks like a six-year-old's attempt at building a teepee. As starts to a glorious adventure go, this isn't very epic."

"Had I been aiming for epic, I would have sent you into the woods to cut down a tree instead of scrounging scrap timber out of Ms. Anzengruber's garage. It doesn't have to look good; it just has to work."

"But what if it falls down while we're on the other side?"

"We'll just put it up again."

They rolled their eyes. "Gio, that would require the damn thing to follow us there, or to exist in two realities at the same time!"

"Yes. And?"

"And I give up. Do your thing."

I took a deep breath, closed my eyes, and gave it all I had.

I didn't need to look to know that it had worked. The smells got to me first. Sun-warmed asphalt. Traffic fumes. The distinctive tang of stale urine, both feline and human. I took a deeper breath than I had in years, and the mixture filled my lungs and made me cough.

I ducked through the portal, opened my eyes, and the familiar sights opened up before me. Rows of tower blocks stretched towards the sky like stubby, grey fingers. The sun beat down on them with rays so hot that they sizzled. The ground was a checkerboard of tacky asphalt and scorched earth, occasionally intersected by brown, leafless hedges. The public works department must have let them get overgrown, like they did every summer, and then cut them so short that they'd be just a collection of sticks until next spring.

I sat on my usual bench, looking down towards the city center. The sea glistened faintly in the distance through a curtain of heat and smog. I nearly put my hands down to feel the warm concrete under me before I remembered to check what I was sitting on. Covering benches in crap, sometimes literally, was a popular local pastime. I'd gotten lucky, by the looks of it: if I'd sat on anything nasty, I couldn't see it. It didn't really matter, anyway. None of this was really real.

Frankie sat next to me, frowning in the glare. "Where are we?"

"My home, as I remember it. This is where I grew up."

They shaded their eyes with their hand and looked around. "I hate to say this, but this is a shockingly ugly place. Something about it makes me want to smash stuff. Is there anything here that isn't made of concrete?"

"There's a chain-link fence near the main road. I'll take you to see it when we're done. They don't call it brutalism for nothing, love. It's not supposed to make you feel good. It's just a cheap and efficient way of cramming too many people in the same place."

"But there isn't a soul around."

"Sunday lunchtime in mid-August. Most people are away on holiday, or to the beach for the day. Those who are left behind are napping."

They put their hand over mine. "All part of your plan?"

"Yeah. I didn't want innocent bystanders. Not even imaginary ones."

"Are you sure about this?"

"No. But I'm sure that we have to do something, and this is all I can think of. If it works, it could solve our problem."

They looked terminally unconvinced, and they weren't wrong. This was one of my worst and most desperate plans ever, which was saying something. I knew it as well as they did.

I tried to smile at them. "Love, I thought that considering all the negatives was my job."

"When it comes to doing shit that could hurt you... Gio, let's bail out."

"And do what? I can't carry on as we have, love. I just can't."

"And you won't let me step in."

"We've discussed that. Too expensive."

"And you won't just leave me?"

"No."

A muscle twitched in their jaw. "Alright. I don't like this, but I respect your decision and I will help you as much as I can."

"Noted. And thank you."

I made them close their eyes before I summoned my helpers. I didn't know how that was going to look, and I didn't want to creep them out with the slow coagulation of bodies out of some kind of primordial ooze. As it emerged, the process was fairly innocuous: the air shimmered, like a mirage from the heat, and out of the shimmering emerged three shapes. Three copies of me, of various ages and in various stages of fucked. I was oddly pleased to see that none of them looked alarmed or surprised in the least. Withdrawn, hostile, and vacant, respectively, but not alarmed.

It didn't take me long to explain my plan to them. I was expecting some resistance from Littlest-Me, but it didn't happen; I guessed that they were used to imagining bad things and seeing worse ones. The hardest part was witnessing the response from Middle-Me. As I got into the details of what we were going to do and why, a strange light had started to burn in their eyes. By the time I was done, they were practically drooling.

"So, we're going to fuck up a bad guy?"

I would have prevaricated, explained that none of this was quite real, but the glee in their eyes made my mouth dry up, so I shrugged instead.

Their lips split in a grin so menacing that it ought to have contained fangs. "Great."

Middle-Me grabbed Little-Me's hand and set off towards the tree line behind us. I started to follow them, but Frankie called me back.

"Are you sure I can't help?

"You are helping. You're staying here to guard the portal and look after me. They're staying here so there's a me for you to look after."

Frankie glanced at Eldest-Me, who sat on the ground with their arms wrapped around their knees, looking blank.

They turned to me and whispered, "Bullshit. *You* are you. *You* are going in there. *You* are going to be in danger."

"Imaginary danger, mostly. In the unlikely event of everything going to shit, I want you to get the fuck out of here and take them home. That way, I'll still be out there, with you."

"You won't. They'll be out there, not you. If they're unreal, it won't work. If they are, I'd risk creating a massive paradox. This isn't a computer game, Gio."

"I know. I also know that, if push comes to shove, you won't give a damn about that. I am pretty sure that it won't come to that, anyway, and I can't think of another way of doing this. I need a back-up plan. They're it."

I was keeping something from Frankie, again: Eldest-Me was playing a pivotal part in my plan. They were there to keep Frankie away from the action, as safe as they could be under the circumstances. I hated keeping that from Frankie, but I would have hated them getting hurt a hell of a lot more. I resolved to make that my very last lie by omission. If I survived my plan, I would never, ever keep anything from them.

I parked those thoughts for another day, and focused on Frankie. "Love, I need you to look after me."

"That's not fair. You've got me over a barrel."

"I know. But my need is genuine."

They rested their forehead on mine. "What about my need, Gio? I'll look after them, you know I will, but who's going to look after me?"

The pain in their voice nearly made my resolve crumble. All I wanted to do was take them in my arms, get them home, and make sure that they were safe, that they were happy. I couldn't do that without dealing with Jacob, though. In order to get there, we had to go through this.

I kissed them. "I love you. We'll be alright. I'll see you soon."

"You better. Good luck." They gave me a squeeze and let me go.

I walked away from them without looking back. I knew that if I did, the love and fear in their eyes would have made me give up.

I made my way through the tree line. It looked impenetrable from the outside. Someone who didn't know it as well as I did would have been scratched to shreds trying to break through it without a machete, but I knew just where the gap between the shrubs was hidden. I'd been sneaking through it since I was in kindergarten, after all.

Middle and Littlest were staring at the back of the crumbling villa. It looked just as I remembered it – a huge, stately mansion hidden from view by the vegetation that was attacking it. Tree branches penetrated its windows and small plants choked out its gutters. I normally liked trees – hell, I liked them a lot more than I liked most people – but these looked malevolent, as if they hated people on principle and would do me harm if I gave them half a chance.

They didn't look half as malevolent as the villa, though. The crumbling back wall stretched before me like a row of broken teeth, daring me to cross it. The courtyard behind it looked unnaturally still in the glaring sunlight, like a moment in time caught in amber. Umpteenth windows stared at us, dark and brooding. I was about as tempted to walk in as I was to stick a screwdriver up my nose, but, of course, that was the point: this was where we came for scares and dares. It was supposed to feel awful.

Nothing about it seemed to faze Middle-Me. As I recalled, their system could only run three feelings – hate, anger, and spite – so it didn't surprise me. Littlest was clearly terrorized, but they were used to that. They both looked at me expectantly.

"I'm going up the front. Wait until our man shows up before you do anything, alright? And don't get caught." I locked eyes with Middle. "You both need to get out. There is a chance that if something happens to you, it will create a paradox and wipe the rest of us out. It's unlikely, but—"

Middle glared at me. "I'm not stupid."

"I didn't say... Alright. Sorry."

I looked towards the villa. Now that I was faced with the practical consequences of my plan, I knew that I really didn't want to go ahead with it. It was too risky, too vague, but mostly it was just too fucking scary. I also knew that I couldn't back down now, and not just because bailing out would have put us right back where we'd started. The thought of having Middle think me a coward filled me with bile. Having them around must have been bleeding some of their particular blend of stupid into me; I would have rather gotten hurt than faced their contempt.

I nodded at them. "If it works at all, it shouldn't take long."

"If it doesn't work, you've just wasted our time."

I swallowed down a rant about how valuable their time was, given the crowds of loving friends and wonderful array of hobbies they had to fill it with, and set off towards the side of the villa. I heard them scramble over the wall as I was walking off. I was almost sure that I could trust them, which meant that I didn't quite trust them. Maybe that should have freaked me out, but I was used to not being able to trust myself.

I walked back along the tree line. I could see Frankie sitting on the bench, right where I left them, apparently engaged in conversation with Eldest-Me. I was suddenly struck with terror: what if meeting that version of me put them off me for life? I kicked myself for all the holes in my plan and sped up. Another scramble through the bushes took me to the garden wall. I walked along it until the ground before me started to drop, then climbed up on it and walked along the top. I had to chant to myself that it was no different from walking on the pavement, that all I needed to do was stay balanced and not look down, but a part of me knew that I was about twelve feet up and that a landing would really fucking hurt. Thankfully, I reached the breach in the wall before my legs had a chance to go wobbly. A quick scramble, and I was in the garden.

The trees were taller here, majestic monsters that probably pre-dated the villa and would doubtlessly outlive me. Their branches chopped up the sky and turned the ground into an irregular patchwork of glaring light and total darkness that hurt my eyes. I found myself walking on tiptoes, trying to sneak past the trees, as if they might wake up and attack me. When I got out from under them and reached the paved area that surrounded the front of the villa like a moat of dazzling sunlight, I was momentarily relieved. Looking at the main door made my relief evaporate.

It was half-open, as always, half of it held permanently shut by the collapsing wall above it while the other half rotted on the ground a few feet away. I knew what lay beyond it, and I knew that I had almost nothing to fear from it, but that didn't help. I took a deep breath, screamed at my stomach to shut the fuck up, and walked in. A few steps later, I was standing in the middle of the ballroom. It was not as cavernous as I remembered it, but it was still massive, three stories tall and ringed by a high gallery on three sides.

I fucking hated being in there. I'd always hated it, always had the feeling that the villa was going to collapse behind me and swallow me up – which, given the condition it was in, was not impossible. Chunks of plaster on the floor made me look up and reminded me of my most realistic risk: the fresco on the ceiling was crumbling, slowly giving way in patches and adding to the dust smothering the place. Only about half of it was still up there – enough to brain me if it came down, and also apparently enough to still "protect" the property. It was ironic, really: the building was listed as a scheduled monument because of the fresco, so nobody could redevelop it. As a result, the fresco was left to self-destruct, along with the villa. As soon as the fresco was damaged enough, the building would not be protected by law, and developers would doubtlessly swoop in. This was the only patch of ground this side of town not covered by blocks of flats, after all. The trees around it, as majestic as they were, would not be able to stop the tide of bulldozers.

For now, though, the villa and its treasures were left alone and mostly forgotten. The only people who remembered it were the children who flocked to it. It made for an unlikely and dangerous playground, but it was also the only space grown-ups hadn't shaped into unbearable, rigid squares, the only place where we could play, or simply be. Provided that we didn't let anyone know that we were here, obviously.

I was about to break that rule, which was why my insides were clenching. Still, it had to be done. I took a deep breath and tried to make my voice sound loud and steady.

"Horsefucker! Come out, come out, wherever you are!"

My words resonated unnaturally, even in that cavernous room. A few moments later, the shadows in the corners became darker and denser. My stomach clenched, and it took all my strength to stop myself from cowering and scurrying off. My eyes kept darting from side to side, trying to spot the shadows moving. A part of me was willing to swear that they did, that they were inching towards me as soon as I averted my gaze, and retreated when I looked at them. Another part of me thought that I was seeing things, and a third one was screaming at me that I was being a coward, as usual, and I should be disgusted with myself. It all made my brain very loud, which was probably why I didn't notice him straight away.

When I spotted him, I forgot all about the shadows. Jacob was standing on the gallery, about 20 feet above me, leaning nonchalantly against the metal railing. It was rather brave of him, given the condition the building was in, but he didn't seem at all worried. He was as relaxed as a cat, and twice as predatory.

When he spoke, his voice sent shivers down my spine. "Hey, little girl. Are we going to play?"

I got so scared that my brain actually pulled together. Instead of running in all directions, all parts of me turned towards the threat right in front of me. I remembered that I needed to breathe, and managed to suck in a lungful of air before attempting to speak.

"I don't want to play with you. You don't play nice."

A lazy smile spread on his face. "You must enjoy it, or you wouldn't have called me here."

He was loving every moment of this. He had terrified me for weeks, he had forced me to visit parts of my brain I'd sealed shut years ago, he had sabotaged my relationships with everyone I cared about, and he was loving it.

My fear converted into anger. It flooded into me, filling me with an overwhelming, burning need to hurt the person who had dared to terrorize me. When a little internal voice reminded me of the hurt he'd caused Frankie, hurting him back became my sole consideration. I was going to get my revenge, whatever the cost.

"Did I call you? So, I was right: you do fuck horses."

His eyes darkened. "Careful now. You don't want to make me angry."

"I wonder if the rest of the stories are right. With you, it's hard to tell. The things you do are so shitty that it's impossible to distinguish between slurs and factual accounts."

His face contorted for a second, but he calmed himself down. "If you have heard the stories, then you should know what happens to those who piss me off."

I heard the sound of smashing glass in the distance. I glanced out the window at the courtyard beyond. Middle-Me held Littlest's hand with their left hand, and threw a stone at a window with their right. Their throw was horribly uncoordinated, but it did the job. Another window shattered.

I forced myself to ignore them and look up at Jacob. I needed him to come down to the ground floor, and to be angry enough to ignore his surroundings until it was too late.

"Yeah, sure. Miserable lives, horrible deaths, blah blah blah. It's funny how you don't seem to realize that all the malice you spread around you never achieves anything. I mean, you think you're clever, and everyone else seems to agree with you, but I don't see it. If you're so clever, how comes none of your plans ever come to fruition? How comes people less bright than you constantly kick your ass? And how comes you don't seem to realize this? My people have the lifespans of gnats compared to you, but we learn. We adapt. You're clearly incapable of learning, even from you own experience, and you still think yourself smarter than us."

"Mortal, if you had any idea of what I'm capable of doing—"

I scoffed and cut him off. "Oh, yeah, your divine powers. Do you genuinely think they make you special? It's quite sad, really: there are plenty of tricksters who are not giant assholes. It's not a requirement for the job. But you went all out in that direction like a Satan fanboy, and you still somehow managed to fuck it up. You're definitely not loved, but you're not feared, either. Half the people I know fear their uncles more than they'd ever fear you. And if you're going to use your origin story as your excuse, I know people who can beat that, too. Didn't it occur to you that just because you're a bastard, it doesn't mean you have to act like one? Anyway, half the kids who break into this building are more dangerous than you. They're smarter, too. You're nothing special. If you didn't have your powers, you'd be utterly irrelevant."

I turned my back to him and started to walk towards the front door. It lay open right in front of me, the green of the trees beyond it beckoning me to run to safety. I didn't get a chance to let it tempt me, though: Jacob appeared right in front of me, cutting my exit.

He was wearing his interpretation of Frankie's face. Combined with the murderous glare in his eyes, it made me feel queasy.

"But I *do* have my powers. I can squash you like a fly."

"You could. So could this ceiling. It makes neither of you special."

I turned around and walked off towards the windows to the courtyard. He appeared in front of me again.

"Mortal, up to now you've been mildly amusing. That is the only reason I've tolerated your existence."

"Huh. I thought you must be lonely or something. I mean, it has to be pretty lonely, being so evil that nobody nice can love you but so incompetent at it that the evil people don't want anything to do with you. Nobody likes you, nobody trusts you, and nobody respects you. If you weren't such an unmitigated asshole, maybe you could gain people's pity. As it is, nobody wants to know you. And you still think you're better than everyone else, in the face of overwhelming evidence."

I turned a right angle, towards the left wing of the building. I knew that that door was stuck shut, but it didn't matter: Jacob cut me off again.

His voice dripped down my spine like sugary poison. "I am going to have so much fun with you that I don't know where to start. Should I break your body and leave your mind fully capable of realizing what is happening? Or should I leave your body untouched and break your mind, so you can enjoy the fruits of my labor for the span of your natural life?" His eyes half-closed, as if his lust for my pain was taking him over. "No. I will leave you untouched for a while, and play with your little friend. He's mine, after all. It's only right I should start with him."

The noise of breaking glass in the courtyard suddenly stopped. I started to back away from Jacob, towards the right wing of the building. I wanted to bolt, but I couldn't. Not yet.

My voice came out as a pathetic squeak. "They. Frankie is a they. Misgendering them doesn't make you stronger. And this is why you never, ever win at anything: you're nothing more than a petty, vindictive, pathetic bully."

I was wondering what would come next, another bout of threats or something infinitely worse, when Littlest-Me came hurtling through a broken window, as if they'd been thrown. They landed badly and started crying. A moment later, Middle-Me flew through the same window and scooped them up. They raced right past me and through the front door.

I knew that I needed to move, but I couldn't: I was rooted to the spot, frozen by conflicting fears. Then the monster came through the window. He didn't leap through it: he just ran through the wall, leaving a hole behind him, like in a cartoon. He was much bigger than I remembered, much bigger than any human had a right to be, but everything else about him was the same: the army jacket, the face furrowed by years of hard living, and the axe.

He saw us and roared in rage, his mouth splitting his face into two and showing way too many teeth. My body informed me that I'd peed myself, and the next moment he'd set off running at us.

Jacob didn't get a chance to move before the axe caught him at the junction of neck and shoulder. A flash of red filled my vision and broke me out of my freeze. I let my fear take me over and ran out of the door as fast as my legs could carry me.

The garden stretched before me, dark and endless, the gap in the wall invisible through the trees. Time started to misfire and took my sense of distance with it. One moment the wall was miles away, and a moment later it was so close that I nearly smacked into it. Another second later, I was running out of the tree line with no clear idea of how I'd gotten there.

Frankie was standing up by the bench, looking out towards me. My three younger mes stood next to them, but all I could see was Frankie's eyes, luminous and terrified.

I screamed as I ran towards them. "We've gotta go. Now!"

"Are you alright?"

"I think so." I threw myself into their arms.

"And Jacob?"

I started shaking. "Not good. I don't know. We need to get out of here!"

"Alright. Beam us up."

I turned towards my younger versions. Eldest-Me looked vague and Littlest-Me was still crying, but Middle-Me was laughing so hard they were having stitches.

"Thank you. I couldn't have done this without you."

Middle-Me grinned savagely. "It was a pleasure. It really was."

I held onto Frankie as hard as I could as we stepped through our portal.

15. STANDARD BITTER LOVE SONG #8

I didn't think there was any chance of us sleeping that night, or maybe ever again. After I told Frankie what happened, which took forever because I kept freaking out, they freaked out, too. We freaked out together, like true companions, going through the same phases – self-blaming, panic, regrets, compulsive apologizing, utterly pointless attempts at planning what to do next – until we were both too worn out to carry on.

I put up a circle, and we collapsed in a heap in our nest, in our bed, in our room, in our home. Even that didn't make me feel safe. Tiredness got the best of me, though, and I eventually passed out.

They came after me in the middle of one of my nightmares. It was one of the standard ones, the ones I used to have all the time before I moved into Ms. Anzengruber's house. I was stuck in a large, dark building. I desperately needed to get out, but all the doors and windows were stuck shut or too narrow. I wandered through a maze of passages and rooms, searching for an opening that would allow me to escape, while something or someone hunted me down. It was a nightmare I'd woken up from so many times that I ought to know that it was not real. While I was inside it, though, I could never remember that. All I could do was go along with it, do my best through my rising panic, and watch it all be for nothing. Whatever I did, whatever solution I engineered, the nightmare always adapted, always managed to keep just ahead of me and eventually to beat me. I always woke up just before I died, which I was thankful for. Sometimes I wondered if those deaths were real, if that was what death was: the erasure of our consciousness right at the point where carrying on with our life would be worse than giving it all up. I only wondered that when I was awake, though; while in the dream, I had no time for that.

I was creeping down the dark hallways of my dream – which were strongly reminiscent of the dark hallways of my old school – when I found a doorknob that actually turned. It should have been a relief, but it filled my insides with lead. I'd played this game enough to know that it was more likely to be a trap than a way out. Whatever was chasing me was closing in on me, though, so I had to take my chances. I opened the door as quietly as I could, peered through the crack, and found myself standing in the middle of a room so cavernous that I couldn't see the walls and ceiling. I couldn't see the floor either, though, and that didn't seem to be causing me any problems, so I decided not to worry about it. Across from me, far enough for me to have to strain my eyes to see them, were seven people enthroned on vast chairs. They looked mostly like people, anyway, but I was sure that they weren't. People didn't ambush me in my sleep. Living people didn't, anyway. This was the end of the line. I was done for.

As my body and mind relaxed in the knowledge that I had nothing left to worry about, a voice boomed in my head without passing through my ears. *"You know why you're here."*

I thought about just thinking at them and seeing what happened, but my brain was in too much of a mess to get any kind of message across clearly, so I cleared my throat and tried to sound casual. "Actually, no, I don't. Well, I assume that it's because you want me here and you don't care about where I want to be, but I don't know why that would be. I mean, I know that you don't understand about consent and basic politeness, but I don't even know where 'here' is."

"That is not your concern. You are here to be judged for your misdeeds."

"That doesn't clear things up much. What are we talking about, exactly? Was it that time I stole a toy horse from kindergarten? That would seem like overkill. I genuinely didn't understand about private property back then, and my mom made me bring it back. Or was it that time—"

"SILENCE!"

The shout rattled the inside of my skull. It shut me up for a moment, but it didn't do much to improve my mood. I had already gone way beyond fear, and getting yelled at pushed me further towards rage. Knowing that I was utterly powerless just made me more belligerent. They could do whatever they wanted to me, so what did I have to lose?

I rubbed my ears with my fingers. "I beg your pardon?"

"In the matter of your activities against Jacob..."

Frankie's voice, coming from two inches behind my left ear, drowned out the rest of that sentence. "Hey. You keep leaving me behind."

I turned around and kissed them. "Next time I get abducted, I'll ask if I can bring a plus-one. What the hell are you doing here?"

"Your breathing went all funny. It woke me up, and when I checked you out, you weren't all there."

"You should be used to that, and you should definitely not be here."

They shrugged. "You should be used to me being where I shouldn't be. So, what's new?"

"We've not gotten to that yet."

"Great. So I didn't miss anything much?"

"Nah. It's been mostly yelling and blustering up to this point."

A giggle as melodious as silver bells filled my head, and a soft voice followed it. *"Mortal, most of the blustering has been on your part."*

"You might have a point, but I didn't get to pick the settings. I didn't even get a fancy throne. I have to make up for that somehow."

"Are you not in awe of our powers?"

"To be perfectly honest, shit has been so weird of late that I think I burnt that circuit out. Plus I've never been a fan of intimidation."

"But you trapped and killed one of our kind. Was that not intimidation?"

Frankie took a step forward and grabbed my hand. I knew exactly what they were going to do: they would throw themself in the middle of this to defend me without considering the possible costs. I loved them for it, but I did not have the energy to deal with the inevitable fallout. Their intentions were good, but they had the tact of a tsunami, and I needed them to stay safe.

I tightened my hand around theirs. "Love, will you let me drive?"

They frowned. "Are you sure?"

"I think so. Yes. I'll tag you if I need you, alright?"

They didn't look happy, but they nodded. "Alright. Do your thing."

I turned to face the assembly. "Technically, I never touched him. I didn't even ask him to come over. All I did was create a reality for myself. It was his decision to barge in."

"You taunted him."

"He wouldn't have heard any of that if he'd not been stalking me."

"But you knew that he was stalking you, and you knew that he would not ignore your taunts."

I briefly considered lying, but I decided against it. "I had a good idea that he might come along, but it was still his choice. I just wanted him to leave me alone. As he refused to do that, I thought I'd teach him a lesson."

"Is that why you spilled his blood?"

"I didn't do that. I never laid a finger on him."

"You put a killer in his path."

A flashback of Jacob's last look before the axe hit him made me shudder. "That I did. I didn't mean to, but I don't suppose that matters."

Frankie wrapped his arm around my waist and whispered, "Are you alright?"

I whispered back. "Yes and no. I still wish it'd not gone down like that."

"It was an accident."

"I know, but I still feel terrible about it."

The angry voice boomed in my head again. *"Your feelings on the subject are wholly immaterial."*

Getting yelled at shook me out of my melancholy. "Everyone's feelings on any subject are wholly immaterial. That's just how feelings are."

The soft voice murmured, *"Now you're just being a smartass."*

"Yes. Sorry. But I really didn't mean to get Jacob hurt like that. That guy in the villa never actually hurt anyone. He was just a homeless person who lived there. He chased after us if we started to get too naughty, and scared the crap out of us, but that was it."

"But you remember him as a monster. That was his role in your childhood."

"Yes. That's why I got my littlest me to summon him. He was a lot bigger when I was smaller, kinda thing, but I had genuinely forgotten how much he used to scare me. I thought he might give Jacob a good scare, like Jacob had given me. I honestly didn't think it'd go down like that. I would take it back if I could, but I can't. Is Jacob alright? I mean, gods can't really die, can they?"

A chorus of imaginary voices exploded in my head. They all talked over each other, so I couldn't make out anything they were saying, until a piercing shriek cut through them all.

"Make them give it back!"

One of the distant figures advanced on me so fast that I didn't have a chance to panic until a face distorted by hatred hovered just inches from my nose. When it spoke, it revealed a mouth full of row after row of needle-sharp teeth. *"Thief! It's mine! Give. It. Back!"*

It was just a bit too much for me. I dissociated so fast and so far that I lost all sense of my body. I was floating a few feet away from the scene, looking at myself looking at the monster, and nothing mattered.

Frankie took a look at me and held me tighter. "Firstly, don't call Gio names. I've warned you about that before. I won't do it again. Secondly, if you want something from us, you better learn to use the magic word."

The face growled at them. *"You have exhausted your very limited charms. If you don't give me back what's mine, I will—"*

Frankie snorted. "You can cut that shit out, too. If you thought that you could bully it out of us, you would have done so already. So, how about you tell us what you want and why we should give it to you? And you might wanna consider what kind of attitude is more likely to make us want to do you a favor. At the moment, you're not doing great."

"Mortal, I will—"

Frankie's eyes narrowed and blazed, and their voice got that eerie echo that meant that they were about to do something supranatural. "Call me mortal again, and this conversation is over."

A new voice filled my brain; calm, deep, and mildly amused, it reminded me of Ben's, but it was infinitely more confident. *"If you have finished throwing threats around, maybe we could get to the bottom of this."*

Everyone shut up. My head got so quiet that my ears started ringing. I wasn't at all surprised, because that wasn't the sort of voice one would want to defy, even though there was no menace in it. There was something really absolute about it, as if what it said could define the reality around it.

The voice carried on. *"You didn't intend to harm Jacob?"*

I managed to squeak out a "No. Well, it depends on what you mean by harm. I wanted to teach him that I could scare him as much as he'd scared me. That's a type of harm. But I didn't want him to get hurt like that."

"And you did not intend to spill his blood?"

"No. Definitely not."

The voice sighed. *"But spill his blood you did, and now we have to deal with the consequences. You have his blood. He wants it back."*

"What? I don't have his blood! I didn't even touch it!" I found myself blinking back tears, and realized that they were tears of shame. I felt ashamed about that, too, and that second wave of shame finally pushed the tears out. "I just ran away. Maybe I should have tried to help him, but... I didn't. I couldn't."

"You would have gone back to help him?"

"No. Not really. I would like to be the kind of person who does that kind of thing, but I'm just not brave enough."

Another storm of disembodied murmurs started. The confident voice cut through it with a, *"Oh, for the love of all that is holy..."*

The scene changed suddenly. The seven gods were sitting on a half circle of matching leather armchairs only a few feet away from us. I still couldn't see them clearly, and I couldn't work out why. Every now and then my perspective shifted and it seemed that they were still far away, but so large that my brain couldn't process the distance. Either way, my eyes didn't like it, and it was giving me a rancid headache.

The confident voice whispered, *"Would you like to sit down? This is likely to take a while."*

I looked behind me and saw an armchair, and another one behind Frankie. We looked at each other, nodded, and sat down. My armchair was way too big for me, its arms so high that they reached nearly to my armpits. It reminded me of being a tiny child in the dentist's waiting room. I reached over to grab Frankie's hand. I had to bend and stretch in a way that was rather uncomfortable, but it made me feel better.

The confident voice mumbled to itself, *"This won't do."* A nanosecond later, Frankie and I were snuggled on a two-seater, surrounded by a heap of comfy cushions.

"That's better. Would you like something to drink?"

I looked at Frankie. They seemed as perplexed as I was, but they shrugged, so I shrugged too.

A woman got up from one of the armchairs. She had one of those voluptuous bodies which, once they are set in motion, seem to flow through the world without any actual expenditure of effort, like ocean waves. As she advanced towards us, I found it very hard to keep my eyes on her face. Frankie didn't seem to be even trying.

When she got to our couch, she looked down at Frankie with a smile and nodded towards a cup and saucer next to them. I could have sworn that they hadn't been there a moment before.

"What would you like?" I recognized the soft voice from earlier. It sounded as if maple syrup was being poured all over my brain.

Frankie made a small, strangled noise before clearing their throat. They then proceeded to emit a long series of meaningless monosyllables.

The woman giggled. *"Sure. Hold up your vessel."*

I elbowed Frankie. They spun around in shock, blushed crimson, and spun back to pick up their cup. The lady filled it up from a pitcher that came out of nowhere. When she was done, she floated over to me.

I knew the drill, so I held my cup up without being asked and managed not to look surprised when whatever she was pouring started steaming. Frankie's drink had not done that.

When my cup was full, she nodded at me, winked at Frankie, and meandered back to her chair. When she got there, she sat down. The pitcher was nowhere in sight.

I elbowed Frankie again and mumbled, "Close your damn mouth!"

They jumped a foot in the air. "I'm sorry! I love you!"

"And I love you, even when you drool over busty women."

They blushed crimson and took a sip of their drink. They choked and coughed, and then they took another one. "Holy shit."

"What did you get?"

"It's either a really good single malt, or someone dissolved a chunk of peat and a horse turd in turpentine."

"And you're going to drink that?"

"Oh hell, yeah! It's fantastic! What did you get?"

"Hot cocoa with mini marshmallows. They're shaped like hearts."

They beamed at me. "I love you so fucking much."

A polite cough brought me back to the present. *"If you don't mind,"* the confident voice said, *"We really need to get this issue resolved."*

I put my cup down. "Sure. I'm still confused as to what the issue is."

"Jacob's blood was spilled, in copious amounts, in a reality of your making. Every part of that reality was a part of you, including his killer. That makes

you responsible for his death."

"None of it was real, though. I just made it all up."

"It was real within itself. Everything that happened there really happened there. Does that make sense?"

"Not really. I mean, I understand the words you are saying, but they don't make much sense. I can take it as a given, though."

"Good. The blood was spilled within your reality. The earth of your reality absorbed it. Well, that and a wall, apparently. By all accounts, it was a thorough but messy job."

My stomach tightened up. "I am sorry about that. I really am."

I kept scanning the seven gods, trying to guess who was speaking. I knew it wasn't the voluptuous woman, and I was willing to bet that it wasn't the other woman there, either. The other five seemed to be guys, although I obviously couldn't be sure. Taking Jacob out of the equation left four of them. My eyes kept travelling back to a man wearing a tatty blue hoodie and John Lennon-style sunglasses. He was the worst dressed of everyone there, but there was something about the way he lounged in his chair, attentive but relaxed, that made him look in charge.

The voice continued. *"I believe you. That doesn't alter the facts, though. You have Jacob's blood. Do you understand what that means?"*

"Nope. Not a clue."

Lennon started laughing. I couldn't hear him, but I could see his chest heave. *"Oh, this is funny! You killed a god and took his blood, and you don't even know what that means?"*

Jacob turned towards him, his lips parted in a snarl. His teeth had gone back to normal, but he didn't look any friendlier. *"It may be a joke to you—"*

"It definitely is. You'd see the joke too, if you weren't so bitter about it all."

"It has my blood!"

"She does. But he wouldn't have it if you'd not goaded her. He had asked you to leave her alone, and you didn't. You started this, and it turned around and bit you on the ass. I don't feel sorry for you."

"You have to fix this!"

"Do I?"

There was nothing inherently threatening in that question or how it was posed, but it still put a knot in my stomach. Jacob seemed to be just as affected. His eyes widened, and he shrunk back into himself. *"No. Of course. I didn't mean to... But if mortals start challenging the gods—"*

"It would be good for you. It would teach you to keep on your toes, instead of wasting your days and your powers on petty nonsense. It would do all of us good: we have grown slack with overconfidence."

"But—"

"*Spare me. I will deal with this as I see fit.*" He turned towards me. "*Do you believe that you have Jacob's blood?*"

I could see Frankie nodding out of the corner of my eye. "Yes."

"*Are you willing to give it back? That would bring about the quickest resolution.*"

"I don't know. What would that entail?"

Lennon scratched his beard. "*Bloodletting. We'd give you your blood back, naturally. It would be not unlike donating platelets in one of your hospitals, except that the process would be a bit more old-fashioned.*"

Frankie's hand tightened around mine. "Old-fashioned how?"

"*Instead of using a needle and a machine, we use a blade and a chalice.*"

"Out of the question!"

Lennon leaned forward in his chair. "*You give yourself the right to speak for your partner?*"

"Not generally, but I draw the line at exsanguination!" They turned to me. "Gio, I fully respect your bodily autonomy and I'm not gonna tell you what to do, but I would really appreciate it if we could discuss this."

"No need. I have no intention of having my blood poured into a chalice, or any other drinking vessel, for that matter. Sorry and all that."

Jacob exploded. "*Do you hear it? It defies us.*"

Frankie exploded back. "What is your fucking problem, anyway? People donate blood all the time! Eat a few steaks, drink plenty of fluids, rest, and you'll be back to normal in no time!"

Jacob had just opened his mouth to screech when Lennon's laughter cut him off. "*Oh, this is great fun. You really don't get it, do you?*"

"No! And I'll probably continue not to get it unless you decide to actually explain it to us!"

"*Sure. What do you know about sympathetic magic?*"

Frankie glanced at me, dread exuding out of them. "Huh. Not a lot. Gio explained it to me last term, but I'm not sure I really got it and my memory is crap." And they launched into a painfully detailed explanation of the laws of similarity and contact that would probably have gone on for a half hour, plus ten minutes for references, if Lennon hadn't lifted a hand to stop them.

"*Great. So you will understand. Your partner created a world out of herself. In that world, he bested Jacob. Not only that, but she bested Jacob at his own game.*"

Frankie beamed. "He tricked a trickster."

"*Yes. And Jacob's death took place inside your partner. When his blood was spilled, not a drop was lost. And blood is the essence of life."*

"But Jacob is right there. I mean, he looks pretty good for a dead guy." Frankie tilted their head. "Wait. I can actually see him. Normally he's all pixelated, kinda. What the fuck is going on?"

"Killing a god is not as simple as swatting a fly, though some of us are just as annoying. Jacob isn't altogether dead, but the part of him that entered Gio's world died there. More importantly, the blood symbolized the transfer of Jacob's essence and, with it, some of his powers."

"So Jacob can't shapeshift?"

Lennon smirked. *"He can, but he has to actually shift his shape. He can't just use his glamour to baffle mortals. Sorry! Humans."*

"No worries. And how long is that going to last?"

"Until he gets his blood back."

"Even though none of what happened was really real?"

"Yes. We are not entirely sure of how it came about, to be perfectly honest. That kind of thing can happen temporarily, in a ritual setting, but to have it happen by accident, as part of a prank..." He shrugged. *"Our people are investigating the issue. We have some theories, but nothing has been proven yet. Gio seems to have the ability to create a very concrete reality around him."*

Frankie beamed. "She does. I live in his home, and it doesn't get homier than that."

"Huh. Interesting. Anyway, the blood, representing Jacob's essence, was soaked by the earth, representing Gio. That was enough to do it. When the reality was cancelled, Jacob found that some of his powers were missing."

Frankie reeled. "Hot damn. A powerful enough metaphor really grows its own truth."

Lennon looked impressed. *"Where did you learn that?"*

"You wouldn't believe me if I told you. So a part of Jacob is inside Gio?"

"Basically."

Frankie turned to me. "Do you feel alright?"

"I feel totally grossed out, but otherwise fine. Remind me not to kill any more gods, alright?"

"If the need arises, we'll put some tarps down first."

"Sound strategy." I turned to Lennon. "If I give Jacob his blood back, will I die?"

"No. It would, however, be somewhat uncomfortable."

"And Jacob will get his powers back?"

"Yes."

"And if I don't?"

Jacob started shrieking in incoherent rage, but he was cut off by Lennon getting up. *"Would you like to come for a walk with me?"*

Frankie and I looked at each other. Their eyes were full of uncertainty, but they nodded. I wasn't half as keen.

"I don't want to make a fuss, but I'd prefer it if there was a floor. And I'd really appreciate it if it wasn't the floor of my old school."

Lennon winced. *"Of course. I'm sorry. Your place or mine?"*

"What?" I squealed.

"Would you like to open a portal?"

"I can't. I don't have any timber."

He smiled. *"You don't need it, not unless you believe that you need it, particularly when you're somewhere like here. None of this is quite real. Well, it's not the kind of real you're used to."*

"Are there different kinds of real?"

"Yes. So, would you like to do the honors?"

I thought about opening a portal and letting him through, and it felt way too intimate. Maybe it was just that my portals had always been a private thing, something between me and Frankie that only Ben knew about. Maybe I'd been hearing too much about gods spilling their bodily fluids into me. Either way, I found myself profoundly disinclined to let a stranger through any portal of mine.

I shook my head. "Your place. If you don't mind."

He shrugged. *"No problem."*

He reached out as if to grab an invisible door handle. Sure enough, as soon as he turned it, the door was there. He opened it and waved us through into a scene right out of an old Italian movie: we were in one of those bars where the smell of coffee is enough to raise your blood pressure and they sell every type of pastry a mind could imagine. The smells were so delicious and distracting that it took me a while to realize that we couldn't possibly be in Italy, because all the prices were in dollars.

Frankie looked around, their eyes big enough to swallow half the display. "Where are we?"

"St. Paul, Minnesota. We can go somewhere else, if you want, but the coffee here is to die for."

We both jumped up. Lennon had actually said that, using his actual mouth. His voice didn't sound much like the mental voice he'd been projecting; it was softer, more musical, and with a trace of an accent I couldn't quite identify.

He smiled at us, or at our discomfort. "This is my treat. What would you like? If you're hungry, they sell pizza just around the corner."

I looked around. The place was absolutely crammed with people. It didn't surprise me in the least, because everything on display looked delicious, but the density of the crowd put such a knot in my stomach that I didn't think anything else would fit in. I did my best to smile and speak loudly enough to be audible. "I'm OK."

"You don't want anything?"

"No, thank you."

Frankie flinched. "Gio, if you're gonna do that, at least warn me?" He turned to Lennon. "Gio would like to eat literally everything this place holds, but his stomach is too small. That's not the problem, though. She doesn't really like to eat in front of people."

Lennon smiled. "That's a problem I can fix."

Frankie bunched their fists and started to shake in excitement. "Are you going to make us invisible? Or stop time for everyone but us?"

"That's some creative problem-solving right there, but I was just going to ask for take-out."

Frankie blushed. "Yeah. That'd do it."

They turned back to me to check that I was OK. When I nodded, they shooed me off to a relatively quiet corner so I could catch my breath, then walked over to wait in line with Lennon while he ordered. As their conversation progressed, they got more and more into it. I could tell the exact instant when they totally forgot our circumstances and fell fully into whatever it was Lennon was telling them; they were suddenly so alert, alive, and present that everything around them seemed to fade. They turned, beamed at me, and raced over.

"Gio! You're never gonna guess this!"

"Very likely. Are you going to tell me?"

"He's seen John Darnielle live! Four times!" They stared at me, burning with excitement.

"Love, I hate to burst your bubble, but I don't know who that is."

"What?! John Darnielle! The Mountain Goats!"

"Ah. Sure. That's... interesting?"

Their energy dissipated, leaving them limp and clearly vexed. "Yes, Gio, it is! What's your beef?"

"It's just that you've been talking to a god who kidnapped me in my dreams and opened a magical portal into an Aladdin's Cave of the most delicious food on god's green earth—"

"Which god?"

"What? Oh. OK. That was an unfortunate turn of phrase. Frankie, love, I am very, very happy that you have a new friend and he likes the music you like, but there are other considerations we should probably keep in mind, one of them being that we still don't know who the fuck that guy is."

They scoffed. "You should start trusting me. Of course I asked him that! His name is Lance. Well, that's the name he's using, anyway."

"What, Lance as in spear?"

They blinked. "I kind of assumed that he was a Voltron fan, but yeah, that makes more sense." Their brain did one of its about-turns, and they were suddenly grave. "You're not really considering going along with this, are you?"

"I don't know. The whole bloodletting thing isn't really my scene, but I don't know how else we can get Jacob off our backs."

"Do you think that'd do it?"

"I don't know. He's been a pretty persistent pest up to this point."

"I hope that alliteration wasn't aimed at me." Lance was standing behind Frankie, holding a large paper bag and a loaded cup holder. "You want to get out of here?"

I nodded. "Please." It was one of the most beautiful places I'd ever been, full of perfect food, but discussing the pros and cons of getting bled half to death while getting jostled by a crowd was just too much.

When Lance opened the door, I expected him to take us into a different world. In a way, he did: we stepped out of 1950s Italy and into modern America, but no magic was involved. He led us down the road for a few minutes until we reached a park by a river, where he found us a quiet spot under a tree.

As he opened our bag of treats, he smiled at our surroundings as if greeting a friend. "The Mississippi. Have you seen it before?"

Frankie nodded. I shook my head.

"I really like it here. Of all the cities I've lived in, it's probably my favorite. Great music scene, great food, and just about enough trees to make me feel like I can breathe. I miss the sea, though."

Frankie picked up their cup and smiled shyly at him. "Why do you stay here, then?"

"I'm self-employed. Do you know how hard it is to find reliable staff?"

"Nope. But I work for my uncle, and I don't think he would have put up with me if he wasn't desperate and I wasn't family."

"I don't know. He speaks very highly of you."

Frankie blushed crimson. "You know him?"

"Yes. Not well, but I don't know many people who do. He's not terribly sociable, but I've never known another person that good around a forge. It seems like such a waste that he chooses to work with water."

Frankie frowned. "I don't know. I haven't asked him, but I figured that after years of working with fire, he wanted a change."

Lance looked stricken and went quiet. It suited me fine, because Frankie had just deposited not one, not two, but four delicious-looking little pastries right in front of me. I looked up at them with a question, and they smiled.

"We get two each, and you get to pick, because I had to guess what you wanted. I don't care, anyway. You know me: if it's got sugar in it, I like it."

"This is perfect. Thank you."

"So, why are you not eating?" They grinned. "Homeslice, are you having an 'Alice in Wonderland' moment?"

"Yes! How could you tell?"

They leaned over and kissed my cheek. "Magic. That, or I know how your brain works. Eat up, before I decide that I want all of them."

Instead of answering them, I shoved half a pastry in my mouth.

"Gio, I was joking. Can you please try not to choke yourself?"

I swallowed and shrugged. "It would be a pretty good way to go."

Lance was looking more and more uncomfortable. I was fairly used to that: a lot of people found my relationship with Frankie discomfiting. When that happened, it never failed to give me pause, but then so did most social interactions. Over the months, I had learnt to ignore that feeling and carry on, provided that doing so wasn't going to result in us getting a stomping. We weren't doing anything that a binary couple wouldn't do in public, after all. Frankie liked Lance, though, so I decided to tone us down a notch until he was used to us.

We behaved ourselves properly all the way through our meal. Even so, Lance hardly said anything, and he looked relieved when we were done eating.

As he packed up our trash, he fashioned his face into the semblance of a smile. "If you want me to leave you to discuss the situation, I'm more than happy to do that. That's largely why I got you out here. I figured you needed some time and space."

Frankie beamed at him. "That's very kind of you."

"No, it's not. I believe that what I want is the right thing, so I obviously assume that you'll come to the right decision if you get a chance to think this through. My people have a tendency to assume that bullying and manipulation will get them what they want."

"Yes! I can't say that I appreciate it."

Lance shrugged. "I always assume that I'm the wisest person in the room. We all have our faults. So, do you want me to clear off?"

I took a deep breath and spoke up. "In a bit, maybe, but first we really need more information. I can't quite get a grip on what happened. I mean, I take your word for it, but it all seems surreal. And I definitely don't know enough about what's going to happen if I give Jacob back his blood."

"You will experience some temporary discomfort, and Jacob will get his powers back."

"When you put it like that, it doesn't sound like a great deal for me."

He shrugged. "The flipside is what may happen if you don't give him what he wants. He's unlikely to take that lying down."

"So he'll be on our tail forever?"

"Most likely. The flipside of that is that, at the moment, you are evenly matched. Theoretically, anyway: you need to learn to use your new powers. Until then, they are functionally useless. When you do, however, you should be more powerful than he is."

"What? Why?"

"You would have your three gifts, your human abilities, and his powers. He just has what's left of his powers."

Frankie guffawed. "And a few centuries of doing stuff and learning things! I mean, Gio has read about half the books ever written and knows how to do pretty much anything, I'm not knocking that, but we're barely grown-ups. In the grand scheme of things, we don't know shit. How long has Jacob been around?"

Lance looked uncomfortable. "That's classified."

Frankie goggled. "Say what?"

"He can choose to tell you himself, but we don't out each other."

"Is it one of your rules?"

"Yes. Anyway, Jacob's age is fairly immaterial. One can be old and ignorant, or at least limited in one's experience. My people are fairly prone to that. We have a tendency to stick with what we're good at and skate by on our powers."

Frankie's eyes became perfectly round. "Huh. Gio has never skated by on anything. I mean, he's the smartest person I've ever met—"

I mumbled a, "Stop it!"

"You are! But you haven't had it easy, have you? I mean, you've been swimming upstream most of your life. That's probably why you kick so much ass."

"Yeah, right." I wasn't inclined to talk about all the things I struggled to do in front of Lance, which was just as well: it would have taken me forever to list them all.

"Yeah, right! I'm glad you agree! Anyway, you're really good at triumphing over adversity and all that kind of shit."

"Do you want to make it sound more epic?"

"Not really, but I can if you want me to. Are you going to shut up long enough for me to get my point across?"

"If I do, will you make any sense?"

"Tons of it. What I'm trying to say is that you're so used to making do with not enough that can do almost everything with almost nothing. If you had enough, you could achieve so fucking much!" Their eyes went soft and dreamy. "I can't wait to see that. And if you had more than enough, what you could do would be just amazing. I just know it."

"I could say the same about you."

"Nah. I had plenty of opportunities and blew them."

"Like what?"

"Like my parents being loaded, and me barely graduating high school."

"There's a bit more to that story."

"Yeah, but... You know me. Give me all the resources in the world, and I'd still not get anywhere. I'd never get my shit in order, or I'd start something and drop it halfway. That wouldn't even be a bad thing; half of what I'd try to do would be bullshit, anyway. But you could do so many good things. Think about it, Gio: you, with Jacob's powers—"

"We don't even know what those powers are." I turned to Lance. "I know he can shapeshift, and I know that he's an asshole, but that's about it. What else can he do?"

Lance frowned. "He's a genius."

Frankie muttered, "So's Gio," but I hushed them up.

"Anything else?"

"He is a skilled sorcerer."

"I thought that was a matter of training. Learning spells, and so on."

"Yes and no. Sorcery is... complicated. You need a certain aptitude for it. Spells help, no doubt, but they aren't it. Magic is about raising the natural energy that exists in all things – people, animals, plants, stones, but also immaterial things like sensations and emotions. Once that energy is raised, it has to be shaped, to be given a purpose, and then released with a certain intention. If the energy is sufficient and applied accurately, the desired effect will take place."

Frankie whistled under their breath. "No wonder I suck at it, then. I can't focus for shit."

I elbowed them. "Will you cut it out with the self-deprecating shit? I've never met anyone who can focus as hard as you do."

"Yeah, but it's hardly ever on what I need to be focusing on."

"We could fix that. I don't think I want to, though." I turned to Lance.

"Is there anything else Jacob has got that I might possibly want?"

Lance shook his head. "Are you seriously telling me that you are not interested in magic? Most humans would kill for that. Many have, in fact."

"Not me." The memory of Jacob getting butchered flashed through my brain. "Well, not intentionally, anyway. I mean, magic is nifty, but it's been way too much trouble up to now. I like a quiet life."

"Alright. Well, Jacob can be very persuasive. In fact, the most surprising thing about this entire episode is that it went this far. I would have expected him to get what he wanted from you just by talking you into it."

"I'd file that under 'being an asshole,' and it's hardly a superpower, anyway. The world is full of manipulative bastards."

"I don't think many of them are as skilled as Jacob, but I see your point. He's also unencumbered by rules."

"Again, asshole."

Frankie ran their finger on my hand. "I'm not too good at rules, either."

"That's because most rules make no sense, and you see that. You don't just break them for shits and giggles."

"Well, if you look at my past record..."

"I'd rather not. And you always do your best not to hurt people, so it's a totally different situation. You have a million zillion rules you live by, and they're all sound. It's the official ones you don't always buy into."

A little smile crept on their lips. "So you still love me, even though I'm a rebel?"

"Outlaw, technically. But yes, of course I do." I tore my eyes from their face, even though it was a struggle. "Love, we need to keep our thinking brains on. We're nowhere nearer coming to a decision about this."

"We're not? It seems like an obvious choice. You can do a lot more good with Jacob's powers than he ever will."

"Sure, but I don't know if I want to. I don't want to have supernatural powers. All I want is for things to go back to normal."

"Homeslice, things were never normal."

"Alright. Then what I want is for things to get normal, and for us two to live happily ever after. I don't really care what that looks like, as long as we get there."

"Oh, shit." Their smile faded, replaced by a stricken look. "That. Of course. How the fuck didn't I think about that?"

"About what?"

"Jacob's age." They turned to Lance. "If Gio got a chunk of Jacob's powers, is she immortal now?"

Lance looked really uncomfortable. "That's unlikely. We don't know for sure, but half of immortality is mortality, after all. But he is almost certainly going to live for a very long time."

"But that's great!" They whirred around to face me. "Isn't it?"

I was starting to feel physically ill. Odd magical powers didn't really bother me anymore; we'd had to deal with them for months, and they weren't anything more than a minor hassle. All we had to do was not use them, and things could be basically normal. This was different, though. This was real. And something about it felt really, really gross.

My thoughts were spinning out of control so fast that I was caught in a vortex of nausea, but I tried to make them congeal into something coherent for Frankie's sake. "Taking away someone's lifetime is a sick thing to do."

They picked up my hand and held it tight. "Gio, we got him killed."

"I did. You didn't. And it was an accident, anyway, and it didn't feel as bad. Taking his time while he's alive makes me feel like a leech."

"That's his tough shit for going after you. Just think about this, alright? You wouldn't have to be scared of dying."

"To be honest, dying doesn't scare me half as much as living does."

"You're not thinking straight! Think of all the things you could do, all the stuff you could learn! You could read all the books, Gio. You could read until your brain got so full that stuff would start leaking out the other end. And think about me!"

"What about you?"

They smiled. "I'd never lose you. Only..." A thought had been gathering at the back of their eyes, dimming their light. "Nah. Doesn't matter."

"The hell it doesn't. Out with it."

They looked straight at me, beautiful and desolate. "Will you still love me when I get old? I mean, I know you'd still love me if we both got old, but if I get old and you don't, will you still love me?"

I froze. I thought about them getting old, how cute and funny they would be, how they'd be the terror of any retirement home, charming and exasperating the most hardened nurses. I knew, I just knew, that their inner light would dazzle me forever.

Until it stopped shining. One day that light would die out, leaving the world utterly dark and empty. The sun may come up in the morning, the stars may stay up in the sky, the days follow one after the other, but there'd be no joy in it, no magic, no meaning. If the world carried on, it would be an empty parody of its former self.

I thought about how it'd feel to know that I'd lost them forever, that they'd never come back to me. I knew that what I was feeling was only a fraction of the real horror of it, a tiny taste of a pain I could hardly comprehend, but it was still awful enough to put ice in my veins and fill my throat with bile. Then I thought about an eternity of that, endless days mourning the loss of the only person I'd ever loved and would ever love, the only person worth loving, and a huge sob wracked my body.

Frankie snapped to high alert. "Gio, what is it?"

I wanted to tell them, but I just couldn't. I was feeling too much. Sob after sob exploded out of me, until I lost all control of my body. A little voice at the back of my head informed me that this was why they called them 'paroxysms of grief,' while the rest of me was wracked by despair.

In the pale, dim world outside the storm in my chest, Lance mumbled something, got up, and cleared off. Frankie wrapped their arms around me and murmured soothing nonsense into my hair. It still took forever and a day for my episode to be over, and even then I could hardly speak.

"Forever... Without you."

I felt Frankie go rigid. "Oh. Shit. Yes. But you'd get over it, Gio. I mean, it's not as if you can stop me dying, one way or the other. You'd meet other people—"

"No! Don't make me! Please!"

I dissolved into a tsunami of tears and snot all over their shoulder. They didn't seem to mind; they just held me and rocked me until I stopped crying. When I was done, they peeled me off them, wiped my cheeks, and stared straight into my eyes.

"Are you sure?"

I didn't trust myself to speak, so I nodded.

"You wanna think about this? When you feel better?"

I shook my head.

"Alright. If you're really sure." They wiped a few stray tears off my face and made me drink the rest of their coffee. I didn't want to let go of them, so they held the cup up to my lips. A lot of it went down my chin, which made them swear, which made me giggle. I felt better afterwards, even though my chest still hurt.

When Lance walked back towards us, as tentative as if I were a rabid dog, Frankie squeezed my hand and looked a question at me. I nodded.

They took a deep breath. "Gio has decided. She's going ahead with it. Can you get your ceremony ready?"

It wasn't hard for us to guess what Lance had hoped I would decide to do. As soon as Frankie explained my decision to him, he cooled off towards me so suddenly and comprehensively that I started to shiver.

"You're going to give up the chance to be a demigod because you don't want to outlive your partner?"

I couldn't speak yet, so Frankie answered for me. "Yes."

"And you are going to let her go ahead with this?"

"I never tell him what to do. And anyway, I'd do the same. I can imagine a life without her, but I'd rather not."

Lance stiffened. "Fine. But, for the record, I do not understand you."

Frankie sagged slightly. "I'm sorry. I really am."

Lance shrugged the apology off, opened a portal, and waved us to go through. "Eight tonight, your time. Wear clothes you don't mind getting bloody."

Frankie frowned. "Where?"

"Immaterial. We'll find you."

We stepped through the portal together, holding hands, and found ourselves in our back yard. The sun was up in the sky, but the world still felt new. The breeze put a chill in the air. That was mostly why I shivered.

Frankie pulled me along. "Let's get inside before you catch something."

I patted my pockets. "I don't have my keys."

"Me neither. Hey, I'm glad you dreamt yourself some clothes before they picked you up."

"Shit. My nightmares are not *that* bad. Don't give my brain any ideas."

"We really need to make provisions for this kind of eventuality."

"I refuse to go to bed with you wearing a fanny pack."

They snorted. "You'd go to bed with me if I was wearing a flamingo costume, and you know it."

It was at that point that I bashed my knee into an invisible barrier and swore at the top of my voice.

Frankie turned back to look at me. "What is it?"

"The fucking circle! I can't get through!"

Their face hovered between hilarity and awe. "Wow. You've circled yourself out of your own home. You really are a demigod, hey."

I turned the circle off and stepped through. For the first time ever, I really felt my own circle: it was only a light vibration in the air, but it was definitely there.

I started shuddering. I felt alien and gross, which I was used to, but this new sensation was much worse than my usual self-loathing: I wanted to rip my flesh off and soak my brain in bleach to remove every trace of Jacob from me.

Frankie took a look at my face and hugged me. "Come on. Let's get inside."

"I don't know if I want to be in the house right now."

"Why?"

"I don't want to soil it. Frankie, home was our happy place."

"It still is. We've been through some shit, and we're still here. Come on. I'm sure it's time for breakfast."

"We can't get in! And everybody's out!"

They grinned. "You've forgotten our special skills."

They dragged me to our bathroom window and squinted at it. Two seconds later, I heard a popping sound.

"What did you do?"

"Broke the latch." They lifted the window open and waved me through. "In you get. You're way smaller than me."

I hated to leave them out there in case they just disappeared, so I raced to our patio door. When I opened it, they were already out there. They walked in and hugged me in a single movement.

"Gio, I don't tell you enough: I love you so. Damn. Much."

"I love you, too. What time is it?"

"Time you got some food into you."

"No way. I'd just throw up. How long do we have to wait?"

They checked their watch. "It's not even 8 yet."

"I can't do it. I just can't. If I sit down, I will literally explode."

They kissed me. "Don't sit down, then. If you need to move, move."

"I'm just worked up."

"Small wonder. And that doesn't change the fact that you feel like moving."

"But—"

"No." They gripped my shoulders and locked eyes with me. "Your response to this isn't right or wrong: it just is. Do what you need to do. What's the alternative? Trying to stand still and driving yourself up the wall in the process?"

"But I'm in no fit state to do anything useful."

"Do you give a fuck? Because I don't. If doing useless stuff makes you feel better, it is useful."

They dragged me over to the garage, walked over to the sink, filled a jug with hot water and dishwashing liquid, threw a rag in it, and handed it to me. "Clean. Dust. Break stuff. Run around screaming. Whatever works."

"And you?"

"And I'm going to park my ass on the couch and brood. Get on with it."

I set off to clean our kitchen. Two minutes later, I was caught in a whirlwind of barely-coordinated action: I charged about with no clear goal and no system, dealing with whatever came up, washing and dusting and tidying whatever was in front of my nose. An indefinite amount of time later, the energy that had been driving me just ran out. I found myself sitting on the floor, a wet rag in my hand and a dusty baseboard before me, but the thought of cleaning it up was just too much. I dragged myself to the couch and lay down over Frankie. They wrapped their arms around me and kissed my hair. We stayed like that for a while, then they rolled me gently off them.

"Homeslice, you need to eat."

"I'm not hungry."

"That's irrelevant. You still need to eat."

"First you tell me to listen to my body, Now you tell me to ignore it?"

"Yes. I told you to do what was good for you. Right now, that means getting some damn food into you. You'll need your strength." They tensed up. "Gio, if I could spare you this I would. You know that, right? If there was absolutely anything I could do to make this right, or just make it go away—"

"I know. But there isn't."

"Right. But I can make sure you eat your fucking meals when your system is out of whack. Do you have any requests?"

"Something quick, so you'll be back soon."

They kissed me. "I love you more than I can say. Anything else?"

I tried to think about it, because Frankie wanted me to. "Something soft? My head hurts and I don't feel like chewing.

"Right. Great idea." They kissed my forehead and got up.

I crawled into the warm spot they'd left on the couch and tried to imagine that it was a part of them, a phantom limb they'd left behind to keep me cozy and warm. Between that and watching them bustle around the kitchen, so focused on looking after me that all other considerations had been driven from their mind, I felt warm inside and out, as if I were wrapped in a cocoon of their love.

When they turned up with two plates heaped with noodles, I felt almost calm. I ate every morsel, largely because every time I put my fork down they gave me A Look. When I was done, they took my plate from me and replaced it with a glass of chocolate milk. When I was done with that, too, they smiled.

"Good kid. You're bearing up with this awfully well."

"Are you kidding? I'm terrified."

"That's because you're not a fool. And anyway, I'm terrified, too."

"What of?"

"You getting hurt. Me having to watch you get hurt." They marched me off to the couch, scooped me up, and sat me on their lap. "When we were caught in the last of Jacob's traps, I made a vow to myself."

"What was it?"

"I wanted to vow that nobody was ever going to hurt you again, but I'm not twelve anymore. Hell, I don't know if I would have believed it even when I was a kid. So I vowed that I was never going to sit idle and watch you get hurt. I don't even know if that was for your benefit or mine, because having to sit and watch that shit unfold nearly did my head in. And here we are, just a few days later, and I'm going to sit by and watch you give up something that could be so good for you, and get hurt in the process. It's precisely what I vowed to never do. This kind of shit doesn't do much for my self-respect, you know?"

"But I'm asking you to do that. You're doing it for me."

"All of this is my fault. That you're in this situation, and that you want to get out of it. Anyone else would kill for a half chance at immortality, and superpowers to boot."

"Nobody else has you. They don't have what we've got."

They snorted. "Other people are in love, Gio."

"Not like we are."

"And you know that how?"

"If they loved like I love you, there'd be no spectator sports, no advertising, no fashion industry, no stock exchange—"

"What? Why?"

"Because nobody would bother with all that crap. They'd do the bare minimum required to get food, clothes, and shelter, and then they'd go home to be with you. That's what I'll do, soon as I have a chance to."

They chortled. "When you put it like that, it makes sense. Just as well we're special, hey? Having too many of us around would be the end of capitalism."

"Yeah. And what a shame that would be."

"A tragedy, indeed. There would still be music, though. I'm sure of it."

"Of course. Music is a basic human need."

"Right. But all the songs would be about you."

"Huh. It's probably for the best that's not the case."

"Nonsense. All the best songs are about you now." They lifted me off their lap and got up. "Come on. Up you get."

"What? Why?"

"Because something terrible is about to happen and I want to spend the time we have until then doing the most wonderful thing I can think of."

I started off towards our bedroom, but they caught me by the hand. "Nah. Here's better."

"We can't! If Ben comes back early—"

They turned the stereo up without looking at it. "He wouldn't care in the least. Gio, what's my favorite thing to do?"

"I'm not quite sure. It's either having sex or playing guitar."

"Pah! You are utterly wrong, even though you're kind of right."

"What is it, then?"

They stepped close to me and held my waist. "Dancing. Obviously."

"I've never seen you dance."

They pulled me closer to them. "That's because you never take me dancing."

"I can't. I can't dance."

"You can. Everyone and everything can dance. The light dances, and so do the stars in the sky and the waves on the sea. Even the dust dances. Everything that's alive dances. That's what being alive means."

"You just said that the dust dances, and the dust is not alive."

"Precisely. Do you want to let the dust kick your ass? Come on." They pulled me towards the middle of the room.

"I can't. I told you. And anyway, Jimi Hendrix isn't dance music."

They stiffened. "Gio, don't swear at me. All music is dance music."

"If you believe in yourself?"

"No. If you believe in the music. Can you waltz?"

"No! Why, can you?"

"Naturally. Did you think that my folk would have let me reach adulthood without all the skills pertinent to a gentleman?" They took a few steps towards me. I tried to keep up, but I tripped them up anyway.

"I thought your folk were against anything fun on principle."

"Ballroom dancing is not supposed to be fun. It's a socially sanctioned public display with the implicit purpose of assisting one in securing a worthy mate. It utterly negates what dancing should be all about."

"Which is?"

"Making love with music."

"Then we've done that hundreds of times. We've always got the music on when we make love."

They started swaying slowly in time with the music. "No, Homeslice: making love *to* the music. That's what dancing is, or should be. Just let your body fuck the music, Gio, and let the music fuck you. Let it happen."

They pulled my hands behind them and stuck them in their back pockets.

"I can't. I don't know the steps."

"You don't know the steps when we're doing it, and you don't let that stop you."

"That's completely different."

"It's not. You get in time with my body and do what feels right. Just get in time with the music instead."

"I can't! I don't know what to do!"

"Whatever you want. There are no wrong steps, same as there are no wrong notes."

"You've not heard me try to sing."

"I haven't. I look forward to that. But for now, we should dance."

"Why?"

"Because dancing is the opposite of being dead."

We'd somehow made it over to our table. I realized that when I felt it behind my ass. They put their hands against it, one on each side of me.

"You can hear the bass, right? That's usually where you're at."

"How do you know that?"

"Because you're forever humming along to the bass line when you don't stop yourself. Can you feel it?"

"What?"

"Don't think about it. Close your eyes and tell me where you can feel it."

Not looking at them was torture, but they were close enough to me that I could bear it. I found the bass line with my ears, and then followed it to where it was in the room. I pointed to it.

They giggled. "Gio, that's my sternum."

"I know. That's where it is."

"I was thinking more in terms of your body."

I shrugged. "That was not specified in the instructions."

"Noted. I'll revise my method for next time."

They squished themself right up against me, so I could barely move. With my eyes closed, I could feel the bass line in their chest. I followed it as it travelled up and down, trying to work out whether it was beating along with their heart or it was beating their heart for them. When they stepped back from me, I realized that what I was feeling was in my own chest, and I determined to express my awe in the most poetic manner I could come up with.

"Well, shit."

They chortled. "Told you."

"But now I lost it!"

"So what? You'll find it again. I love you so fucking much."

"Why?"

"Because I have excellent taste, as well as the best luck of any person who ever lived."

I kissed them. They didn't seem to mind; in fact their response was rather enthusiastic. They still kept moving to the music, though. After a while, I had to say something.

"Frankie, this is weird."

"What is?"

"There being three of us in here: me, you, and the music."

"Get used to it. This is only the first stage, anyway."

"More than three would be a crowd."

"True that. But when you get your head out of it—"

"Don't you mean around it?"

"Absolutely not. Anyway, when that happy moment comes, you'll come to realize that there's only ever one of us."

"Love, that is very Zen."

"Thank you."

"I meant to say that I think it's bullshit."

"I know. I'll still take it as a compliment."

They closed their eyes. Their lips parted slightly, so I put my tongue through them. They put up no resistance. I could feel the music in them: the bass beat in their chest, the guitar travelled up and down their spine, and the drums drove their hips against mine.

I disengaged our mouths and lifted my ass up on the table.

They half-opened one eye. "Hey. Whatcha doing?"

"You'll find out soon enough."

I undid a couple of their shirt buttons. That wasn't quite enough, so I undid them all. I let my hands follow the beat on their skin, and a smile blossomed on their lips.

"Is that strictly necessary?"

"Yes. Trust me."

"It's very distracting.

"That's unfortunate. Do you want me to stop?"

"Nah. I'll cope."

When I undid their zipper, they let off a soft, questioning moan.

"Love, is that a problem?"

"Nope. I am, as always, utterly at your mercy."

Thirty seconds later, they were fucking the tune into me. The music travelled through them, and their body pinned it into mine. Every now and then, they'd remember who they were and what they were doing, and they'd open their eyes to check on me. I'd kiss them, and five seconds later they'd lose themself again.

As the guitar solo peaked, so did we. They finished the song sprawled over me, humming gently into my neck. I could still feel the music tingling through their skin, or maybe through mine. I couldn't really tell, and I didn't really care.

They sighed. "I don't want to get off you."

"Don't, then."

"I also don't want Lance to walk in on us and find my naked ass up in the air."

"Are you worried that it's going to give him ideas?"

They blushed. "He's pretty cute, but he's straight."

"I bow to your superior knowledge. He's also a bit of a dick."

"Yeah." They took a deep breath and pushed themself up. "It's a bummer. I thought that maybe we could hang out."

They didn't look forlorn, not quite, but they wore the saddest expression I'd ever seen on them post-coitus. A thought hit me and filled me with fury: I was an antisocial piece of shit, but they weren't. They'd been isolating themself to make my life more comfortable, to meet my needs, and in doing so they'd totally failed to meet their own. It was intolerable, and I wasn't going to stand for it.

"Love, next term you've got to join a club or three. Form a band. Take up yodeling. I don't care, as long as it involves you hanging out with people you like."

They frowned. "But you hate people."

"I don't. I just don't want to be near them."

"Same difference."

"But you like people, and you miss them. So that's your choice: either you go and socialize without me, or I'll have to socialize with you."

They morphed into a horrified five-year-old. "You mean that."

"I do. It will be good for you, and you'll come home with a ton of stories to tell me, which will be good for me."

"How often?"

"Hmm. Considering you've got work and school, I could let you get away with twice a week."

They shook their head. "You drive a hard bargain."

"That should not surprise you." I was watching them put their socks on when a thought made me shudder. "Shit. What time is it?"

They checked their watch. "We've got about ten minutes."

"I forgot all about that! For a while, anyway. How the fuck did that happen?"

They straightened up with a wink. "Magic, Homeslice. The only kind worth knowing."

"I think you're right, Doom. We should do this every time something awful is about to happen."

They blinked. "Two points. Point one: Doom?"

"Yup. Doom of Humankind, trespasser extraordinaire, epic breaker of things and bender of time, and all that jazz."

"I'll bend you, if you're not careful. Point two: we don't always know in advance when something awful is about to happen."

"Good point. So we should do this all the time, just in case."

They pulled me upright and kissed me. "I like your thinking. Cup of tea?"

"Hot chocolate."

"Again?" Their eyes twinkled. "You're getting positively debauched in your old age. And, before you ask, I'm all for it."

After we had sex, there was always a period of time when Frankie wasn't remotely interested in anything sexual. The length of that period varied, but it could be up to twenty minutes, particularly if we'd had a good session. That was probably why, when they opened our front door and found the busty pitcher-wielding blonde from the previous night's shenanigans smiling at them, they didn't turn into a gibbering wreck. They still got tongue-tied and overly formal, which made them seem younger and almost unbearably cute, but that was it. The blonde responded by beaming at them, which flustered them even more. She seemed to be enjoying their discomfort a bit too much for my taste, so I converted my nerves into action and waded right into the situation, literally and metaphorically.

After nudging Frankie out of the way, I stretched my hand out to her. "Hi. I'm Gio. This is Frankie."

Her smile sounded like silver bells and smelled like jasmine, or something; I wasn't too sure, because something about it was scrambling my brain. Her voice didn't help, either: it was as soft as a pillow and as fragrant as fresh bread.

"I know. You're the talk of the town."

"Which town?"

"Mine." She tilted her head and smiled an even prettier smile. "You can call me Anna. I asked Lance to be your escort for the event. He wasn't terribly happy, but he never says no to me." She stood up a little straighter as she said that, which made her figure even more attractive. Frankie, still firmly in his no-fuck zone, didn't seem to pick up on that.

"Lance is pissed off at us, isn't he?"

Her smile faded a fraction, which made it almost tolerable. "He's disappointed. I wouldn't worry about it; disappointment is his natural state of being. He spends too much of his time trying to herd cats, if you ask me. He can't let things just happen."

"He let Jacob come after me for weeks," I mumbled.

She looked uncomfortable. "Yes. Well, he only gets involved if he thinks an issue is important... I'm sorry."

Frankie went rigid. "What are you sorry about?"

"About how things went between my people and your household. I would have done things differently."

"Why didn't you, then?"

She murmured, "It's not up to me to intervene in such matters. It isn't my place."

"Fucking move, then."

"What?" She stared at them, her mouth open in a perfect O.

"If you can't do something because it's not your place, and you want to do it, change your place. Simple."

"It may be simple for you, but for my people—"

"Honestly, if having supernatural powers makes you unable to do what you really want, then I don't see the point." They turned towards me. "Are you still up for this?"

"Yes. Is that OK?"

They smirked. "It's not my place to say." They put their hand in mine. "Ready when you are."

"Ready for what?"

"Whatever you need me for. This is your show."

I took a deep breath, made a mental note to check out what "girding one's loins" actually meant and what the etymology was, and stepped out.

The portal – a white wooden gate only as high as my waist – stood unsupported right in the middle of the railroad tracks. I wondered briefly what would happen if a train went through it, but I pushed that thought out of my mind. I needed to focus on what lay ahead and I knew full well what my brain was doing: it was latching on petty details in order to pretend that nothing was out of kilter. With every step I took, I was less and less keen to go. All I wanted to do was to go back to my room and hide under a blanket, ideally forever. When I remembered how literal that "forever" might be, I shuddered and sped up.

As soon as I pulled the gate open, a soothing medley of sounds, lights, and smells washed over me. I stepped through the portal and into a cherry orchard. It wasn't any old orchard, either: the trees were of one of those double-flowered varieties that looked equally wonderful and ludicrous, like brides who don't know when to stop with the lace and trimmings. The sun shone, the air was warm and sweet-smelling, the occasional breeze sprinkled pink petals like confetti, and all I wanted to do was to sit on the ground and wonder.

Frankie stumbled next to me with a gasp. "Wow."

"Yeah."

"I mean... wow."

"Not too shabby, hey?"

"I don't know. My eyes hurt. It's like being inside a wedding cake."

"Say what?" I looked at them, their face a perfect picture of amazement, and my nerves dissolved into giggles.

They frowned at me. "Are you mocking me?"

"Yes. I love you."

"Why?"

"Because you make everything better."

Anna guided us further into the orchard. As we walked, the twinkly music in the breeze got louder. It was half pleasant and half annoying, like very high quality elevator music with a folk twist. My brain was busy trying to work out whether I actually knew the tune or if it sounded familiar because it was so bland, when we reached a round glade. At the center of it stood a large round pedestal, a bit like a band stand, surrounded by pink and white marigolds and topped by a huge flower arch.

Frankie nudged me. "What did I tell you?"

"Alright. That is a bit wedding-cakey."

At the far end of the glade were three musicians dedicating all their energy to filling our ears with Generic Pastoral Folk, for which I didn't feel terribly thankful. Scattered around the edges of the glade were tables covered in an astonishing array of foods and drinks. People, or creatures who looked very much like people, were gathered around the tables, eating, drinking, and making merry.

As soon as one of them saw us, they all turned to stare at us. Even the music faltered. My stomach decided to inform me that it didn't like that kind of attention by trying to implode, while my throat constricted so much and so fast that I didn't even have a chance to gasp.

Frankie caught my arm and whispered in my ear, "You're alright."

I managed to squeak back at them. "I don't feel it."

"I know. But you're brave, you're clever, you're beautiful, and you are perfectly capable of going through this if you want to. I, on the other hand, am perfectly willing to throat-punch anyone who bothers you."

"Have you been watching Bruce Lee movies?"

"Nope. Remind me to do that when we get home. For now, I'll have to make it up as I'm going along."

"I love you so fucking much."

"Right back at you." They smiled at Anna. "Ready when you are."

She smiled and waved us towards the middle of the throng. We didn't get very far before Jacob descended upon us, his arms open and a huge smile on his face.

It was his actual face, I guessed: he looked like a man in his forties, a bit weather-beaten, neither heart-achingly handsome nor terrifyingly ugly. I wouldn't have noticed him in a crowd, were it not for his sky-blue and cherry-pink floral shirt and for the hunger at the bottom of his eyes. The former hurt my eyes, and the latter made my pervdar scream in alarm.

He either didn't notice or didn't care, because he stretched his arms as if he was going to embrace me. "Welcome! It's so nice to see you."

I was so worked up that I wanted to screech, but Frankie saved me. They stepped between us and spoke in a low, cold voice. "Yeah, right. Can we just get this over with?"

Jacob stopped a couple of feet away from us and put a hand to his chest, looking mortally offended. "Does it have to be like this? I thought we were here to make up."

"You thought wrong. We just want to give you back what's yours, go home, and never see you again."

He scowled for a fraction of a second. "That's hurtful. I thought we could spend some time together, like in the good old days." He waved his arms around. "I made this just for you. Don't you like it?"

"It's adorable. Can we get on with it?"

Jacob flounced off theatrically, mumbling something about "ungrateful youngsters" just loudly enough for everyone to hear him. Frankie stood next to me, straight and rigid, a strange tension running through them. They looked oddly vivid, oddly real. It took me a while to realize what was going on: they were wholly focused on this moment, their brain entirely dedicated to evaluating the situation, their senses stretched to pick up everything around us. The intensity of their focus spooked me a little, so I stuck my hand in their pocket.

They turned with a start. "I'm sorry, but this feels like I imagine an arranged wedding would. One of the bad ones. Everyone fucking celebrating, apart from the bride."

"That's me, isn't it?"

"Yeah. Sorry."

"It's fine. But you're not happy, either."

They snorted. "Of course. As the bride's lover, I'm hardly going to be impressed. Gio, I don't like this. No part of it."

"Me neither."

"You can still bail out."

"Can I? What are we going to do, fight our way out of here?"

Their eyes narrowed. "If it comes to that, yes. It's not as if you're under contract. I wouldn't care, anyway: if you change your mind, for whatever reason, I'm going to put a stop to this. You know I could."

A lump congealed in my stomach. "Are you saying what I think you're saying?"

They swallowed. "Yes. I won't do anything you don't want me to do, because you don't want me to do it, but if you decide that you want out of here, I'll get you out, whatever it takes."

"I can't let that happen."

They turned and hissed right in my face. "For fuck's sake, Gio! How about you look after yourself and I look after myself for a change? I know you care about me, and I love that, but I think we need to learn to trust that we can take care of ourselves, too." They blinked. "I'm sorry. This isn't the time. But please trust me to be able to decide what I'd rather go through. I know I'm scatty—"

"You're not!"

"I am. But I'm still an adult. I can decide for myself. I can tell you if I don't want to do something, even when it's for you. And right now, I'd much rather bust us out of here than let you go through with this if you don't want to." They picked up my hands and looked into my eyes. The anger that had filled them a moment earlier had been replaced with a mixture of love and sorrow. "You'd do the same for me. Wouldn't you?"

"Yes. Of course. If I had any useful powers—"

They shut me up with A Look. "If you're not careful, I'll write you a list of your useful powers when we get home, and then I'll throw it at you."

"I can probably defend myself against a sheet of paper."

"Less so against an encyclopedia. Homeslice, shut up and focus. Do you still want to do this?"

I glanced at Jacob. He was holding court with his guests, looking exceptionally smug. I thought about giving him what he wanted, and that didn't seem like a good idea. Then I thought about keeping what belonged to him, and that idea seemed infinitely worse.

I nodded. "Yes. But we need to come up with a way to make him promise to leave us the fuck alone once we're done, and to make it stick."

"Alright. That's Plan A. What's Plan B?"

"You bust us out of here, we run home, and we hide there until we can come up with a Plan C."

"Sounds good to me. Sit down, relax as much as you can, and have a good think. Whatever promise we extract from Jacob, it needs to be solid. The guy is slipperier than an eel, and not half as cuddly."

"What are you going to do?"

"Mingle. I'm going to bumble around like the spaced-out fool that I am, and see if I can overhear anything useful. I won't be far, alright?"

I didn't like the idea of them leaving me alone, but I nodded. They kissed the tip of my nose and wandered off.

I sat myself under one of those outrageous cherry trees, hidden by a curtain of gaudy pink, and tried to come up with a way to tie Jacob down to a promise. Doing that would have been infinitely easier if roughly 80% of my brain had not been busy telling me that I should have done this sooner, that I shouldn't have wasted the day indulging my whims, that anyone with more than two neurons would have known that, and that I was fucking this up same as I fucked everything up, because I was a fuck-up. I was used to it, so I tried to ignore it and think through the din, but doing that took up another 5% of my brain. All in all, I was operating well below capacity and getting rather vexed.

Next thing I knew, I was having a minor heart attack. I'd been staring at the trunk of the tree, purely because my eyes needed somewhere to point at. After a while, I'd half-noticed that a chunk of tree bark looked just like a face. The next instant, my vision flipped: there *was* a face in the bark, and that face was attached to a person.

Being a true hero, I squealed like a flattened hamster. That startled my opponent: it tried to back away from me, whacking its head against the tree in the process. When we were done with our respective, highly successful fight-or-flight responses, we found ourselves staring at each other. I clutched my chest, just to make sure that my heart hadn't actually managed to pounce out of it. She – I thought she was a she, anyway – rubbed the back of her head.

I didn't know who she was, but that didn't worry me half as much as not knowing *what* she was. She looked broadly humanoid, and very cute with it, but something about the way her face was put together suggested that I was facing another mythical person. It had taken me that long to see her partly because I was wrapped up in my own problems, but also because her skin was almost the exact color of cherry bark, and with the same rich shine. About three and a half feet tall, she was the smallest adult I'd ever seen. She was slender, but a second glance revealed that there was a solidity to her, an undeniable strength. Despite her size and her apparent klutziness, I wouldn't have wanted to mess with her.

I'd almost managed to catch my breath when another realization knocked it out of me again. Something about her looked really familiar, as if she was someone I used to know as a child and I'd forgotten all about. That made no sense, though: I was pretty sure that not even I would forget someone who looked like that.

I managed to get some air in and blurted out, "Sorry. You scared me."

She looked horrified. "Oh. Sorry."

"No, it's OK. Hi."

"Hi."

"I'm Gio."

"I'm Minna." When she stuck her hand up about shoulder-high and waved it about a few times – the international sign for "introvert desperately trying to be friendly" – my fear evaporated. I knew her now, sure as I knew myself, and having her here felt wonderful.

It also felt really fucking awkward.

My social skills had improved dramatically since I'd started university. I knew that, largely because Frankie wouldn't quit harping on about it every time they got the chance, but I also knew that, when you start from rock bottom, the only way is up. I could now reliably manage a conversation with a total stranger without choking on my own tongue. I could even speak in front of up to three people I knew without throwing up afterwards. Those were improvements, no doubt, but I was painfully aware that my main social strategy was to hang out with people who had actual social skills and let them do all the work.

It was supremely easy for me to survive social interactions when I was standing next to Frankie, who could have a riveting conversation all by themself and who always covered for me when I got uncomfortable. Ditto when I was with Ben, who was so chilled out that everyone around him automatically relaxed. I relied on them to grease the gears of my social interactions, which they never failed to do, and I managed to look good-ish as a result. But that didn't mean that I had developed any social skills of my own, and it definitely didn't mean that I could manage a conversation with someone who seemed at least as socially inept as me.

I wanted to talk to Minna, and I knew that she wanted to talk to me, because otherwise she wouldn't have come out of a tree right in my face, but that didn't make it any easier to get started. She was uncomfortable, I was uncomfortable, and the build-up of raw discomfort in the air was such that the mere thought of breaking the silence sent me into a cold sweat. I knew from experience that the longer I waited, the worse it'd get, because the build-up of expectation would require me to think of something truly amazing to break the ice with. I also knew that there wasn't a fucking thing I could do about it, so I sat and fretted while a maelstrom of insults battered my brain.

It had gotten so bad that I was considering saying something, anything, just to break us out of that hell, when I spotted the cavalry: Frankie ducked under the tree canopy. They were still oddly focused and they looked preoccupied, but, under the circumstances, that didn't worry me.

They didn't spot Minna until they'd sat down next to me, their hand in my lap. When they did, they looked surprised for half an instant, and then they smiled a rather complicated smile, which they pointed at the floor.

"Hey. Hi. I'm Frankie."

I grabbed their hand, just to make sure that they were real. "Hey, you. This is Minna."

They peeped through the curtain of their eyelashes. "Your godparent?"

Minna blushed and shrunk into herself a little, nodding.

I blurted out, "How did you know?"

"Family resemblance."

"What? We don't look anything alike!"

They blushed. "Nah. But you feel the same." They sighed. "Anyway, I have been almost useful. I have some bad news and some good news, plus some news I can't interpret."

"Just throw it all at me. I'll add it to the soup."

They turned slightly and did that wonderful thing they always did when they were talking to someone shy; instead of speaking just to me, cutting Minna out of the conversation, or to her, spooking her, they aimed their words at a spot between us all. I could never quite work out how they did it, but it worked: everyone was involved, but nobody was under any pressure. I wanted to sit and marvel at how clever, kind, and wonderful they were, and how lucky I was to have found them, but we had too much to worry about. I promised to myself that, as soon as we got home, I'd let them know just how much I loved them. If we got home.

"Bad news: apparently we were supposed to ask for guest rights as soon as we got here. They're kind of a big deal. We could have done with them."

"Fuck. I should have thought about that! They're in literally all the stories! Is it too late to ask about them now?"

"Yup. Good news: nobody expected Jacob to actually respect them, so we'd be just as screwed. He kind of has a bad rep around here. Nobody seems to like him."

"I'm shocked."

"More good news, I think: you each get to have a party, with a second and a third."

That baffled me entirely. "What are you on about? Cakes?"

Frankie and Minna both giggled. The sound was so joyful that instead of feeling embarrassed, I felt happy I'd managed to make them laugh.

Frankie poked my nose. "No, Homeslice. Although, if you venture out from under this here tree, you will find that one of those tables holds a range of delectable desserts. When the time comes for... for that thing, you'll have to go up on that dais—"

I shuddered. "Oh, fuck. With everyone watching? Why can't I just slice myself up in peace and quiet?"

Frankie wrapped their arm around my shoulders as Minna's hand found mine. Even through my misery, it felt pretty good.

"You'll be OK," said Frankie. "You won't be on your own. That's the point. You will have a second and a third, kinda like in duels."

"What, so if I back out, the second will get sliced instead?"

"Nope. OK, so it's not exactly like in duels, but you will have two people with you. So will Jacob."

"Wait. Who gets to pick them?"

"I dunno, but they've been picked. Two people per side, and that's it. Everyone else will have to stay the fuck out of the way, and there will be people in charge of making sure that everything goes according to plans."

"Whose plans, though? I'm sure Jacob is plotting some shit."

"Me too. Everyone is, really, but I'm sure we can get around that."

"How?"

They beamed at me. "Use me. You're not obligated to do jack shit. Make Jacob promise to leave us the fuck alone forever. If he lies, I'll know. If you make the promise specific enough and you make him swear by his troth, there'll be repercussions if he breaks it."

"By his troth? Did we fall into an epic myth?"

"Yeah. Months ago."

"What kind of repercussion?"

"From what I understand, Lance and his goons will kick his ass."

"So, a promise is not going to stop him, but it's going to cost him?"

Frankie winced. "Ain't that always the case? But it's something, right? And if he refuses to promise, we'll know he's up to something and we can fuck off home and try something else."

My stomach sank. "You're asking me to go up in front of everyone and make a scene."

They blinked. "Yes. Shit. But Gio, we've got to do it. It's our best bet."

I closed my eyes and concentrated on breathing, and on the feeling of Frankie's body against mine. Minna's hand stroked mine.

"I will be in your party," she whispered.

I opened my eyes and looked up at her. "You don't want to make a scene, either."

"No. But if there is a need..."

"I can do it." Frankie was staring at her, their eyes two green beacons fixed on her face. "Bow out, and I'll step in. That's got to be allowed."

She was so startled that she looked right at them. "Yes. But..."

"I don't mind if you don't mind. Gio won't mind, either." They turned to me. "You won't, will you?" They didn't give me a chance to answer before turning back to Minna. "I mean, I'm not saying you can't help, and it's great to have you here, it really is, but I am totally cool with making as big a scene as is needed. I'm used to it. Half the time, I make one without even meaning to. And I'd rather not be too far from Gio. But it's up to you, obviously. You know more about this kind of thing than I do."

Minna shook her head, her hair making a cloud around her. "Not really. This kind of thing isn't done often, and I'm never involved. If you need me to step aside, I will."

They both looked at me. I thought about my two options – walking up there with a goddess beside me, or with Frankie's hand in mine – and it wasn't even a competition. "I'd rather go with Frankie, if you don't mind. Their truth-telling is pretty handy, and they're used to calming me down."

Minna smiled, looking more relieved than disappointed. "Of course. I understand. I'm glad it's worked out like that for you."

"What has?"

Her voice was no louder than the breeze rustling the cherry flowers, but I could still hear her. "Finding a home. I'm glad it's a person, rather than a place. It's risky, but when it works, it's worth it."

My heart did some complicated gymnastics and my eyes got very itchy, but I held it mostly together. Frankie, on the other end, ended up looking as dazed as if someone had whacked them on the head with a bat.

They murmured to themself, "It's really real. Oh, man."

I stifled a giggle. "Very eloquently put, Doom. Anyway, is there any other intel?"

They shook themself off. "Oh, yeah! I forgot the most important bit." They leant their head against mine and whispered in my ear. "Gio, you'll never guess what I found."

I whispered back, "You're almost certainly right."

"This place has a fruit salad bar."

"Say what?"

They stuck their hand in their hoodie pocket and dragged out a handful of cherries. "Here you go. They've got all sorts, but I know these are your favorite. And it's safe for us to eat here. I asked."

I wanted to thank them, but I only managed to mumble vaguely through a mouthful of fruit. I'd not finished that first handful when they dragged out another one, and then another. They just kept piling fruit in my lap until it was covered in a pile of cherries. I couldn't believe my eyes.

"What else do you have in that pocket? A white rabbit?"

They shook their head. "That was it, I'm afraid. I swear, sometimes I wonder whether I ought to give up having sex with you and take up horticulture. You'd enjoy the fruits of my labor—"

"Talk of sex as labor, and you won't have to worry about it again."

Frankie turned to Minna. "You see? This is what I get. I guess he doesn't want me to go back for more."

"There's more?" I squeaked.

"Yup." They leaped to their feet with a dazzling grin. "Stay put. I won't be a moment."

I watched them go with a sigh. Minna's hand found mine again, and that put a little bit of warmth back in my heart.

I was pretty sure that I knew the answer, but I thought I'd ask anyway. "When this is over, will you come visit? I think you'd like our home. It's quiet. We have a housemate, but he's nice. He gets it."

I had the feeling that she was blushing, but I couldn't be sure because her complexion was too dark. Maybe goddesses like her didn't blush, anyway. I was blushing, but for once I didn't mind.

"I would like to, but it's difficult. It's not my home."

"Your home is a place?"

She smiled beatifically. "Yes. You should visit. It's not easy to get to, but I could open a portal for you."

I was just about to ask her a million questions about that, when I spotted Frankie heading back towards us. They were walking somberly, with their head bowed and no bounce in their step. When they looked at me, their eyes were filled with a mixture of dread and defiance. I realized why a moment later, and I was so stunned that I didn't even get a chance to swear.

As Frankie sank to the ground next to me, Marin towered over us. He was composed, but I could hear his teeth grinding.

I racked my brain for words that may begin to explain how we'd ended up in this situation, and why he shouldn't just blow us up with a fireball, but I didn't get a chance to.

He took a deep breath and growled, "We will talk about this when we get home." His tone brooked no argument. We sat roasting under his glare for roughly a million years, until he finally turned away from us.

When he turned to Minna, I panicked: I didn't want him having a go at us, but I wanted him to have a go at her even less. He just nodded, though, and when he spoke, his voice was almost soft. "It is a pleasure to finally meet you. I am sorry it is under these circumstances. Kids, hey? I will call you when it's time, if you wish."

Frankie piped up. "I'm taking her place."

Marin wheeled around with such speed and ferocity that I gasped.

"Haven't you done enough?" he growled.

"No. If I'd done enough, we wouldn't be here." They held Marin's gaze for a few seconds before dropping their head. "We want the same thing. Let me help."

Marin growled, "I can't tell you what to do. All I can do is mop up the mess." He turned on his heels and stomped off without a backward glance.

As soon as he was out of sight, we all drew a breath.

Frankie sighed. "Before you ask, he's in your party. He's your third."

"But how the fuck did he know that this was even happening? Isn't he supposed to be in fucking Kennewhatnot?"

"He got called in. In case you missed it, he is not a happy bunny. Ms. Anzengruber is driving herself home. As soon as we all get there, we're in for it."

"No shit."

Frankie looked up at me with a dazzling smile. "Isn't it great?"

"What? Did you bump your head or something?"

"Nope. He said we're not gonna talk until we get home, right?"

"Yeah. So what?"

"So there's no way in hell he'd miss out on the opportunity to yell his lungs off at us over a fuck-up of such epic proportions. The fact that he's willing to wait means that he's totally sure that we're gonna make it home.

We're gonna be alright, Gio. It's in the bag."

They let off an enormous sigh and lay down on the grass. I lay down next to them, my head in the crook of their arm.

"Doom, I never thought I'd look forward to getting a roasting from your borderline psychopathic, fire-tossing uncle—"

"But now you do?"

"But now I do."

As it emerged, the protocol for this particular ceremony required that we should all be kept waiting just long enough for our emotional responses to reach their peak and start congealing before getting down to business. By the time Marin came back to call us, I was rigid with terror and Frankie had gone slack with boredom. I felt sorry for them, because I knew how they hated it when their inner motor ground to a halt, but their stillness brought me some relief. Before succumbing to their ennui, they had been so twitchy that I'd been tempted to nail them to a tree. That would have spooked Minna, though, and she was already spooked enough. All in all, the three of us couldn't be said to be doing great. Luckily, we were all used to that.

Marin's low growl made us all jump. "It's time."

I managed to get off the ground, even though my body felt like it was made out of sticks held together by too-tight elastic bands. Frankie struggled even more than me; they had to tear themself off the ground limb by limb, as if they were stuck in a high-gravity field. We managed to get up, anyway, and we did our best to act normal. I wasn't sure that we were pulling it off, but we were doing our best.

I tried to smile a goodbye at Minna. She tried to smile back at me, but didn't get very far. Her hands were bunched into fists and clutched tight against her body, making her look terrified and vulnerable. I realized that mine were doing the same; I'd just taught myself to hide them in my pockets first.

I took a deep breath and tried to reassure her without lying to her face. "We will most probably be OK."

She nodded. She looked about as comforted as I felt, but I didn't have the time and energy to spend on making her feel better. Frankie tugged at my arm, and we walked on.

As soon as we stepped out from under the tree, all eyes were on us. With every step I took towards the dais, my feet got heavier. I could feel people's eyes on me, each gaze adding a pound to my body. I was terrified of crumbling under the weight, of collapsing in front of everyone, of letting everyone down, of looking like a total waste of space. I was also afraid of what was to come, of the knife-and-blood aspect of the affair, but that fear was minuscule compared to the paralyzing agony of being on display. Knowing that letting myself get wound up was increasing my chances of fucking up did nothing to calm me down.

By the time I got there, I was both incoherent and uncoordinated. My body felt like it didn't belong to me, as if it was a robot I was operating through a series of badly-calibrated levers, and without a manual. My brain was so occupied screaming about various impending dooms that I couldn't think at all. I couldn't even process what I was seeing and hearing; everything just turned into a fuzzy, buzzy mush that assaulted my senses without making any sense.

I managed to get to the dais without falling over, but that took all of my resources. I found myself staring up at it, with nothing left to give and the whole damn ceremony still ahead of me. The only part of my brain still functioning was wholly occupied with wondering whether I could will my heart to stop beating. Then Frankie turned around and caught me.

They literally caught me: I wobbled just a little bit, and next thing I knew their arms were around my waist. When I looked into their face, they looked concerned, but also supremely pissed off.

"I'm OK," I croaked.

"You're not, and this is my fault. I should have put my foot down. This didn't need to be such a circus. I can tell them to clear off, if you want."

"What? No!"

"Yes." They stared right into my eyes, their eyes burning with fury. "Tell me to stop this, and I will. If they don't like it, that's too bad. You have all the power here, Gio. Don't let yourself forget it."

A weird sensation washed over me, as if my entire body was taking a deep breath. I could bail out, and, if I did, Frankie would back me up. They didn't discount how I felt because it made no sense to them. They wouldn't punish me for being a weirdo. They actually gave a fuck about me, and they were willing to do pretty much anything to look after me. As pissed off as they were about the situation, they would punch the sun right out of the sky for me. This wasn't a repeat of a zillion situations I'd experienced growing up: this was a whole new thing, and I could go through it in a whole new way.

Frankie kept looking at me, their face slowly relaxing. When I felt confident that I could do it without falling over, I nodded.

They nodded back. "You wanna do this thing?"

"Yes. I want it over with."

"You want me to tell all the gawkers to fuck off?"

"No. It's alright. It'll be quicker this way, and there's less chance of Jacob trying something nasty."

"OK. Let's do it."

They hooked their arm under mine and we stepped up on the dais. Marin, Jacob, and two people I didn't know were already up there.

Jacob looked mightily peeved, but something about his expression didn't sit quite right. I would have bet good money that he was using anger to cover up a different feeling, but I couldn't tell which.

He sneered at Frankie. "What is he doing here?"

Rage exploded inside me, blowing everything else out of its way. "*They* are here because I want them to be here. If you've got a problem with it, we can call it a day."

Jacob looked startled for a second, as if he'd not expected me to speak, and then locked eyes with me. He eyeballed me so hard and for so long that my eyes started hurting, but there was no way in hell I was gonna back down. Nobody talked to Frankie like that.

I was wondering how the fuck that kind of stand-off actually worked – was there some kind of provision for disengaging without losing face, or were we just going to spend eternity like that? – when a commotion in the crowd distracted me. I looked over and spotted Lance making his way towards us, the crowd parting in front of him like the Red Sea for Moses. Seeing him gave me a bit of a jolt. Seeing our Guardian striding up behind him, a hand casually resting on the pommel of her sword, gave me a bigger one. She exuded such an air of calm, confident lethality that Lance, frowny-faced and bustling, looked like a peeved toddler by comparison.

Frankie leaned over and whispered in my ear, "What is this, a convention of our biggest fans?"

"Seems like it."

"Ho-hum. At least nobody's going to try and do anything they shouldn't with those two around."

"There's that."

Their sigh tickled my ear. "When we get home, we have to talk about something."

My heart sank. "I'm in trouble with you, too?"

"No. We just need to talk about how your anxiety evaporates when you're doing something for me. It's not urgent, but I'd appreciate it if you could file it for later. I know that I'll forget about it, and it's important."

I was going to ask what the fuck they were on about when Lance and the Guardian climbed up on the dais. She positioned herself just out of arm's reach, but well within sword's reach. Lance came to stand between me and Jacob, and cleared his throat.

"Is everyone ready?"

Jacob huffed something about being kept waiting, but Lance wasn't paying any attention to him. I just nodded.

He nodded back. "Has the ceremony been explained to you?"

I shook my head.

"This is the sword."

He held up a leaf-shaped blade about a foot long and a million years old. The surface looked faintly patterned, like a Damascus knife, but it was so pitted and corroded that I couldn't be sure. It looked like crap, but it also looked like it embodied a whole lot of swordness in a very small space. It was, unequivocally and unashamedly, an instrument for killing.

Frankie peered over my shoulder. "Gio has got to cut himself with that?"

"Yes. Along the life line of her left hand."

"Life line? Like in palm reading?"

"Yes."

"That's going to be a righteous pain in the ass! He needs to be able to use her hand!"

Lance shrugged. "It doesn't have to be a big cut. It's largely symbolic. Once the blood starts flowing, it will collect in this chalice." He held up a smallish glass covered in a pattern of swirls.

"Huh. I was expecting a drinking horn or something. Gio's got to drip into that?"

"No. That's what the dais is for. It didn't have to be quite so ornate," he flicked a glance at Jacob, "But it serves a purpose. How detailed an explanation do you require?"

Frankie blinked. "Not very. I'm not braining well."

"The dais will transfer Jacob's essence from the blood into the cup. No dripping. It's relatively neat, as centuries-old ceremonies go."

"Huh. Does Gio have to fill that? It looks like a lot."

I nudged them. "They take more than that when you give blood."

"But you're so little! And that blade looks like tetanus waiting to happen!"

"Yeah, I'm not totally sold on that." I looked up at Lance. "Do I have to use the gladius?"

He frowned. "You are into swords?"

"Not even a little. I'm into old books. I know a gladius when I see one. It does look pretty crusty, though I'm sure it's sharp. Is it essential?"

"The sword has... a power."

"Is that power essential to these proceedings?"

"Not really, but unless you brought your own blade—"

"Here." I stuck my hand in my pocket and brought out the utility knife I'd stolen from my own bedroom in Jacob's trap. "It's sharp and it's clean."

Frankie grumbled something under their breath, but I couldn't catch what it was and I didn't have the time to worry about it.

Lance frowned, but he eventually nodded. "It will probably hurt more."

"Maybe, but I know it. Let's get on with it. I want to go home."

Jacob lurched forward and made to grab my knife. I pulled back and Frankie stepped forward, so they collided. Before they had a chance to start anything, Lance split them up.

He looked at me. "Jacob has to make the cut. That's the only way this would work. The cutter's essence—"

Frankie pulled at my sleeve. "I don't like this. I don't trust him."

Marin placed a hand on their shoulder, and another one on mine. For the first time in my life, I felt comforted by his presence. "It's gotta be done, kid. There's no other way. If he steps out of line, I will deal with it."

"Yeah, but what's the point in you dealing with it after Gio's thumb is on the floor?"

"That won't happen." He looked up at Jacob, his face utterly emotionless. "Jacob will cut Gio as little as needed. Right?"

Jacob's face twitched. "Yes."

Frankie straightened up and aimed all of their focus on Jacob. "And you swear this."

"Do I have to?" grunted Jacob through gritted teeth.

"Yes. And you also have to swear that, as soon as the ceremony is over, you will leave me and Gio alone forever. You won't make contact with us in any way, you won't send any goons at us, you will have nothing to do with us at all, in person or via a third party."

Jacob glared at them, his face totally blank, and didn't say a damn thing.

Frankie put their arm through mine. "Alright. I guess we're not going to do this after all. Have a nice half-life."

We stepped towards the edge of the dais and were about to climb down when Jacob barked, "Fine!"

Frankie stared at him. "You swear this?"

"Yes."

"By your troth?"

"Yes! Now, can we get this over with?"

Frankie looked at me. I nodded at them. They nodded back. As we walked back towards our spot, they whispered in my ear, "Remind me to look up what the fuck a troth is."

I was probably tenser than I'd realized, because that made me giggle. Once I started, I couldn't stop until I was out of air. I should have been mortally embarrassed by that, but when I saw Frankie's face smiling at me, I didn't care about anything else.

They stroked my hand. "You still up for this?"

"Yeah. Let's get it done and go home."

Handing Jacob my knife was the hardest thing I'd ever done, until the time came to hold my hand out while he cut me. I had to focus so hard on staying still and not hitting him than I barely noticed the pain. When the blood started welling out of the cut, I gasped. When I realized that it was flowing out but not actually going anywhere, I felt dizzy.

"What the fuck?"

Frankie pointed at the glass in Lance's hands. "Look." The vessel was filling up, slowly but surely.

"Well, shit."

"Does it hurt?"

"A bit."

Their face dropped. "I'm so sorry." They picked up my hand and were about to kiss my wound when Jacob screeched.

"Leave it alone! Don't touch it!"

Frankie turned around with exaggerated care to stare him down. "Will you calm the fuck down? You're getting what you want."

"Damn right, I am!" He was looking feral and smug again. I hated to see that, so I stepped back towards the edge of the dais until I was as far from him as I could be.

Frankie looked conflicted between coming after me and lumping Jacob in the face. The latter option seemed to be gaining, but Marin's hand landed on their shoulder and pulled them out of the way.

Then Marin took a step forward towards Jacob, and it was like watching a mountain move. He was massive, ponderous, unstoppable, and about as friendly as a glacier. "You leave the kid alone."

Jacob sneered. "He's your kid now? That figures."

"Care to elaborate?"

"He's useless. They both are. They can't plan! They can't think!"

"And where did all your clever planning get you?"

Jacob took two steps towards Marin, his chest swelling up menacingly under his ludicrous shirt. "Where did it get me? It got me what I want. It always does. While you people grope and toil, my people–"

"Your people? What people would that be? Nobody likes you!"

"See who's talking! You're only tolerated because you're useful. Even your mortal—"

"You leave her out of this!"

They kept walking in circles around each other, growling louder and sharper insults. Each of them made motions suggesting that they were just about to flip out and beat the crap out of the other one, except that neither was actually doing a damn thing. They were giving me a hell of a headache and I was feeling dizzy, so I tried to tune them out. I leaned into Frankie and they wrapped their arms around me, shielding me from the world.

I tried to relax into their chest, but my brain weasels had other plans. They kept running around in circles, screeching words I couldn't string together. Blood. Essence. Cut. Chalice. The cutter's essence, into the chalice. Jacob's essence, into the chalice, for Jacob to devour.

It didn't have to be like that. The problem wasn't that I'd gotten a chunk of Jacob's powers. I could live with that. My only issue was that Frankie didn't get any.

I took my knife out of my pocket and held it between us.

Frankie tensed up. "Gio? What the fuck?"

"Do you trust me?"

"Yes. Always."

I pressed the blade against my palm, just below the cut Jacob had made. When I was done, I handed the blade to Frankie. "Now you."

They looked shocked for a second, then nodded. "OK." They pushed the blade against their life line until the blood welled out. "Now what?"

"Now we've gotta find a way to drink that blood before Jacob does."

"Shit. Alright. No sweat."

They turned around, stuck their cut hand into my back pocket, and walked us over to Lance, who was hovering at the edge of Marin and Jacob's performance.

They pointed at the glass and smiled. "Hey, can I have a look at that?"

Lance flinched. "What?"

"I've never seen a chalice fill up with my partner's blood via magical means. It's kinda cool, you know? I mean, I've never really seen a lot of blood. I've had a couple of blood tests when I was a kid, and I tried to donate blood, but they won't take it because I've had sex with guys, which was super fun to explain away to my parents, I tell you, and this is, like, pretty fucking cool, even though it sucks, and I won't ever get to see it again, hopefully, so, like, can I have a look?" They sounded so chirpy and innocent that they could have been five years old.

Lance looked unconvinced, but he lifted the glass up. "Alright."

Frankie leaned over until their nose nearly touched the glass. "Shit. So the blood just magically transfers into there?"

"Yes. More or less. The blood has a high symbolic value—"

"But it only works if you hold it, right?"

"No. The nature of the chalice and the runes on the dais are doing all the work. That, Gio's intention, and Jacob's will when he made the cut."

They straightened themself up. "I don't believe it. I don't believe there are magical glasses that fill themselves. Can I try it?" They stretched their hand out with a huge smile.

Lance spoke clearly and slowly. "Fine. But you have to be really careful, alright? Don't spill it."

"I won't." Frankie grabbed the glass and held it up to their eyes. The level of the blood kept going up. "Wow. It does work! How do you know when it's enough?"

"It's not really a matter of volume. It is a symbolic gesture. It just has to happen. How it happens is largely immaterial, provided that everyone really means it. A powerful enough metaphor, like you said. Willingly spilt blood is one of the strongest metaphors out there."

Frankie turned to me with a grin and shoved the glass right in my face. "Do you see this? Nearly full already."

"Yeah. It's super gross."

"It's gonna get grosser." They stared into my eyes and murmured, "Bottoms up?"

"Yeah."

They'd taken a huge swig and passed the glass to me before Lance's yell had had a chance to leave his lips. By the time his hands grabbed the glass, I'd emptied it. For a moment the whole world went quiet, and then noise exploded around us. Everyone was screaming, Frankie was bent in half, gagging, someone was shaking me by the shoulders, and I couldn't even tell which way was up. The confusion increased until it was almost unbearable, and then it suddenly stopped. In the deafening silence, I could hear a hissing, crackling sound. I looked towards it and spotted the Guardian standing in the middle of the dais, her sword held so casually in her hand that it looked like an afterthought. It was a four-foot-long, fiery afterthought, though, so people were really paying attention.

Hands I'd not even noticed let go of my throat, and I took a huge gulp of air. Jacob stood up, unfolding himself over me. "I demand retribution."

The Guardian tilted her head. "Retribution? Whatever for?"

Jacob erupted. "They took my blood! Again!"

"How could it be your blood, when it wasn't in your veins?"

"Are you shitting me?"

Her voice got colder. "I beg your pardon?"

Jacob totally lost it. He started gesticulating wildly and bellowing semi-incoherently. "The ceremony! My blood! Cheats! Thieves!"

The Guardian waved her sword to and fro. It wasn't an intimidating gesture – she just looked as if she was enjoying the resulting swish and crackle – but it was still scary as hell. "I'm sorry, I have no idea what you're talking about. I was brought here to facilitate the uninterrupted completion of this ceremony. Evidence suggests that it is now completed. You can all go home."

She turned towards Marin. He took a slow, tentative step towards Frankie, who was still gagging quietly. When nobody reacted, he walked to them, grabbed their arm, and half-dragged them towards me. He reached down into his cargo pocket and extracted his portable portal. He opened it with a single flick of his hand, threw Frankie through it, dragged me upright, and threw me after them.

I was in our back yard. Frankie was on the ground, looking nauseous, but they got up as soon as they saw me. They went to kiss me, then recoiled back and wiped something off the corner of my mouth.

"Blood?"

They nodded. "Yes. Jesus, Gio. What did we do?"

"I don't know. It just seemed like a good idea at the time."

Marin's bear-like paws grabbed us and split us up. For a moment I thought he was gonna smack our heads together, but he let Frankie go. "Kid, go get your aunt. You," he squeezed my shoulder, "Come with me."

He set off towards the front of the house without letting go of me. I could either follow him or be dragged, so I chose the former. Frankie charged after us, looking panicked.

"Ms. Anzengruber? But why? And where are you taking Gio?"

Marin stopped, his face utterly expressionless, and spoke at half his normal speed, etching every word into the air. "I am taking both of you to hospital."

I squealed, "Hospital?"

He pulled me along. "Yes. Your hand needs medical attention."

I'd forgotten about my hand. I'd forgotten I had hands, to be honest. I looked down and immediately regretted it: the blood was pouring out of the cuts and running through my fingers. The weirdest thing was that I couldn't feel it. The pain was somewhere out there, I knew it, but I couldn't actually feel it.

Frankie squealed and ran off. I looked up just in time to watch them disappear around the corner of the house. My ears started to buzz and I thought I was going to pass out, but Marin dragged me on.

By the time we got to the driveway, Frankie was waiting for us by Ms. Anzengruber's car, twitching frantically. When I got near them, Marin let me go, and I stumbled into their arms.

After I'd caught my breath, I whispered in their ear. "Frankie, I don't want stitches. I really don't. Please, don't make me get stitches."

They let off a strangled wail. "But you need them! And you can't tell me that you faced a bunch of angry gods like there was nothing to it, but you're scared of getting stitches!"

"I can't? But it's true! I'll be alright!"

They kissed my neck under my ear. "Come on. It's gotta be done." They went to stroke my face but stopped at the last moment. "Shit."

"What?" I looked at their hand, and it was dripping blood. "Frankie! You need a doctor!"

I looked up and caught them staring at me, slowly shaking their head. "Gio, you know, I really love you, but I'll be damned if I can understand you half the time."

I was about to ask them to explain that when Ms. Anzengruber descended upon us. She handed us each a dish towel and waved us towards her car.

"Get in. Try not to bleed everywhere."

Nobody said a damn thing all the way there. It wasn't far, just at the far end of campus, but getting there seemed to take so long that I had a chance to calm down about what had happened and get wound up about what was about to happen. Ms. Anzengruber was so pissed off that her knuckles were white over the steering wheel. I had no idea what she was going to do to us once we were fixed up. Marin kept turning back and looking at us, his face so impassive that it gave me the chills. Frankie was bleeding profusely and looked way too pale. Everything was fucking awful, and only about to get worse.

I managed to keep it together until we got to the medical center and they tried to split me and Frankie up. I started crying then, even though I was in public and I knew perfectly well that I would probably never stop. Frankie wrapped themself around me like an octopus and didn't let go until the doctor consented to see us together.

My cuts were worse, so she saw me first. I sat on Frankie's lap, my face buried in their shoulder, while she did whatever she had to do. Once I had been sorted out, I sat on a chair right next to Frankie, leaning against their uninjured side, with my eyes shut tight so I couldn't see anything. I just couldn't bear to watch them get hurt, particularly when it was my fault, but they didn't seem bothered in the least; in fact, they were extremely excited about it all. They kept asking how everything worked and exclaiming how cool it all was. At the end of it all, I half expected the nurse to offer them a lollipop for being such a good kid. He didn't, though; he just told us that we were done with a sad, weary smile, so we wandered off towards the waiting room with our arms linked.

That was when things got really bad for us. I'd coasted through most of the day on a wave of adrenaline and confusion. Now that those were spent, there was nothing to cushion me from what lie ahead.

Ms. Anzengruber and Marin had waited for us. He looked truculent, which was so normal for him as to be a non-event, but she was so angry that she'd gone cold. Her stare made the contents of my stomach curdle. Thinking about what those contents were didn't help at all.

Frankie, buoyed by their infinite enthusiasm, launched on a cheery and gory description of our recent medical adventures before the chill in Ms. Anzengruber's stare froze the words on their tongue. In the ensuing silence, their arm tightened around mine.

"It wasn't Gio's fault. None of it."

Ms. Anzengruber closed her eyes and kept them shut for about ten seconds. When she opened them again, she looked furious. Frankie flinched, but I welcomed that change: I'd rather have her angry at me than freezing me out. I was still terrified, though.

"Come on." She marched out of the medical center and we all followed her. She didn't say anything all the way home. I felt that I was sinking deeper into hell, falling into a nightmare from where I may never emerge again. Even the sight of our home didn't make me feel any better. When we walked in and she directed us upstairs, I knew that we were done for.

She sat us at her table and was heading towards the kitchen when Frankie spoke up, their voice quiet but clear. "If we're in the shit, I'd rather you just gave it to us straight. If you go off and start angry-washing dishes at us, I'll... Well, I'd rather you didn't. But you need to know that it wasn't Gio's fault. It really wasn't."

My heart broke for them: they were tired, upset, injured, and scared, but they were still doing their level best to protect me. They were the most wonderful person who had ever lived, and I'd put them through so much already. All I wanted to do was open a portal just for the two of us, walk off somewhere safe, and never come back. This was our safe space, though. This was our home, and Ms. Anzengruber held the key to it. Right at that moment, she looked more likely to throw said key at us than to welcome us back into the fold, but this was the only fold we had. We had to try and get back in.

Ms. Anzengruber crossed her arms over her chest and scowled at Frankie. "I was going to get you some soup, actually, because it seemed the right thing to do. But if you want to do this now—"

"I'd rather."

"Fine. Would you care to tell me why you think I'm upset with you?"

"Because we waited until you were out of the house and we got into a whole mess. But we didn't start it, and we didn't mean to cause such a stink. We just wanted to teach Jacob a lesson so he'd leave Gio alone."

"That explains half of it, if you can call it an explanation. And the rest?"

They winced. "The rest just kinda followed."

"Obviously. After suffering the unintended consequences of meddling with things you do not understand, jumping with both feet into something else you do not understand is the most logical solution."

"Yeah, but... We knew we'd fucked up, and we were trying to undo it."

"That's why you couldn't wait until we came back? Did you think we wouldn't find out?"

"No, it wasn't that at all! You're not getting it! Gio was upset! We had to do something!"

Marin grumbled, "Gio is upset every day ending in 'y'."

I felt the heat rise up my cheeks just as every good feeling I'd ever had seeped out of my body, leaving me in a pile of shame and misery. I was about to sink right into my despair, but Frankie's mood shifted so quickly that I forgot to pay attention to my own.

They straightened up and spoke in a voice a full octave lower than normal. "You watch how you talk about Gio."

Marin threw his hands up in the air. "Why not? I'm watching everything else, and it's like watching a car crash. First you get involved with a fucking trickster—"

"I didn't pick him, same as I didn't pick you."

"You didn't tell him to fuck off, either."

"Actually, we did, clearly and repeatedly. Turns out that stalkers are not so good at respecting boundaries. Who could have guessed?"

"Very funny."

"It fucking isn't, actually." Frankie poked the table hard enough to make Ms. Anzengruber's centerpiece jump. "We did the best we could with what we had in the circumstances we were thrown into. What's your actual problem: what we did or how we did it? Because I think we did pretty great, actually, all considering."

"Considering what? That you're a clueless idiot? That you got your partner to give up a gift she hardly understood?"

Frankie swelled up so much that their shirt strained over their chest. "First of all, I didn't get Gio to do shit, because I'm not an asshole and he's not a mat. Secondly, something you don't actually want isn't a fucking gift! If the lot of you would finally get that into your heads—"

Marin barked something at them, they barked something back, and the two of them carried on throwing sentences at each other, disgorging old resentments and poking at each other's sore spots with increasing accuracy and vehemence. When their voices had gotten so loud that they were almost screaming, Ms. Anzengruber tugged at my sleeve. I'd not even noticed her walk over, engrossed as I was in the shouting match.

"Come on," she mumbled out of the corner of her mouth.

She walked over to the kitchen and I followed her. Frankie didn't even seem to notice me getting up. She put a pan on the stove and turned around to look at me. Her eyes weren't cold or angry anymore: they were sad and tired, and made her look older.

I took a deep breath and let it all out. "I'm sorry and Frankie is wrong: it was all my fault. I just couldn't take it anymore, so I did the only thing I could think of, and that degenerated, and then we had to keep on going. I didn't know what I was doing. I still don't really know what we did."

"According to Marin, you tricked a trickster. He's rather impressed with you."

"Yeah, right! That's why he's screaming bloody murder at Frankie?"

"No. He's screaming because he was extremely worried about both of you. You might think that he's an insensitive clod, and I can't blame you, but the amount of time and care he has invested in the two of you should give you a clue as to how he actually feels."

My eyes were feeling itchy and I really didn't want to have another public episode, so I did my best to hang on to my indignation. "He's screaming at Frankie. They don't deserve that. They did their best."

"So did you, I have no doubts, but I am sorely tempted to do a lot more than scream at you."

We stared at each other and it suddenly hit me that none of us were actually angry. We had all been terrified and now we were all relieved, and none of us had the skills to navigate that. Anger was easier all round. It was bullshit, though, and I was fed up with that kind of thing.

"I'm sorry. And I feel like shit, and I want to go home."

She grabbed my shoulders. "You are home."

"It's not home where people scream."

"Sometimes it is, dear. Sometimes people need to scream at each other for a bit to clear the air."

"I've never seen that working."

"I promise you, if they're not done by the time dinner is ready, I'll stop them myself."

"Can I help?"

"With the cooking or the stopping?"

"The cooking. I'm definitely not up to anything else."

She patted my shoulders and let me go. "I'm not sure you're up to cooking, either. That hand looked bad."

"It's not that deep. I'll be OK in a few days."

"How are you going to cope with your classes?"

"I can write with my right hand, if I have to. I'll figure something out. I did crap at this one, anyway."

"What are we talking about, a B?"

"Christ, I hope not. Probably an A-."

She didn't say anything, so I looked up at her. She was staring at me, shaking her head.

"What?"

"Nothing. I hope you can make do with a grilled cheese sandwich, because that's all I'm up to making."

She looked at me with a tiny, fragile smile, and that undid me. The tears started to fall out of my eyes and I just couldn't stop them. She patted me for a bit, but that just got me more wound up because I didn't want to cry in front of her, so she grabbed my arm and marched me over to Frankie. They were still engrossed in their shouting match, but they stopped as soon as they saw me. They pushed back their chair, pulled me on their lap, and cuddled me until the food arrived. We ate sitting like that; it was awkward as hell, but I didn't want to move, and Ms. Anzengruber had cut up our sandwiches to make it easier for us to eat one-handed, so it was alright.

When we were done eating, I felt exhausted and Frankie looked awful, so Ms. Anzengruber sent us to bed. Frankie was asleep before their head hit the pillow. I managed to stay awake and enjoy the feeling of their body next to mine for at least four seconds, and then the darkness claimed me.

16. FRESH BERRIES FOR YOU

All the way through our little adventure, I knew just how I was going to feel when it was over: relieved, overjoyed, optimistic, and generally just fucking happy at getting my life back. As soon as that living sword of Damocles was out of my way, I would be skipping and hopping through life like Tigger in Frankie's book.

I was right, mostly. I woke up with a jolt on Monday morning and remembered that I didn't have to worry, that I didn't need to look over my shoulder all the damn time, that I could wander off to see Frankie at work if I had the inclination, that I was actually free to stroll all around the place to my heart's content. I took a deep, long breath of freedom, and promptly started crying. That woke Frankie up with a jolt, too. It took me a while to calm down enough to explain to them what was wrong with me. We ended up kissing and cuddling for so long that they had to run off to work without their breakfast.

I spent the day floating on a cloud of relief. I walked to campus to see Frankie for lunch, even though I could have 'ported, just because I wanted to enjoy my freedom. I enjoyed every step I took down our railroad track. Everything looked new, picturesque, and exciting.

After lunch, I stayed on campus and waited for Frankie to finish their shift under a tree. I wanted to read, but the day was too beautiful for me to throw myself into a book. I just lay down, closed my eyes, and listened to the breeze singing the song of summer while the light coming through the canopy drew patterns on my eyelids. It was pretty, but after a while it made my eyes ache, so I covered my face with my hair. When Frankie finally turned up and saw me, they laughed so hard that they gave themself a stitch and fell over. We spent the evening mock-arguing. They called me "Cousin It." I called them all sorts. We didn't officially make up until we got to bed, which worked out rather well.

The day after, I woke up feeling just as great, and the same happened again on Wednesday and Thursday. My high lasted just long enough for me to think that maybe this was it, that I could actually feel good forever. Then, on Friday morning, something clicked in my brain and all the joy drained out of it in an instant. I didn't just go back to being my usual, miserable self; all my normal feelings got washed out, too. Even my anxiety left me, and I found myself stranded like a fish on dry land. The rest of the day stretched out in front of me, and I didn't even have the energy to worry about not having the energy to deal with it. I felt totally drained, and all I wanted to do was drop to the floor and stay there until I either got better or decomposed. Frankie had left their lunch at home, though. I couldn't even think about walking over, so I 'ported to them.

They were waiting for me in a shower stall. It made a nice change from a toilet, but it also made it pretty hard for me to hide that I wasn't feeling right. With my face only a few inches away from theirs and under a glaring neon light, it took them roughly a third of a nanosecond to work out that something was up.

"Gio? What's wrong?" They touched my forehead. "You're not hot. Do you have a headache? Have you eaten? Drunk enough water?"

"It's not that. My head is broken. Inside."

"Oh." They pulled me to them and hugged me. "I love you."

"I know. Thank you. I love you, too."

"It's all been a bit of a rollercoaster, hasn't it?"

"Yeah. I'm so sorry."

"Why?"

"I should feel—"

They rested a finger on my lips. "No. That's not how it works. You can't decide how you should feel and bully yourself into feeling that way. Feelings are real, Gio."

"The hell they are. They're all in my head."

"So's your amygdala, and you wouldn't dispute its existence, but that's not the point. You feel the way you feel, and that's OK, even when that feeling isn't good. It's OK for you not to feel good about something, or to just not feel good."

"Anyone else in my position—"

"No!" They were so upset with me that they kissed my nose in punishment. "Aside from the fact that most people in your position would have crumbled weeks ago – no, months ago... Actually, scrap that: based on what I know of your life, it's a miracle you made it through your teens. But that's not the point. Stop distracting me!"

"I didn't—"

"You did. Gio, I love you, and I'm not going to tell you how to think, not ever, but you have this bad habit of assuming things only count as bad if they suck equally for everyone on the planet. Things that only suck for you still suck. And when it comes to evaluating your own life, that's pretty much the only criteria worth using."

"But—"

"No. Sorry, but no. For whatever reason, you feel like shit right now. That's all that matters."

"But I don't like it!" I was trying to sound like a rational adult, but it came out as a pathetic whine.

"Of course you don't! I don't like it, either. I hope we can fix it. But how you feel, right now, is OK, even though it's not OK."

"You're not making a lot of sense."

"Don't listen to what I say; listen to what I mean. Homeslice, you're not obliged to like everything life throws at you. And sometimes you'll feel like crap for no valid reason, and that's OK, too, as long as you don't take it out on other people. And you don't."

"If I'm miserable around you, isn't that what I'm doing?"

"No. I'm talking about stuff like using me as a punch bag."

"I snap at you plenty of times."

"Only when I do something that pisses you off." They rubbed their nose on mine. "Gio, I would be very happy if we always felt great all the time and things between us were perfectly harmonious, but we're people."

"Are we? We don't even know that. Not anymore."

They rolled their eyes at me. "We're mostly people. We're going to have bad days. I don't think the way to get over them is to ignore they're there and plow on regardless."

"I don't want to wallow in my shit."

"Me neither. It's gross, and you'd use up all the hot water to clean up. But there's a line between honoring your feelings and wallowing in them."

"Where do you draw it?"

"No fucking idea. You'll have to work it out, I guess. I'll help, if I can."

I sighed. "OK. So what do we do now?"

"Now? We have lunch."

"And after?"

They shrugged. "We make it up as we're going along. At least we have practice."

I had hoped that my whatever-it-was would be just a quick blip, a momentary lapse that would be gone by morning. Instead, I woke up on Saturday morning and there it was, sucking the life right out of me. I felt utterly dejected about feeling dejected. Even the prospect of a weekend alone with Frankie – no work, no homework, and our part of the house all to ourselves for the last time until the Thanksgiving holidays – didn't cheer me up. As it turned out, my lack of enthusiasm was appropriate: my funk was so great that even Frankie's optimism didn't cure it. Instead, it infected them. A few hours stuck with me, and they were as droopy and

miserable as I was. They insisted that it wasn't my fault, that we were just experiencing the same emotional backlash, but they couldn't convince me. We spent the whole weekend sunk in apathy, only rousing to make increasingly desperate attempts at cheering each other up.

When Monday reared its ugly head, I woke up to Frankie sitting up in our bed, staring into space. When I snuggled up to them, they bent down and kissed my hair.

"Hey."

"Hey, you."

"Gio, I have to go to work."

The non sequitur blew the left-over sleep out of my head. "I know. It's Monday."

"No, that's not what I mean. I want to stay here with you, because you feel like shit, and I also want to stay here because *I* feel like shit, but I honestly believe that if I don't get moving right now, I will totally seize up. This is gruesome. It's kicking my ass. I have to fight it, and I can't fight it from here. I need to be up and moving. I need to feel productive. I have to go to work."

They looked so beautiful, brave, and desperate, that my heart nearly exploded. "You're so much better than me."

They snorted. "Not hardly. I'm running off to work because I'm scared of how I feel, and leaving you behind. That's a super shitty thing to do."

"No. You're doing what you need to do to feel better, so you can look after me. Oxygen masks, Doom."

"Say what?"

"You have to put your own on first, otherwise you won't be able to help anyone else. You're doing the right thing."

I said that and I meant it, but watching them go was torture. I couldn't bear the thought of a day without them, but the thought of re-infecting them with my downer was even worse, so I'd sent them off with a packed lunch and told them I'd see them that afternoon.

I was braced for their departure, but it didn't do me any good; the sound of the front door shutting behind them unclogged something in my chest, and I dissolved into sobs that seemed to last for eons. Once I was done with that, I felt sore and exhausted, but also a tiny bit lighter, as if a tiny part of the awful weight that had been crushing me had dropped away. It was enough of an improvement to give me some hope, but not much.

When they rolled in from work, I was sitting on the floor, staring out of the patio doors. I'd been there all day; I'd sat down for a moment after clearing up our breakfast, and discovered that I couldn't muster the

motivation to move. I couldn't go to sleep, but I wasn't quite awake. I couldn't call it vegetating, because plants were useful.

They took a look at me and sighed. "Hey." They put their backpack on the floor with some effort and a thump.

"Hey, you. Whatcha got there?"

"Our schoolbooks." They walked over and snuggled next to me on the floor. "I went to the admin office at lunchtime and sorted out my classes. It needed doing, and I couldn't stay still, so... Anyway, I did it. I dropped down to eleven credits. It puts me in the part-time bracket for fees, so it makes sense, and I think I can handle those classes and work. Is that OK?"

"I am not going to tell you what to do, love."

"I know. But you know me, you love me, and you're infinitely more clever than I could ever dream of being. That's why I ask for your advice."

I tried to get my brain to focus. "You checked with Marin about times?"

"Yeah. He's fine with it. In theory, anyway. Did I do good?"

"I think so. If it doesn't work out, we can change it. I'm sorry I wasn't there for you. I'm being so fucking useless."

They gave me a squeeze. "You were here for me. That's just as good. Anyway, when I got that sorted, I was feeling all grown-up and shit, so I went to the bookstore and got us the books for next term. I remembered how you did it last term, and it seemed like it was the right time, so—"

"It was. I can't believe it, but I'd forgotten all about it. Thank you." I let my head rest on their shoulder. It felt really good, even though it made me feel bad. I was resting too much of my weight on them, literally and metaphorically. I knew that they didn't mind, but I did.

As always, they picked up on my mood. Their voice dropped to a sickbed whisper. "How are you feeling?"

"Fuck-awful. Thank you for asking."

They croaked, "I'm sorry. What's up?"

"My head hurts. My back hurts. My life hurts."

Their bottom lip wobbled momentarily, but they steeled themself. "I don't know how to make it better, Gio. If I could, I would."

"I know. You always do that for me. You're great like that. This one is kind of a biggie, though. I think I'll just have to sit with it until it goes away. I'm just not ready to come out from under the porch yet. But I still love you. I love you all the bits."

I looked inside their eyes, searching for that fear that had eaten them inside so badly at the start of summer. I could see a trace of it there, but they were fighting it. When they'd got it under control, they nodded.

"That's great, Gio. You're taking care of yourself."

"I miss you, though. I miss you so fucking much."

Their eyes filled with tears. They slipped their arm behind me and gave me a squeeze. "I miss you. But I'll be here when you come out."

"That's the thing, though." I picked up every scrap of courage I had, but my voice still came out half-choked. "Frankie, would you like to come under the porch with me?"

Their eyes went all a-flutter. "You mean that. You want me to be with you? Under the porch?"

"Yes. If you want to come."

They looked away, smiled, wiped off a couple of tears, then looked back at me. "Yes. Of course I do. But I don't know what that means."

"Neither do I. I thought we could figure it out together."

"I'd like that very much." Their voice sounded choked, too. They stared into space for a bit, then cleared their throat. "Would you like a hot drink? Tea? Hot chocolate? Soup? I know it's not going to fix anything, but…"

I thought about it. "I would, actually. That would be bloody marvelous."

"Are you making fun of me?"

"No. A hot drink would be splendid. Just don't be gone too long, OK?"

They nuzzled my neck. "Never. Would you like cookies with that?"

"Do bears shit in the woods?"

"No idea. I'm a townie, remember? I'll see what I can do. About the cookies, not the bear poop."

They gave me a last squeeze and got up. Even though it was only a few steps to the door, they still checked on me again before walking out. It made me feel cared for, but sad, too: they shouldn't have to worry about me. They had enough on their plate.

I let my head drop back onto the bed and tried to loosen my neck. It felt way too tight, as if my spine was trying to insert itself into my cranium, and I just couldn't make it relax. I tried rocking my head from side to side, to see if the movement would untie the knots in my neck, or perhaps break it. I would have been good with either, but my efforts didn't do shit.

I flopped towards the door to find Ben staring at me, looking perplexed. "Hi. Are you, huh, alright?"

"You're back early."

"Not really. I have to, like, get my shit in order, have meetings and stuff. And Frankie called, and… You know."

"Ah. So you've heard all about it?"

"Yeah. It sounded…" He winced. "How are you?"

In lieu of an answer, I shrugged.

"I have a thing you might like." He walked in and handed me a bundle

of VHS tapes.

"What's this?"

"'The Power of Myth.' Joseph Campbell. It's not mine. My mom got it for me, and my sister kept it. It's pretty cool. You need to read his books. You'll love them. The guy used all the words."

Even through the fog in my brain, that piqued my curiosity. "Oh. Like what?"

Ben's brow furrowed. "Lemme see. Cosmogony? Antipathy? Extirpate?"

I shrugged. "Sorry. Nothing new there. Anything else?"

"What about 'effulgence'?"

"Huh. I've never heard that. What does that mean?"

He smiled. "You'll have to find out, won't you? Anyway, I just thought you might like something to watch, if you're not up to much else."

"Thanks. That'd be cool."

His eyes narrowed. "Are you, like, doing alright?"

"Dunno. Sometimes I think I'm doing crappy. Sometimes I think I'm doing great, considering what went on, and then I feel crappy about that."

He crossed his arms over his chest. "You did what you had to do. You should feel great about it. You're a fucking hero."

"The hell I am! Heroes do heroic stuff. I just got caught in a series of escalating blunders."

"You faced a god, stole his powers, and shared them with your partner. That's classic heroism."

"All I did was trick a trickster. If you want to find a hero, I can get you the address of a woman who's got fucking wings and a for-real-and-no-shit fiery sword."

"That's not how it works. You did what you did *without* a fiery sword. That's the whole point. The Guardian has got the arsenal, the skills, and the backup. You don't, but you still went for it, and you genuinely didn't know if you were going to make it."

"I also had no choice."

"Doesn't matter. It's still serious hero shit."

"Please, don't mythologize me. I have had enough of that kind of crap to last me a lifetime."

His voice dropped to a croaky whisper. "I don't think I can help it. I kinda do that with everyone I have a crush on."

The words fell out of his mouth and landed between us with an audible thud. Their echo resonated in my head. When it finally stopped, I had no idea if I'd been staring at Ben for a second or an hour. I was sure I had to say something to him, though, and I had no fucking idea what it was.

I tried to get a breath in and to find the right words. "Ben, it's not that I don't like you. It's just... I don't want to fuck things up with Frankie."

He smiled at me, though he didn't look terribly happy. "If I thought I could fuck things up between you and Frankie, I'd move. I have no intention to get between you. I'm thinking more in terms of, I don't know, something else. On the side. Literally. Or, you know, nothing. My crush is not your obligation."

A suspicion arose in my mind. "You have spoken to Frankie about this. That sounds like them."

His face went rigid. "Yes. Sorry. It's not that I wanted to go behind your back. I just needed to check with them..." He took a big gulp of air. "I went behind your back. I wasn't going to cut in on them. It's just... It's not about ownership. It's about territory. No, wait, that sounds even worse."

"It's cool. I get it. You're Frankie's friend. I'd do the same if I got interested in your Guardian."

He looked horrified. "But you're not. Are you?"

"Hell, no. I try to avoid falling in lust with people who terrify me."

"That's very wise on your part."

"I'm trying to make up for the rest of my life. What did Frankie say?"

"That it was none of their business. That you don't belong to them. That I was a good friend to you and maybe I could be more. They wished me luck. They slapped me on the back and everything. You know what it's like when they're being all dudely and shit."

"Yeah. It's adorable."

"Yeah. Anyway, you know them: they want everyone they know to love each other."

"Sure. I just didn't think they meant biblically."

He blushed. "I don't know if they mean that. I, huh, don't know if I do, either. None of us has a damn clue, frankly."

"So, business as usual?"

"Yeah. But I told them that I didn't want to be Lancelot, and they said, and I quote, that that wouldn't be a problem because you'd rather eat your own shit than be Guinevere."

That made me chortle. "They're not wrong."

"They also said that tragic love triangles can suck their dick."

"They'd probably enjoy that, in the short term. In the long run, the drama would get on their nerves." I took a deep breath and told him the truth, even though it was ugly. "I don't think this is a great time for me to make my life more complicated than it already is."

He stared at the floor. "Does this have to complicate things?"

"Generally speaking, when you're living with your partner and you start to get interested in a third party... I don't know. It creates extra friction. Potentially, anyway. More moving parts."

"I'm not saying we should jump into it. I don't even know what we'd be jumping into. Mostly I just wanted you to know, so things would be straight between us. But, like, maybe we could go on a date or something."

I squealed, "A date?"

Ben looked up and chortled. "Is it really that far out? Just because you didn't date Frankie, it doesn't mean that you can't date me."

"I've never dated anyone. Not really. I don't even know what it means."

"What do you normally do?"

"Jump into bed with people, regret it almost instantly, and sit with my bad decision until things get so awful that I have to bail out."

He stared at me, blinking. "Could we, like, not do that? It sounds kinda shitty."

"Roger that. So what would we do?"

"I don't know. Catch a movie. Or I could cook for you."

"You cook for us all the time. We live in the same house, man."

He shrugged. "I'll think of something. If you want me to. Or you can."

I started to nod, but a cramp stabbed me in the back of the neck, so I ended up twitching and swearing instead.

Ben frowned. "Bad back?"

"You have no idea."

"Want a backrub?"

"You know how to do that?"

"Dude. I lived in a hippie commune for three and a half years."

He walked over to the bed and sat behind me, squeezing his knees behind my shoulders. It was really comfortable, but I still felt myself go rigid. I tried to make myself relax, but I couldn't.

Next thing I knew, he'd flicked me in the back of the head. "Look, man, if you don't want me to do this, just say."

"I'm alright."

"You're not. Just chill, OK? Nothing's changed. This isn't about... I'd give Frankie a backrub, if they needed it and they could stay still long enough. You want one or not?"

"I'd like a new back, ideally."

"Can't help you with that." He rested his palms on my shoulders and ran his thumbs up the back of my neck. For someone with hands the size of shovels, he was surprisingly gentle. Then he found a knot and pushed into it hard enough to make me yelp.

302

"Sorry. It's gotta be done. Your back is a mess. How do you even move?"

"With great difficulty and immense pain. Please, have mercy upon me."

"I'll do my best."

By the time Frankie reappeared, Ben had started to work on my shoulder blades, and I was oscillating between whimpering and drooling. Frankie didn't just walk in: they peered around the door first, their eyes immense and questioning. When they saw us, they smiled their biggest smile ever. They waltzed in, literally, balancing a tray loaded with three mugs of something steaming and three slabs of toast and jam. They put a drink and a toast on the nightstand for Ben and placed the tray on the floor, next to me. Then they lay down between me and the patio doors and plopped their head in my lap. Their smiling face swimming in a pool of curls was the most beautiful thing I'd ever seen.

"Don't mind me, Doom. Just make yourself at home."

They ran a hand up my leg. "That was my plan. Does that feel good?"

"It does, apart from the bits when it makes me want to scream."

"Maybe I can learn to do that."

"To make me scream? You do that plenty of times."

Their eyes twinkled. "No, you pervert. To disentangle you."

"I'm sure you can, love. Maybe I can, too. Then we can all give each other backrubs."

Their smile turned up a notch. "All three of us?"

"Yeah. But don't get ideas. It doesn't mean anything, you know?"

"Does too! Means we can all get a ton of backrubs." They closed their eyes, still smiling, and snuggled their head deeper into my lap. "Hey, wanna open up the portal? There may really be a moon out there."

I tried to go into the place in my head where portals happened, but I couldn't. It took me no time to work out why. "Sorry, love. If you want it open, one of you is going to have to do the honors."

They flipped over and lifted themself up on one elbow, looking up at me. Their smile had disappeared. "Are you scared to do it? In case it's a trap again?"

"No. I think we're done with that."

"Does your head hurt? Do you need anything? Painkillers?"

"Nah. It's just... I can't open a portal right now. I can't find the intention. There's nowhere else I'd like to be."

Ben's hands stammered over my back, and Frankie's smile blossomed. As they snuggled back down into my lap, my heart did a couple of somersaults. I had really made it. I was home.

DISCOGRAPHY

I normally like to include a discography with each of my books, but the last few months have been weird. I started listening to The Mountain Goats in February (2018), and, six months later, I haven't stopped yet. In my defense, John Darnielle is a *beast*, so they have something like over 40 albums out (though I only own 21 – send help). It's still weird, though, even though they are Frankie's favorite band *ever*. And they would know, because they've had a ton of favorite bands ever.

If you're going to get in there, I'd recommend you start with "All Hail West Texas" and just don't stop.

The only exception to this TMG domination has been 'Wintermore' by Nicky Murray, but that has only been with me for a couple of scenes. It's absolutely great and you should get it, though. If we don't support the artists making the things we love, we'll have to learn to go without.

ABOUT THE AUTHOR

Robin Banks finds writing in the third person intensely creepifying, so I won't.

I was born a while ago, and these days I don't regret it too often. A fan of peregrinations with a terrible tendency to get myself marooned, I currently dwell with an excessive number of dogs right at the end of the big cabbage field. That's the big field with the cabbages, not the field with the big cabbages. Don't be silly.

I enjoy road trips, dogs, guitars, and getting into scrapes. My favorite writers are Tom Robbins, Spider Robinson, and Matthew Stover; Rory Miller for non-fiction. I refuse to be landlocked, because you need to have some standards. I like Irish coffee with condensed milk in lieu of cream. You can't help some people.

There is a rumor going around that I might in fact be a collection of raccoons hiding inside a hoodie, but that's not been confirmed to date, possibly because I bite.

I hope this didn't suck for you. If you enjoyed this, please check out:
https://www.amazon.com/Robin-Banks/e/B01MU5VWGL
https://www.facebook.com/HeinleinsFinches
https://godsbastard.wordpress.com/heinleins-finches/

Made in the USA
Las Vegas, NV
24 January 2022